Soho Honey

A. W. Rock

Clink
Street

London | New York

Published by Clink Street Publishing 2016

Copyright © 2016

First edition.

ISBN: 9781911110248 paperback
9781911110255 ebook

WITH MANY THANKS TO:

Georgia : for her hours of patient editing and creative input and much more.

Maya Whitehead-Nash : Studio Nash website design and social media.
Alistair Nash : Cover Design.
Jonathan Knowles : Cover photography.
Lord Foster of Bath : Political advice.
Christopher MacLehose : for his encouragement.
Melanie Hurdley : lawyer.
Terry Hardy : Bee Keeper.
Roger Rolls : Chemistry advice.
Mark Strutt : The source of many things including whisky.
Carl Erikson : The armourer.
Ian Cousins : The policeman.
Crispin Wigfield : Neurosurgery Consultant.
Andy : Bishops of Bath for motor scooter advice.
Alan Williams : Journalist at the Bath Chronicle.
Andy : Buckler's Hard harbour master.
Charlie Davis : map illustration.
Jay Villiers : actor / audio book.
Stephanie Tasker : website film editor.
John Parker : website music composer.

And last but very importantly –
Kate, Hayley, Gareth and Josh (in the USA) : Authoright & Clink Street Publishing.

This book is dedicated to my close friends, some of whom gave up their valuable time to help with practical and editorial advice.

Please read the book slowly because it took me a long time to write.

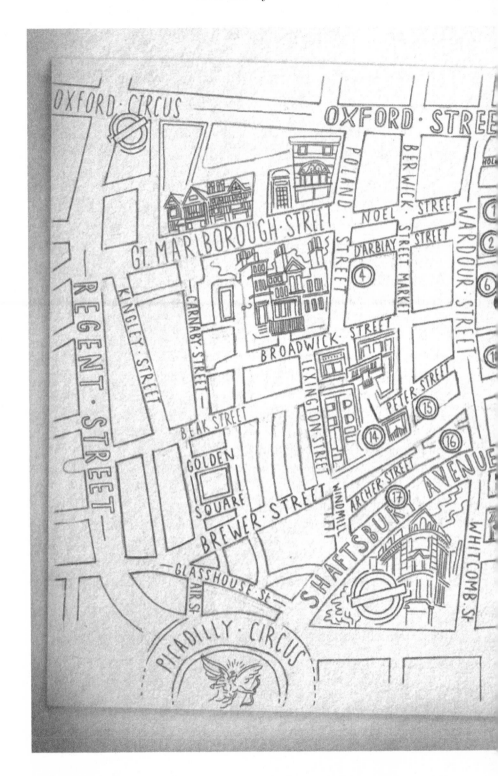

1. SOHO GAZETTE
2. THE SHIP
3. ST. BARNABAS'S
4. SNOWMAN'S FLAT
5. CARRIE'S FLAT
6. COSTAS'S LOUNGE
7. REDCLIFFE'S APARTMENT
8. HARRY'S FLAT
9. EUREKA'S FLAT
10. MIKEY'S APARTMENT
11. EMPIRE ROOM
12. RONNIE SCOTT'S
13. BAR ITALIA
14. GIOVANNI'S SHOP
15. MADAME LULU'S
16. HOTEL CALIFORNIA
17. RED LABEL CLUB
18. DENNIS'S CLUB
19. CHINA HOTEL
20. MASONIC MANSIONS

List of main characters and their adopted and/or their nick-names :

1. Ben – Benny – Branen.
2. Rita – jazz singer.
3. Jane – Branen's ex-partner and mother of Carrie.
4. Carrie – code name CHARON – Branen & Jane's daughter.
5. Errol – doorman at Ronnie Scott's.
6. Costas – owner of Costas's Lounge.
7. Jack – Costas's barman.
8. Melissa – Costas's paramour.
9. Charlie – a regular at Costas's bar.
10. The Black Brothers, mini-cab company – Saul – answers the phone. George – sorts out the problem customers. Stewart – runs the street and calls the cabs.
11. Harry White – Whitey – Tommy Farr – the fat man.
12. Snowman – also known as 'the mutant' by Harry.
13. Myrtle – Snowman's partner.
14. Darren – Snowman's flunky.
15. Ayo – owner of The Empire Room in Dean Street.
16. Anthony – the barrister.
17. Michelle de Lavigne – Mikey – also known as 'the hermaphrodite' by Harry.
18. Fred – Mikey's Special Forces explosive expert.
19. Sabrina – Mikey's manager.
20. Tilley – Serbian waitress at Madame LuLu's.
21. Sean – the bar owner in Dean Street.
22. Busby Bob – a regular at Sean's bar.
23. Herbert Redcliffe – the Senior Civil Servant – also known as the SCS.
24. The Associates – a secret cadre run by the Senior Civil Servant within the Home Office.
25. Helen – the Controller at MI5.
26. Antoinette, James and Janet – the Controller's researchers.
27. The Chief – the Controller's boss at MI5.
28. MI5 – also known as The Firm.
29. MI6 – the Secret Intelligence Service – also known as SIS.
30. Dean Beck – Chairman, local BNP.

PROLOGUE
The history of The Associates

All governments carry out secret operations and they must be more savvy and brutal than the criminal gangs and terrorists who inhabit their countries. The more democratic a government, the more illicit its operations have to be. Despite sophisticated technology, the Government also employs deniable Operation Officers and their agents for covert assignments, without the knowledge of politicians or the public.

The Associates is a project run by the Senior Civil Servant within the Home Office and total secrecy is essential to its existence. He is known as the SCS, is answerable only to the Home Secretary and is protected by the Public Interest Immunity Certificate.

The Associates' employees are known only to the SCS and his personal assistant, and are usually ex-Home or Foreign Office. They set up small legitimate businesses and employ agents assigned to them by the SCS; these agents are usually former SIS officers, security screened mercenaries or retired Special Forces soldiers.

The Operations Officers and their agents are given backup personnel when necessary. These operatives are only given case-specific information on a need to know basis.

In the 1970s and 80s a similar secret cadre called Group 13 was set up by the SIS to infiltrate the IRA and execute Margaret Thatcher's alleged 'shoot to kill' policy. It was hidden within an organisation known as the Increment or 'Inc' and employed a dozen ex-Special Service soldiers to carry out assassinations and deniable operations in Ireland. When a controversial mission became compromised, it had to be disbanded before its activities became public knowledge.

Two Group 13 agents were then employed by the SCS as Operations Officers to set up The Associates. In the UK there is a photographic bureau, an Indian travel agency and a Chinese fruit wholesaler, employing in total seven agents.

1

The SCS can brief the Operations Officer or an agent directly by secure satellite phone. The agent validates the operation with his catch-word, known only to his Operations Officer and the SCS.

Simple but effective.

INTRODUCTION
Ben – (his early years)

An hour must have passed before he came round. He was on the floor with the shotgun in his hands and Rita's lifeless body slumped on the sofa above him.

He was floating; he wanted to vomit and was struggling to deal with the scene in front of him. She had been so full of life and now she resembled a white china doll splashed with blood.

Ben was twenty-two and hadn't wanted to settle down, but he loved Jane and when they had a kid he did try to make it work. But three years on when he met Rita, a jazz singer at Ronnie Scott's, he couldn't resist; even if she did have history.

He was at her flat having a smoke one night when the door was kicked in and three Chinese hoods barged in.

The boss stared at Ben, then turned to Rita. "What the fuck is he doing here?"

"What do you want…?" asked Rita, "…get out of my flat…"

"Are those my drugs you're smoking?"

Ben stood up, held out his hands and stepped towards the boss. "Look mate…"

The man pulled a sawn-off shotgun from under his coat and pushed the barrels into Ben's face. "Keep the fuck out of this…" He gestured to the two hoods with him and they grabbed Ben's arms.

He turned to Rita, "You owe me… you slut… and what's this pretty boy doing here?"

Rita screamed at him, "You and I've got nothing… I owe you nothing… you get the fuck…"

Rita's three-year old daughter came in from the bedroom. As she went to pick up the child, the boss slapped Rita round the head. She dropped the baby, who then clung to her legs screaming.

Ben broke free and grabbed at the gun. "Leave her alone..."

The two hoods jumped on Ben and as they struggled to overpower him the shotgun went off, blowing Rita back onto the sofa with the hysterical child trapped under her body.

"No... no... fuck no," cried the boss, cradling Rita in his arms.

He laid her gently on the sofa and stood up slowly, tears in his eyes. He looked at his blood-stained hands, then turned on Ben. "You fucking gwilo."

He hit Ben with the stock of the shotgun. The last thing he remembered was the trance-like sobbing of the child.

As Ben regained consciousness he felt he was swimming in space; the feeling was familiar, it was a heroin trip. His head was floating and he attempted to get to his feet. On the table was an empty syringe and some wraps. They must have tried to overdose him, but he was lucky; either they had got the mix wrong or he was able to tolerate it. He couldn't feel his heart beating and was fighting to cope with the horror in front of him; and where was the child?

It looked like a set-up ready for the police to arrive. For all he knew they were already on the way; how would he explain what had happened here? His legs were jelly, he had to clean up his finger prints. He searched in vain for the child. He was gagging as he staggered down the stairs to the street.

* * *

He was seventeen when he was first seduced by Soho. In the early hours one Saturday morning as he was wandering down from the 100 Club to Bar Italia for an espresso he saw this big black guy, on the opposite side of the street, locking up Ronnie Scott's Jazz Club.

Never one to miss a trick, he went over to him. "Any chance of a job, mate?"

The man must have felt sorry for him. "Hang on a minute."

Another man appeared from the doorway.

"This bloke wants a job..."

Checking Ben out, the second man said, "He looks fit... do you reckon he could handle the punters?"

"He don't look too soft."

"Okay, put 'im on the door, Errol."

It was night work so Ben needed something to fill his days, and with Errol's introduction he arrived at Costas's Lounge.

"Errol said you could use some help."

"Errol's the one who needs help... and I need you like a second arsehole," said Costas, looking Ben up and down. "You got any experience...?" he asked, "...what's your washing-up like?"

"Clean..." said Ben.

Costas needed a cheap bottle-washer and offered him a job and somewhere to doss down. Costas didn't trust Ben to work with the general public so he spent his days as a dogsbody, restocking the bar and doing other menial stuff.

He supplemented his earnings at Ronnie's by selling a bit of coke and dope while he worked the door. Before his grandfather died, leaving him £10,000, Ben had already saved a couple of grand. He put a deposit on a small workshop off Broadwick Street and got a bank loan.

Soho had become his home.

He first saw Jane a couple of years later at the Marquee in Wardour Street when he went to see a punk band called Ferking Nouveau. She was wearing a thin sweater and tight leather trousers. She was sex on legs and dancing with a man who didn't have a lot of natural rhythm. Ben sat in the shadows and waited nearly an hour for a chance to talk to her. Eventually she went up to the bar and he slid in beside her.

"Hello... can I, er... buy you a drink?" he asked her.

"No thanks... but maybe later," she said.

"What's your name?" Ben asked.

"I'll save that for later too..." she said, smiling.

"Will there be a later?"

"You'll know later..."

"I can hardly wait..."

"I hope that doesn't apply to everything you do," she said, turning back to the dance floor.

Ben was left hanging. He kept making eye contact, which left him with a permanent wooden smile and his mind frozen in the flashing lights. He was infatuated and completely at her mercy.

He went out onto the street. He had been set up by the most desirable woman he'd ever seen and his nerve had given out. But if he went home now he would never forgive himself.

The rubber stamp on the back of his hand, proving that he'd paid to get in, had faded.

The guy on the door, who was only slightly smaller than an elephant, blocked his way.

"C'mon... you remember me..." said Ben, "...I only just left."

"Let me see the stamp on your hand..."

"C'mon man... don't be a..."

"I can't see no stamp... I can't let you in without the stamp, so you can piss off, mate."

She appeared from behind the bouncer.

"He's with me," she said, smiling.

"What's her name?" the doorman asked Ben.

"I'll tell you later," said Ben.

They fell in love and their daughter Carrie was born nine months later.

Ben loved them but could never really deal with the responsibility. They were too young to have had a child and over the next year a distance developed between them.

For three more years they lived in the workshop whilst he laboured for Costas during the day and worked at Ronnie's in the evenings. Most of the time he was out of it.

* * *

Jane took care of Ben after he was attacked by the Chinese gang, but her feelings for him had cooled. He read about Rita's murder in the Soho Gazette and listened to the gossip on the streets; but after a couple of weeks the press lost interest and he heard no more.

When he'd recovered from the overdose he returned to his old haunts and it was then that he got involved in a scam with a bunch of lads he'd met outside Ronnie's.

One evening after a few drinks in The Ship they had approached him. "We'd like you to join our team... what's your driving like?" they asked him. "...We're in a hurry and we need a wheelman on a job we've got planned... it's easy enough, you'll just have to drive us out of the West End and dump the car we've nicked. No tricky stuff... we don't want to get caught for speeding."

Ben didn't stop to think; he wanted the adrenalin rush.

The gang had knowledge of a consignment of heroin from Hong Kong due to be delivered to a restaurant in Chinatown. They were in position at the bottom of Greek Street by eleven thirty the next morning. They had to wait for a call from the snitch and then drive straight across Shaftesbury Avenue to the restaurant.

The team consisted of two with shotguns who were the assault team, and a footman with a sawn-off hidden inside his jacket; he was already in position. The footman was to guard the entrance while the two army-trained men had to make the first floor flat, and Ben was to stay in the stolen Range Rover. It was a simple plan, always the best; but they were set up.

They never found out who had grassed them up but they believed the Triads had 'persuaded' the Chinese snitch to talk; they'd substituted the heroin with noodles and told the police that they were being persecuted by a London gang who were demanding protection money.

No sooner had Ben pulled up in Newport Place and the lads gone through the door than he was looking down the wrong end of a police shooter.

The only one to get away was the footman. He'd noticed the disguised policemen as they broke cover, and slipped away into the astonished crowd.

Ben was twenty-two years old when he'd agreed to be their driver. He'd joined the caper for the buzz and there he was, pleading guilty and facing seven years in prison.

Carrie was three years old when they arrested him, and Jane made it clear that for her, it was the end of their relationship.

* * *

At his trial Ben's brief told the court that he had nothing to do with the planning of the robbery and had been roped in at the last moment.

Because he was unarmed and had pleaded guilty he would be eligible for parole after serving one third of his sentence, if he behaved himself.

Prison taught him how to survive in a hostile environment; 'stitches for snitches' was the code and he kept his nose clean. He was forced to stop and think about his life. He was still in love with Jane and loved his daughter, but realised it was all too late. Jane had given him love and support but he had done irreparable damage to the relationship; and while he was inside she had moved out of their home.

He asked his solicitor to sell the workshop and pay off the mortgage. He gave half to Jane and put £50,000 on deposit at the bank.

He completed three years in prison, but before being released he had to appear in front of the Parole Board. They droned on about the terms of his licence after release, which included non-association with any of his former partners in crime. This wasn't difficult because, except for the footman, they were all still in prison. The court had also imposed a geographical exclusion zone which meant Soho and its environs; and he had to report on a weekly basis to a parole officer.

* * *

Then he was out in the big wide world, breathing fresh air and able to make decisions for himself. In prison he had worked hard on his fitness in order to survive; he now no longer had to watch his back.

He tried to renew his relationship with Jane but she didn't need him as she had another man, and Carrie hardly recognised Ben; there was no place in their lives for him. However hard it was, he had to accept it. He had not given them a second thought when he had agreed to do the robbery and now he had to pay for his selfishness.

He was twenty-five with no job and had lost his only family.

He managed to keep his first appointment with the parole officer, but inevitably ended up in the West End.

He came up the subway steps at Piccadilly Circus and at once felt at home. He had a coffee and relaxed in the sunshine. It had been three years since he'd seen an attractive woman or heard a carefree conversation. Instead he'd endured the aggressive banter of prison and the smell of disinfectant and sweat. The West End was a hive of activity and it felt good to be alive and free.

When he woke early the next morning he was back in the heart of Soho, in Costas's basement room with a hangover. He had committed a breach of parole by being in Soho, and his next appointment with the parole officer was the following day. In prison he'd read a book called A Mouthful of Stones, about a man who runs away and joins the Foreign Legion.

Disappearing wasn't difficult if you had the bottle to do it. The Foreign Legion had been formed two hundred years before and offered sanctuary, immunity and a change of identity. It was what he needed to break the emotional bond and to make a fresh start.

He went straight to Waterloo, caught the train and crossed over to France.

BEN – A.K.A. BRANEN & THE LEGION :

The port of entry for the Foreign Legion was Fort de Nogent in Paris.

Only one in twelve applicants pass the induction course and, if chosen, travel down to Marseilles for a further three week trial. Then the recruits who make the cut suffer sixteen weeks at Castel Nordre in south-west France in an attempt to get through the brutal training regime. The few who are left finally earn their white cap and become Legionnaires.

He was determined not to fuck up again. The Legion offered him the chance to make a new start, but military life required team work. The recruits were put into groups of seven to carry out exercises and complete missions. But he couldn't tolerate the others' lack of foresight and planning. He could always see a better route to achieving the objective and would invariably go off on his own.

As punishment, he would have his head shaved and made to wear a metal helmet with the lining removed; then carrying his rifle above his head he would be forced to run round in the midday sun. With a rucksack full of rocks and wire straps over his shoulders, on command he would have to do knee bends and press-ups for up to two hours in the relentless heat.

However many punishment routines he was forced to endure, he still carried on working on his own. Adopting this masochistic attitude, he saw the extra exercises as a way of getting stronger and fitter than anyone else.

Eventually he was pulled up in front of the Colonel and found himself seconded to a special unit formed to operate behind enemy lines. The unconventional nature of this suited him. Practised in close combat and speaking passable French, he operated as a lone sniper.

After five years of being treated like a disposable handkerchief he left the Legion. They offered him the option of keeping his adopted name of Branen with a French passport or reverting to his true identity; but since he'd screwed up his parole and was still a wanted man in the UK, he kept his new name.

After demobilisation he made his way to Paris and rented a room on the Left Bank. As summer arrived, so did the time for decision.

He was thirty-one years old and travelling on a French passport when he arrived at Heathrow. The immigration officer put his passport number into the computer and there was a pregnant pause. He was taken to one side and after sitting in an office for an hour they gave him back his passport and released him without explanation.

He was standing outside Terminal 2 waiting for a bus into London when a chauffeur-driven car pulled up.

A man in a smart suit got out. "Branen... I wonder if we could have a chat?"

"That depends on what you want."

"How about a coffee in the bar here... we're very interested in offering you a job that would utilise your considerable skills."

Branen was curious and in the airport lounge the man, who said his name was David, continued, "You've come to our notice through the Directorate Générale de la Sécurité Extérieure. We asked them to keep an eye out for Legionnaires who showed potential... and you came up on their radar."

"Who's we?... Who are you?" asked Branen.

"I represent the Government... we're looking for a French-speaking agent for a particular project... and you've got all the necessary qualifications."

The Secret Intelligence Service had been given the brief by the Senior Civil Servant but they were not told why.

* * *

Branen accepted the Secret Service's offer but was transferred by the Senior Civil Servant to The Associates, an organisation that the SIS had little knowledge of.

After six months of training he was given a grant and enrolled on a photo-journalism course at The Spéos International Photography School in Paris.

Soon after he was told to go to Milan to meet World Pictures, who would employ him on a freelance basis. He was to pursue his career as a photo-journalist with the guarantee that he would earn good money from the syndication rights.

Via The Associates' secure satellite phone Branen received a call. "Branen, you've passed our training programme and I've got your..."

"Who am I talking to?"

"We don't deal in names, dear boy..."

His attitude irritated Branen. "What's the password?"

"LEGION, and I'm your boss. Now as I was saying before you interrupted me I'm going to give you the catch-word for your first mission."

'Pompous prick,' thought Branen.

World Pictures, with its Government sponsored introductions, offered him an advantage many photographers would have killed for.

He had to stop questioning the morals and politics that caused him to kill for his country. He was destructive in the interests of British security but could be creative with his photographic work. He knew he was being naïve, but it was the excuse that allowed him to live with his conscience.

At least for the moment.

BRANEN & THE BARRISTER :

A few months into the new job, whilst he was back in London to photograph an anti-government demo, Branen decided to drop in on the
Empire Room in Dean Street.

He was familiar with the club from his early days in Soho and he
wanted to catch up with the owner, Ayo Wood.

"Look who we've got here, darlings…" said Ayo, as Branen hesitated
in the doorway. "…My God man, come in… where have you been?"

There was the sharp smell of spirits mixed with stale cigarette smoke.

A punter sitting at the bar turned to look and fell off his stool.

Branen squeezed in and put his camera on the bar.

"What can I get you, Ben?" asked Ayo, who only knew him by his
real name.

"Give me a whisky and water and get yourself a drink… how's
tricks?"

"Same as ever… same old faces, hiding from reality, not wanting to
go home. I hate 'em and love 'em… and they pay the rent," said Ayo,
turning to the man who had struggled back onto his stool. "Time to
face the real world, Nigel."

"The real world is an illusion… reality is here in the bottom of my
glass…" said Nigel as he tried to stand up. "…Fuck the real world…"
He smashed his glass down onto the bar. "…I want love."

Ayo showed him the door. "I don't want you kissing my customers
again… be careful on your way down the stairs."

Nigel descended the stairs one by one swearing revenge at every step.

The man sitting next to Branen asked, "You a photographer…?
Expensive camera."

The man looked reasonably sober so Branen acknowledged him.
"Yes, a tool of the trade. What do you do?"

"I work at the bar…"

"This bar?"

"No, the legal bar… for fifteen years I've been a fucking lawyer…
but when I tell people, all I get is their problems… bit like being a
doctor. Do you earn well taking pictures?"

"Not as much as you."

"That depends… I earn too much for some people but not enough to support an ex-wife, a daughter and Ayo's extortionate prices... divorce can be expensive."

"Me too."

"What's that mean?"

"For me it was expensive emotionally... I've got a daughter too."

"Don't tell me... tell Ayo over there, he's used to listening to sob stories..." said the barrister, holding up his empty glass, "... do you want another?"

Branen saw the man had a glint in his eye. "Someone once said, 'Anyone who trades alcohol for happiness deserves neither'."

"I think you mis-quote Aristotle, my friend... but I give you the Bard, 'Alcohol provokes the desire but takes away the performance'."

"I don't think you need to worry about that at the moment..." said Branen, looking round the bar. "...You won't score in here tonight."

After that first meeting they agreed to keep in touch. Whenever Branen visited London on photographic assignments, they made a point of meeting up and in time became good friends.

He told Branen that he owned a yacht and invited him to go sailing; but like a lot of drunken invitations, it never happened.

The barrister had a contact in the stock market who fed at the top table and had advance notice of major deals. He had placed what was left from his divorce into the markets and was making 20% per annum. Even after tax it was good money. Branen decided to invest the £50,000 he had from the sale of the workshop using the barrister's contact as a broker.

Branen continued working undercover for The Associates as a photographer until he was ordered to carry out a mission that was to have devastating repercussions.

THE PLAN :

She could not be allowed to continue.

The latest of many incendiary rumours was that she was pregnant and might marry a Muslim whose billionaire father posed an unacceptable threat to the social, religious and political status quo.

Ignoring them was no longer an option. The threat had to be neutralized.

The plan had to be deniable otherwise it would have catastrophic consequences for the Government. It had to be flexible to allow for the unpredictable target. There would be no time for complicated set-ups, rigged machinery or tampered electronics. It had to be capable of being authorised or stood down at a moment's notice.

The planners called such schemes net concepts.

The project was ideally suited to The Associates.

Several strategies were put in place but since The Associates was small it did not have sufficient resources or personnel for complex operations, so reluctantly on occasion officers from MI6 or MI5, also known as The Firm, had to be called in.

All net concepts had to undergo exhaustive scrutiny and all of the options had to be operable within days if not hours of a green light. The current plan involved a car crash. It was originally conceived to get rid of Slobodan Milošević; but as he had been arrested, indicted and put on trial the plan was never implemented.

The Associates could not rely solely on a motor accident; the odds of survival were too high. There had to be a back-up plan.

PARIS : (AUGUST 1997)

The operation was mobilised as soon as The Associates received information that the target was going to visit the future father-in-law's hotel in Paris.

Central to The Associates' plan was an allegedly corruptible individual who was deputy head of security at the hotel and also conveniently the senior chauffeur. The Secret Intelligence Service knew the man well and had been paying him for his inside knowledge. His position in an important hotel that entertained ambassadors, politicians, criminals and other influential VIPs was invaluable. It was alleged that he was in the pay of more than one secret service and had money deposited in bank accounts all over the world.

A complete dry run of the plan had been rehearsed three weeks before the job was authorised. Using a different identity and different hotel from the final mission, fall-back scenarios were planned to cope with the unpredictable. Branen hired a bicycle and cycled the whole route, including his escape, and observed the patterns of behaviour of the staff at a motorcycle shop under the Route Périphérique.

Back in England, he contacted the Firm's Research and Facility department through his Operation Officer. Without knowledge of any details they produced a skeleton key and false French number plate for a Honda 750cc Africa Twin motorcycle.

PARIS : (SATURDAY 30 AUGUST 1997)

On that fateful Saturday, Branen crossed the channel at five thirty in the morning on the Eurostar from Waterloo.

It took nearly three hours to reach the Gare du Nord.

From the railway station he caught a taxi to Les Deux Magots on the Boulevard St Germain. It was a short walk to the family-run Hotel Gem.

In the small foyer stood a mahogany reception desk with one of those brass bells straight out of a 1940s Hollywood film. After he had rung the bell three times the owner finally appeared.

The hotelier contemplated him through hungover eyes, surprised to be receiving a guest so early in the morning, and took Branen's money with nicotine-stained fingers. A typically warm Parisian welcome. Branen checked in using a false name and passport.

Finally in his room he sorted out his kit and ordered a pastry and coffee from room service. A knock on the door revealed a less reserved hostess dressed in a baggy smock and apron with a dollop of jam on her rotund breasts. He checked the croissant to see if she had taken a bite on her way up. She gave him a wide inappropriate smile and wiped her mouth with the back of her hand. He wasn't sure what kind of tip she had in mind.

After a few pleasantries he eventually managed to ease her out of the door. She had to be the proprietor's wife and he couldn't have invented the pair of them.

Later, dressed as a tourist, he left the hotel carrying a grip containing his motorcycle leathers and false number plate. He crossed the Seine and then doubled back checking for tails. He walked up the Left Bank and crossed the river again and caught a taxi to the Marché aux Puces at Porte de Clignancourt. A hundred metres north of the flea market, under the Boulevard Périphérique, he went to a tool shop he'd found on the recce and bought a pair of tin snips and a screwdriver. On the far side of the flyover he found an alleyway. Keeping out of sight he changed into his leathers, and put his clothes into the bag.

There was a café within eyeshot of the chosen motorcycle shop. He sat in the window watching for a couple of hours.

Around the middle of the day the shop's staff turned their attention to lunch. This was his opportunity.

The shop had been chosen because it hired out motorbikes whose off-road capabilities would be useful for his mission. Five bikes were regimentally lined up on the pavement outside, leaning on their foot stands in perfect formation.

Branen had had several espressos and was feeling fairly wired when the time came to move. He stood looking through the shopfront for a few moments checking the four staff, who were all with customers. Two of the bikes were out of eyeshot from the shop interior. Pretending to try the end bike for balance, he slipped the skeleton key into the ignition and fired it up. With his bag in his lap he revved the engine quietly and rode off.

He drove into the centre of Paris and found a back street where he swapped the number plates. With the operation waiting for a green light, he was keyed up and anxious to get going.

His first contact was with a journalist who worked for the French Secret Service. The researchers had discovered his pederast peccadilloes and used a combination of blackmail and a large sum of money to persuade him to become involved. They told him they were a press syndication bureau and wanted an exclusive scoop on the passengers in the limo. His role was to delay the Ritz Hotel's Mercedes in one of the tunnels along the Seine. They gave him the planned route along the river and told him to wait for instructions. Half the money up front sealed the deal. Branen rang his mobile, gave him the catch-word and informed him that the project was ready to go; he told him he was to park his car beside the river on the Place de la Concorde and wait for his call.

Branen returned to the Ritz and waited to make his second contact.

When the hotel's senior chauffeur took his customary afternoon break he followed him; it was his habit to spend time in a bar close to his apartment.

Branen joined him at the bar, bought him a Pernod and engaged him in conversation, telling him that he was a press photographer. He explained that he had followed him and would pay him a substantial amount of money if he made sure he chauffeured the famous couple staying in his hotel. If they decided to go back to their apartment that evening, he was to convince them that he should use another route to avoid the hungry press pack. He explained this would allow him to get exclusive pictures and coverage of his prestigious passengers and make them both a lot of money. The chauffeur liked the idea and agreed to keep Branen posted.

They arranged to rendezvous in the Place Vendôme later in the day.

As the evening progressed the plan became increasingly viable.

As soon as he could slip away unnoticed, the chauffeur confirmed to Branen that he would drive the couple along the detour they had discussed.

An hour later, while the chauffeur was waiting for his passengers, he received a text message suggesting that he visit the hotel bar. One of The Associates' watchers had been allowed to break cover. She introduced herself as Branen's friend and showed him a cheque which she would give him in the morning when he had completed his side of the agreement. Then she bought him his favourite tipple, another large Pernod.

When the chauffeur went to the lavatory she spiked his drink with a strong solution of Prozac and Tiapridal from an eye-drop bottle. If his blood was ever tested, the traces in his system would be put down to his existing use of these prescription drugs.

Ten minutes before the target couple left the hotel by the rear entrance the chauffeur gave the pre-arranged signal to Branen who then alerted two agents on a second motorbike and called the journalist in his white Fiat in the Place de la Concorde.

When the limousine left to take the couple and their bodyguard back to their apartment on the Champs-Elysées, it was followed by Branen and the other motorcycle.

When the paparazzi in the Place Vendôme realised they had been duped they set out in hot pursuit on motor scooters and in cars.

The plan had been well conceived. The target's car was travelling at 120 kph as it entered the Pont de l'Alma tunnel. The operatives on the second bike accelerated alongside the Mercedes. The pillion passenger made eye contact with the chauffeur, tempting him to speed up. The bike slowed from 140 kph to match the speed of the limousine, which was closing on a white Fiat in front. The passenger on the bike twisted in his seat and turned on a 1000w strobe light that flashed twice per second. He focussed the light directly into the chauffeur's eyes. If anyone observed the flashes they could be blamed upon the ubiquitous paparazzi camera-flashes.

The Fiat brake-tested the limousine, which swerved and clipped the back of it. The Mercedes then careered into the central reservation, hitting a concrete pillar with an enormous impact throwing the car up in the air and spinning it round through 180 degrees. The Fiat continued on its way.

Branen was about seventy metres behind and had to brake hard and swerve round the condemned vehicle as it finally came to rest.

The crash was far more spectacular than anyone had expected and made his job easier. A heart attack could be brought on in relatively minor accidents but the severe nature of this crash made The Associates' plan even more believable.

Branen parked the bike ahead of the wrecked car and ran back through the smoke. The car's horn was jammed on. The raucous wail was unnerving. The tunnel was claustrophobic.

When he reached the vehicle, the horror of it made him hesitate; it was as if he were about to open a coffin lid without knowing what was inside. The extreme heat of the wreck, the noise and the smoke stopped him in his tracks. He pulled open the rear door of the car.

The pitiful sight smacked him in the gut. The heat was stifling and the acrid smell of burning oil turned his stomach.

The front passenger on the far side wasn't wearing a seat belt. He was screaming, blinded with blood, his face was a mess, a shotgun blast of glass particles; he must be the bodyguard. Branen knew this man had not and could not see him so he spared him.

The chauffeur was trapped over the steering wheel. The Arab was bent double in the distorted seat behind the bodyguard. Both appeared dead.

The target was dumped unceremoniously on the floor at his feet. She was slumped forwards and trapped behind the front seats; completely at his mercy. She was gasping for breath, moving her arms and trying to speak. She was dying.

Using the car door Branen blocked the view of anyone who might be approaching and took a hollow pin which was hidden in the hinge of the camera and looked for a flesh wound. There was a trickle of blood running down from a graze on her forehead where she had collided with the front seat and there was also a flesh wound on her thigh. As he went to insert the pin into the cut and release the neurotoxin he hesitated. This job had exposed him to the darkest workings of human nature and he felt a genuine pity, even sympathy for her; he had never had a target so vulnerable. He wanted to de-personalise the situation but it wasn't possible. Here was a fallible and beautiful woman and although she was almost dead, his job was to make sure.

The poison was an undetectable compound of oleandrin extracted from the oleander bush designed to cause a heart-attack; what he didn't know was that her pulmonary artery had already been torn and she was about to die anyway, literally of a broken heart.

Branen didn't want to do it; he couldn't go through with it.

He pressed the shutter release on the camera. The flash fired erratically, giving the impression of a stop-frame staccato action film.

The paparazzi and journalists were arriving. He heard the echoing footsteps as they ran towards the wreckage. Battle-hardened as some were even they stopped, assaulted by the noise and inevitable carnage that faced them.

Branen took a couple of wide-angle shots that might offer protection in case this assignment ever came back to haunt him.

As he looked through the viewfinder, a civilian with an emergency medical pack entered the edge of the frame. He was shouting into a mobile phone calling the emergency services. Branen pushed the car door closed without slamming it. One of the paparazzi arrived and pulled it open again. The man with the medical pack was a doctor. He pushed past the journalist and climbed into the wrecked car.

Branen slipped back into the meleé.

The trees along the side of the boulevard flashed by casting ominous shadows from the street lights. It looked as surreal as it felt.

He entered the Bois de Boulogne, a favourite hangout for transvestites. The park was networked with small roads and with a lake in the middle. He cut off-road onto a track towards the north of the lake, which led through the trees to a boat house. He changed the number plate back to the original. Removing his leathers he stood naked on the foot pegs and drove the bike at speed off the bank. The water was nearly two metres deep; enough to completely submerge the bike and remove any traces of DNA. The quagmire on the bottom swallowed the bike. If it was ever found and traced to the hire shop it would look as if it have been dumped by a joy-rider.

As he clambered back to shore, a figure emerged from the trees. Branen climbed up onto the bank and, pulling his feet out of the deep mud, tried to look as if it was something he did every day.

"Bonsoir... are you waiting for someone?" Branen asked in French.

"Do you always swim in the evenings?" the man asked. His false eyelashes blinked slowly and self-consciously like butterfly wings.

Branen was compromised. "Have you any plans for tonight?" Branen asked, trying to decide what to do.

"Only with you," he answered, and with a coquettish tilt of the head he flicked henna streaked hair off his face.

"Let me get dressed and perhaps we could have a beer."

The transvestite didn't want a love affair, he wanted to turn a franc in a hurry. "If you have me now, it will be a lot cheaper." He stood provocatively close with one hand on his hip pouting at Branen.

Branen pulled on his leathers and stepped into the boots, "Let's take a walk."

They walked into the woods.

"Ca va, ici," Branen said, turning to face his new friend.

"Deux cents francs pour le blow-job et quatre cents francs pour autres choses," he said, caressing his buttocks.

Branen took four one-hundred-franc notes from his wallet. The transvestite gently took the money and then the moon-light reflected off a blade, long enough to go right through Branen, that had appeared in his right hand.

"Donnez-moi votre portefeuille," he said, holding out his hand for the wallet.

That made up Branen's mind. He grabbed the hand and twisted. He heard the wrist crack as the tranny screamed and was forced to turn away. Branen kicked his legs away and he fell face down. Branen dropped his knees onto the back of the tranny's arms, making sure the blade in his right hand was trapped against the ground.

Branen leaned over him and hooked his left forearm round the man's throat and locked his left hand onto his right bicep. Putting his right hand onto the back of his head, he pulled him backwards, throttling him. He was strong and agile but Branen's grip was sound. Then the tranny's neck broke.

Branen walked back to the edge of the lake and changed his clothes. He put the motorcycle gear into the grip with some large stones and walked a hundred metres along the bank. Spinning round like a discus thrower he hurled it out into the lake. He stopped for a moment and watched it sink out of sight. After the splash, the only sound was of distant traffic. A calm, balmy atmosphere pervaded the lake as the ripples from the sinking bag reached the bank.

He stood there looking out over the water. The adrenalin was wearing off and a wave of doubt overcame him as he realised the enormity of what he was involved in.

The next morning he cut the false number plate into shreds with the tin snips and checked out of the hotel. Back at Deux Magots, the newspapers and television were saturated with the news of the deaths in the tunnel.

After depositing fragments of the number plate in the waste bins surrounding the Gare de Lyon, he caught a train south.

LONDON : (AUTUMN 1997)

Following the sensational press coverage of the accident Branen had to disappear. He'd had enough and now he wanted out of this world of violence; Paris was to be his last operation.

It was three months after the Paris job and nearly two years since he'd invested his money when a rise on the stock market led to his shares being worth nearly £100,000.

On one of his evenings with Anthony, the barrister warned him that the stock market was a circular bazaar and the recent rises would not continue forever.

When Branen told him he was looking for a way out of his job Anthony told him about a podere, a small-holding a friend was selling abroad. Instinctively Branen took the plunge and sold the shares. He told Anthony that his separation from Carrie and Jane was hurting as much as ever and he had decided to make one last attempt at reconciliation.

With the barrister's help, he bought the derelict stone farmhouse with a barn and six hectares of vines and olives that was to be his retreat.

It was a warm September day when Branen met Jane and Carrie at the Soho Café. They sat at an outside table in the sun; he had his arm round Carrie, who was now fourteen years old.

"This is hard…" he said, "I don't know how to ask you this, other than just saying it… would you give me another chance to make things right between us… I still love you… and Carrie. I've got a place abroad… we could start again… Carrie could go to school there…"

Carrie looked at her mother hopefully.

"Sorry darling…" said Jane and turned to Branen. "You can't ask me this now… it's too late… I'm in another relationship and I want to make it work."

Branen couldn't look at her.

"We had something really good but you kept breaking my heart… I had to move on," she whispered to him.

"I know…" He had no excuses.

Knowing that she was going to see her father, Carrie had written a letter and as they parted she gave it to him.

He kept the letter, along with a Polaroid he took of them that day.

THE JOURNALIST, THE CHIEF & THE SCS :

Even though it was a few years since the Paris mission the press coverage had not abated.

Conspiracy theories escalated and with the unrelenting publicity paranoia intensified within The Associates. It was not Associates' policy to assassinate one of its own unless the agent were to defect or turn double, but this case was unique.

Then the journalist who had driven the white Fiat in the Pont de l'Alma tunnel decided that the time had come to sell his story for enough money to secure his old age.

He wrote a five thousand word article and approached Le Monde. He could not have chosen a worse time. The editorial staff were in dispute with the management and the article was opened by a team leader with connections within the DGSE; they in turn contacted MI6.

On the day the Chief of MI5 heard the news from MI6 he happened to be lunching with the Senior Civil Servant. He suggested to the SCS that they share a taxi back to his office. "I've something to show you that might interest you." He was pleased to have one over on his higher-ranking colleague.

When the SCS saw the classified email he was shaken. The Associates was at risk of exposure in the same way that Group 13 had been when the Littlejohns, the IRA double agents, had tried to avoid prosecution in the UK by revealing that they were working for the SIS. This email could similarly threaten the very existence of The Associates.

The DGSE had not forwarded the complete article to the Chief but had merely outlined the accusations.

In order that nobody else, including the Chief, saw the whole document the SCS flew to Paris on the next available flight.

Even though the journalist had not known the whole truth, the facts he presented could destroy the credibility of, and permanently damage, the British Government; it did little to aid the SCS's digestion.

Unfortunately for him, rumours spread within Le Monde and although nothing could be confirmed yet another conspiracy theory began to circulate.

With this latest publicity refusing to die down the SCS's paranoia intensified. He wanted the Fiat journalist out of the way and he needed to guarantee Branen's silence. Branen could help cover up The Associates' involvement in Paris, so the SCS contacted him to explain that he wanted the Fiat journalist removed. Branen refused, telling the SCS that he had retired and didn't want anything to do with his previous life and he'd only agreed to be contactable via satellite phone because of his previous involvement.

Branen's reluctance led the SCS to the conclusion that Branen had become unreliable and that he would have to resolve the problem himself.

A month later the journalist was found dead with a hole in his head in a burnt-out car, in remote woodland near Montpellier. The Associates' agents searched his flat and removed any evidence of his ever having been involved in the assassination. The team leader at Le Monde was contacted and told to suppress the article.

The SCS needed to reinforce his hold over Branen. He could threaten to take retribution on his family if anything was ever revealed but the civil servant in him made him consider a more subtle approach; a psychological advantage, to show Branen that his daughter was within arm's reach and could easily have an accident.

To enable this, but without revealing his true intentions, he invited the Chief to another lunch at the Athenaeum and with a conspiratorial arm around his shoulders asked for help.

"Dear boy, I want you to take on and train a young woman who's the daughter of one of my best agents. He masterminded a major operation... of a highly sensitive nature that was crucial for this country's future and I want to look after his offspring."

Normally the Chief made a point of not letting personal matters interfere with professional decisions, particularly when in this case it involved the SCS doing someone a favour. But he also didn't want to cause any problems so close to his retirement. "Conveniently we do have a case where we are looking for a young female agent to infiltrate a Pakistani terrorist group. We suspect they are being financed by the sale of drugs... and we've located the distribution network run by some eccentric character called Michelle de Lavigne... we want to put someone on the inside. But your girl would have to pass through the training course..."

"I don't want this girl's life put at risk... I want her in one piece," the SCS said.

After carrying out background research, the Chief reluctantly agreed to enrol her on their training course.

PART ONE
Present day

1. CARRIE :

Carrie's earliest memories of her father were vague.

She was fourteen when he had unexpectedly turned up again. She had been excited to see him but her mother told her that he couldn't stay and he was soon gone again. She remembered him as a quiet man who had swept her up in his arms and held her close. As she grew up she began to understand how sometimes relationships didn't last, but she missed her father. His visit had made a deep impression on her and she couldn't forget him.

She didn't hold any resentment towards him and because her mother never said a bad word about him she realised Jane still held a candle for him. Her mother rarely mentioned him after that, but if she did it was always with affection.

Carrie left school at eighteen and went to a provincial university to study psychology. College life proved to be a difficult time for her. Her self-possession alienated the other girls who were wary of her, while the male students were never comfortable in her presence. Although it was nearly seven years since she had last seen her father, she still held a deep desire to see him again. It affected her attitude towards men and instead of dating her contemporaries she became involved with one of her tutors. Their affair came to the notice of the Principal and in the summer of her second year, at twenty years old, she left university. She convinced herself it was all too boring. She wanted results now, not years in the future.

She had no income and returned to London to live with her mother, who now had a twelve month old baby Georgie with her new partner Paul.

They lived a comfortable middle-class life in Hampstead; something Jane said she wanted after her experience with Branen.

The approach came in early January while Carrie was still searching for employment.

It was a cold sunny afternoon, and she was walking the family labrador on the Heath. She sat down on a bench looking out over London as the sun descended in the west.

A smartly dressed woman, whose appearance was unusual for someone walking on the Heath at that time of day, hesitated and then sat on the bench beside her. A minute or two passed. Carrie shifted uncomfortably. She glanced at the woman's tailored woollen coat. There was a strong scent of rose petals. As Carrie stood up to leave, the woman turned to her. "Carrie, I wonder if I could have a chat with you?"

Carrie stared at her, "How do you know my name?... Who are you?"

"I've got a proposition for you..."

"What's this all about?"

"I can help put you in touch with your father..."

"How do you know my father?"

"He is doing work of a highly sensitive nature for the Government... I'm offering you a job... the work would be secret and you'd receive proper training and a good salary."

"What training... Why should I believe you?"

"Your father is abroad but you will have opportunities to meet. You'll be able to give each other support." She deceived without guilt.

"Where is my father..?"

The woman saw Carrie's excitement at the mention of him.

"I can't give you that information yet."

"I'll need to discuss this with my mother."

"Of course... but it's probably better to keep it simple. Tell her it's a job with the Civil Service... for her own benefit."

Jane, only twenty years older than Carrie, was more like a sister and friend and she had no reason to disbelieve Carrie about the job. But she found it hard to understand why Carrie had to go away for six months 'on a training course'.

28

To spare her mother's feelings Carrie didn't mention the connection with her father. She sensed her mother's anxiety and tried to reassure her that she would keep in regular touch while she was away.

Jane knew that to become too inquisitive would alienate her daughter, who had inherited her father's independence.

By July Carrie had finished her training and returned home.

"It worries me that you don't tell us about your work," said Jane.

"There's nothing to tell... it's just a job."

"Your mother's concerned about you," said Paul.

Carrie turned on him. "It's none of your business."

"Don't talk to Paul like that... you look tired..."

"I am tired... there's nothing to worry about... I just need to be on my own. I've got to move out of London anyway."

"Where are you going?" asked Jane.

"I don't know yet..."

"The more evasive you get the more concerned your mother's going to become," said Paul.

"Who asked you?"

"Why are you forcing an argument?" asked Jane.

Carrie picked up her bag. "It's better for everyone if I move out."

Carrie didn't want to deceive her mother but the Controller had told her that she would be protecting her mother by not letting her know about the role she was going to play.

Jane had no real reason for her worries and tried to assuage her fears by convincing herself she was laying her own personal baggage on her daughter. But her intuition told her all was not well. In the end, Jane decided that Carrie was having an affair and did not want to discuss it.

Carrie felt guilty so made sure she regularly texted her mother to stop her worrying, promising to visit when she had sorted herself out.

Carrie was turning out to be an ideal agent for the Firm's plans to infiltrate the drugs ring in Soho; and the SCS had Branen's daughter within easy reach.

The full implications of the plan the SCS had put in place, and the extent of the fraud that had been plotted long before that fateful meeting on Hampstead Heath, would never be known to Carrie.

2. SOHO, LONDON – (PRESENT DAY)

Soho was a village in the heart of London but it kept its own heart hidden and beating within the bars, clubs and dark alleyways.

So! Ho! was the hunting call when Henry VIII chased wild boar in the woods where Soho now stood. If you listened carefully today you would still hear the snorts of male boars as they copulated in tarts' rented rooms.

Winter was closing in but the smell of autumn was still in the air as the cold wind gusted down the narrow streets.

The wind spun the remaining leaves down from the trees in Soho Square and blew them high up beyond the neon glow that hung over the buildings silhouetted against the sky.

Entering Soho, there was a change of atmosphere from London's traffic-congested metropolis; a distinct atmosphere of veiled tension, excitement and anticipation of forbidden fruit, available to those who knew where to look. Couples romanced, sitting out at pavement cafés. Girls touted for business in strip-club doorways. Messengers wearing aerodynamic sunglasses carried silver film cans from processing laboratories to production houses.

The tourist-guide version was on show throughout. But underneath the sociable veneer of the cafés, bars, restaurants and delis existed a world of racketeering, extortion and a thriving drug industry. Since the second World War the Greeks, the Maltese and more recently the Asians had fought with the London mobsters for control of sex joints and drinking clubs.

3. HARRY : (MONDAY 2 NOVEMBER)

Harry was a thickset man who, although fat, looked powerful and full of threat. He was wearing a grey roll-neck sweater over grey baggy trousers and worn trainers. He didn't stand out in a crowd; that is, unless you looked into his eyes. The few people who did would not hold his gaze for long.

He wearily looked up from the old computer screen. It was grey outside and beginning to rain. He went over to the dinette and took out two tins of Tate and Lyle syrup and a slab of Stilton cheese from the melamine cupboard. He cursed as he tried to open the drawer which was stuck in its runners. He stuffed a chunk of cheese into his mouth and stabbed holes in the bottom of the syrup tins.

Harry's flat was on the corner of Dean Street and Bateman Street with windows that looked out over both. The computer sat on a desk against the wall between two casement windows overlooking Dean Street. Alongside the workbench on the adjacent wall was a table with an old television and a battered DVD and VHS recorder. As well as a cheap office chair he had a generous armchair with a folding-out leg support and sliding drinks tray. The leatherette was permanently dented from the hours he spent watching DVDs and tapes. Tatty canvas blinds hung loosely in all the windows and the flat smelled of stale cooking oil and sweat.

Taking the syrup with him, he wandered across to the wooden steps. Using his free arm he unlocked the roof-light and pushed up the heavy glass door until it locked vertically.

The rain fell lightly through his thinning greasy hair. He shivered as he emerged onto the roof. From this dark vantage point he could, unseen, watch people without their knowledge. He found solace up on his roof in the night with his bees. He took a deep breath of city air. He loved the anonymity of urban life, little realising that his stature and arcane presence gave him an aura that couldn't easily be ignored. His other refuge was the numbness generated by his cocktail of drugs. For that and other sins he had to suffer the repercussions of the hangover, the anxiety and the contrition.

Going to the first hive he turned the tin upright and put it on the hole in the top of the crown board, allowing the syrup to drip slowly through into the brood box. He missed out the middle hive containing the camera, and repeated the task in the third hive.

"That'll keep you fat for winter." He walked to the edge of the balustrade and looked out over Soho.

The constant buzz of the bees went deep into Harry's psyche. He would sometimes, like now, feel reassured by the sound. At other times it would trigger his paranoia and leave him desperately anxious. The bees went about their business uninterrupted by the prejudices and platitudes of others. They didn't encroach. They left him alone and he admired their self-sufficiency.

A gust of wind whistled through the hives and across the darkness came the sound of a thumping bass. He stood hesitating at the edge of the roof. Another blast of wind and he felt himself being pushed over the low balustrade. He looked down, drawn into the abyss. There was no mid-ground, only the edge of the building and the road four storeys below.

There in the flat across the road they danced, smoking a joint and swaying to the music.

"Blow me, honey," Harry said as he crouched down behind the balustrading; hiding from the wind, and them.

When Carrie had moved into the flat opposite it hadn't been easy for Harry to observe her from his window without being seen. So he had sacked the temple and built his own Trojan horse; the hive camera had solved the problem.

4. HARRY & SNOWMAN : (EARLY HOURS, TUESDAY 3 NOVEMBER)

Soho Cars' office in Old Compton Street used to be a tobacco kiosk.

The Black Brothers took it over in the eighties and still ran it from the pavement. The brainy one, Saul, stayed in the kiosk answering the phone and quoting fares. The biggest brother, George, was security, sorting out the drunks and the debates. The third brother, Stewart, was the streetman who called in the cabs with a piercing whistle. The lucky ones, parked within eyeshot with engines running, had the advantage. Harry preferred to cruise past letting them know he was available, then park up waiting for them to call him.

Harry White was the name on his licence and he had been given the nickname 'Whitey' by the Brothers as he was the only white man on the fleet.

They knew Whitey didn't like to go far from Soho but he would work the early-hour shift when demand was high, punters intoxicated, and cabs hard to find.

It was 3.45am on Tuesday morning when the mobile rang. Harry was parked in Greek Street, just round the corner, in his scruffy red Datsun with tinted windows. He was wearing a straw hat, narrow brimmed with a woven rafia chequered band. When he put it on he became Jack the lad, a facade which allowed him to hide the anguish and deep conflicts within him.

"One for you, Whitey?"

"Yeah."

The odd-looking man waiting on the pavement by the kiosk was a regular. The man didn't bother with the half-eaten sandwich and newspapers on the front seat; he got straight in the back.

Snowman was of mixed race with white hair. He was anomalous; he had negroid features, pale skin and blue eyes. He was lean and laid-back and the way he listened attentively made him attractive to women.

"Poland Mansions," said Snowman, "That's Poland Street... where you've taken me before." He felt he had to repeat himself.

Harry had been Snowman's chosen driver for the last few months; three or four times a week he had run him a few hundred yards around Soho and Harry wondered who the man he called the mutant was trying to impress. He didn't like him. In fact, if he ever thought about it, Harry didn't really like anybody.

He turned out into Charing Cross Road, up to the junction and turned left at the no left turn into Oxford Street. He drove west across the top of Soho and turned into Poland Street.

"The block on the left."

The passenger's command brought Harry out of his ruminations. Before he realised it they had arrived. He often drove on automatic pilot and couldn't always remember making the journey.

He jumped the lights on amber and swung the car over to the nearside kerb.

"Five pounds."

The man didn't argue. It was 4am. He slammed the door.

Harry took out a little notebook and filled in a record of his trip in his tight handwriting. His account with the Brothers was religiously settled at the end of each week. They would subtract the cost of his amphetamines and amylnitrate along with 30% of every fare they booked for him.

Harry wound his way back past a street-cleaning lorry trundling along the kerb, its giant circular brushes sweeping up the city's refuse.

'Enough,' thought Harry and went home.

5. SNOWMAN : (EARLY HOURS, TUESDAY 3 NOVEMBER)

The Otis lift didn't work. This wasn't unusual. The old accordion gates often stuck in the floor groove, which was filled with a lifetime's grime.

Snowman had been on his feet for eight hours touring Soho's clubs and bars, checking his contacts and selling to his clients. It had been a good night; he had collected nearly three grand today. He unlocked the top and bottom Chubbs and found the middle one wasn't double locked.

She was still awake and waiting for him, or perhaps he woke her but she wasn't telling. He lay on top of her, his strange pallor against her rich dark African skin. In the glow of the sodium light coming through the net curtains they looked like a slice of chocolate cake topped with vanilla ice cream.

Snowman jumped awake at 11am when a taxi braked viciously outside his flat, blasting its horn and trying unsuccessfully to avoid an old man with a walking stick.

Looking down at the street he thought, 'Now he'll need two sticks.'

Myrtle had already gone. His heart was palpitating. He closed his eyes. He tried not to make a habit of joining in with his clients' indulgences but last night he had been tempted. And now he had to let his body recover its balance. He drank a pint glass of water and blew his nose. It started to bleed.

"I should fucking know by now."

Blocking his nostril he settled back onto the bed.

The three room flat was glowing with wintry sunshine.

The building on the opposite side of Poland Street was a modern glass office block that had made some local Westminster councillor rich when the demolition order for the old terrace town houses was signed. The new building only reached up as far as the third storey, allowing Snowman's windows to see the sky.

The resurrection for Snowman was at about 3pm, but not before a tumbler of Fernet Branca did he feel ready to face the day. He showered and completed fifteen, ten and then five chins on the bar followed by a series of fifty, thirty and twenty press-ups. He flexed his wiry body in the bathroom mirror and practised a range of lightening punches. "Not bad at my age."

Then he went back to bed.

The second coming was at about five that afternoon.

Myrtle had returned home an hour before and now Snowman felt ready to face the day.

He got up and started to dress.

"Ain't you gonna have a shower?" asked Myrtle.

"I already did… fuck it's getting dark… here comes winter."

He pulled on a tight white T-shirt and a pair of dungarees with many pockets. Then he donned a black hunting vest he'd bought in Los Angeles that had even more pockets; some he still hadn't discovered. If he was fleeced by the old bill or a mugger was stupid enough to hit on him, the many pockets would add to the confusion. He had secret pockets where he kept his stash and obvious pockets where he kept small amounts of cash; the old Bill weren't beyond keeping a hundred quid and letting him go.

He put on a black pork-pie hat and a padded nylon flying jacket, kissed Myrtle good-night and stepped out into the hallway.

He kicked the doors of the Otis and walked down the stairs.

Meanwhile Myrtle was on the phone planning her evening.

Back on the street Snowman went into his favourite coffee shop. He ordered a mocha for the chocolate and an almond croissant for the sugar. Breakfast tasted good and he smoked his first small cigar of the evening. Then another coffee; an espresso for the caffeine and a Danish pastry to settle his stomach.

He was just about ready to start his day's work.

6. CARRIE & SNOWMAN :

It was the previous August when Carrie had moved into the top floor flat, above The Crown and Two Chairmen, that her MI5 Controller had rented from the landlord. The pub was on the corner of Dean Street and Bateman Street on the opposite side to Harry's flat.

Her cover story was that she was working as a photographic model represented by the London Model Agency. She was comfortable in front of the camera and enjoyed living and working in Soho, where her parents had lived when she was a child.

Her first objective was to make contact with the Snowman at Costas's Lounge. She spent a few days wandering around, visiting her model agency and checking out Soho.

As dusk descended the neon lights from the bars and cafés replaced the disappearing daylight. The streets came alive and like her mother, Carrie took to Soho's conviviality. The summer nights buzzed with people hanging out in pavement bars, drinking too much, laughing and arguing and strolling arm in arm down the middle of the road. It made Carrie feel alive and vital.

On the day she decided to have the meeting it happened to be her twenty-first birthday, so she phoned her mother. "Hi Mum…"

"Happy birthday, darling. Can we meet up? I've got a present for you."

"I'm working outside London…" She hated deceiving her mother.

"Where are you? What are you doing?"

"I'm enjoying my work but I can't tell you about it 'cos it's confidential…"

"Are you seeing someone?"

"Don't worry, Mum, I will explain it when I see you."

"When will that be?… I never see you…"

"I've got to go, Mum… I love you. I promise I'll be in touch."

That evening she turned up at Costas's for a couple of cocktails; she deliberately wore a provocative décolleté top which stopped above her midriff and a short skirt cut low on her hips.

Costas's Lounge was not strictly a private bar, but if a visitor was antisocial it became a members' only club. A buxom woman with bottle-blonde hair sat at the bar with the glazed expression of a person who had given up blaming alcohol for her predicament. Her face had the texture and colour of dough.

Costas was resting on his elbows behind the bar talking to her, and when he saw Carrie his expression changed.

Jack the young barman was first on the scene. He put down the tumbler he had been drying and made straight for Carrie, ignoring a man moulded to his stool in the corner of the bar who was holding up his empty glass and calling for more.

Costas broke off from his conversation and edged Jack aside. "Go get Charlie his drink."

"This lady was first," said Jack.

"I'll deal with her."

"You're too old, Guv."

"You're too young, Jack."

"Do you think Charlie ought to have another?" Jack didn't want to leave the conversation.

Costas cupped his hand by his mouth so Carrie couldn't see his lips and mouthed, "Fuck off."

Jack reluctantly withdrew, mumbling. Carrie winked at him; he hesitated, but seeing Costas's expression decided to get Charlie his drink.

"I haven't seen you in here before," Costas said, maintaining eye contact with Carrie.

"This is the first time I've been here..." said Carrie. "Is it alright if I have a drink? I'm not a member."

Costas leaned over the bar in a conspiratorial manner. "Any time... make yourself at home, darling... do you live round here?"

Carrie held his gaze and smiled.

Snowman arrived at Costas's about an hour later and was welcomed by a loud-mouthed cockney sitting at a table by the door with a young blonde woman who looked as though she had been drawn by Vargas.

The loudmouth had come on to Carrie earlier, letting her know in a voice loud enough for everyone around to hear, "I'm a show-biz agent... I represent London's top talent in stand-up comedy."

When his girlfriend turned up he'd had to cool it. But this hadn't stopped him eyeing up Carrie every time his woman turned away.

Carrie recognised Snowman from the covert mug-shots she had been shown during her briefing and now her work started for real.

Snowman noticed her when he shook hands with the cockney agent, who instantly reached for his wallet.

"Relax and buy me a drink," said Snowman.

While he spent as little time as he could with the cockney he kept an eye on Carrie who was sitting alone at the far end of the bar. Again Snowman shook hands with the cockney and smiled at Carrie; not something he did very often.

She returned his smile.

Snowman went over to her, "Don't you have any friends?"

Carrie looked around. "I can't see anyone else."

"What's your name?"

"Carrie."

"Would you like a drink, Carrie?"

She checked her watch. "Why not?"

"Indeed…" Snowman waved to the barman. "Another cocktail for Carrie, Jack."

"Unusually generous of you," said Jack, looking pissed off.

Carrie looked into Snowman's cerulean blue eyes, which had not been apparent in the photographs.

Snowman smiled for the second time. "Do you come here often?"

Carrie ignored the cliché. "I moved into Soho recently."

"What do you do?"

"I'm a model."

"Really?"

"Fashion and advertising… not what you're thinking. What about you?"

"I'm an entrepreneur."

"What's that mean?"

Snowman smiled for a third time that night. "Let's go somewhere else for a drink?"

"I'm happy here."

"If you came with me I could show you what an entrepreneur is."

"It's okay, I already know… I wanted to see if you knew."

It wasn't often Snowman was lost for an answer.

Carrie decided to take a chance. "I couldn't help noticing you passed that man a wrap and I wondered if..."

"So that's why you're so friendly."

"Well, partly..."

"What's the other part?"

Carrie picked up her cocktail.

Snowman put the flat of his hand on the counter. "Try a taster, you might not like it."

Snowman hadn't noticed a group of girls at a table in the back corner of the bar. One of them was Myrtle and she hadn't missed the tête à tête. She broke away from the others and went over to the bar.

"Hello."

Snowman didn't like surprises.

"Hi," said Carrie, she reached out a hand, "My name's Carrie."

Myrtle shook her hand. "Myrtle," and turning to Snowman, added, "Surprise."

Snowman scooped up the wrap and smiled for the last time that evening.

7. CARRIE & HARRY & SNOWMAN :
(WEDNESDAY 4 NOVEMBER)

It was now almost three months since Carrie had moved into Soho and persuaded Snowman that he could use her flat as a safe house for his cash and his stash. He found her sexy and was attracted by her independence; he had no idea that he was being manipulated.

Harry sat transfixed. He watched and wished.

Using the remote control he tightened the zoom on the beehive camera. The image of all his fantasies was on the monitor with the DVD burner recording on the desk in front of him. He was aroused, observing a beautiful woman without her being aware that he was watching.

She was in her dressing gown at the computer on a desk in the window. She leaned back for a moment looking up at the ceiling. Then she stood up, took the mirror off the wall and carried it over to the coffee table. She pulled a wrap from her pocket, chopped out and snorted a line of coke, splitting it between each nostril. She shivered and found temporary escape.

The Firm had not foreseen the possibility that Carrie could be seduced by cocaine; let alone the irresistible hit she had recently discovered from a lung-full of crack smoke.

The drugs had allowed her some space to deal with the constant pressure of deception and pretence that she had to maintain twenty-four hours a day.

The idea had first occurred to Harry after an argument with the Brothers. He'd been watching Snowman coming and going from Carrie's flat for the last few weeks. The vast amounts of cash the mutant would throw on the table, the flashy necklace and the gold Oyster Rolex dangling from his wrist angered Harry. While he ferried self-important film people around Soho earning a few measly quid, that extravagant white haired piss-head made a fortune and fucked Carrie whenever he wanted to. Life wasn't fair. "Wait till you see what I've got planned, you fucking mutant... I want to see you suffer... and I want some of that tart."

Snowman cut through the alleyways to Carrie's front door in Bateman Street. He went through his pockets and then rang the bell. Carrie answered the intercom and let him in.

Harry heard himself say, "He must have forgotten his key."

He watched the monitor as the mutant undid the top of his dungarees and tied the braces round his waist. Harry moved irritably in his chair. "He's playing it cool and she loves it."

Snowman put a bottle of Delamain brandy on the coffee table. He noticed the remains of the coke on the mirror and looked at Carrie, who was calculatedly ignoring him.

"I thought you were looking perky," he said sarcastically.

She kept her back to him.

"Haven't you got any work this week?" he said, as he rolled a joint.

She continued to ignore him. He took a metal toolbox from the sideboard and opened it with a key hanging from a bootlace round his neck. The ritual preparation of his product involved the use of chemistry scales, Stanley knife blades, cling film and three-inch squares of paper. He sat down in front of the mirror surrounded by his equipment. Adrenalin coursed through him as he planned the night ahead; his routine of bars and clubs with the punters laying all that cash on him.

He turned to Carrie, "Stop fucking around with that computer and give me a hand."

He would cut the 28 grammes of cocaine with twelve grammes of crushed Proplus tablets and Vitamin C powder. The process of measuring out and wrapping would take over an hour. Carrie would have to fold the wraps for him.

She was finding it difficult to stay in character; she had to play the bimbo and Snowman was no fool. She couldn't let her guard drop for a moment. She did enjoy Snowman's company and the occasional line and drink helped her relax into the role. But when she agreed to lead this double life she hadn't realised how difficult it would be to maintain the depths of deceit and to manage the strain from months of under-cover work. Her training and psychological examinations had been thorough, but until an agent was out there on their own it was impossi-ble to predict how they would react after months and sometimes years of stress.

Snowman poured himself a large cognac and went to work, adding the caffeine powder and vitamin C to the coke, then shaking the polythene bag to mix it up.

"The healthiest charlie in the West End," he said, holding it up to Carrie.

He tipped it out onto the mirrored altar and halved it, weighing it repeatedly, until he was left with forty one-gramme piles. Chopping and dividing his stash was a therapeutic process and with the help of the cognac and a spliff Snowman had reached a trance-like state.

Carrie was cutting and folding paper, until she finally tossed the last wrap onto the table. "I'm going up the road for ten minutes... don't go away."

He handed her a wad of cash. "Take that... and take the rubbish down when you go."

Harry was still slumped in his battered armchair, a pint glass full of mead and vodka in his hand, watching and recording.

Snowman only really had one problem in life and that was how to launder all the cash he made. He couldn't put it in the bank because without a satisfactory explanation they were obliged to alert the authorities.

So he set up Myrtle in a cash business and kept his immediate earnings stuffed in a Slazenger tennis bag under the bed. Myrtle bought a massive cast iron range and opened an African restaurant at the top end of Berwick Street. She cooked three dishes a day, two meat and one fish, each accompanied by sweet potatoes, yams and African beer. Her customers were regular and adoring.

Eventually Snowman's profit had become too substantial for the small restaurant to launder. He needed another business with potential for a considerable cash turnover so he bought the building next door to the restaurant under his company's name Heavy Duty Limited, and set up a jewellery shop. It allowed Myrtle to turn over larger cash amounts without attracting attention.

She fiddled the turnover in an attempt to keep the figures realistic, and paid a local accountant extortionate hourly rates to authenticate the books. Her annual turnover was declared and the tax paid with no questions asked.

Myrtle and her man lived very well indeed; but then they did tend to pay for a lot in cash.

8. HARRY : (WEDNESDAY 4 NOVEMBER)

Harry was wearing XXL yellow rubber Marigolds as he went through Carrie's rubbish.

He had watched her dump it by the door before she wandered off. Checking that the coast was clear he trudged downstairs, past her front door, casually picking up the bag.

He found what he wanted; her email address. He sat at his computer and went to work. It had to look as if his email was from an enemy at street level. Someone the mutant had come in contact with during his business transactions around Soho.

Ten thousand pounds was a lot of money but judging by the bundles of cash he had watched Snowman playing with, he would pay it to keep out of jail.

Setting up a new identity had not been a problem for Harry. Before moving into Soho he had registered in the false name of Harry White for driving lessons at the British School of Motoring in Oxford Street; he would laugh to himself as he pretended to drive like a learner.

Six weeks later he had taken the test and passed first time. Using the mailboxes outside Giovanni's store as his address, he eventually received his new driving licence. Then he opened a bank account in the name of Harry White and with that he rented his flat; it wasn't difficult. At the same time he'd launched a proxy email account through Amsterdam and configured his address as a random collection of numbers and letters. He didn't have to give a name and had paid with a money order through the Bureau de Change on Shaftesbury Avenue.

Harry's hands shook with anticipation as he composed the email. He made it sound illiterate, as though he were an uneducated punter who had been let down by his drug-dealer. 'I hope I haven't overdone it,' he thought, as his finger hung nervously over the send button; once he hit the key there would be no going back. 'I need a plan to collect the money, without getting caught...' He took his hand away. 'I'll have a drink and a line... and then decide.'

9. CARRIE & SNOWMAN : (WEDNESDAY 4 NOVEMBER)

Snowman tucked the tongue of the final wrap back into itself and stubbed out his spliff. He was feeling mellow.

He cleaned the scales and put them back in the toolbox. From the bottom compartment he took out two piles of fifty pound notes and distributed the cash into the many pockets of his waistcoat. As he was counting out several more piles, Carrie returned with a carrier bag full of shopping. He emptied the bag onto the floor and filled it with the money.

"I've got to go and earn a living," said Snowman.

"Can I come with you?"

"If I get any aggro and you're with me, it makes me weak. I have to watch my back… I don't want you getting hurt."

"How long will you be?"

"A couple of hours."

"You always say that."

He gathered up his wraps and the carrier bag. "See you later."

Snowman's routine was important. He had to be in a given pub or bar at a regular time. The punters came to rely on this and would be waiting for his arrival. Most punters were subtle enough not to make the business transactions too obvious, but a noticeable frisson of expectation would run through a bar when he entered.

His routine was necessary but at the same time could be dangerous if his cover was ever blown.

10. HARRY, CARRIE & SNOWMAN :
(WEDNESDAY 4 NOVEMBER)

Harry was in charge. He was supreme. The speed had hit home.

He went over to the window and watched through a gap in the blind as Snowman came out onto the street.

With the rush of amphetamine-induced adrenalin he entered the unknown; he pressed the send key and set the scam in motion.

Back at his monitor he watched Carrie's face closely. She was beautiful. She looked troubled. She was reading his email.

He reached down and started to massage his crotch.

Carrie stared at the screen in disbelief. She called Snowman. The phone rang and rang. She threw the phone down in frustration; he must have be in a noisy pub or club. She read the email again. "What is this? It's got to be a joke." She sent Snowman a text; it was 8.15pm.

Snowman was one hundred and fifty metres from Carrie's flat, in the Ship in Wardour Street, having his first drink of the evening.

He was preparing himself for the night ahead. He sank a couple of pints of strong bitter; its mildly hallucinogenic quality would help him deal with the punters who were usually drunk. His self-confidence reassured them that they were dealing with the main man, and it deterred them from becoming too lippy.

Fortified against external forces Snowman left the Ship and set out for Madame LuLu's with the carrier safely under his arm; before starting his rounds he had to meet Mikey.

Snowman never sold to a face he didn't know. If an existing client wanted him to supply a friend, he had to be introduced personally. In fellow workmates' eyes there was a certain status for a punter to be recognised by his drug dealer; to enter the rigmarole of exchanging money with the opening handshake, a short conversation, and the final handshake when the elixir was handed over. The mutual trust that the amount of money was correct and that the measure and purity of the drug was consistent was, until abused, taken for granted. The deal was done as a secret ceremony, which only the chosen few were allowed to attend. A ritual supposedly unobserved by the bar staff, who in this scenario represented authority, yet if it were totally unobserved would not give the purchaser the necessary kudos.

As Snowman left the pub his mobile beeped. It was a text from Carrie.

'Impatient bitch,' Snowman said to himself, and ignored it.

11. MIKEY : (WEDNESDAY 4 NOVEMBER)

If it had existed at all, Mikey's childhood had been brief.

She spent her early years in and out of institutions and had learned how to protect herself. Without her spikey, bleached hair and year-round suntan she looked unremarkable. But she was intelligent and street-wise and that had allowed her to build her property and night club empire. She was of average height and medium build, but her ego compensated for any lack of physical presence.

Mikey pulled the silk sheets up over her head, rolled over and stretched out an arm. The bed was warm and the sound of purring comforting. The Persian cat arched its back and stretched the sleep from its body. It crawled to Mikey, rubbing its face on hers; it was ready to eat.

Mikey opened one eye and pulled the cat down into her arms. "Okay, greedy cat... what's the time?"

The Bang & Olufson alarm started its gentle beep.

"Shit... I'm sure I set it for midday."

It was midday.

She got up, holding her head and shielding her eyes from the sun streaming through the damask drapes. She pulled on a robe and stumbled into the living room, which was decorated theatrically with velvet drapery and expensive Gothic furniture. Picking the cat up she went over to the panoramic window. From her penthouse she could sense Soho was awake and ready for her.

She fed the cat and made a pot of coffee. She showered, dressed in a man's Armani suit and rubbed gel through her hair.

Mikey had grandiose political ambitions. She had wealth, but not the respect and power she craved and believed that she deserved. It was no secret that she despised the Jews and hated the nouveau-riche bourgeois Pakistanis who were becoming ever more dominant and, more worryingly, gaining political influence. But they supplied her with raw cocaine and it was in her interest to ingratiate herself with them. She was an important client; even though she was a woman dealing in a Muslim world she was accepted despite, or perhaps because of, her bizarre and androgynous appearance.

The Pakistanis worked hard and were taking over an increasing share of the drug and pornography trades in Soho. Not only did they seem to Mikey to be unstoppable, they had reneged upon their original agreement and were diluting the product. "Why should they be over here gaining credibility in society when I'm English born and bred?" she asked the cat. "One day, if I don't stop them, they'll be dictating my future and my life... I need to destroy them... undermine their religion and their very existence."

Her plan was simple in essence but complicated in its execution.

It was a couple of months since she had started a rumour around Soho of a terrorist group operating in the area. The story had spread amongst the local gossips and the original source was lost. It was these rumours that reached the ears of the police and subsequently been passed on to MI5.

Whilst Mikey was canvassing as the candidate for the local British

National Party she handed out leaflets around Soho. She would not normally mix with people on the street, but leafleting allowed her to be the centre of attention. If her pompous preaching was challenged it would incite her to become even more vociferous, which in turn fuelled her sense of self-importance.

It was while she was door-stepping in Soho that she noticed the flags of St. George outside the George & Dragon pub in Chinatown; an English symbol hijacked by the extreme right-wing. The pub was a Caucasian island stronghold; an invitation to the fascist elements.

Closer inspection revealed a black door, right next to the pub. 'Masonic Mansions' was carved into the stone above the door. The building consisted of three flats on three floors above the pub. She noticed the first two floors were let to local Chinese businesses but there was no name on the top bell.

She got into conversation with the landlord of the pub and discovered the top floor mansion flat was vacant. Pretending to show no particular interest in the flat Mikey didn't find it difficult to persuade the landlord to vote for BNP at the next local election.

Later she called Snowman and told him to rent the top floor apartment under the name of Harold Singh and to tell the landlord they intended to import spices.

To swing the deal and discourage any further questions, Snowman gave the landlord a fistful of fifty pound notes and promised all future rent would be paid in, "... notes of the Realm." They duly signed a lease and shook hands on the deal.

Over a couple of drinks the landlord commented on the contradiction between Snowman's appearance and his Asian name. Snowman explained that it must have been some distortion of names in his forefathers' history.

The landlord claimed he didn't doubt the explanation.

Now Mikey had her premises and through her Pakistani contacts found two illegal immigrants desperate for work to run her factory. They didn't know it but they were destined to be Mikey's sacrificial lambs.

12. SNOWMAN & MIKEY : (WEDNESDAY 4 NOVEMBER)

Snowman walked through Soho to Madame LuLu's in Brewer Street.

Sabrina was on the door and typical of the club's clientele. He or she was a hangover from the 80s New Romantics. She wore a gold lamé smock over skin-tight satin trousers and a white bowler hat on her head; her face was sculpted with thick make-up. She was responsible for the running of Mikey's clubs and acted as Mikey's confidante; giving support when Mikey suffered her drug-induced bouts of self-doubt. She was irreplaceable.

Sabrina didn't look up as Snowman entered.

"We're closed love… don't bother to come back until midnight… no action until then." Sabrina still had her head down.

When the visitor didn't leave, she looked up. "Darling, why didn't you say it was you?"

She welcomed Snowman with open arms. The bright red lipstick kiss on his pale face beneath the black pork-pie hat made him look like a cartoon character.

Snowman went through the velvet curtain and down the dark mirrored staircase into the club. The decor was a modern mix of art nouveau and art deco; neither one nor the other and missing the point of both. The room was infused with the plush and sleazy atmosphere that pervaded the club whatever time of day or night it was.

Mikey was sitting at a table by the bar. She saw Snowman and beckoned him over. "There you are," she said, pointing to a chair. Snowman sat down and put the bag on the floor under the table.

"Drink?"

"Just a coffee," he said, lighting his second cigar of the evening.

Not to be outdone, Mikey opened a box of Sobranie Black Russian. She ostentatiously put a pink cigarette into a holder and lit it with a jewel-encrusted lighter.

Mikey turned to the bar. "Tilly… a coffee and another iced Stoli," then to Snowman, "Is that my bag?… It's overdue."

He nodded.

"And?" asked Mikey, frustrated by his enigmatic manner.

"Everything's okay… apart from a few Paki dealers…" he stopped in mid-sentence. The moment he said it he regretted it; the less she knew about his end of the business the better.

She gestured at the carrier bag. "Is it all there?"

"As always... less five hundred for the Masonic Mansion flat."

"I can't supply you any more at the moment, m'dear."

"What about next week?"

"You are doing very well, aren't you? You kept me waiting, now you'll have to wait."

Snowman ignored her, "I'll take two Ks... one of each," he said.

Mikey leant forward and stared into his eyes. "I hope you're not spreading into the Garden... ARE YOU?"

"Mikey, I'm your main man in Soho and if I want to spread my wings a little that's my decision... remember I do the streets... you don't know fuck-all about it... you wouldn't last long where I work."

"You remember who butters your bread."

"If I move into the Garden I'll do better for you than anyone else."

Snowman didn't like her but he had to deal with her otherwise he didn't deal. "I'll handle them... I'll make more money... You'll gain... we'll both gain."

Mikey reached over and wiped the lipstick from his face. She felt threatened by his territorial aspirations. "Remember... there's a lot of fish in the sea, and I'm the fisherman... and don't you worry your pretty little head about the Pakis... I've got plans for them. I want you to come to my apartment at three tomorrow afternoon... I want to talk to you."

Snowman picked up his coffee and thought to himself, 'I'm close to the top of the feeding chain. I need to cut Mikey out and meet the big cheese who supplies her. I'll buy bigger, cheaper, increase my profits and I wouldn't have to deal with Mikey's crap.'

Covent Garden offered rich pickings and since he had Soho covered he wanted to expand his territory. The advantage of both 'the Village' as Snowman called Soho, and 'the Garden', was their size. They were both less than a mile across and with a couple more of his corner boys he could handle all the main bars and clubs.

Recently they had been telling him about some Asian dealers on the streets and had considered having a word in Mikey's ear. In the past Mikey had mentioned a Chinese enforcer, known as the Butcher, who would hang around the 'infected area and quickly amputate the offending cancer'. The Asian dealers were a problem for Snowman, who didn't know that Mikey had given up her Chinese connections and was now being supplied by the Pakistanis. He saw a weakness in Mikey, because she hadn't insisted that he couldn't sell in the Garden; but she was not to underestimated.

'Maybe she's already got someone trading in that territory,' he thought to himself. A kilo of coke and a kilo of smack was a significant order and represented fifty grand in cash when sold on the street. Snowman was sure he could shift that amount in less than a month if he widened his jurisdiction.

As far as Mikey was concerned, Snowman already knew too much and she had decided to involve and entrap him rather than alienate him.

"It will be done," said Mikey, breaking into his reverie, "...but be careful where you get rid of it... I don't want you overselling yourself and getting caught... you've got a nice little business at the moment... don't fuck it up."

Snowman hated being patronised. He got up from the table, doffed his hat and strolled out leaving the carrier-bag containing £23,500.

She called after him, "Don't forget, come round at three tomorrow afternoon."

13. CARRIE, SNOWMAN & HARRY : (3AM, THURSDAY 5 NOVEMBER)

Carrie had been asleep for two hours when Snowman returned.

She gave him the printed email.

"Have you seen this?... Is it a joke or something?"

Snowman read it. "When did you get it?"

"Last night."

"Why the fuck didn't you tell me?"

"How could I?"

"You could've left a more urgent message!"

"I rang you but it went straight to your message service... and you ignored my text."

"You should've tried again."

"Why? I'm not your fucking secretary."

Snowman was still dealing with the effects of the night's excesses. "Fucking bitch!" He paced the room, "I'm not going to pay... if I do the bastards will keep coming back."

"You've got no choice... if you don't pay we'll have the police all over us. If you go along with it perhaps you'll catch them out."

"What do you fucking know about it, you've never dealt with these cunts. How do they know I've got that sort of money? They might have seen me do a bit of dealing but it's not as though anybody except you knows how much money I've got... and how did they know they can contact me through your fucking computer?"

"How should I know?... It's nothing to do with me... I'm trying to help."

"I don't need your fucking help."

The argument raged for a while until they were both almost hysterical and then it turned to passion.

Snowman peeled the silk nightdress up over her head.

Harry couldn't believe his luck when he saw her wandering around talking to Snowman. He'd finished off the vodka and was desperate for one more line of speed, but there was nothing left. In his strung-out state he saw her body moving inside the thin silk, just for him; her nipples, her breasts as she leant forwards, just for him.

He watched, transfixed, and now came his reward. After Snowman had pulled off the nightie Harry ejaculated for the third time that night.

It was gone 5am when Harry finally fell into bed, unable to sleep. He tossed and turned in a half sleep, his mind tormented by amphetamine-induced nightmares. He jolted awake. The illuminated clock/radio said 7.28, then 7.29, then 7.30; he watched without blinking as the seconds pulsed away. The radio came on making him jump. The dour announcer gave the morning traffic reports for those lucky people trying to get to work in the rush hour. What seemed like hours were minutes as he forced his eyes closed again, only to open them when the thumping of his heart brought the anxiety rushing back to the surface.

He woke again at about 11am, his heart still pounding from the speed; he felt like shit. He buried his head in the pillow and listened to his heart beating, wondering how long his nervous system would stand the strain. His eyes were dry and he had to force himself to blink. He reached out, blindly fumbling for a packet of diazepam. The Valium would relax the tension and regulate his breathing and hopefully allow him to sleep. He swallowed two and pushed his face back into the pillow.

The next time he awoke it was 4pm. The light was going and he was overwhelmed by a feeling of despair. He lay there thinking of his bees. The honey season was over and there was nothing to do after supplying their feed. He had to leave them to survive the winter.

He forced himself out of bed and made a brew. He pressed the power button on the monitor to check what the hive camera was seeing.

Snowman and Carrie believed the windows of the flat were not over-looked, and fortunately for Harry they didn't always bother to close the curtains.

He would wait for Carrie to appear and provide him with more hours of flaccid masturbation.

14. CARRIE, SNOWMAN & HARRY :
(THURSDAY 5 NOVEMBER)

Carrie didn't wake up until the late morning, while Snowman was still asleep.

She left him snoring in bed while she visited her agency to show her face and encourage them to send her to more castings. Although she didn't find it intellectually challenging, she enjoyed modelling and acting as long as the photographers weren't too full of themselves. The girls running the agency invited her to stay for lunch and later in the afternoon they sent her to a casting at a film company in Wardour Street.

It didn't go well. The casting director was friendly enough but the director of the commercial wasn't sure.

When she returned home in the late afternoon it was dusk and she was still anxious about the confrontation she'd had with Snowman in the early hours.

He was at the computer. "How am I gonna find these fuckers?"

Carrie ignored the question and poured herself a glass of wine.

"Chop me out a line, I'm tired… I need a pick-me-up… How long did you sleep for?" she asked.

Snowman ignored her question and produced the mirror from the sideboard with three lines on it. He snorted one and offered one to Carrie. She snorted both lines.

"Don't worry there's plenty more where that came from…" he said sarcastically, "… where've you been today?"

Carrie pointed at the mirror. "I see you started without me… I went to a casting for a coffee commercial but the director couldn't see talent if it jumped on him."

"I hope you didn't… make me a coffee… have you had anything to eat?"

"Yes."

Snowman returned to the computer. "Who with?"

"Some friends." She went into the kitchen and put the kettle on.

"I didn't know you had any… How am I gonna to find these fuckers?"

"Maybe I can help you."

"How?"

"I'll ask around."

Snowman was intrigued. "Who the fuck do you know?"

"Why not let me try and help?"

Now Snowman really wanted to know. Carrie wished she had not opened her mouth.

The coke had kicked in. They were both wired.

Snowman went over to her. "Y'know… I always wondered about you… turning up at Costas's… with a flat a couple of doors away. I'd never seen you before and nobody knew you… and you knew nobody." He got up from the computer and stood in the kitchen doorway confronting her. "Tell me about it."

Carrie stared at him.

He grabbed her by the shoulders. "Fucking tell me the truth."

Carrie pushed him back. "Don't be stupid."

"Is this anything to do with you?" he asked, pointing to the computer.

Snowman slapped out at Carrie.

She put up her arm in self-defence. "I'm trying to help you."

Realising he had lost it, Snowman closed his eyes and turned away. "I've got to find the bastards."

15. HARRY : (THURSDAY 5 NOVEMBER)

Dressed in a shabby dressing gown, Harry was slouched in his armchair watching the recording on the monitor. He was transfixed by Carrie, recording her every move, his heart beating and his brain buzzing. They were swarming again. They wouldn't leave his skull. 'Why the fuck does it have to be like this?..FUCKING BUZZ BUZZ BUZZ.'

His tortured mind would not stop plaguing him with scattered thoughts that went nowhere and resolved nothing. Unable to quieten the paranoia, he sat still and tried to control his jittering nerves.

His stomach churned and he knew what he had to do. He crept down the stairs carrying his boots. The building had a faded grandeur left over from when it had been an elegant town house; long before the ground floor became an Italian restaurant. The passage leading to the street door had an elaborate ceiling rose and the floor was carpeted with point-of-sale mailers and fast food leaflets. He had to duck around the gas and electricity meters that hung at head height behind the door. The lock was stiff and the door creaked as he opened it. He didn't want any of the tenants to hear or see him but he didn't know why.

He wandered out into the dank early morning streets. His obsession took him up Greek Street and through the archway in Manette Street. He stopped outside St. Barnabas's Chapel.

He pushed the gate and entered into the world of religious ritual. A chapel was attached to St. Barnabas-in-Soho, a house offering care and support to homeless women. It was the vulnerability of these women that fuelled his fantasies of power and domination. Sometimes when he visited they were kneeling and praying.

His luck was in. The young woman was kneeling humbly before the altar. He crept into the cloister beside the nave and from behind a pillar had a view of the supplicant woman.

Grinding his teeth together he imagined the woman begging him for mercy.

16. MIKEY & SNOWMAN : (3PM, THURSDAY 5 NOVEMBER)

The doorbell rang at exactly three o'clock that afternoon.

Mikey checked the CCTV camera to the street door and there he stood, arrogant and uncouth, characteristics she most disliked, but he had what she needed to complete her project.

She ejected the Sinatra CD and replaced it with classical music to create the right atmosphere.

Snowman sauntered in.

Mikey gestured to him to sit down. She poured two brandies then opened an ornate ivory box and took a bag of coke, a mirror and a solid silver blade from her Aladdin's cave. She chopped out a couple of generous lines.

Snowman refused the line and the lit spliff she offered him.

Mikey stood over him and accompanied by Wagner said, "I've made you a fortune…" She stared at him waiting for a reaction.

"We've helped each other…" he said, not wanting to put himself in a compromising position since he didn't know what was coming.

She bent forward, "I've decided to stand for Parliament.. and I want you to help me."

It took a lot for Snowman to be nonplussed so he just nodded; it was better than bursting out laughing.

"Well, what do you think?" she asked.

"What do you want me to do?"

"I'm going to make a major hit."

"Would that be… a record, a drug deal or a murder?"

Mikey was irritated by his lack of respect. "The latter."

Snowman tried to look unconcerned. "Okay, who?"

"One thing at a time."

"Okay… who?"

Mikey returned to her side of the table and chopped out two more lines and as slowly and as elegantly as anyone could, bent forward and snorted one. As she pushed the mirror across to him her mobile rang. The timing, as far as she was concerned, was perfect.

She flicked it open, "I'm in conference at the moment… call me later and we'll do some business together… I'm looking forward to meeting up with you." A little reminder to Snowman that she wasn't totally dependent on him and that he was not all-important to her business.

Snowman wasn't comfortable with the amateur dramatics but he went along with them. 'After all...', he thought, '...this queer has made me fucking rich and I don't want it to stop now.'

She leant forward in a conspiratorial manner. "I need to leave my mark in Soho... people need to know who I am... I am nothing without being known. I want to be seen as a benefactor to English society... someone who helped us white folk survive the infestation of foreigners. That's why I am standing for candidate and leader of the local BNP."

Snowman shook his head in disbelief; she seemed to have totally ignored the fact that he was of mixed race.

The toot had hit home. She leant closer to him and in a stage whisper said, "It's a major politician but I'm not telling you where, or when or how, yet."

Snowman was in the presence of her Majesty the Queen of Soho, planning the assassination of one of her subjects.

Keeping a straight face, he asked, "What do you want from me?"

"I want to know that you're with me all the way... I'm going to need your help with the logistics."

She offered him the mirror and again he refused. He suspected there was nobody else she could turn to. Life was good; he had his mistress and his lover; he had money and he felt safe; that was apart from the cunt who was threatening to blackmail him. He did not to mention the threat to Mikey because he didn't want to appear vulnerable.

The chance of a substantial financial killing was the only reason he would put his present lifestyle at risk. Mikey was worth millions. Eventually he would separate her from enough of it to let him retire and live on a beach for the rest of his life and this might be his opportunity. "Is that flat at Masonic Mansions part of this?"

She nodded and went over and closed the door, even though there was no-one there.

"I want the Pakis out of Soho, they're stepping on my toes... I can't start a war, that won't resolve anything... there are too many of them... they'll just keep on coming. I've got to disgrace the lot of 'em. I've got to get the locals on my side... appeal to their baser instincts, to their insecurities... that's why I'll become the BNP candidate... a major political assassination linked to Islamist terrorists would mean that their credibility would be ruined. Then add a catalyst... the Government's neurosis about Islamic fundamentalist groups, and I'll have all the ingredients I need. With public opinion united behind me I can chase the Pakis out of Soho." Mikey's enthusiasm had reached a crescendo.

'So far,' thought Snowman, 'we've got the BNP and we've got murder.'

"What makes you think that will solve anything?" he asked.

"I'll swing public opinion against the Asians... I'll drive them out of Soho. A crime will have been committed against English society... and the old bill will chase them away into someone else's territory." The coke was adding to Mikey's delusions. "I'll kill two birds with one stone. I'll get them off my back and I will gain recognition as the Saviour of Soho."

Snowman stood up.

She was in full flow. "The factory will be the HQ for the terrorist cell... and it will be called Group X. I love the X, don't you?... it reminds me of a swastika." Mikey was standing too, staring into Snowman's face. "After the assassination we'll douse the place with petrol and torch it. It'll look like gang warfare. The old bill will discover a crack factory run by two illegal Paki immigrants... and the rifle used to shoot the politician... they'll think they've discovered a terrorist cell!"

"Okay," said Snowman. "Where do I come in?"

"Well, first of all I need an untraceable rifle... then I'll need someone to fire it."

17. SNOWMAN, CARRIE & SEAN :
(6PM, THURSDAY 5 NOVEMBER)

As well as the rifle for Mikey, Snowman wanted a pistol in case the blackmailer got too close.

After his meeting with Mikey he went back to Carrie's. "Hi darlin', sorry about this morning, I got carried away... whoever's fucking with me got me going."

Carrie looked uneasy. "I don't want to discuss this morning."

Trying to find out what she really knew, he said, "Got any clue who sent that email?"

"How would I know?" Carrie said, worried that he was suspecting her.

"Whatever... I just met up with this crazy fucker called Mikey, who I do some business with... she wants to represent the local BNP and she's setting up some sort of terrorist group called 'X' or something, to get rid of the Pakis... I dunno what she's thinking."

"Who's this Mikey?" she asked.

"Never mind... I've gotta go out now."

Halfway down down Dean Street there was a brown door which led to a brown painted staircase lit by a single strip-light. Up the stairs through another brown door was the Irishman. If he didn't know you he'd ask, "What the fuck do you want?" But if he did it was okay. He stood behind a brown bar in a brown room with brown linoleum floor tiles. It could have all been battleship grey, but they probably hadn't had any in stock that day. Curved tubular metal chairs surrounded half a dozen circular tables with plastic tops. In the centre of each table stood a raffia-encased Chianti bottle topped with a red lampshade; the only other colour in the room. This was a place for the professional drinker.

Snowman entered. Busby Bob, who always sat in the same place at the bar, ran his fingers through his impressive afro. He always did this when he was feeling insecure. "I need some shit man," he said, looking at Snowman.

Snowman leant over the bar. "Sean... I want a word?"

"What'll you be wanting other than a word then?"

Busby Bob stared at them.

"A large Delamain for me and..." he turned to Bob, "I'll buy you a drink then get out of my face."

"Nice, man," said Bob, moving away.

Sean took the cognac bottle off the shelf and poured three fingers. "What do you want?"

Snowman leant closer. "I need a shooter."

"Animal or mineral?"

Sean wasn't going to ask what for, and Snowman knew that. "Both."

"Do you want to frighten 'em with a big one or shoot 'em with a little one?" asked Sean.

"Something I can carry easily."

"It'll cost you."

"I'm not going to sleep with you."

"I hope you know what you're doing, 'cos once you up the ante your friends will do the same."

"I'm not sure who's involved but I'm in a hurry. Can you do it tonight?" asked Snowman.

"I can lend you something… but if it's used I don't want it back…"

"How much do you want?"

"If you use it, it'll cost you a monkey… hang on a minute."

Sean disappeared into a room behind the bar. After a couple of minutes he returned with a lumpy, padded Jiffy bag. "It's a small revolver, I got from the old bill… and there's a box of ammo… it's untraceable… make sure you keep the safety catch on, unless of course you want to shoot somebody. If you do, remember I don't want it back."

Snowman took the bag and tucked it inside his jacket. "Is it alright if I drop the money off to you in the next couple of days?"

"Sure."

Snowman sank his drink, reached into his pocket, pulled out a wrap and went over and shook Bob's hand.

"Have this one on me."

18. CARRIE & THE CONTROLLER :
(7PM, THURSDAY 5 NOVEMBER)

While Snowman was out, Carrie retrieved the Firm's mobile phone from its hiding place in the top of the wardrobe.

She speed dialled number 7 and 'Office' appeared on the screen. All their mobiles had built-in scrambling devices.

"Yes" said a voice, without emotion.

Carrie paused.

"Catch-word?"

She spelt out, "C.H.A.R.O.N," which was pronounced 'care-on' like the mythological Greek ferryman. A smart-arse in the Service with a first in Classics and a morbid sense of humour had come up with the idea. The mythological ferryman's cargo had been cadavers. Her code didn't have to be complicated; it just had to be delivered without hesitation and without any other words or letters mentioned. The Duty Officer also had the benefit of the mobile number appearing on the screen in front of him and a voice-print check through his computer.

With all three tests confirmed he answered.

"Yes."

"I have a problem."

"Wait."

A minute later the Controller came on the line. "What do you need?"

"A meeting.. I've got ..."

The Controller cut in. "Don't explain... when do you want to meet?"

"Now."

"Recommended RV?"

"Yes."

"We'll be there in one hour." The line went dead.

It had been dark for an hour when Carrie, whose counter surveillance training had been short, walked the figure of eight block and dropped into Viva la Diva, a lingerie shop on the corner of Dean and Old Compton Street. It had wide windows facing both streets with underwear displayed on racks in both windows. She could peruse the racks while observing people on the street. As she had been trained to do, she memorised a detail on each loitering passerby for later reference, including the fat man wearing a straw hat.

Moving on, she ordered an espresso at Bar Italia and took it out onto a pavement table. She sat for a while drinking it and observing. Then, without hesitating, she got up waved at nobody in particular and ran up Frith Street. She turned into Bateman Street and into the first shop doorway on the left. She watched the street carefully and waited for a couple of minutes. The owner of the shop, Hollywood Videos, appeared in the entrance behind her.

"Fancy a job luv?"

Preoccupied by watching the street, she hadn't noticed him.

"Did I startle you?" he asked.

"Er... no... no thank you." Seeing no-one on the street she recognised, she moved on. She believed that Snowman was her only threat and if she was not being followed by him she felt safe.

19. HARRY & CARRIE : (7.15PM, THURSDAY 5 NOVEMBER)

Harry's mobile rang.

The voice on the other end took him by surprise. He had tried to stay calm and collect his thoughts. He needed to appear on top of the situation. After repeating the instructions he had been given, he confirmed that he would fulfil the order and report back.

Harry had seen Carrie put on her coat and leave the flat a few minutes before. He grabbed his coat, straw hat, camera and voice recorder and rushed down the stairs. He opened the street door just after she had passed by and followed her down Dean Street. He didn't see her disappear into the lingerie shop. He walked on by. Even though her attempts to avoid being followed were amateurish, Harry lost her within a hundred metres. He got as far as Shaftesbury Avenue before he gave up and turned back.

He was wandering back when Carrie appeared on the opposite pavement. She came out of Bateman Street and turned in front of him. He took the digital camera from under his jacket and turned to aim it at a building across the road. He zoomed in and at the last moment swung the camera over towards Carrie. She stepped off the pavement and was standing between two cars looking down the road, checking the traffic. His shock at seeing her apparently staring straight down his lens caused him to press the shutter in surprise. The flash of the camera in the darkness momentarily caught her attention, but tourists taking photographs in Soho were a regular event and she thought no more of it. She swooped in front of Harry and turned into St Anne's Court. He was so close to her he could smell her scent. He had to hesitate as she swept past him.

Carrie went straight into The Piano Bar. Harry entered through the glass doors directly behind her and she held the door for him, but as far as she was concerned he didn't exist.

The bar was busy with evening revellers. Carrie ordered a vodka and Red Bull and sat at the counter.

A man in a suit, his tie loose at the neck, who'd had a drink said, "Can I buy that for you?"

Carrie hesitated as the barman put her change down. "It's too late…"

"It's never too late."

"That depends on what you're doing."

"Well now, what do you do?"

"I take care of myself."

"I can see that, and you're making it hard for me to hit on you… but I like you."

"What do you do?" asked Carrie.

"I don't take care of myself."

"I can see that," she said, smiling, and got up to leave.

"Stay and have another drink."

"If I wanted another drink you'd know by now."

The man watched her walk away and sit on a stool in the window.

She wondered whether he was her contact but when he didn't follow her she assumed he was just looking for fun. It was small situations like this that made her regret having accepted the job. She wanted to be normal and stop playing this double-life game.

Harry slid onto the stool beside her and she jumped.

"C-H-A-R-O-N," said Harry, "I'm your handler."

"Really?" said Carrie.

"What do you want?" he asked.

"I'm worried Snowman has sussed me."

"What do you want us to do?"

Carrie turned to Harry with a look of disbelief on her face.

Hoping to prolong the meeting, he asked, "Can I buy you another drink?"

She was speechless. 'What's this arsehole think I'm doing here?' she asked herself. But she needed help. "He's suspicious… he thinks I know something or I'm seeing someone… and he tried to knock me about."

"Well, are you?"

"NO."

"You've got nothing to worry about then… but if the situation gets worse let us know… Are you sure you won't have a drink?"

Carrie turned on him. "Nothing to worry about?… It's me who's got to live with him… if it gets any worse I might not be able to let you know… he's a fucking thug as well as a drug dealer… if I upset him he could kill me."

"We'll know about it," said Harry.

Carrie looked at him incredulously. He was staring at her. She desperately needed reassurance. "It'll be too late by then… also he's being blackmailed."

"Who's doing that?"

"He has no idea." Carrie realised she wasn't getting any help from this man. "I have to go."

"Keep in touch… we need more on him before we can make a move."

She gave Harry a look of contempt and left.

Harry reached inside his coat and turned off the digital voice recorder and smiled. It was the first time he had been face to face with her and he had on record that she was afraid Snowman might kill her; he loved to see the fear in her face.

He was so aroused that he couldn't wait until he got home so he went to the Men's room.

20. CARRIE : (9PM, THURSDAY 5 NOVEMBER)

When Carrie got back to her flat she was shaking. This was her first assignment and a covert meeting with a pervy-looking man made her feel that the Controller didn't give a damn about her safety. She needed help and back-up. Suddenly it was all too real.

She poured herself a glass of wine. If she could contact her father he would know what to do. She retrieved the mobile from the wardrobe and dialled.

"Yes," said the Duty Officer.

"3,8,1,18,5,14," said Carrie. This was her emergency code. It told the operator that she was in danger. If it was only partially sent the operator would immediately activate a Crisis Response Team. But if completed the operator would attempt a verbal connection.

"Yes," said the Duty Officer again.

"I want more help."

"What for?"

"I want my father's contact number."

"We are looking after you. Don't use the code again unless your life is in danger." The line went dead.

She slumped down onto the sofa. "Fuck."

She returned the mobile to the wardrobe and took her notebook from the hiding place. She made a note of the meeting with the MI5 officer, whose name she didn't know. She listed the time, date and venue, and the fact that he had offered no real help. She felt totally isolated.

When Harry got back to his flat he too was shaking.

Meeting her face to face, smelling her and seeing her fear had aroused him more than he had imagined.

He went to the monitor and switched it on. There she sat with a drink in her hand, looking like an angel. 'Dear God, if only I had her here beside me. I could take her mind off her troubles.'

He lay on his bed and closed his eyes.

Harry awoke suddenly. It was dark, the phone was ringing, he didn't know how long he had been asleep. He grabbed the phone.

"Catch-word?" demanded the Duty Officer.

"W-H-I-T-E-Y."

The officer checked Whitey's voice print and connected him to the Controller.

"What's taken you so long to report back?", she asked.

"I met her... I told her she is being watched... I reassured her..."

"How concerned was she?" asked the Controller.

"She's worrying for nothing," said Harry.

"Worrying about what?"

"I dunno... that bloke she's with..."

"What do you know about that bloke?"

"Nothing..."

The Controller listened to Whitey's curt report and doubted that Carrie had been reassured by him. When Whitey used the word 'watched' she felt uneasy; she knew nothing about his hive camera and little did she realise the difference between Whitey's watching compared with being watched over.

Helen, the Controller, was in her mid-forties and although a little overweight was still an attractive woman. Her sensitive appraisal of casework and intuitive handling of her field officers gave her the edge over her male colleagues. Her career had always taken priority and after three disastrous relationships she had given up on men. Because she was future leadership material her position at headquarters was vulnerable; her male colleagues closed ranks in an effort to slow her promotion to the top. Hence she was keen to impress those in command and was aware that she must not make any mistakes.

When Helen was allocated Whitey as Carrie's handler she found him awkward to deal with and now she wasn't satisfied with the brevity of his report. Her instincts told her to keep a close eye on him but this investigation was a slowly developing case. She was also managing two other more urgent projects and did not follow up on her suspicions, even after a warning from the Duty Officer that Carrie had used the emergency contact code without good reason.

It would be three days before the Controller would be in touch with Whitey again.

21. MIKEY, HARRY & SNOWMAN :

It had been eighteen months since Special Branch had informed the Secret Service that Michelle de Lavigne was distributing large amounts of cocaine and heroin from Pakistan.

It was because of this Asian connection that MI5 had got involved. It was discovered that Mikey had an investment company, Grande Gilts Inc. with a portfolio of properties in Soho including Madame LuLu's Limited, a lucrative cash business. The Firm was convinced that Michelle de Lavigne was involved in money laundering because she also owned a holding company, Global Industries, registered in the Dutch Antilles which showed no turnover.

After watching Mikey for several weeks they observed her regular meetings with Snowman and decided to include him in their investigation. They discovered that Snowman was in the habit of using one particular cab driver on a regular basis and they suspected the man might be part of his distribution network. They made enquiries into the driver and it didn't take long for the Firm to discover his real identity of Tommy Farr and his nickname Whitey.

When he left school Tommy Farr was without ambition or direction and after six months of unemployment, volunteered to join the army. His subversive, uncommunicative attitude and inability to integrate with any form of group activity meant he was alienated from the other recruits. His Commanding Officer recommended him for transfer to a sniper squadron. There Tommy found his métier. He revelled in the independence and isolation. He became an accomplished sniper who carried out several successful solo missions, which was unusual because snipers normally worked with a spotter. During the first Iraq war, rumours of miscreant behaviour were reported; then he went AWOL. Caught by the civilian police in Vietnam with two underage girls and brought back to the UK, he was decommissioned and served six months in military prison.

After leaving the army he completed a teacher training course in Theology and ended up being employed by a well known girls' public school.

That was twenty years ago.

When the Firm was sure that Tommy Farr wasn't directly involved in Snowman's activities they contacted him.

At first Harry was flattered that he had been approached. But then he thought that they were on to him until he realised that they didn't know his false identity of Harry White.

His army training reassured the Firm that Tommy Farr had the ability to carry out surveillance on Snowman without losing his nerve. As Snowman's cab driver he was the ideal person to keep an eye on him, and hopefully discover something of his distribution network.

As far as the Firm was concerned Tommy was bottom of the ladder and so was subjected only to a minimal security clearance; an ad hoc operative recruited for a single mission and provided only with low grade intel. What the Firm's research department failed to discover was the reason Tommy Farr had been dismissed from the girl's school.

Whitey's role was to supply information gleaned from unguarded conversations in the back of his cab, which could provide valuable intelligence. The Firm expected a lot of his reports to be rumour and speculation, but he was better placed than anyone else they had at the time.

The Firm gave him a small retainer, deposited monthly in cash in his account and the Controller decided to keep it simple and use W.H.I.T.E.Y as his catch-word. Harry reported back regularly and appeared to perform well, and due to staff shortages the Firm decided to put Carrie in the flat directly opposite his so that he could act as her handler.

22. HARRY : (FRIDAY MORNING, 6 NOVEMBER)

Harry's plan to collect the money from Snowman had to be kept simple. The more involved the more there was to go wrong, and as on sniping missions he made contingency plans in case events didn't develop exactly as anticipated.

He put on a pair of glasses with tinted lenses, tucked his hair into a flat cap and wore an extra large pac-a-mac in an attempt to hide his shape. He had assembled a collection of disguises when he set up his false identity and had hung onto these props because he never knew when he might need them.

Then he took his rubbish bag for a walk down Meard Street where he had seen a couple of old dustbins on the pavement. He put the bag into one of the bins and swung it over his shoulder. He strolled down Old Compton Street to the Three Greyhounds Pub. In many parts of the city walking down the street with a dustbin over your shoulder would attract attention but in Soho he was just another weirdo.

Harry dumped the bin out of sight at the far end of the narrow alleyway behind the pub. He had a quick Bloody Mary and checked out the fire door on the stairs leading down to the lavatory.

Then he went to Hamley's toy shop and bought a chemistry set.

On the way back he bought three pay-as-you-go mobiles with cash. He told the shop assistant that they were for his wife and kids. He bought a packet of flowers of sulphur at the chemist and a second-hand car battery from the garage on Brewer Street, and then humped it all back to his flat.

He spent the next couple of hours making hydrogen sulphide. With a handkerchief over his nose and mouth he used the spirit burner, test tube and iron filings from the chemistry set and added the hydrochloric acid from the battery to the heated filings and the sulphur. He poured the pungent liquid into a glass bottle.

He recorded a message on one of the mobiles, which he would leave in his flat, and programmed it to divert to the phone he would give Snowman. When Snowman answered it the signal would trigger the message. He had modified a trick used by the IRA to avoid the source call being traceable. Then he laboriously wrote a note with his left hand, disguising any characteristics of his own handwriting:

'KEEP THIS FONE TURNED ON / PUT 10K IN A BAG / WATE FOR INSTRUCTIONS.'

He put the mobile, the charger and the note into a padded envelope addressed to the 'Top Flat'.

He picked his moment and pushed it through Carrie's letterbox.

He sat and waited nervously watching the monitor. It took him back to a time when he had hidden in a wadi on a promontory overlooking an Iraqi communications centre that controlled their mobile Scud missile launchers. He had waited three days for the Republican Guard Commanding Officer to appear, then he shot him through the heart from five hundred metres. His comms had gone down and the recovery helicopter could not find him. He'd had to lie low in the desert for three long days until the allied invasion caught up with him.

Harry fell asleep in his chair.

He had just woken up when Snowman arrived back at Carrie's flat. He was gesticulating angrily at her and waving the padded envelope.

Harry couldn't believe his luck; there she was in her underwear. He loaded a fresh DVD into the machine and pressed record.

Half an hour later he decided the time had come to tighten the screw. He sent another email:

'NO TRIKS NO TRAKING OR I CALL THE LAW'

Lounging on the sofa, Snowman heard the computer announce the arrival of the email.

Harry zoomed the camera for a closer shot on Snowman's face as he read and re-read the email; then he started typing.

Harry went over to his computer:

'I DON'T HAVE THE MONEY I NEED TIME TO FIND THE CASH.'

Harry laughed at the screen and replied:

'FUCK OFF / PAY TONITE / CASH OR ELSE'

Harry was amused as he watched Snowman smoking a cigar and pacing the room in frustration. He decided to give them an alternative and sent another message:

'IF U NOT GOT MONEY WAT ELSE U GOT'

Back came the reply: 'WHAT DO YOU WANT?'

'WHAT HAVE YOU GOT'. Harry signed this one: 'AN ADMIRER'.

He watched. It gave him power. He felt he could manipulate the characters on his TV at the touch of a button. They were his puppets and he wanted to extend their misery. He imagined Carrie in black lace underwear standing in front of him.

'He's taking the piss… he wants paying tonight. I'm at the cunt's mercy,' Snowman said to himself. 'It's got to be someone who knows me from the street.'

Should he pay or take a chance and move out of Carrie's flat to see if they followed him? He wandered over to the window which faced a brick wall on the other side of the street. He looked up and saw the bee-hives and thought to himself, 'Bee-keepers aren't blackmailers.'

The first email had angered more than worried him but now he had to take it seriously. If the police turned up at Carrie's door he was fucked. His own corner boys handled the majority of his sales and it wasn't in their interest to blackmail their boss. They were dependent on him and wouldn't risk their relationship or their lives for just 10K. Then there were his numerous face to face civvy punters who came from a cross-section of Soho night-life. He couldn't finger any one of them as a blackmailer and anyway none of them knew where he lived, let alone Carrie's email address. Even Mikey didn't know where he lived. The only contact point for his customers was his mobile, which was pay-as-you-go and registered in a false name. Then there were the Paki street dealers; but how could they possibly have traced him? He even considered the cab driver, Whitey. He was a possibility, but unlikely because he had never taken him to Carrie's place. Every avenue he went down was a dead end.

He split his time between Myrtle and Carrie. It was Carrie's computer that was being used as the blackmailer's contact point.

'Perhaps the bitch has opened her mouth to someone in a bar or over a line in a lavatory... or maybe she was involved?' he thought.

He retrieved the toolbox from the sideboard and began to count out 10K in fifty-pound notes. He only had a thousand pounds left. Carrie watched him without comment. She realised he was going to pay up and she didn't want to aggravate him.

Harry watched the monitor, realising that if everything went to plan he was going to be ten thousand pounds richer tonight.

As Snowman counted out the money the same question kept going round his head: 'Who knows about me being at Carrie's flat, other than her?' The seeds of doubt had been sown and were beginning to germinate.

23. HARRY & SNOWMAN : (5PM, FRIDAY 6 NOVEMBER)

Harry paced up and down anxiously; he managed to swallow a few biscuits and sink a cup of coffee.

In the deluded belief that it would settle his system he had a line of speed, a mead and vodka cocktail and a pop of amylnitrate. He wasn't sure why, but he decided to put on his shiny mohair suit. The jacket bulged between the buttons and the trousers cut in at the crotch. It was too tight for his heavy frame, but he felt more professional wearing it.

In an attempt to relax he made himself walk slowly to the parking lot in Wardour Street to collect his car. Then he drove slowly round and checked in with the Brothers.

At six o'clock Harry used the third mobile to call Snowman. He assumed an Irish accent and muffled the phone with a handkerchief. "Take a taxi to the northwest corner of Soho Square at seven o'clock tonight. Stay in the taxi and wait for us to call." He heard Snowman start to shout something and switched off the phone; he was shaking.

As Harry had hoped, the call to the Brothers came within fifteen minutes of his ringing Snowman.

Snowman wanted a cab to collect him from the corner of Bateman Street at precisely a quarter to seven and he asked for his regular driver.

Harry had told Saul he was expecting his regular client to call and would not be taking any other jobs until then.

When Snowman rang for Whitey, Saul said, "Yes, I know."

Thinking that Saul meant he knew where Bateman Street was he didn't attach any significance to the comment; it almost went unnoticed. Snowman was also preoccupied with thinking about Darren, a doorman friend who he wanted as backup to grab the fucker who came to take his money. He was going to give Darren the revolver, reckoning that if there was any shooting to be done Darren was better equipped to do it than he was.

As Harry drove along Bateman Street in the dark, Snowman stepped out from between two parked cars into his headlights. He was carrying a black Nike hold-all.

He hailed Harry down and got in the back, as usual.

"Where to, Guv?" asked Harry.

"Take me up to Soho Square."

"Is that all?"

"Just do what I say."

They turned into Soho Square and Snowman told him to pull over in the corner. Harry double parked and switched the engine off.

As they sat in silence Harry pressed the dial button twice on the mobile connecting to the rigged phone in his flat, which in turn dialled Snowman's mobile.

Snowman answered it. Harry's disguised voice kicked in. "We're watching you. Put the phone in the bag with the money. Tell the driver to take the bag and leave it in the men's toilets in the Three Greyhounds, repeat the basement of the Three Greyhounds… we're watching every move."

Snowman asked, "How do you know I've got the money?"

There was no response. The line had gone dead.

Snowman switched off the phone and put it into the money bag.

He turned to Harry. "I want you to take this bag and leave it in the basement toilets in the Three Greyhounds."

Harry assumed an expression of astonishment. "I can't do that, Guv… How do I know it's not a bomb?… and anyway I've only earned a fiver on this job."

Snowman got out and slammed the door. He looked around, trying to see if anyone was watching. There were far too many windows, doorways and people. There was no way he could spot his blackmailers.

Harry got out of the car. "Careful with my door, Guv."

Snowman held the bag above his head and hurled it down on to the pavement. "See, it can't be a fucking bomb."

Darren, who was hidden in a doorway, ran forward. "Everyfing alwight, Boss?"

Snowman waved him away. "Just watch my back."

A couple walking past stopped and stared at Snowman, who turned on them. "What the fuck are you looking at?" They moved away.

Harry wanted to laugh. "I still don't think I can do that," he said.

"I'll give you a hundred notes."

"I'll have to phone my office."

Snowman just managed to control himself.

Harry pulled the phone from his pocket and pretended to dial the cab company. "I've got a customer here who wants me to deliver a bag to a pub... without him there."

Harry pretended to listen. "They say it's up to me."

Snowman reached into his back pocket, pulled out a wad of notes and peeled off two fifties.

Harry shrugged, took the cash and picked up the bag. He expected Snowman to accompany him as far as the pub but he stood there on the pavement talking to Darren.

As Harry started the engine the back door of his car was suddenly opened. He turned round to see Darren lying in the foot-well under the back seat.

"Face the front and keep driving," ordered Darren.

Harry drove round the Square and down Greek Street with his mind racing; had Snowman set him up? The traffic was solid and as he crawled along he started to sweat. He pulled over at the corner on double yellow lines and turned off the engine.

Without turning round he asked, "Shall I take the bag now?"

"Do what he told you."

"Leave the bag in the toilets?" asked Harry.

"If that's what he told you, do it."

Harry picked up the bag. "I'll have a quick drink while I'm in there... so it doesn't look too suspicious," said Harry, buying himself time.

"Okay, but don't fuck about."

"Keep an eye on the car 'cause I can't afford a ticket... I'll leave the keys in."

"I'm not driving the fucking car," said Darren, "If you get a ticket that's your problem."

"I'm not going then."

Darren pushed the snout of Snowman's revolver into the back of Harry's neck. "You don't go and you're dead, pal."

Harry eased out of the car and disappeared into the pub. He bought a large vodka, took a slug and waited a while to check no-one went down to the lavatories.

The fire door to the alleyway was not alarmed, as Harry had discovered on the recce earlier in the day. He slipped out leaving it ajar behind him. The space between the tall buildings surrounding him went straight up to the night sky. There were no other doorways. The dustbin was where he had left it with the bag of rubbish inside.

He opened Snowman's bag and checked that the mobile was turned off. He counted the cash quickly; it looked about right. He put the bag in the bottom of the bin and covered it with the rubbish. Hands shaking he nearly dropped the glass bottle of hydrogen sulphide as he poured it into the dustbin. The stink caused him to retch as he jammed the lid back on.

With his heart pumping he hid behind the door on the stairwell as a woman came down to the lavatory. When the coast was clear he closed the door behind him and trudged back up the stairs.

He went back to his glass and was draining the dregs when Darren whispered in his ear, "You done it, mate?"

Harry jumped out of his skin. The shock combined with the drugs in his system nearly stopped his heart. He couldn't speak at first; then he managed an answer. "Yeah."

Darren sniffed, "Have you farted you dirty old man? Go on, fuck off."

Harry fucked off.

24. SNOWMAN : (11PM, FRIDAY 6 NOVEMBER)

Snowman was pissed off and decided to call it a night as far as business was concerned. He was turning the whole blackmail event over in his head when he remembered what Saul had said on the phone, about Whitey expecting his call.

He rang the cab company, "Saul… when I called earlier you said you knew I was going to call. How did you know?"

Saul didn't get involved in punters' problems, it wasn't good for business. "I don't know what you're talking about."

"Come on Saul, don't fuck me about."

"Look man, I run a cab company, I'm not a fucking clairvoyant."

Snowman realised the conversation was going nowhere and phoned Darren.

"Anyone leave the pub with the bag?"

"No Boss, nobody came up with it and when I went down to check out the bog it was gone."

"What about that cab driver?"

"He did as he was told and when he came back up I told him to fuck off."

"Did you see him leave the bag in the lavatory?"

"No Boss, I didn't want to expose myself."

Snowman hesitated and then continued, "Is there a back way out?"

"Dunno, Boss, I'll 'ave a look."

"Meet me at Sean's in half an hour and bring the shooter."

En route to Sean's, Snowman dropped into Carrie's flat. She was asleep in front of the TV so he collected five hundred pounds from his bag and crept out. It had turned into an expensive day.

Then he went down to Costas's Lounge and had a couple of large brandies. He was having trouble dealing with the humiliation.

He was coming to the conclusion that someone connected to Carrie must be involved. He was obsessed with the fact that some arrogant arsehole had his money. As the alcohol seeped into his system he made up his mind to show the blackmailing cunts they'd made the worst decision of their miserable lives.

Snowman was in a sombre mood when he met Darren at Sean's. He gave Sean the five hundred pounds in a sealed envelope. He had a couple more drinks and told Sean he wanted to hang on to the shooter for a while.

It was eleven forty-five when Snowman decided to go over to The Three Greyhounds to check it out for himself.

25. HARRY : (MIDNIGHT, FRIDAY 6 NOVEMBER))

Harry had gone back to work for a couple of hours and then he couldn't wait any longer.

He parked in Greek Street and strolled into the alleyway. He put his scarf over his face as he tipped the fetid garbage from the bin. Having wiped Snowman's bag clean, he dumped the scarf and headed back to the car.

A drunk was pissing in the alcove halfway up the alley. He stepped back into Harry's path and was as surprised to see Harry as Harry was to see him.

The drunk drew himself up to his full height and puffed out his chest, "What d'you want, pal?"

Harry had to make a quick decision; knock him over or try to placate him. He didn't want to draw attention to himself carrying a bag full of money in a dark Soho alleyway. He reached into his pocket and pulled out a ten pound note.

"Hey, thanks pal," said the drunk and started to sing as Harry pushed past him.

Snowman arrived at the Three Greyhounds ten minutes before Harry. He had another large brandy and then went down to the toilets. Halfway down he pushed open the fire-escape door and found himself in the alleyway. He saw the drunk staggering out into Greek Street singing 'Thanks for the Memory' and waving the ten pound note. And there was Whitey crossing the road, carrying his Nike bag.

Harry was having trouble with the boot lock, cursing as he bent back a finger nail. Eventually he managed to open it and throw in the bag. The drunk attempted to put an arm around Harry's shoulder. Harry pushed him away and he tripped over the kerb. Harry didn't see

Snowman approaching. As he slammed the boot shut and got into the driving seat Snowman arrived at the other side of the car.

The drunk was back on his feet and heading towards the Datsun. Snowman climbed into the rear seat with the revolver in his hand. Harry turned, expecting to see the drunk, but Snowman already had the gun pressed to the side of his throat. This was the second time in a few hours he'd had that weapon stuck to his neck.

"Start the car and drive."

The drunk was running at the car, arms flailing. He pressed his face against Harry's window. "What the fuck, pal?"

Harry pulled away and the drunk stumbled and slid down, out of sight. Harry was in shock; one thing his plan had not included was getting caught red-handed.

Snowman told Harry to drive down into Chinatown. In the less policed world of the Cantonese they were unlikely to draw attention to themselves. He ordered Harry to park the car outside Masonic Mansions.

"Gimme the keys to the boot and wait here…" he said, waving the revolver around, "…and don't even fucking dream about running away."

26. MIKEY, FRED & THE ILLIMS : (EARLY OCTOBER)

As far as the landlord was concerned the top flat at Masonic Mansions was rented by Harold Singh and used by Group X Products; and as long as he got his money, he didn't give a damn.

Mikey found an ex-military explosives expert through the security company she used at Madame LuLu's. To protect her identity she had an unregistered mobile phone passed on to him with instructions to use it only when he contacted her. His call came the same day and she arranged to meet him that night in Falconberg Court, an alleyway behind Soho Square.

She turned up wearing a hooded top, a scarf over her face and with a ten-inch carving knife up her sleeve.

The military man introduced himself as 'Fred' and, in a Liverpudlian accent demanded, "…A grand up front." Mikey had anticipated this and had brought along a couple of thousand pounds. She told him that she wanted two devices that would be construed as Islamic terrorist bombs, and which were small enough to conceal between floor joists.

Fred gave her a shopping list for acetone, hydrogen peroxide and hydrochloric acid. He told her that the ingredients were readily available but warned her that they could attract attention if they were all bought by the same person.

She bought the first two ingredients over the internet using stolen credit cards that she obtained for another grand from her friends in the Soho underworld. For the hydrogen peroxide she posed as a hairdressing salon and for the acetone she became a decorating company. She bought the hydrochloric acid from a builders' merchant, saying it was for a blocked drain. Then she sent Snowman out to buy half-a-dozen copies of the Qur'an from Foyles, using cash.

The deliveries were made to an empty flat at the top of Wardour Street that she had temporarily rented for an extortionate fee from another of her 'friends'. Sabrina, who had no idea what was going on, was told to stay at the flat until the products had been delivered.

To stabilise the recipe, Fred mixed the ingredients with M118 military explosive, which he had stolen in small quantities during his army career. He packed the finished cocktail tightly into a couple of 2 litre pressure cookers that were no more than six inches high, and fitted specially-made detonators in place of the pressure valves. He had made two TATP bombs, a favourite of Al-Qaeda.

When he delivered the bombs to Mikey he told her to handle them with extreme care and to avoid excessive temperature changes.

Mikey then used Snowman to purchase all the equipment needed for a crack factory from different suppliers, again using cash. And Sabrina was told to buy six cold packs from the chemist.

Through her Pakistani contacts she sent two sets of keys, a pay-as-you-go mobile and three hundred pounds in cash to the two illegal immigrants, who she called 'the Illims'. She told them to wait at Masonic Mansions for her call, then via the mobile instructed them on how she wanted the factory to be set up.

When everything was ready Mikey arranged for Snowman to show them how to produce a sample batch of crack.

He arrived wearing a balaclava and checked that all the preparatory work had been completed according to instructions. He had brought the raw materials with him and a measured amount of cocaine, which would be kept in a small safe bolted to the floor.

Their job was to make a solution of powdered cocaine, sodium bicarbonate and ammonia which when boiled would produce a gelatinous substance that separated from the mixture. The blancmange would be removed and dried in microwave ovens. The resultant lumps of 'white' would then be chopped into two sizes weighing a tenth of a gramme and half a gramme. Selling the small rocks at £10 each, which were often smoked every twenty minutes, would make Mikey rich faster than selling the coke for snorting. She paid the Illims £150 a day each to keep their mouths shut. Every week Snowman would push an envelope containing their wages through the letterbox without meeting them face to face.

One night, after she had told Snowman to make sure the Illims went out for the evening, Mikey took a taxi to Masonic Mansions laden with the pressure cookers and all the ingredients. She also took the copies of the Qur'an and two ten-litre cans of diesel disguised in olive oil tins. She asked the driver to drop her off a hundred metres from her destination and as she unloaded the heavy, wheeled suitcase from the cab the driver nipped round to help her. She refused but tipped him generously and waited for him to drive off.

She laboured with the overloaded case and was exhausted by the time she had made it up to the top-floor factory.

Fred had to complete one more job for Mikey. She met him again in Falconberg Court and, after retrieving the mobile phone from him, explained what she wanted done. For a large amount of cash, 50% of which he wanted up front, he allowed himself to be ferried to and from the factory in a taxi, with his eyes taped up. Mikey made him wear dark glasses to cover the tape and supplied him with a white stick. To avoid having to mention their destination, so that Fred didn't know where he was going, Mikey handed the driver the address of a Chinese restaurant and a twenty pound note. By the time they reached Lisle Street Fred had no idea where he was. In the middle of the night and wearing her hood and scarf, she led him up the stairs of Masonic Mansions and set him to work planting the bombs.

He positioned the first one at the far end of the room, under the floorboards and away from the boiling vat. He squeezed the second bomb between the joists under the doormat at the entrance. To ensure the bombs would destroy the whole factory, he split open the cold packs containing ammonium nitrate and poured the powder into the cans of diesel which he placed between the joists at both locations.

He showed her how to activate the bombs by flicking a hidden switch which would trigger a built-in four minute time delay.

Only Mikey and Fred knew of the booby-traps and how to trigger them. She felt safe that he would never admit to being involved in the bomb-making or to the wiring of a building with explosives; especially if it was eventually revealed to be a terrorist hideout.

27. SNOWMAN & HARRY :
(12AM, SATURDAY 7 NOVEMBER)

It was close to midnight when Snowman led Harry across the pavement. The wind whipped down Lisle Street, driving the rain into the pavement like nails.

Snowman collected the money from the boot and led Harry into Masonic Mansions. "If you try anything I'll shoot you..." He shied away from Harry. "What the fuck is that smell?"

Harry entered the building like a lamb to slaughter. They stopped inside the entrance and Snowman rang the Illims. Eventually they answered.

"I'm coming into the factory now. Stay out of the way... I'm going into the office."

Harry climbed the three flights of stairs. His nerves were shattered and he was gasping for breath, wondering how long his heart could deal with the stress.

The Illims were wrapped in blankets at the far end of the room. Snowman led Harry to the office and ordered him to strip. He taped together four dustbin bags on the floor and put the office chair in the middle. Then he taped Harry's arms to the chair. With a strip of tape over his mouth, Harry was finding it hard to breathe through a nose damaged by years of snorting speed.

Snowman put on a pair of surgical gloves and rang Mikey.

"I've caught a cunt who tried to rob me... I'm at the factory... I need your help to get rid of him."

"What the fuck are you doing compromising the factory?"

"It's alright, he won't be leaving here."

"It's not alright... what about being recognised... fingerprints... DNA?"

"He won't leave anything... I've taken precautions."

"What if he identifies you?"

"I told you, he's going nowhere."

Mikey was shouting, "You fucking idiot, don't do anything 'til I get there."

It was 1.30am when Mikey arrived at the factory. She wore a long dark overcoat and a balaclava rolled up like a skull-cap. She climbed to the third floor, wondering what potential disaster Snowman was going to present her with. However practical and profitable he was to her, he was a loose cannon and she didn't like events to get out of her control. She rolled the balaclava down over her face and let herself in.

The Illims lying hunched up in their blankets didn't move. She savoured the smell of ammonia and the sound of the bubbling vat as her crack factory continued to make her money, but she was furious with that fucking oaf bringing his shit into her life.

She entered the office where Harry sat secured to the chair; the room stank of bad eggs. Mikey thought it was the fat man farting with fear.

Harry was naked and lit by a single light-bulb hanging from middle of the ceiling.

Mikey was struggling to control herself. "This looks like a bad movie... it had better be worth getting me out of bed for."

Snowman sat behind the desk in the shadows. "He tried to blackmail me... he wanted ten grand... or else."

"Or else what?" asked Mikey, wondering if the blackmail attempt was linked to her factory. "How does he know about you?"

"He was my cab driver... but I don't know how he knew so much about me... that's what I'm going to find out."

"We'll find out," said Mikey.

Snowman left the office and came back carrying the blow-torch used for heating up the cocaine solution and a ghetto-blaster. He turned on the gas and Mikey lit the flame; she was looking forward to this.

Sweat was running down Harry's body and puddling in his crotch. He tried to shout but the only noise he could make was a subdued grunting, hardly enough to disturb the Pakistanis in the next room.

Mikey leaned close to Harry's face. "You'd better talk or your life won't be worth living."

Snowman put the flaming blow-torch down on the desk in full view of Harry and switched on the ghetto-blaster. He turned the volume up and the small office was filled with Arabic music.

Mikey retired to a chair in the corner and rolled a joint.

Snowman sat on the edge of the desk and toyed with the blow-torch. He intended to let Harry suffer the anticipation of the pain that was about to be inflicted.

Mikey put on a pair of gloves and lit the spliff with the blow-torch. She took a long slow toke then rested the cigarette on the edge of the table. She went up behind Harry and covered his eyes.

Snowman turned up the flame and passed it slowly across Harry's chest. He let out a howl, like a wolf, and wrenched at the arms of the chair. Not a lot could be heard through the duct tape.

The smell of burnt hair and flesh combined with the smell of the hydrogen sulphide turned Mikey's stomach; she found the man disgusting. She removed her gloved hands from Harry's eyes. They were bloodshot and bulging. His chest was raw, red, sore. His head hung down, his chin on his chest. Soaked in sweat, he glistened in the electric light. His groaning was pitiful. Snowman returned to the edge of the desk and picked up the spliff. Nothing was said. They both stared at Harry. He kept grunting. He was trying to show them he wanted to speak.

"Do you think he's trying to tell us something?" asked Snowman.

Harry started to nod furiously.

"I don't think so," said Mikey.

"Let's warm him up again," said Snowman.

Harry was writhing furiously. Snowman reached out and adjusted the flame on the blow-torch to a hotspot of blue, but left it standing on the table. Harry began to sob.

"Perhaps we should give him the chance to talk to us," said Mikey.

"He's had his chance."

"Well, he could tell you how he knew about your business."

Harry nodded urgently, his eyes begging them. Snowman picked up the blow-torch. Harry was crying and pleading.

"If you scream out, you're dead," said Snowman as he ripped the duct tape from Harry's mouth.

"I'll tell you anything you want to know... I can tell you something you don't know," said Harry in a hoarse whisper.

"What?" asked Snowman.

"Your girlfriend works for the Government."

Snowman's face creased up in bewilderment. What was this piece of scum telling him?

Harry was desperately trying to sound believeable. "I know Carrie is in Soho to investigate you."

"How do you know?" asked Mikey.

"Cos, I got involved with her."

Snowman and Mikey looked at each other in disbelief. Snowman lost it and ran the flame over Harry's chest.

Harry screamed and sobbed with pain. The chair creaked under the strain of his contractions.

Mikey went to the office door, "For fuck's sake, remember I've got those Pakis in there... I don't want them running away."

Snowman leant forward and hit Harry across the face. "You're fucking lying... what the fuck are you talking about?"

Harry was losing consciousness.

Mikey held Snowman's arm. "Let him talk."

"The fuckin' cunt," said Snowman. He went to the sink and filled a glass with water and threw it over Harry.

Harry took an enormous breath and choked. The pain was unbearable. The cold water on his raw chest made him howl like a submissive dog.

Snowman turned off the music and sat back on the edge of the desk; the room went quiet.

The only sound was the splattering of rain on the window.

"You'd better tell me everything," said Snowman quietly.

"Carrie fed me the information we needed to blackmail you. How do you think I knew to contact you through her computer?" He lied that he'd met Carrie when she had phoned the taxi company and asked for him personally, to take her on a shopping expedition.

"How did she know about you?" asked Snowman.

"I dunno… she told me she knew I was your driver. She told me the blackmail idea and that she was trying to get information on your operation… if we worked together we could make a lot of money."

"Maybe she's an undercover cop," said Mikey.

"Then why would she encourage him to blackmail me?" asked Snowman, "I don't get it."

"To fool the idiot so he would give out what he knew about you," suggested Mikey. "Either way we've got to get rid of her."

Snowman's suspicions were confirmed; Carrie was behind the blackmail attempt. "How were you going to split the money?"

Harry told Snowman what he knew he wanted to hear, that Carrie hadn't revealed any information about him other than his dealing.

They continued questioning him and discovered that he had been a sniper in the army.

Mikey took Snowman over to the corner of the room and spoke quietly. "He could be useful."

"If we let him go he might double-cross us… and what about Carrie?"

"We'll have to get rid of her… we'll use him to do it," said Mikey.

Snowman had to accept the inevitable but he knew that if Carrie was killed he might come under suspicion; he'd need to have a cast-iron alibi.

Mikey realised Harry was a gift from the gods. He was the piece of the jigsaw she had been looking for to complete her Group X project. It was in her interest to keep him alive.

She took Snowman by the arm. "We'll get him working for us. Carrie has to be removed from the scene, and if he does it we've got him… I'll make it worth your while.. I'll give you two hundred K to see it through."

Snowman wasn't sure. "He's seen me. If we let him go he might…"

"Not if we give him the blackmail money…"

"But that's my money."

"You got me into this… I'll split it with you… we'll use him for the big job. I won't tell him about it until after the girl's disposed of… and I'll promise him more when both jobs are done. Tell him he'll be killed if he tries to double-cross us. Remember, he's a crook, otherwise he wouldn't have tried to blackmail you… money's what he wants… and he's smart… look how he set you up."

Snowman was amazed. "You're going to use him for your shooter?"

Mikey smiled. "Once I've finished with him you'll dispose of him."

She went back to Harry. "We've got a proposition for you… but the way things are for you it's more of a fait accompli… we'll let you live and let you keep the money if you get rid of that girl for us."

Harry was prepared to accept any offer.

28. SNOWMAN & HARRY :
(DAWN, SATURDAY 7 NOVEMBER)

Snowman wanted to know where Harry lived, and when he told him to take him back to his flat he was surprised to see that he lived so close to Carrie.

Harry was struggling to deal with the pain while Snowman told him to get Carrie out of her place by 4pm because he wanted to remove any evidence that he'd ever been there. And before she was disposed of, Harry was to find out about her connections and how much they knew about Snowman's business.

Snowman told him, "You'll get five thousand pounds now and the other five grand after you've dealt with her."

While he was giving Harry instructions he lifted the blind and looked out of the window towards Carrie's flat. He wondered if, from this oblique angle, Harry had ever tried to watch him. He never asked the question and never found out about the video link in the beehive.

Harry decided to carry out the mutant's instructions. He would do the job on Carrie, collect the money, change his identity again and disappear.

29. HARRY : (SATURDAY MIDDAY, 7 NOVEMBER)

Now it was Harry's turn to inflict pain and the thought of it aroused him.

He needed a plan. He hadn't been given a contact number for Carrie and he was left with the problem of contacting her without the Firm knowing and without raising her suspicions. He would tell her that the Controller had given him her email address. He also needed a reason for the meeting that would persuade her to leave the flat. He had been briefed by the Firm before his last meeting with her that she might go on about contacting her father. He would exploit this and hoped she wouldn't ask too many awkward questions. This time his email could be literate but he needed another address to send it from.

In case the internet café in Brewer Street had CCTV cameras, Harry put on his disguise and thin leather gloves. This time nothing was to be left to chance.

He entered the café and headed between the two rows of screens to the back where he was confronted by a pale skinned, heavily pierced and tattooed man who didn't hide his disgust at the sight of another pervert turning up to use his facilities. He took Harry's money and gave him a password then continued reading his porn magazine.

Harry tapped into Google mail and opened an account using 'Office' in the title. If anyone were to search in the future the source of the email could only be traced back as far as this internet café. He needed the address for one message and he was confident no-one would ever trace it. He made a note of the password so he could check later on from home, in case she unexpectedly replied.

He noticed it was nearly midday when he hit the 'Send' button:

C.H.A.R.O.N. FATHER WANTS TO SEE YOU. MEET COSTAS LOUNGE – 16.00 HRS. TODAY – OFFICE.

30. CARRIE, SNOWMAN & THE CONTROLLER : (SATURDAY 7 NOVEMBER)

Carrie hadn't slept well and she had not heard from Snowman since yesterday.

This was not unusual but she had a deep sense of foreboding since he'd crept in the previous night. He had taken a bundle of money and left without a word.

She called her agency to see if she had any castings for next week. When they told her nothing was happening she decided to chill. The closing winter weather wasn't conducive to hanging out or shopping so she planned to have a slothful day at home. She slipped her coat on over her nightdress, then made a quick visit to Berwick Street market to get coffee beans, vegetables and a bunch of fresh lilies to lift her spirits.

She was back at the flat within half an hour and heard an email come in.

She decided to make a coffee before checking it out.

She was caught off guard; this was the first email she had received which was headed with her code-name. She didn't know that they had her private email address; Snowman could have read it. Since the meeting with that fat, lecherous handler she felt her MI5 employers didn't really care. She pushed her suspicions to the back of her mind, because at last she was going to meet her father. She felt her confidence returning. She assumed the Controller must have contacted him after she had told them about her concerns. She knew he wouldn't let her down. She was excited. She poured out some of Snowman's brandy and chopped herself a small line.

'I'll see him soon… he'll help me,' she confirmed to herself. The stresses of the last few months were surfacing again. She was grateful to the Controller for arranging the reunion. And in an effort to fulfil her role as an agent she decided to ring the 'Office' to report what Snowman had told her yesterday about Mikey and the 'X' terrorist group, even if Snowman had been sceptical and dismissed the information as the ravings of a megalomaniac. But since then things had become fraught and it had slipped her mind.

She retrieved her mobile and the Controller came on the line. She was unusually friendly. "Hello Carrie, good to hear from you." She was relieved to hear Carrie's voice after the report from Whitey.

"I've got news… he's met somebody who…" Carrie was about to tell the story when she heard the creak of the apartment door behind her.

There was Snowman standing in the entrance staring at her.

"I've got to go now. I'll talk to you later."

Snowman slammed the door and stared at Carrie. "Who was that?"

"Just a friend."

"Who was it?"

Carrie's mind was racing and she said the first thing that came into her head. "It was my father…"

"You said, 'he's met somebody'… is that to do with me?" Snowman was standing menacingly over her.

Carrie turned away, slipping the mobile into her dressing gown pocket and trying to be cool. "I was talking about my brother… he's met a new woman."

"You never told me you had a brother."

"You never asked."

"Why did you suddenly end the call?"

Carrie was struggling to answer and beginning to panic. Snowman knew it. She was so close to meeting her father but she felt more vulnerable than ever.

"You took me by surprise… and I thought I'd call back later."

Snowman knew she was lying but unless he tried to beat the information out of her he wasn't going to find out any more. Catching her making that phone call helped to substantiate what Harry had told him, and because her time on this earth was limited he decided to let it go. All he could do was wait and hope she didn't call the authorities and fuck up his plans. He made a collection from his toolbox and left without saying another word.

Carrie returned the mobile and notebook to their hiding place. She wanted to call her mother, to hear her reassuring voice but she couldn't let her know the danger she was in. When she had accepted the job it had appeared exciting and an opportunity to see her father again. But now the fantasy had worn off, leaving her disillusioned and afraid.

She went to the drawer and took out a pipe. She prepared it as Snowman had shown her. She stretched a fresh piece of tin foil over the rim and held it in place with an elastic band. Then she put a small pile of cigarette ash over the hole she had pricked in the foil and laid a small rock of crack on top. Taking her gas lighter she turned up the jet and fired it at the crack. The ash slowed the burning of the rock, allowing her to leisurely inhale the fumes.

She was out of her depth. During her training she had performed well in the physical and psychological stress tests, but the drugs had lowered her resistance and being caught on the phone by Snowman had shaken her.

She slowly inhaled, held the smoke in her lungs and a tremor shook her body. A shiver shot up her spine and exploded into her head. Her stomach tightened as the feeling of euphoria soared through her. A tear ran down to her cheek; its path seemed to cut a cold track through her skin. Time dissolved into space. She watched her worries drift away with the smoke. She lay back on the sofa and allowed the elation to flood her mind. After a few minutes she got to her feet, put on a CD and danced slowly round the room.

Had she phoned the Controller back, life for her would have turned out very differently.

31. HARRY & CARRIE :
(SATURDAY AFTERNOON, 7 NOVEMBER)

Harry went to the chemist and bought a packet of latex gloves and some dressings for his chest.

He returned just in time to see Carrie dancing slowly around the room hugging the towelling robe to her body. She must have received the email by now. By her glazed expression and the way she was moving she appeared to be out of it. He hoped she wouldn't lose it altogether and forget to turn up to their meeting. When she let the dressing gown fall from her shoulders he hardly dared look; he imagined that she knew she was being watched and that she was doing it for him.

At the back of the wardrobe he found some old clothes which he could destroy afterwards. He decided to wear his Doc Martens boots because they would clean up easily and his straw hat to avoid leaving hairs and traces of DNA.

He dressed his wounded chest and with his beekeeper's veil and gloves on, he eased himself through the skylight and belly-crawled to the nearest hive. The lukewarm afternoon sun had brought a few docile worker-bees out on to the flight board. Staying low behind the hive he removed the crown board to reveal the brood box. His luck was in; the queen bee was visible in the middle of the chamber. He took an empty matchbox from his pocket and gently plucked her from a cluster of bees. The buzzing intensified as the aggravated bees realised their queen was being taken. He slipped her quickly into a matchbox and replaced the crown board before the swarm had time to react. Making sure he did not appear above the balustrade he crawled back down into his flat.

He put a Polaroid camera and the latex gloves into a supermarket bag and slipped a half-bottle of vodka into his back pocket. His last act before leaving was to put a DVD into his recorder and set the timer for 5pm.

He walked over to his car to collect the black-jack and then wandered over to Costas's to have a glass or two of red wine. He was struggling to control the sexual anticipation of what lay ahead.

It was late Saturday lunchtime and Soho was teeming with provincial tourists and Chinese families who ventured across Shaftesbury Avenue at the weekends. The contrast between cultures was evident. Even though the weather was inclement the congested streets were full of the chattering invaders, creating a very different atmosphere from the week.

By his fourth glass of wine Harry had convinced himself in his warped imagination that he was justified in carrying out his perverse assignment. He indulged in the fantasy that he was carrying out a freelance mission, working as a double agent with the bonus of getting his hands on the most perfect body he had ever seen.

Carrie arrived at a quarter to four and sat at the bar.

Harry had taken the table behind the door. He let her stew for fifteen minutes until finally, with her frequent and expectant glances towards the door, her gaze eventually landed on him. She hardly recognised him in his hat. A shiver of horror ran through her. She was there to meet her father, who she believed was due at any moment. Her face fell as Harry got up from the table, carrying his plastic bag.

As he got closer the first thing he noticed were her dilated pupils. In his own weird way he was concerned for her.

"What are you doing here?" she said. "Where's my father?"

"I've been instructed to accompany you... we have to wait here until I get a message." He had already drafted the text message on his mobile and all he had to do was recall it and send it to himself. He had practised before leaving home and could execute it without glancing at the screen.

"Why isn't he here?"

"I don't know... we just have to follow instructions."

Time dragged by as she suffered this man's attentions. He had introduced himself as Larry and tried to charm her. He still harboured the fantasy that she might like to invite him back to her flat of her own accord. However hard he tried to engage her in conversation, she didn't want to know. She was only interested in knowing when her father would show up. Harry stalled and she drank a couple more glasses of wine. On two occasions she disappeared into the loos. Harry sweated those moments out, hoping that she hadn't dumped him.

32. SNOWMAN : (SATURDAY AFTERNOON, 7 NOVEMBER)

Snowman had been surprised when he turned up at Carrie's flat to find her still there. Then he overheard her phone call and any feelings of guilt left him.

He returned to the Dog and Duck, which had a view of her front door. He had a couple of pints and kept an eye out for her to leave. He was selling a gramme to an old Fleet Street hack when Carrie left to meet Harry and Snowman didn't see her go.

At 4pm he left the pub and rang her doorbell. Having established that she'd left, he climbed the four flights of stairs, realising that this would be the last time. He had to keep moving because he didn't know how long it would be before she returned. It would be impossible to get rid of every hair and skin trace but since he'd never had a DNA or fingerprint sample taken he felt safe. He put the bed sheets into the washing machine and went through every room methodically cleaning every surface and all the floors. Then he repeated the exercise, looking for any traces of his presence that he might have missed the first time. Fortunately most of his clothes were at the flat he shared with Myrtle. He reckoned that if he were ever traced to Carrie's flat he could always claim to have met her at Costas's Lounge and to have had a one night stand.

Then as a final farewell he snorted one of the lines of coke on the coffee table and left.

33. CARRIE & HARRY : (5.30PM, SATURDAY 7 NOVEMBER)

It was five-thirty when Harry sent the text message to himself.

His phone buzzed in his pocket. He read the message out loud. "Return to Carrie's flat. Her father will arrive at six." He held out the phone for her to see the message as though this proved its legitimacy.

Carrie panicked. "I can't go back… there might be someone there."

"We'll have to go back… I can't change the RV… I'll wait outside and stop anyone coming up," said Harry, believing Snowman had left by now.

She was furious but there was nothing she could do. The message was clear; if she wanted to meet her father she had to go along with it. She told him to ring the doorbell when her father arrived. If she wasn't alone she would answer saying, "Not today, thank you." Then he should take her father back to Costas's and she would join them there.

When she arrived at the flat she noticed several things had been rear-ranged. Had Snowman tidied up? He never cleaned up. And why was the washing machine on? She was confused and distracted. And she had Larry or whatever his name was waiting downstairs at the front door. She went straight to her computer looking for any new mail. There wasn't any.

She sat down and tried to relax. Should she phone the Controller again? She paced up and down and the minutes passed slowly. Every time she looked at the clock the hand had hardly moved.

Eventually she couldn't wait any longer. She picked up the intercom. "Is there any sign of him?"

Harry's voice came back calm and precise. "No sign... but I've got another message."

"What's it say?"

"I'll come up."

Carrie pressed the door release.

Inside the street door Harry pulled on the latex gloves. He took a phial of amylnitrate from his pocket and took the hit. He sucked in air resting his spinning head against the door jam. All the nerves in his body were tingling with the euphoria generated by the popper. He began to float up the stairs towards her flat.

When Carrie opened the door she didn't see the black-jack in his right hand. She was annoyed at the arrogant way he pushed in. "What are you doing?"

Harry pointed behind her. "Look out!"

She was wondering about the latex glove on his hand but in her confused state she turned round. Harry pole-axed her with the black-jack just above her right ear. It was an accurate aim; her knees folded and she dropped to the floor.

She came round slowly but she couldn't move her head; her neck seemed paralysed. She couldn't move her body. She could feel all her limbs but they wouldn't move. She opened her eyes as the adrenalin coursed through her body. Her head and neck ached unbearably. She was only wearing her underwear. Her legs were taped to the chair and her arms taped behind her back. Her mouth was taped shut and she could only breathe through her nose.

Harry was sitting facing her. He was gently bathing her face with a cold, wet dishcloth. He reached down and slid his hand inside her knickers. She tried to beg him to stop but with her mouth taped-up it just seemed to excite him even more. She played possum until he had removed the gag. He stood in front of her and pushed his erect penis into her mouth. She bit him and screamed frantically. He pulled back in agony and hit her hard. The chair fell backwards and her mouth filled with blood. He pulled the chair back up. She was helpless in the hands of this bastard. She decided her best chance of survival was to suffer his abuse without panicking. She apologised and hung her head hoping her submissive attitude would satisfy his needs. He bent over the coffee table and took a long line of her cocaine. He took a slug of vodka and sat down in front of her again. The pain in his penis was easing. He ripped her bra off and sat staring at her naked breasts.

Carrie realised she was in full view of the window but there was a blank brick wall on the other side of the street. There were a couple of bee-hives, one floor up, on the roof. She'd never really noticed them before. She remembered her childhood, when she had been taken away from her father in London to live in the country with her mother. Perhaps one more scream at the right time and maybe, hopefully, someone would hear her.

Harry cut her legs free and pulled her to her feet. He pushed her towards the window and stood in front of her computer. She had no idea what he was going to do. He walked round her, fondling her body. "Stand still," he ordered. Feeling a surge of power over this defenceless goddess, he pulled her knickers down to her knees. He went over to his shopping bag and took out the Polaroid camera. He made her face him, turn with her back to him and twist her shoulders round to face the camera so he could see the sides of her breasts. Then he bent her over the computer table, each time making her look into the lens. The Polaroid camera whirred, ejecting photograph after photograph.

"Stand up and face me."

He ripped off her knickers leaving her totally naked, her arms still bound behind her back.

Her legs were shaking so violently she could hardly stand.

He took her in his arms and kissed her passionately on the mouth. She didn't resist and she didn't comply. She remained passive waiting for her opportunity.

Finally he turned her round and pushed her over the table facing the window. He lifted her taped arms and pulled her head back by her hair. Then he forced himself violently into her.

Her face was inches from the window. She let out a blood-curdling scream, hoping someone close by would hear and take notice. The scream made Harry hesitate for a moment. She stamped on his foot, jammed her arms back into his raw chest so that he released his grip. She made a break for the door. She only managed two paces before he grabbed her and swung her back to the table. The last thing she saw, as he viciously thrust her head forward, was the vase of lillies she had bought that morning from Berwick Street market.

He repeatedly banged her head on the table then crammed her knickers into her mouth and wound fresh tape round her face.

He raped her again from behind. The knickers were sucked down into her throat as she gasped for breath. She couldn't defend herself. She vomited and started to suffocate. Her convulsions encouraged Harry's ejaculation. Unable to expel the vomit, she went into spasm and choked to death.

But Harry hadn't finished with her. She had gone limp and in his resentment and frustration he tried to masturbate himself erect again. He tried to ejaculate over her naked body, but his failure magnified his exasperation. Pulling her up by her hair, he ripped the tape from her mouth and pulled out the knickers. He grabbed the vase of flowers from beside the computer and tipped the water over her face in an effort to clean away the vomit and revive her. He dragged her off the desk and laid her on the floor. Tilting her head back, he pressed his mouth against hers and blew down her throat. But she was dead.

He grabbed her by the hair and let out a desperate howl. There was so much more he wanted to do to her.

34. SNOWMAN & COSTAS :
(SATURDAY EVENING, 7 NOVEMBER)

After cleaning Carrie's flat Snowman took everything back to Myrtle's on foot. There would be no taxi drivers to witness him move his bags from Carrie's.

He needed to get drunk to try to forget about her. He went to Costas's Lounge. He would make sure he established his alibi by being the centre of attention; he would not go missing for a minute.

The problem he had to deal with was that, while he was at Costas's, a couple of hundred metres away Carrie was being killed. He didn't usually have a conscience when it came to business but every time she crossed his mind he shuddered. Regret was fucking with his head. She might have been a good lay and a handy place to keep his stash but she was also bright, cheerful and intelligent and he'd liked her. There, he was already thinking of her in the past tense. He knew drinking and tooting would only kill the guilt temporarily and in the morning he would have to face his demons again. But she had double-crossed him; hadn't she? That was his justification for what was happening right now. But each time he used the excuse to relieve his conscience it became less convincing.

He was standing at the bar when Costas came up to him. "Did you see Carrie? She was in here earlier."

Snowman was visibly shaken by the question and the mention of her name. Fortunately the drink had numbed him sufficiently to allow him to stumble over his answer without appearing to arouse Costas's suspicions.

"No... I, er... I haven't seen her for a couple of days... you know, fucking women." He managed an artificial laugh.

It was awkward and out of character; something Costas wasn't going to forget.

35. HARRY : (SATURDAY EVENING, 7 NOVEMBER)

Harry dragged Carrie's body across the floor and dumped her in the middle of the room.

His fantasy had not gone to plan. He had wanted her to be more co-operative. To beg him for mercy. To drop to her knees and suck him off. But nothing, fucking nothing like that had happened. What if the people who paid him to watch over her found out? He was still wearing his gloves and hat. He had left no finger prints and hopefully no hair. He wanted to place the blame for the murder as far away from himself as possible. He needed to show a motive for her murder.

He went to the kitchen and found a carving knife. Perhaps he could implicate the Chinese and make it look like a drug killing. In a deluded frenzy he chopped at her body, naively attempting to imitate a Triad murder. A revenge killing, carried out in a fit of rage. He had better remove the tape. But it would leave traces of adhesive for the forensic people. Harry was confused. What should he do to protect himself? He had ejaculated in her, which would have left his DNA. He searched the bathroom and found a bottle of bleach. He filled her vagina with the bleach. He was in a blind panic and had lost all reason. He had to slow down. Snowman was not coming back. He had time to clear up. But everything seemed to be escalating out of control.

Then the buzzing started.

He looked out of the window to his roof opposite. It was as though the bees had left the hive and were in the room with him.

'Buzz.. buzz.. FUCKING BUZZING...'

In his continued rage he returned to hacking and slashing at Carrie's body. Blood oozed from the wounds. Gasping for breath, he worked himself into a state of hysteria before falling back sweating and exhausted. Then he lay down on the floor beside her and held her hand.

Time passed; how long he didn't know. His head seemed to quieten and the buzzing faded. He took the matchbox from his pocket and shook the queen bee into Carrie's mouth. He pushed her teeth together and listened to the bee's aggravated buzzing as it tried to escape. He kissed Carrie's cold, unresponsive lips and lay crouched over her body, trying to relieve the great sense of loss that pervaded him.

Finally he took a last Polaroid and returned the pictures and camera to the plastic bag.

Harry waited behind Carrie's front door until the street was clear.

He turned his cardigan inside out and held the carrier bag in front of him to hide the blood stains on his trousers. It was dark and he only had fifty metres to cover before he got to his doorway.

Back in his flat he paced the room. "Those bastards tortured me... I loved her and they came between us. People always intrude and fuck up my life."

In the small Victorian fireplace he methodically burned the cardigan, trousers, shirt and hat, cutting each garment into strips. Then he compulsively cleaned his Doc Martens over and over again.

He put on his pyjamas and, with tears running down his face, tried to destroy the memories by drinking mead and vodka and snorting speed until he began a trip into oblivion. He tore off his pyjamas and started slapping his head. He went up onto the roof and stood there naked, the cold rain stinging his raw chest as he tried to do penance for his sin. But with the fragment of reasoning he had left, he knew nothing would ever relieve his agony.

Through the fog he became aware that it was 6am. He sat at the monitor watching his recording of Carrie's rape.

He couldn't and wouldn't admit to himself that he had murdered her. She had died before she was meant to. "It was not my fault... if things had worked out we could have escaped together."

The hive-camera had captured all the action on the desk until he had dragged her into the middle of the room, where because of the reflections on the window it became less clear. He had to turn away from the screen when he saw himself repeatedly and futilely masturbating over her dead body.

She was no longer there for him to watch. Nothing was as it was meant to be. He had done what he had been told to do and they still owed him another 5K. If he kept his head down, with time the pain and regret might pass.

36. THE CONTROLLER & HARRY : (AFTERNOON, SUNDAY 8 NOVEMBER)

The Controller woke early with Carrie on her mind; she had not paid enough attention to Carrie's last phone call. She was overloaded with work and she had been preoccupied.

She tried to read the Sunday papers but was too distracted to concentrate. Finally she gave up and went to the office. She would arrange a face to face with Carrie; even if that meant stepping outside the rule book. Her instincts told her that a situation was developing and she decided that from now on she would contact her every forty-eight hours. She tried Carrie's mobile and left a couple of messages. When at 6pm she still had not heard from her, she decided to ring Whitey.

Harry had been up for thirty-six hours and finally at 8am put away the drugs and alcohol.

He was in the middle of a nightmare when the call came through.

He tried to ignore the mobile's incessant ringing, but as he surfaced he recognised the ring-tone. He fumbled around, heart thumping. "Fucking bastards."

"Have you had any visual contact with the subject recently?"

Harry's voice was thick with sleep. "Not really."

"What's that mean?"

"Well... she was at the window."

"What was she doing?"

"Just hanging around."

"Doing what?" The Controller shook her head; it was like trying to get blood from a stone.

"Well... she was dancing... and, er... it looked like she was doing some drugs."

"What kind of drugs?"

Harry played the naive card. "How should I know?"

"Was she smoking, injecting or snorting them?"

"She was snorting them."

The Controller was confused. "How do you know what she was doing inside her flat?"

Perspiration soaked his shirt. He didn't know whether Carrie's body had been found yet. With his hung-over brain he was vulnerable.

"Hang on a minute," said Harry, "I think there's someone at the door." He put down the phone and went over to the kitchen sink. He stuck his head under the cold tap, gasping as the freezing water brought him to his senses.

The Controller slumped back in her chair.

He came back on the line. "From my flat I can just about see her window."

"Who was at the door?" asked the Controller.

He hesitated. "I was mistaken."

The Controller wanted to pursue it but realised it was going nowhere. "She was doing drugs in the window?" she asked.

"Yes," said Harry, haltingly.

"How did she look?"

"What do you mean?"

"Was she tired, stressed, happy... what?"

"She looked fine..." The Controller's questioning jarred on his already frayed nerves. Trying to move the conversation on, he panicked. "… I've got a photograph of her."

This caught the Controller completely off guard. It wasn't part of Whitey's brief to photograph Carrie. "What are you doing photographing her?"

Harry didn't answer; in his confusion he was digging himself deeper.

There was a long pause before the Controller said, "Okay, email it over to me… I want the photograph and the report now."

Harry was stuck; he couldn't refuse without arousing more suspicion. "What about today? Have you seen her today?"

"No."

"I want you to keep a regular check on her. I want you to call me immediately if she looks as though she's in any kind of trouble."

Harry didn't answer. 'She doesn't know Carrie's dead,' he thought.

"You're not up to the job… send the picture over now" she demanded, deciding to bring the call to an end. "Is there anything else I should know?"

"I don't think so."

She rang off. Whitey's answers had filled her with apprehension.

Harry felt humiliated by being ordered about by a woman and having the phone put down on him. At first he thought, 'Fuck you.' But the last thing he wanted was a visit from the Firm. He swallowed his pride and settled down at the computer. He emailed a sketchy report to the Controller with the picture he'd taken of Carrie in Dean Street.

While the Controller sat there worrying, Whitey's email arrived; it did nothing to alleviate her concern. He had been unhelpful and agitated on the phone and his report was superficial. She wouldn't risk asking Whitey to make face to face contact and activated a Crisis Response Team to check Carrie's wellbeing. She gave instructions to the team's leader that they were to be discreet and must not unsettle Carrie.

Now there was nothing more she could do until they got back to her, so she went home.

37. THE CRISIS RESPONSE TEAM :
(10PM, SUNDAY 8 NOVEMBER)

It was Sunday evening and the Crisis Response Team was off duty.

Eventually the team leader located and deployed them. The team of two men and a woman were in the bar of The Crown & Two Chairman within three hours of the Controller's order. They were indistinguishable from the rest of the weekend punters in the pub. Sunday was the quietest night of the week in Soho, and the evening crowd consisted mostly of early clubbers who wanted a few rippers before moving on when the pubs closed.

The female member of the team rang Carrie's doorbell but couldn't get an answer. One of the male operatives joined her and while they chatted in the doorway he used the Firm's duplicate key.

The third member of the team took his pint out onto the pavement and stood in Carrie's doorway, pretending to be drunk. He had a pager in his pocket to contact the other two if an unexpected visitor turned up.

When they reached the flat their plan of action was determined. The woman went straight back down to the street door to inform the agent on guard, then brought him inside to seal the door. Meanwhile the other man rang the Controller to tell her what they had found, and while he was waiting for instructions drew the curtains and put on the light.

The Controller was on her second glass of wine and was sitting down to a ready meal when the phone rang. The news hit her hard. She was devastated and angry with herself. She was responsible for this inexperienced agent who had not been given the support she needed. The Civil Service bureaucracy had not allowed her the budget for the extra staff required to handle the recent increase in workload. She had been shafted by her Chief who was trying to show that his department was financially viable, and now she had lost one of her operatives. "Contain and seal the site and wait for instructions," she ordered and slammed down the phone.

Carrie's case had not been given a high priority rating. And the Controller had never felt comfortable with Whitey as her handler. Now it had all blown up in her face. Her anger burst over. "Too many fucking cases," she shouted at her empty flat. The tears of regret and frustration came without her expecting them. She had to pull herself together. She could not allow the police to discover the murder. The last thing the Chief needed was to have them sniffing around and upsetting the department. They were like rats up a drainpipe when anything happened with the Firm. If she allowed them to become involved, her job would be on the line. She called a clean-up team and ordered them to be on site as soon as possible.

The Office Cleaning Company's van was parked, with two wheels up on the pavement outside Carrie's door and the bonnet up, within the hour. Photographs were taken and a forensic examination completed. Two hours later the flat had been cleaned.

In the early hours of the morning when the street was empty, Carrie's body was brought down and loaded into the van.

38. THE FIRM & THE ASSOCIATES : (MONDAY 9 NOVEMBER)

After the Controller heard that Carrie had been dead for more than twenty-four hours she rang the Chief.

"This is a priority incident requiring immediate action..." he said, "... remember that Carrie was forced on me by the SCS without any explanation..."

"Harry White was forced on me... and he's behaving strangely..." she said, "I'll deal with this."

The Controller was taking Carrie's death personally. If she had been kept fully informed then the poor girl might still be alive. She would contact Whitey again and grill him; but that would have to wait until after the conference, scheduled for 3am.

The meeting was attended by the Chief, the Controller and the Senior Civil Servant, who brought his personal assistant to take the minutes.

"Let me be clear from the start..." said the SCS, "...I've got the Home Secretary's ear, and his blessing... any disagreement and my decision will be final."

"Carrie was our agent and we must keep this dark…" said the Chief, "… we cannot let the police or anyone know about this…" He pointed to the Controller, "…my case officer will deal with it."

"I accept that it's not in my remit to handle the murder of one of your officers, but I do have a vested interest. I want to use my agent to manage this case… and as long as you are in agreement I am prepared to let him report to you… and you in turn keep me informed. He happens to be Carrie's father and I assure you no-one would be more motivated or do a better job."

"I want to use my agents… has this man any experience of handling this kind of case?" asked the Controller.

"Just as much as you have, my dear."

Ignoring his chauvinism, she said, "Surely his emotional involvement will affect his attitude and his judgement."

"I cannot give you details of his background but take it from me he has been involved in national security, concerning the protection of the Nation and the Royal Family… he is a first class agent."

"I'm concerned that he's being thrown into a situation that he has no knowledge of and it will be massively emotionally upsetting.."

The SCS ignored her. "I do not want the police or Special Branch involved. If the press get hold of this the whole affair could blow up in our faces."

"I don't understand why you want him on the case… what's his background?" asked the Controller.

"You will arrange for Branen to return to this country and his command and control will be handled by you," the SCS said, pointing to the Chief. And realising that the Controller was becoming suspicious of his motives, the SCS turned on her. "Branen's background is none of your business and it never will be."

Now the Controller knew for certain that there was another agenda.

The Chief retorted, "Let's not be patronising… I've spent my whole career working for the Government and in my senior position I do not expect to be left out of important security issues and decisions."

"Remember your previous balls-up when you tried to go over my head…" replied the SCS, "…the Home Secretary won't be as forgiving this time… don't forget you've only got eighteen months until your full pension…" Turning to the Controller, he said, "…in case of any hiccups, ring me if you need permission for immediate action... I want daily progress reports from you at precisely 7pm every evening without fail."

The Controller said, "I hope you're not keeping vital information from us."

The SCS delivered his Parthian shot with a lie. "I believe that Branen is the main suspect... I have reason to believe that he entered the country using false papers and has disappeared."

The Chief and the Controller looked at him incredulously.

The SCS continued, "I suspect that he killed his own daughter to sever all connection with us. If we get him back we could check his credibility... so he could be eliminated from the list of suspects."

"If he did kill her, why would he come back?" asked the Controller.

The SCS was flustered, "This man is wholly unpredictable... he might think that by returning he would not be considered to be a suspect."

The Chief and the Controller were obliged to use Branen because as the SCS had repeatedly emphasised their jobs were at stake. But the Controller could not believe a father would kill his own daughter for the reasons given, and she had her own suspects who included Snowman and Whitey, whose taciturn report was still nagging her; she was also concerned that the SCS had used the word 'eliminated' when referring to Branen.

"Here's Branen's phone number... make sure you get him back... you will inform him of his daughter's murder in all its detail... and give him all necessary help."

"I'll need a photograph of him."

The SCS cut her short. "None exists... you'll communicate via satellite phone... not face to face contact."

It was not in the SCS's interest to provoke an untenable scenario with the Firm which could hinder his actual intentions, but he found it difficult not to lose his temper with these spooks.

The meeting finally ended at 4.30am when the cabal had decided how best to handle and contain the situation.

By then Carrie's body had been removed and the crime scene cleaned.

PART TWO

39. BRANEN'S SMALLHOLDING :
(SUNRISE, MONDAY 9 NOVEMBER)

A breeze rustled through the branches of the eucalyptus tree that had stood for two lifetimes beside the stone farmhouse.

As the sun rose over the hill, the light danced through the leaves and bounced a thousand shadows through the open shutters and onto the roughly plastered wall behind the bed.

The flickering sunlight moved down onto his face. A blackbird perched in the top branches was welcoming the dawn. The slow, regular drip of the leaking tap caught his attention and he persuaded himself to climb out of bed. He watched his bare feet pad over the cold terracotta tiles to the stone basin. The draught from the open window had a winter chill. The brass tap clunked into life and gushed cold mountain water. He pushed his head under the torrent and drank from his cupped hands. Even after living here for seven years, the taste of metal in the water still reminded him of the chemically filtered water he'd had to drink in the desert. He put on some old fatigues and stood for a moment, wondering what the weather was like in London on an early November morning. He was an hour ahead and imagined that Jane and Carrie would still be in bed.

He collected tying wire and secateurs from the barn and wiped the dew from the metal tractor seat. The engine turned over three times before it coughed into life, throwing out a fog of blue diesel fumes. He was out in the vineyard before the sun had cleared the tree line.

The house stood on a promontory overlooking the valley. It was five hundred metres along a track off a narrow road that led further up into the mountains. A row of cypress trees stretched down to a stream which cascaded through the valley to a lake a kilometre away. They acted as a windbreak and offered shade to his six beehives. He had planted lavender amongst the trees to encourage the bees to forage for the pollen which gave the honey its unique taste. Beyond the stream woodlands climbed up the far side of the valley towards the mountains that grew into the sky.

The olive grove lay on the other side of the promontory to the vineyard with its sixty year old vines. The trees produced about a thousand kilos of olives and the vineyard approximately twenty thousand litres of wine each year. His neighbour, Salvatore, advised him that by pruning both the trees and vines heavily, a smaller amount of fruit would produce a higher quality oil and wine. He would come over with his seven year old son Eduardo and half a dozen local men and spend two weeks during the summer and autumn hand-picking. With the help of the local co-operative they made virgin olive oil and good table wine. Branen's income from the podere was thirty-five thousand euros including the truffles he collected with Salvatore's spaniel.

When the wages and taxes were deducted he was left with approximately twenty-five thousand euros a year to live on. With his Associates' pension paid as photographic syndication fees, he was financially self-sufficient in a poor rural community.

These rolling terraces had become his sanctuary. They represented an escape from his earlier violent life, even if it had been a disastrous summer for the vines.

Early spring had started fine and warm but May had been wet. He had walked the rows of vines with the rain running inside the neck of his waterproofs. The lack of sunlight worried him; it would affect the sugar content of the grapes.

By June he was trimming any excessive leaf growth and watching the flowers develop into fruit.

July had turned into a sweltering hot month. He spent the days on his veranda looking out over the sun-baked hill, watching the heat haze move the mountains.

This was his sixth harvest. But this year the humidity had allowed the mildew on the vines to flourish.

Salvatore and Eduardo stood there muttering, then recommended sulphur spraying in an effort to curb the mould.

August had delivered the coup de grace, a hailstorm, the like of which the locals could not recall in living memory. The dark storm clouds came up over the mountains like a rolling fog of burning oil. The tempest tore the vines from their stands and hammered the trees into submission.

He watched as his wine and olive harvest disappeared in a torrent of hailstones that melted into the soil along with his income.

It was as though this last season was an omen.

The hour around sunrise had a magical quality.

He stopped and listened to the roaring of a wild boar in the woods. The animals and birds that had survived the local hunters' recent onslaught announced the dawning day. Autumn had arrived and each day was noticeably colder until the sun had risen.

He was half-way up the second row of vines when the dawn chorus was joined by a distant chirp from the satellite telephone. It was the last sound he wanted to hear. The phone had been on its charger since he first came here; in the barn while he was refurbishing the house, then under his bed by the window for the last six years. He tolerated it because now his daughter was working for the UK Government. The last time it rang was in August when they let him know that Carrie had been recruited. He knew that it had been done deliberately to keep him in line, even though he had no intention of betraying the agreement. He had asked them not to put Carrie into any life-threatening missions but even after their reassurances he was still left feeling insecure; which had been their intention.

He took a deep breath of the herb-scented air, turned away and listened instead to the clip of the secateurs.

The phone rang for a second time as he carried the prunings back to the trailer. He knew that they didn't ring without good reason. He had been decommissioned, but what did that mean? Fuck all. They were mutually dependent; their knowledge of each others' involvement guaranteed his safety and their security.

He worked his way down the vineyard, pruning and re-fixing the vines to the wires. It was going to take three or four days of work and he didn't want to be interrupted.

Some evenings he would sit enjoying the cool night air listening to the cicada's chorus and it was at those moments that he would miss Carrie and Jane. Jane lived another life with another man and Carrie was all he had left. He missed Jane's energy and love of life. The memories were vivid and he visited them all too often. Since the events in Paris he'd been afraid to contact Carrie in case he was being watched. He didn't want the secret services using her as a bargaining chip; but since last August the event he most feared had come to pass; the bastards had persuaded her to join them.

An hour later, as he drove the tractor back up to the house, the warmth of the sun on his back did nothing to relieve the chill he felt inside.

He cut two thick slices of the village bread and poured olive oil into a pan. He fried a couple of duck eggs on the stove and made tea. The smell of the eggs and hot oil filled the room. He stood looking out through the window as the sounds and scents drifted in on the breeze; he wanted to share this moment with somebody.

His reverie was broken by the phone again. He felt his heart beat faster. Eventually he was going to have to answer it; they would never give up. He took the pan off the stove and went up the creaking staircase two at a time.

A woman's voice said, "I'm the Case Controller, I'm afraid I've got bad news... where are you?"

"Abroad, why?"

"I'm the Case Controller. Your daughter is dead."

He knew she wasn't lying. His legs went numb and he fell back against the wall.

He whispered, "When... how do you know?"

"She failed an RV... we went looking," she lied.

"Where?"

"We found her body in a Soho flat."

"Soho.... does her mother know?"

"No..."

Branen interrupted her. "Let me tell her... I'll tell her." He sank down to his knees. He was overwhelmed by a great sense of hopelessness. He felt defeated, beaten. "What happened?"

"I'm sorry Branen, she was murdered... we want you back to help solve this."

"Where is she now?"

"We have her. I'll fax a copy of a left luggage ticket to you. Travel to Stansted Airport in the next forty-eight hours. There will be cash for your expenses and a mobile with our number programmed into key seven… when you arrive, call in and ask for the Controller."

He heard the details through a fog of fury and hopelessness.

"Remember key seven and ask for the Controller."

The line went dead.

He sat staring out over the valley, unable to control the tears.

He was filled with anger and self-recrimination. He hadn't given Carrie what she needed as a child and if he hadn't succumbed to the Associates' overtures she would never have got entangled with the Firm.

He had to detach from his grief and force himself into action; he would not be able to operate clinically under the influence of rage and revenge. If he was going to find his daughter's murderer, he had to return to Soho whatever the risk.

He went online and booked an easyJet flight from Bologna to Stansted.

They were expecting him to arrive by plane but he had no idea what might develop over the next few weeks; he might need to leave the UK in a hurry and by entering the country by an unexpected route it would enable him to leave a false trail; so he confirmed the plane ticket and decided to use his car.

It was ten in the morning and if he left within the hour, he could be at the Mont Blanc tunnel by six in the evening and as long as the sea was calm in the Channel he could be in London by early tomorrow morning.

He went back on the net and checked Stansted's long-term parking.

His cover story for Customs would be that he was selling the rare truffles that he'd collected with Salvatore's dog in the woods. He would go to the restaurants in Soho and the sales would provide some extra income.

He weighed out a kilo of black truffles and half a kilo of the bianco pregiato truffle worth at least three thousand pounds. He put them into an insulated cold-bag to stop the smell permeating his clothes. He packed his kit-bag and loaded the old Range Rover. He put the

French passport, credit card and a UK driving licence all in the name of Branen into his belt-bag. He had not needed a legend since his last operation seven years ago but he had kept the paperwork up to date using the local Poste Restante service as his contact address. He knew SIS had a record of all three so if he wanted them to know what he was buying and where he was, he would use the Branen credit card and every transaction would register on their computer.

He had another credit card with a London post-box address for an account at Barclays Bank in Soho Square in his real name which was unknown to SIS, as was, as far as he knew, the Range Rover. If he used that card it would be hard for them to find him, and it could gain him valuable time if he had to get away quickly. He also took five hundred pounds in euros and sterling, which was all the cash he had left.

He was about to leave when he remembered the insurance policy he had invested in back in Paris in 1997. He retrieved the two photographs he kept with the negatives in the safe, buried in concrete, beneath the first tread of the staircase. While he was securing the stair-tread back into position it dawned on him that now that Carrie was gone, he would not need that fucking satellite phone any longer. Its existence had been an aggravation to him but now it was obsolete. He worked out his anger as he smashed it to pieces with a rock on the terrace. MI5 must have got the number from the Senior Civil Servant, which meant that he had become involved.

He had a one thousand mile drive ahead of him and managed to get onto the autostrada heading north by midday. After six hours of concentrated driving he pulled into a service station, close to the Tunnel di Mont Bianco, and refuelled the car and himself.

The drive through France was numbing. The shock of Carrie's death was taking its toll. As he made his way up through Champagne country and past Rheims, he dropped off to sleep. It can only have been a few seconds later when he woke with a jolt thinking he was in bed. Instead he found himself driving along the hard shoulder.

He stopped and got out. The autoroute was silent and the air cold. He zipped up his jacket and sat on the bonnet of the car. Warmed by the engine he leaned back against the windscreen to stare up at a million stars in a cloudless sky. Since the phone call he'd been preoccupied with preparation for the trip and it had distracted him from his grief. Now it flooded back and overwhelmed him. Carrie was dead. He closed his eyes, imagining she was in his arms as she had been when he'd last seen her. He fixed his attention on a particular star, and that was her; he promised her memory that someone would pay for her death.

A lorry and trailer roared past and in its thunderous wake he was wrenched back to reality.

The rest of the journey to the coast was uneventful.

To make it difficult to trace he used the Barclaycard in his real name to buy a ferry ticket; paying with cash was too obvious and what they would look for first.

He crossed from Calais on the 5.30am boat, arriving at Dover at 6am British time. He only had the passport in the name of Branen and he was forced to use it to check through Customs. He risked revealing his port of entry. The Custom's official gave it a cursory glance and did not record his name or passport number.

He stopped at a twenty-four hour garage on the outskirts of Dover, filled the car with petrol and had a coffee and a doughnut. His stomach was raw and his mouth tasted foul but the coffee gave him a lift.

It was essential that he got to Stansted as soon as possible. Even if they did not reveal themselves, they would surely be waiting for him to collect the parcel from left-luggage. He was forced to compromise in order to get to the airport in time. He had to use the main roads and motorways and his car would be recorded on CCTV cameras. If he had to make a speedy exit in the future and SIS knew he had not flown into Stansted, they would check all other routes including the road and rail connections to the airport. Having discovered his actual route to Stansted, hopefully they would assume he would use the same route to escape. But he intended to use a different getaway and that would give him a considerable time advantage.

As it got light he arrived at the Pink Elephant long stay car park, about a mile from the airport terminal. He took a ticket from the barrier and parked. All he had to do to get out in the future was to insert the ticket and a credit card at the exit barrier, which would avoid any face to face contact.

Once he was in the terminal building the last thing they would consider was that he had arrived by car. If they ever discovered that he owned the Range Rover and searched for it they would eventually find it, but there were thousands of cars parked in that massive space and it could take them several hours.

Instead of taking the ten minute bus transfer he walked to the terminal, trying to avoid any cameras. With the kit-bag over his shoulder and the truffles in the cold-bag under his arm, it took him twenty minutes of brisk walking.

When he got there he went straight to the left-luggage office.

It was 7.30am and Harry was waking up.

40. HARRY : (7.30AM, TUESDAY 10 NOVEMBER)

It was a cold wet morning and the revelry and hubbub of Soho had dissipated with the arrival of dawn.

After the Controller's phone call on Sunday evening Harry had not been able to get back to sleep; thirty-six hours without any sleep. His entanglement with Carrie, his captivity at Mikey's and the pain of his chest wound had left him fucked up.

He'd become even more anxious and paranoid when he saw the team of officers arrive at Carrie's flat on Sunday night. Then they had closed the curtains and he had no idea what was happening in there. Carrie's death existed in his head as a private and secret experience between him and her. It was no one else's business. The people in her flat introduced a sense of reality, a connection with the outside world. He couldn't accept this intrusion on his fantasies.

It was morning again. Another day for Harry to face.

Then the sound he didn't want to hear, the Firm's mobile.

He went through the ritual with the Duty Officer and was put through to the Controller.

She sounded pissed off and aggressive. "I've been trying to get hold of you... where've you been?"

"I have to earn a living... the money you give me isn't enough to live on."

"I rang three times yesterday."

"I was out doing taxi work," said Harry, realising he must have been asleep or totally out of it when she had called.

"I want to know exactly when you last saw Carrie."

"It was Saturday... and I haven't seen her since."

"Why not?" asked the Controller.

"I don't know why... I just haven't seen her."

"You're paid to keep an eye on her."

"She just hasn't been around..." Harry had had enough, he was beginning to panic. "Why don't you get someone else to do your dirty work?"

"She's dead... she was murdered right under your nose."

Harry couldn't work out what to say, so he said nothing.

"Well, haven't you got anything to say?"

"I don't know anything about it."

The Controller thought to herself, 'I've got Billy Bunter here; he didn't know the custard pie was on the top shelf.' She wasn't going to get anything out of him over the phone, so she decided to wait for the forensic results and rang off.

Harry lay back on the bed, soaked in perspiration, still dressed in the same clothes as the previous day. He watched the grey light creep up over the buildings. His brain was a quagmire of chaotic noise and buzzing. Nothing he could do would allow him any relief. His head was spinning and he wanted to vomit. He had to get out of the flat.

Soho was a haven of quiet in the early morning, even though the surrounding city streets roared with traffic as commuters jump-started another day with caffeine. The peaceful streets and foggy light had an ominous air, a pregnant silence waiting for something, anything, to turn up and kick it into life. The occasional motorcycle messenger would throttle through the narrow streets leaving the echo of a Japanese engine to reverberate through the alleyways, grey and forbidding, the shop fronts dingy and dark. The contrast from a few hours earlier was stark.

Harry found himself outside St. Barnabas's Chapel again. But this time Carrie wouldn't allow him to step over the threshold. There was a poster on the wrought iron railings advertising a 'Before You Vote – Wine, Beer and Snax Party', organised by the local British National Party, for the following day. It crossed his mind it might be an opportunity to meet one of those women who were resident at the charity home.

41. BRANEN : (8AM, TUESDAY 10 NOVEMBER)

Branen went straight to the left-luggage office in a kiosk at the back of the airport and was handed a scruffy cardboard box bound with packing tape.

On the drive up from the south he'd thought about all the possible alternatives the Senior Civil Servant might be planning for him. It would be naive to think that they wanted him in the UK just to solve his daughter's murder; they could do that themselves if they wanted to.

He had to assume that he was being watched, but to slip his watchers would arouse suspicion. He wandered through the arrivals lounge and decided the best place to open the box was in the middle of the terminal amongst the meeters and greeters. He slit open the box and on top found what he needed; five hundred pounds in cash. He had spent two hundred pounds of his own money on fuel and food on the way here. Including this money he now had eight hundred pounds, plus a few euros.

He went out onto the concourse and hailed a cab.

Returning to a city he'd known intimately after a five year break meant he was seeing it through the eyes of a visitor. The lush green grass and tree-filled banks at the side of the motorway contrasted with the views into people's houses as they entered central London. The lines of washing in several shades of grey brought back the realities of urban life. Away from the UK it was easy to forget how magnificent the British countryside could be and how it differed from the inner city.

He got to thinking how best to cover his tracks without raising suspicion. He needed a fall-back position and then one after that. As they reached Marylebone Road the taxi's meter said sixty-five pounds. He passed three twenties and a ten through the glass partition and told the driver to unlock the doors if they stopped at a red traffic light.

At the first set of lights he unlocked the doors, but Branen waited.

The next set to show red were at Baker Street and it was busy. The driver unlocked the doors again and Branen was gone as swiftly as his luggage would allow. He disappeared into the crowd and down into the tube station. From another vehicle it would have looked fairly normal and it would have been impossible for the watchers to have every avenue covered. He travelled out of London on the tube and changed lines a couple of times before finally heading back into town and getting off at Piccadilly Circus. He was confident he'd shaken off any watchers; if there had been any to start with.

He emerged at street level and into the cacophony of central London. The first thing he noticed, as he stood looking up at the flashing neon signs of Piccadilly Circus, was the smell of pizza and petrol.

He crossed over to a souvenir shop on the edge of Piccadilly and bought a beret and a pair of sunglasses. On the clothes rack he found an orange jacket with 'London' across the back. With the beret hiding his hair, the collar of the jacket turned up and wearing the sunglasses, it was an obvious but reasonable attempt to look like a tourist. Should he be followed he would make it easy for them and then, by taking the jacket off, become less visible.

He wandered through to Regent Street and bought a large travel bag for the cardboard box and the cold-bag.

He hoped the disguise would give him enough time to establish a foxhole. If everything went wrong he had to be able to disappear. From past experience he knew he would have to find a secondary hiding place and he needed to remain unobserved while he established the fall-back position.

He turned into Gerrard Street and Chinatown came to meet him on the November breeze with the smell of stir-fry and the chatter of Cantonese.

Chinatown was made of London brick and York cobble stones, but it was not England. Entering it was like crossing the border into a foreign country, with the hustle and bustle of street life, where personal space was ignored and people pushed past without noticing his presence. The conventions of behaviour were those of Hong Kong, not London. He loved everything about it, the food, the market stalls, the graphics and the smell.

He wandered down Gerrard Street sidetracking off into alleyways hunting for a small out of the way hotel.

After a plate of pork and wind-dried duck and an hour of searching he walked through a stone archway into Horse and Dolphin Yard. Amongst the four storey terraces he found a flaking black door. Beside it, nailed to the wall, was a dusty hand-painted sign in Chinese. Small lettering below it in English revealed it was called China Hotel. Pushing open the creaky door he found himself in an empty room. Apart from a garish red rug with a gold dragon in the middle, everything else including the staircase on the far side was wood stain and black paint. There was no-one around. He stood in the hallway for a while smelling the garlic and ginger and wondering if he'd walked into someone's home. There was no reception desk; an advantage because if it was a hotel it meant he could come and go without being noticed. It was dark and unwelcoming. It was ideal.

A Chinese woman appeared from a door in the side of the staircase leading him to wonder if the family lived in the cupboard under the stairs. She spoke English with a thick Chinese accent which meant he could speak with an Irish accent without raising suspicion. It would help to confuse any description of him she might have to give in the future. He explained that he was a travelling salesman and would only be using the hotel occasionally. She looked at him suspiciously until he paid two hundred and fifty pounds in cash. She went back into her cupboard with his money. He wondered if he would ever see her again.

After a bellicose verbal exchange in Chinese with a man he couldn't see, she reappeared. Over her shoulder he saw that the doorway opened onto a room at the rear of the building.

She handed him two keys on a ring with a number eight tag and pointed at the stairs.

Room eight was at the end of the corridor. There was absolutely nothing remarkable about it, except of course the smell. As he opened the door there was a scrabbling sound as the wildlife vacated the room ready for him to occupy. He sat on the bed. It didn't submit. Here he was back in the smoke and back at the beginning of another job. He had been in this position several times before but this time it was personal. He had no idea what was going to happen over the next few days and it was important that he did not allow his emotions to affect his actions. He had to be clinical and professional and suppress his personal grief. Imagination could act as protection if used to anticipate danger, but could also get him killed if he allowed it to generate fear.

In the last few years he had found peace of mind managing his crops and making a living from the land. He had promised himself never to return to his previous profession, but he could not have predicted the slaughter of his daughter; now here he was back in this dump hunting for the murderer.

Inside the cardboard box he found a mobile phone. At the bottom was an A4 envelope and amongst the papers in it was a blurred photograph of Carrie. She was standing between two parked cars; she looked drawn but beautiful. The date on the top of the photograph was last Thursday.

'Why were they photographing her just four days ago?' He stared at the picture until the tears came; it didn't take long. He whispered a promise to Carrie: "I will find the bastard."

The next page consisted of a brief report about Carrie and her assignment, without mentioning any of her contacts. It simply stated that she had been murdered in her flat above The Crown and Two Chairmen. Listed on another page was the speed dial contact number '7' for the mobile and his catch-word, V.I.N.T.A.G.E, which made him wonder if they knew more about his new life and wine-making ambitions than he wanted them to.

The information they had given would only contain what they wanted him to know. To start with they would be pulling his strings, but he believed if he survived long enough he could get ahead of them. With Carrie gone and their emotional hold over him removed he had become a risk that they would eventually have to deal with. They had gambled by bringing him back... and so had he by coming back.

He burnt the paper with the speed dial number and catch-word on it and flushed it away. He hid the envelope containing Carrie's papers and her photograph in a slit that he cut in the seam of the mattress. He made the mattress suffer just as it intended to make him suffer if he ever had to sleep on it.

Also in the box were two keys with tags attached. The first one was for a postbox outside Giovanni's grocery store in Brewer Street; he knew the shop. The second was a door key and the tag had Carrie's name and address scrawled on it.

At the bottom of the box, neatly wrapped in a thin flexible lead bag was a SIG 229 with a sound moderator; a compact 9 shot, 9mm pistol used mostly by Special Forces and which he was familiar with. The armourer had included the correct ammo for use with a silencer; a box of fifty rounds of half-jacketed copper shells with lead tips and a 158 grain sub-sonic bullet. The number of rounds was disconcerting because as far as he was concerned he wasn't going to war. Perhaps they thought he was careless and might lose some. His weapons training was ingrained. Without practice the accuracy might slip a little, but the basics never went away.

Why had they given him this weapon? Either they wanted to incriminate him, or they had a problem that they thought he could help them solve. But if they did want to get rid of him, his sentence was being delayed.

He changed back into his jacket and tucked the keys and mobile into the belt-bag with the loaded SIG and strapped it into the small of his back. He put the beret into his pocket and packed the rest of the clothing, including the tourist's outfit into the kit-bag. The empty cardboard box went into the wardrobe with the truffles. He put the two Paris photographs and his documents into the belt-bag and slipped out of the hotel with the kit-bag over his shoulder. The Firm were bound to locate him again in Soho. He wanted them to think he had just taken appropriate avoidance action and was back on the street looking exactly as he had before he'd disappeared.

When he reached the end of the mews he checked the surroundings, wondering when they would catch up with him.

42. BRANEN & COSTAS : (4PM, TUESDAY 10 NOVEMBER)

Dusk was closing in as Branen crossed Shaftesbury Avenue into Soho and headed for Costas's Lounge in Wardour Street.

Soho's porn shops and clubs had flourished throughout the 1960s and 70s. There had always been chic restaurants in the area but in the 1980s Soho opened up to a more diverse range of clubs, bars and restaurants. The gangsters had always been there; their activities conveniently masked by the commercialisation of the area. The extra effort needed to police the proliferation of visitors provided a distraction and a smokescreen for criminal activities. The Soho Branen grew up in had been strip clubs, bars and crime. Soho used to be ominous not auspicious, grey not gay, and he missed its seediness.

Costas's Lounge was well worn but comfortable. The walls had yellowed from years of cigar and cigarette smoke. The room was furnished with small tables and ancient leather sofas that looked as though they were taken from an old manor house. The daylight filtered into the room through wooden venetian blinds, augmented by wall and table lamps with a panelled bar on the left.

An aged couple lounged on a sofa with what must have been their second or third bottle of champagne. He wore an embroidered skull-cap that looked like it had been bought from the souk in Marrakesh. It had slipped down over his forehead. She had a mass of ginger curls and wore a kaftan. She was staring adoringly into his sleeping face. Branen was sure the couple had been there, in the same position, since he'd last visited Costas.

Costas was behind the bar chatting as usual to a couple of pretty young women and as Branen entered, he looked up and did a double take. He took a deep breath and stood back.

After a moment he said, "My God, Ben... where've you been?"

Ben was the name Branen was born with and the name people knew him by when he'd lived in Soho. It had been seven years since he'd last seen Costas.

"What brings you here?" he asked.

"I'm selling truffles."

"You're what?"

"Give me a drink and I'll tell you when you've finished your meeting," Branen said, nodding towards the young women.

Costas put a big paw round his neck, pulled him over the bar and kissed him. "Just like old times, man... good to see you."

"You can let me go now, Costas... I'm not going anywhere."

Costas kissed him again and let go. He reached for a glass and pulled a pint of beer, spilling some on the bar as he thumped it down. Even though he was only four or five years older than Branen he had been his mentor in the old days, and Branen knew he would help in any way he could. A friend like Costas was worth a lot more than a whole gang of Soho acquaintances.

"What's wrong, Ben?"

"Let me have a couple of beers and something to eat."

He got the message. "I've got a good steak."

He disappeared into his small kitchen.

Branen had no plans for the evening, so he stayed on at Costas's. He sat at a table near the door and ate the steak. He was half way through another beer when Costas came round the bar carrying a bottle of Cyprus brandy. "What brings you back to Soho?"

Holding back the emotion, Branen asked, "Did you hear about the girl who was murdered last week in Soho?"

"No... that's strange 'cos I know most things that go on here... I haven't seen the old bill around either."

"It was Carrie... my daughter."

Costas put his arm round Branen's shoulders, pushing him down into the chair. Family was an important part of Cypriot life and as a young man Costas had missed out on that. One night years ago when Branen was working for him, he told him about his delinquent childhood and how he had run away from home. Branen believed that it was his misadventures that had allowed him to identify with him as a kid and to offer him shelter.

He had tears in his eyes when he asked, "How did it happen?"

Branen always carried the Polaroid of Jane and Carrie in his wallet. He showed him the picture. "That's her... seven years ago."

"My God, she looks familiar, I think I know her... I'm sure she's been in here."

"Yes, when was she here?"

"She's been here a few times... "

"What can you tell me about her?"

"The first time I saw her was about three months ago... she was alone and stayed for a couple of hours."

"Did she hitch up with anyone?"

"She got into conversation with a drug dealer." Costas paused; he didn't seem to want to tell any more.

"And...?"

"She came in here with him on a couple of other occasions."

"Who is he?"

"He's known as Snowman... he's been around here for years."

"When did you last see her?"

"At the weekend... she was with a big bloke... I've seen him before too... but only on the street. I don't know who he is or where he's from."

"Which day, Costas?"

"I'm sure it was Saturday afternoon, 'cos we were quiet in here."

Branen looked shaken. "That must have been close to the time she was murdered."

Costas looked away.

Branen's mind was racing. If it was a straightforward murder case, why hadn't the Firm got the police involved? She must have been in deeper than they had let on. As the brandy hit home, he sat and watched Costas make his money. He hadn't wanted to drink; he'd wanted to stay alert. But being in the same bar where Carrie had been just three days ago and meeting up with his old friend was too much to deal with. He was out of practice and wasn't operationally focussed.

After a while Costas came over. "I was thinking... after Carrie left on Saturday, Snowman came by. I asked him if he'd seen her, because she had been in here earlier. His answer was awkward and he made a crummy joke out of not seeing her for a couple of days... he was odd."

"Where would I find him?"

"I don't know where he lives... but he does the rounds every evening."

"Okay, let me know if you see him." Branen scribbled down his mobile number. "I need a reasonable hotel for a few nights... where can I go?"

"There's a place, in Tisbury Court, not far... you'll be alright there." He paused and looked at him carefully, "What are you doing here, Ben?"

He knew Branen hadn't told him the whole story and he was still his concerned benefactor.

"What do you think?"

"Leave it to the police."

"I can't."

"Why not?"

"They don't know about it."

Costas expression turned to unease. "What's going on, Ben?"

Branen reached over and clasped Costas's hand. "Don't worry... I'll keep in touch… if anyone asks, you can say you've seen me… but that's all. Now, about those truffles."

Costas looked irritated. "What bloody truffles?" He didn't want to know about the truffles.

Branen picked up his kit-bag and got up to leave. "How much do I owe you?"

Costas waved the question away.

His first contact had produced a result, but he knew his luck couldn't last.

43. SNOWMAN & SEAN :
(TUESDAY EVENING, 10 NOVEMBER)

Snowman had not slept or eaten well for the last three days and nights.

He had been on edge waiting to get news on the radio or in the newspapers about Carrie. He could not risk contacting Harry in case the police were on to him.

Troubled and agitated by the lack of information, all he could do was wait. He needed to know Carrie was dead. He also had to find a rifle for Mikey's hare-brained scheme.

Eventually he went over to Sean's place. It was late and the bar was closed. Sean would open and close his bar on a whim and tonight he'd had a skinful. To the disgruntlement of his customers, he'd decided to close early and arrange a fuck.

Snowman banged loudly on the door and called out.

A head appeared from a first floor window.

"Oi, mind my fucking paintwork," shouted Sean.

"Sean, I need to talk… it's urgent." Snowman was anxious.

"It'd better be worth it… hang on."

The door was unlocked and unbolted. Sean opened up and examined the paintwork.

"When did you become house-proud?" asked Snowman.

"What do you want?" asked Sean.

"Let me in for fuck's sake."

Sean turned back up the stairs. "I'm busy… close the door behind you."

Their footsteps echoed as they tramped up. When they entered the bar Snowman realised why Sean had been reluctant to let him in. Sitting at the far end, in the shadows, was a girl whose face Snowman vaguely recognised from the street.

Sean took his usual position behind the bar and waited.

Snowman beckoned Sean away to a table in the corner.

"Don't worry about her... she hears no evil," said Sean, waving his hand vaguely in the girl's direction.

Snowman handed him five hundred pounds in cash. "There's the monkey I owe you... I'm keeping the revolver... and now I need a rifle... for a sniper."

"What are you doing... equipping a fucking army?" asked Sean, loud enough for the girl to hear.

Snowman continued, "I want a sniper's rifle, good enough to shoot somebody through the head at a couple of hundred yards... and it better have a silencer."

"It'll cost you," said Sean.

"I'll give you five grand and I want it untraceable."

Sean returned to the bar and poured two glasses of Delamain. "Does that include this expensive brandy we're gonna drink?" he asked.

"I want it soon."

"Give me a few days."

Snowman copied Sean and emptied his glass in one then pushed a stuffed A4 envelope across the table.

"That should cover it," he said.

As soon as Sean had accepted the money Snowman could apply a little pressure. "I want it as soon as possible."

"I'll sort it, pal," said Sean. He looked over towards his date and turned back to Snowman. "Now, fuck off."

44. BRANEN & THE CONTROLLER :
(MIDNIGHT, TUESDAY 10 NOVEMBER)

Hotel California had a small entrance in Tisbury Court, a paved alleyway between Wardour and Rupert Street.

The frosted glass door had a red glow behind it; the kind that brothels have. He mentally thanked Costas and tried the door, noticing it swung both ways, he suspected like some of the guests, and making it easier to eject unwanted customers.

The reception area was particularly attractive. On the right-hand side there was a desk, resembling a cheap pulpit. Behind it sat a tabloid newspaper which didn't reveal its reader.

"I need a room," he said. The newspaper seemed to be studiously ignoring him. "Have you got a room?"

The newspaper lowered revealing a shabby, unshaven man with a thick neck and the shoulders of a wrestler. Without looking up he pushed the register across the desk and the movement of his paper wafted fumes towards Branen; the man had been drinking and hadn't been washing.

"How much?"

He examined Branen then looked past him. Branen followed his gaze and was met by an apparition in black leather sitting on an orange plastic sofa. She returned his stare and smiled from underneath her maquillage. She had a kind face, or was it desperation? The melamine table lamp had an orange shade and the walls needed another coat of maroon paint. He had no idea why red was considered sexy in this environment; it did nothing for her complexion or the view up her skirt.

He could have waited an hour for his answer.

Eventually the owner asked, "Fer 'ow long?"

"A couple of weeks."

"Fifty quid… cash… a day."

Before Branen could answer he pulled back the register and returned to his newspaper. He was reminded of the warm reception he had received at China Hotel.

He produced the cash and his passport. The rustle of notes caused a stir behind him and he had their undivided attention. He thought the owner must have been a magician in a previous life because the hundred and fifty pounds had disappeared; the alcohol hadn't reduced his dexterity. He glanced at the French passport and waved it aside. He gave Branen a key and pointed towards the stairs, "Top floor, Froggy," he said with contempt.

As he started up the rickety stairs the creaking treads reminded him of home. The girl in reception called after him, "Would you like an extra pillow tonight, love?"

He turned to her for a second time. She didn't deserve the reply he had in mind. "No, not tonight thanks, love."

"How about something else to keep you awake?"

She was certainly tenacious. "That's the last thing I need at the moment, thanks."

At the top of the stairs, stretching out in front of him was a long, shabby corridor lit by a spluttering fluorescent light and lined with dusty plastic palm trees.

As he passed 'Mulholland Drive' the door opened and out came a balding man with a strict-looking woman. She was wearing a skin-tight leather skirt, which seemed to be de rigueur in this place, fish-net tights and red stilettos.

He arrived at 'Sunset Boulevard' and unlocked the door.

The street lights shone through the grey net curtains, revealing a cheaply-furnished room. He tried the light switch but nothing happened.

In the room he had déja vu. There in the corner was the same plywood wardrobe they had at China Hotel; there must have been a job lot.

Branen had a base and he needed to formulate a plan. He had to contact the Controller. It was gone one in the morning. They would have some automaton manning the Firm's switchboard twenty-four seven.

"Yes," said the automaton.

He spelt out, "V.I.N.T.A.G.E."

With the benefit of Branen's number on the screen, a voice print check through the computer and the catch-word, the Duty Officer confirmed it was Branen.

"Yes."

"I'm in place... I want to speak to the Controller," he said wearily. He was familiar with the procedure and was tired of the desk monkeys who didn't get their hands dirty but issued instructions as though they were ordering their weekend shopping from the supermarket.

"You'll have to wait a couple of minutes while we patch you through."

While he waited, he imagined a Secret Service flunkey being dragged out of bed, cursing and trying to gather his thoughts.

A voice came on the line sooner than he expected, and it was a woman. Far from being hung over from some bourgeois dinner party she was sharp and wide awake.

"Controller speaking... where are you and what do you need?"

It was the same woman who had phoned him at the podere. She sounded too fresh to have just been woken up. They had been waiting for the call. And he wasn't expecting to be asked what he needed. It was possible that the Firm had been instructed to supply him without being given his full history by the SCS; which could give him an advantage in the future.

"I need to know how she was murdered."

She told him Carrie was murdered at home and gave him the address.

Branen interrupted her, "I already know that... it was in the paperwork." He tried to harass her. "Anything else... what do you think happened?"

She slowed the conversation. "We lost contact last Sunday afternoon... so we went to her flat and found her dead."

"How was she killed?"

"Suffocated then stabbed."

His throat tightened. "Why haven't you contacted the police?"

"Remember, she worked for us and we didn't want her compromised."

He tried pushing her again. "It would be difficult to compromise her now... what you mean is, it's you who doesn't want to be compromised."

"She was working on a drug investigation."

A drug investigation was a case for the police. The Secret Service often worked with the police but it had to be more than drugs for them to get involved. There might be a terrorist connection but she was unlikely to tell him that. If he pushed her she might reveal more than she wanted to. "Tell me what happened to her... I need the details."

The Controller hesitated for a moment; she hardly needed to motivate him when it was his own daughter's death he was investigating.

She decided to tell him. "Okay, she was raped, she was naked and she suffocated on her own vomit. She suffered multiple stab wounds, inflicted after her death. There was half a gram of cocaine on her desk and another couple of grammes and rocks of crack in the flat. There were fresh bruises... forensics think she might have been coshed. She'd been gagged with her own knickers... so no luck there. We found traces of adhesive from gaffer tape on her wrists and legs. We found foreign hair and traces of semen on the table in the window... we're doing DNA analysis at the moment. We also found bleach in the vaginal area... it looked like an attempt to hide his DNA... but he missed the table. Her blood showed alcohol and cocaine consumption within the previous twelve hours."

"What about the DNA on the table?" He was struggling not to break down.

"We have no match, so far."

"Why Carrie?" He had to stop his voice breaking up.

"It was a relatively simple role for a new officer to infiltrate a small drugs organisation... she was chosen because..."

He interrupted her. "Because she was my daughter... you killed her, you bastards." The minute he said it he realised it was a mistake. He had confirmed that he held a grudge.

The Controller didn't react. "Considering the multiple stabbings it is possible the Chinese were implicated... but it might be a red herring because she was dead before she was stabbed... we're looking into it. She was involved with a drug-dealer and she might have got caught up with the Chinese."

He couldn't speak.

The Controller broke the silence. "Prior to her death she had infiltrated a ring supplying quantities of heroin, crack and cocaine, and we suspect the group also had another agenda. We think she was being blackmailed and we want you to investigate."

When she mentioned 'another agenda' he realised that this was the reason the Firm had become involved.

"You haven't told her mother?"

"No."

"I'll let her know."

"Remember this is a covert operation and can't be made public."

The report the Controller received from Whitey prior to the murder had left her sure that Whitey knew more than he was letting on. She could not tell Branen her suspicions because Whitey was the Firm's officer and her superiors would ask how Branen had found him. Branen's job was supposedly to find his daughter's murderer but she could sow the seeds of doubt by mentioning another agenda and blackmail to get him to explore all the possibilities. She had decided to recommend that Whitey be retired from the Service but not until he had been fully de-briefed. She would send a covert officer to get a swab from Whitey's flat for DNA analysis. She could not haul him in on a vague suspicion and she hoped Branen would uncover any information that might incriminate or eliminate Whitey from their investigation.

"Can't you give me any of Carrie's connections?" Branen asked.

"No, we have very little background. It was a new operation, she was in the first stages of getting in place. We had an eye on her… that's as much as I can tell you."

"Why were you photographing her last Thursday?" he asked.

"She contacted us… she was worried her situation was becoming untenable."

"What the fuck does that mean?"

"She was having trouble… that's why I mentioned the…"

He decided to give her the intel he had got from Costas. "Do you mean with Snowman?"

He had to find out why she hadn't yet mentioned the existence of Snowman.

"Yes," said the Controller. She was taken aback that Branen already knew about Snowman but she didn't want to appear naive or in his debt so she didn't ask where he had got the information.

"And you didn't protect her… you bastards." He'd lost control again. Normally they wouldn't put someone into the field who was personally connected to a case, which indicated that they'd brought him in for their own reasons.

His thinking was being confused by his emotions. "I've got to see her," He was almost begging.

"You can't."

"If you don't let me see her I'm going back."

There was a long pause. He might be bluffing. He was unpredictable. He might let Carrie's death go and get out completely.

She didn't want that, "Okay, I'll arrange for a car to pick you up at nine tomorrow morning… where will you be?" she asked.

He wanted to check if she'd located the call. "At my hotel."

"Where's that?"

She might be bluffing, but he wasn't going to win this one so he changed tack. "I'll be on the corner of Old Compton and Dean Street at nine o'clock."

The line went dead before he could ask for more money or ask any more awkward questions. She reckoned that he wouldn't run away before he had settled his account and he knew that she wouldn't have put the phone down if the call hadn't been traced.

He would not need the phone so he turned it off and removed the SIM card and battery.

He lay back on the bed. The room was rotating and he felt sick. He sat up again. He had to sort himself out and remain objective even if he was passionately involved.

Carrie had discovered the exhilaration that cocaine produced and had fallen prey to its temptations. He knew how seductive that could be. He had been introduced to it early on in Soho and had used it for four years until he was imprisoned.

He lay down again and fell asleep: he was seventeen... in Ronnie Scott's jazz club... smoking his first spliff and taking purple hearts, the clammy air thick with dope and tobacco smoke, his T-shirt soaked in perspiration... then he was back on the streets of Soho, doped and drunk, passing the shift workers in the early morning.

45. BRANEN : (6AM, WEDNESDAY 11 NOVEMBER)

In that cheap hotel room and in those first soporific moments of waking, Jane and Carrie's faces appeared to him as they had so often over the last few years.

It still made his stomach churn when he remembered that tiny child calling after him as the police took him away; he'd loved her so much. Jane had been his obsession and he missed her. She had tolerated him, before having to give up and move on with her life.

He drifted in and out of sleep. When he woke again it was still dark. He lay there considering what he would do if the Chinese were involved in Carrie's murder. He realised that he had to find Snowman in order to open up the case. He had to talk to Jane to tell her what had happened, but he didn't want to contact her until he had worked out what to do; he had to be able to give her an explanation for Carrie's murder.

It was six thirty and Berwick Street wouldn't be open yet. He forced himself to get out of bed before any doubts could take hold. He put the kettle on and went down the corridor into the bathroom.

It was a cheap hotel and inconspicuous enough to enable him to function without drawing attention to himself. It was used by the local tarts and he could be just another punter. He had been woken twice during the night as a tart and punter had slammed doors and argued over price. Once, he had gone out and told them to cool it, but he had to be careful; if he was too aggressive and the police were called, a lot of awkward questions would be asked.

A BMW limousine with dark windows drove up Dean Street and crossed Old Compton Street at exactly nine o'clock.

Old habits die hard, so he made a mental note of the first three digits on the number plate. It stopped in the middle of the road; there was nowhere to park. The chauffeur jumped out and opened the rear door. As Branen crossed the road to get into the car, a taxi driver who was being blocked let rip with his horn. The chauffeur smiled and waved to him. The taxi-driver leant out of his window and shouted, "If you're going to a funeral hurry up... otherwise it might be yours."

There was a man in the back seat who looked like the driver's twin brother and he was making no secret of the fact that he was armed. He asked Branen to stretch his arms out onto the partition, separating them from the driver. He'd expected to be searched and had left the SIG well hidden in the bottom of one of the plastic palm pots at the hotel.

All the windows in the rear of the car, including the driver's partition, had small metal venetian blinds which his companion closed. "I must ask you not to lift the blinds, please sir." It was an instruction, not a request.

Did they think that if Branen knew where they were keeping Carrie, maybe he'd steal her body? Paranoia is part of the Secret Service's remit, so maybe... anything.

They drove for about half an hour.

He'd seen dead bodies before. Once it had been a close friend, but they had known and accepted the risks of their business.

The cold harshly lit room, with its stainless steel tables and cabinets had the sharp smell of formaldehyde and disinfectant.

And there lying in front of him was his daughter. This place had nothing to do with her. She should not be here. He realised he was trembling; he had to hold on. He wished it was him lying on the mortuary slab. He wanted to scream. He wanted retribution, revenge, another dead body to even up the score. He loved her and now, here she lay dead, murdered. In his own way he had nurtured her and loved her much more than any physical expression could demonstrate. But he had also neglected her, something he would never be able to rectify. He wanted to show her how sorry he was but it was too late. Nothing could take away the pain and anguish; he was helpless. It was all-consuming. If only he could take her place. He reached out and held her wrist but it wasn't her wrist; it was cold and unresponsive.

Then he broke down.

He was back at the hotel before eleven o'clock.

He was traumatised from seeing his daughter stretched out on that cold, stainless steel table; he hated having to leave her there alone in the hands of total strangers and they still had to carry out an autopsy. He sat in that small grotty hotel room, staring at a crude painting of a nude. He tried to justify the life he had chosen for himself and its effect on the people he'd loved. He had hoped that one day she would have become part of his life again. He couldn't get rid of the image of a forensic surgeon cutting up his daughter's body.

He had to see Jane.

He knew that Carrie had been in a relationship with the drug-dealer and had been in Costas's bar on Saturday afternoon and had left with another man. Whoever he was, he could have been the last person to see her alive. Branen had to find him and Snowman was his only way in.

He sat there waiting. He didn't know what for. Then he couldn't wait any longer. For now, he had to block all thoughts of Carrie. The bitterness and frustration it produced were destructive and were making him vulnerable. He guessed Snowman would not be around until the evening. He had to predict his movements. To set a snare he had to know the tracks he took. Costas had told him that Snowman dealt on the streets, so he would have a routine around the clubs and bars. Branen had to find that pattern.

When he finally pulled himself together he checked the hair-trips he'd placed on the wardrobe, the drawers and his kit-bag. Nothing had been touched. He collected the SIG from the plant pot and put it into his belt-bag.

46. BRANEN : (AFTERNOON, WEDNESDAY 11 NOVEMBER)

He slung the kit-bag over his shoulder and walked across to Berwick Street market.

He forced down a fry-up and psyched himself up for what he had to do.

His stomach became tight with anxiety as he approached Carrie's flat. He looked up at the windows on the top floor and imagined her looking down, smiling and waving to him. This was where he would start the search for her killer, and he had to deal with it.

The lock opened easily and when he withdrew the key it had traces of oil on it and smelt of WD40: the lock had been sprayed by someone to facilitate silent access.

He put his foot on the first tread and it groaned loudly; it would have fucked up any effort to gain a covert entry. He wondered if she had allowed her murderer up these stairs. The front door hadn't been forced and the only other way in would have been over the roof. He stopped for a moment on the top landing and looked up at the fire escape hatch that opened out onto the roof. The paint round the edges was unbroken.

He could feel his heart beating. He took a deep breath and stepped over the threshold; he could feel her spirit in the room. The space was bright and cheerful, just as he remembered her to have been. He sat in a chair by the window and listened to the silence. "What happened in here, my darling?"

He didn't know how long he'd been sitting there, but eventually the persistent buzz of a bee at the window interrupted his concentration. It was a queen bee and it wouldn't live for long now the cold weather had set in. Instead of leaving it trapped, he slid the catch on the window frame and pulled the top casement down. As he reached up he saw the beehives on the roof opposite and realised it might survive the winter.

'Beehives in Soho,' he mused to himself, 'Soho honey?'

The desk with its computer filled the window. He wondered if she had stood there looking down into the street exactly as he was now.

Soho was alive. Taxis hustled their way through the afternoon traffic, honking their horns and forcing other vehicles into making alternative plans.

He turned back into the room. He had to go through the whole flat methodically. There was a sideboard with a mirror on the wall above it.

He only had a small shaving mirror back at the podere and seeing himself surprised him; through his weather-beaten skin he looked knackered. His padded green coat looked just as tired as he did. His hair was short and ragged and he was unshaven, which didn't look out of place in Soho, neither with the fashionistas nor the tramps. His grey sweatshirt was loose at the neck and he looked like he needed an overhaul. He looked to see if he could still see the remains of Carrie's reflection; she must have looked into this mirror many times. There were marks on the mirror's surface and traces of white powder in the edge of the frame. He took it off the wall and laid it on the coffee table. He turned the mirror over and checked the back. There was no other information it could give him.

The next thing he found that didn't fit with Carrie was a bottle of cognac. She might have been into drugs but he thought it unlikely she could have afforded Delamain; it was usually an indulgence of the wealthy. She must have been given it; possibly by Snowman.

Branen wanted to believe that his daughter wasn't a drug user but he had no reason to be righteous. When she was recruited by those bastards to infiltrate a drugs ring, they would have known she would be exposed to and tempted by it.

He took a deep breath and tried to remain objective. He put himself into Carrie's head. Where would she keep her private possessions? He remembered Jane once told him how she had found drawings and messages written by Carrie under the floor of her wardrobe. At six years old a wardrobe is a very secret place. He searched an ornate French armoire in the bedroom and after a couple of minutes of ferreting around, concealed in the carved vertex he found a phone and a notebook.

There were only two entries in the phone contacts menu: 'Snowman' and 'Home' which was speed dial 7. He thought at first it was her mother's number. Then he realised it was the same number he had been given for the Firm.

He opened the notebook and a photograph fell out. He'd forgotten that she'd also taken a polaroid of him the last time the three of them met at the Soho Café. At the sight of her handwriting he choked; it reminded him of the letter she'd given him at that same meeting seven years ago when he'd tried to revive his relationship with Jane.

He read: 'Thursday 5 November 8pm – met officer in The Piano Bar told him I needed help. He was weird – didn't like him – he was useless – feeling totally isolated.'

'Friday 6 November – 'S' told me about meeting a well known Soho person who was a BNP politician – and about Group X, a secret organisation that wants to get rid of the Pakistanis – I contacted Home but 'S' arrived before I could tell them.'

'Saturday 7 November – At last they've promised me I'm going to meet my father – I can't wait.'

This last entry left him unable to move. He had to pull himself together.

He pocketed the phone and the notebook, convinced that they had not been found by the Firm. He went back to the computer and searched for her emails. The 'Inbox' contained five messages. He read the first one out loud :

'U IGNORED ME / U PAY £10K / I NO WERE U LIVE / I FOLOED U / I WILL LET U NO / NO TRIKS OR I TELL POLICE TO FIND STUFF'

He opened the 'Sent Items' to see if she had replied to the message. There had been a negotiation between the blackmailer and Carrie. In the fourth message the blackmailer was asking what else she had to offer; possibly suggesting he was after her rather than the money.

The fifth message confirmed this; it was from 'AN ADMIRER'.

Branen felt a chill run through him. In the last message, the spelling and the grammar had improved. It looked like the whole exercise was a set-up for something else. The sender had used a proxy email address. He had the feeling that these messages were not addressed exclusively to Carrie. Where would she get ten thousand pounds from? If she had enough 'stuff' to justify her being blackmailed, she could have been keeping it for someone else; which meant Snowman. He wondered how the blackmailer knew she had the 'stuff'.

He leaned back in her chair, confused by what he'd read. The emails left questions but provided no answers. But more questions were better than nothing at all. The Firm must have checked the computer, seen all these emails and taken a copy of the hard-drive. They would already be trying to track the source; but proxy email addresses were virtually untraceable. Also they could have deliberately planted false information and left the mobile behind for him to find. There was too much he didn't know; he was their puppet and they were pulling his strings.

All he could do for the moment was continue his search and duck and dive at the right moment.

While he was turning all this over, he went back to the window as the sun was setting behind the buildings. With the dusk closing in, the rain drops were gathering on the glass, making a kaleidoscopic effect from the sodium lights below.

It was past four o'clock and the last low rays of sunlight caused a flare on one of the bee-hives on the opposite roof. At first he thought his eyes were deceiving him. He couldn't be sure. Was he looking down the end of a camera lens inside the hive?

47. HARRY & BRANEN :
(AFTERNOON, WEDNESDAY 11 NOVEMBER)

Harry had put a four-hour tape into the VHS recorder before going to work; he wanted to keep an eye on Carrie's flat.

It recorded until the tape ran out a couple of hours before he got home. He'd spent the night working for the Brothers until the early hours, and was exhausted when he got home so he put on a porno film and fell asleep on the sofa.

He woke up groggily as it began to get light; then fell asleep for another few hours until dreaming of Carrie made him wake with his heart pumping. He was soaked in sweat.

When he eventually got out of bed he reviewed the tape at high speed, wondering why there wasn't any sign of the police. He turned on the monitor with the camera still pointed at Carrie's window and started to cook himself a late lunch. A movement on the screen caught his eye. He left the frying pan and went over to see a man standing at her window. He put a new tape into the recorder and turned it on. He watched intently for an hour. The man hadn't turned the lights on and it was difficult for Harry to see through the reflections on the window panes. When the man stood in the window looking up at the beehives, Harry froze. He checked the blind was closed then pulled on his overcoat and went down to the 'Crown & Two'.

He ordered half a pint of beer and sat in the window with a clear view of Carrie's door.

He was halfway down his second drink when the man appeared from Carrie's front door, a few yards away. He bought a Soho Gazette from the street vendor. Harry followed fifty metres behind him, as he walked through to Frith Street. The man sat down at a table outside Bar Italia, with a clear view of the street.

Harry stopped in his tracks, wondering what to do with himself.

Branen sat at a table on the pavement and unfurled the newspaper.

It was early evening and cold. There were only two tables outside Bar Italia at this time of year, and no one else was braving the damp breeze that blew down Frith Street.

The rain had stopped and the sunset had gone, leaving a dark sky with streaks of deep red hardly visible beyond the street lights. He ordered an espresso and sat, reminiscing; he was waiting for the Empire Room to warm up.

He checked out the street to see if the Firm had put a tail on him. When he'd first sat down he'd noticed a man in an ill-fitting overcoat who didn't seem to know where he was going. At first he dismissed him as a wino but then he saw him look in his direction a couple of times. The man stopped and looked into a shop window on the opposite pavement. Branen couldn't see the reflection of his eyes but his body language was uncomfortable. Then he moved off round the corner into Old Compton Street.

On the corner there was a coffee bar with full height glass windows on both sides. After he'd turned the corner he stopped and stared back, diagonally through both windows directly at Branen.

'Who the fuck was he?' Branen picked up his bag and walked slowly up towards Soho Square, giving the man plenty of time to keep up. As he wandered round the Square he kept an eye on the corner of Frith Street where he'd had come from. Sure enough, as Branen walked along the north side he noticed the man was standing on the south west corner. He couldn't believe the man was from the Firm. Watchers normally work in teams and a solitary eye would not have shown himself outside Bar Italia. He had to be an amateur; but who and why? Branen wondered if he had any connection with the camera he'd seen in the beehive; but that looked more like one of the Firm's deployments.

Branen went into a café in the north-east corner, bought a sandwich and went down to the lavatories. In the cubicle he changed into his orange tourist's jacket and beret. He was going to make it hard or easy for his watcher, depending on how good he was. The new jacket was conspicuous and easy to follow but at the same time the radical change of appearance would outwit an amateur. When he got back onto the street the man had vanished, which was frustrating because he had planned to turn the tail on him.

48. MICHELLE DE LAVIGNE :

If the Pakistanis had not moved into the sex industry in Soho, Mikey would not have come across them and would still be buying her drugs from the Chinese.

The Pakistanis soon moved into the importation of heroin and cocaine. That's when Mikey tripped over them and started buying quantities of supposedly un-cut coke at much lower prices per kilo than the Chinese were prepared to offer.

Having been lured in, she now had to deal with their trading conventions; they changed the terms of business including stepping on the coke they supplied her.

Then they started to move in on her distribution. They had seen the potential profits of selling diluted coke by the gramme at street level. By distilling it into crack they could also make another 60% profit, and it was not difficult for them to recruit street dealers from the Asian enclaves of north-west London.

Mikey realised that if she did not do something about it, they would eventually cut her out of her own market. She planned a two-pronged attack: she would use her invented terrorist cell, Group X, to exploit the authorities' fear of terrorism; and she would tell the Chinese that the Pakistanis were undercutting them, leading to a war which she reckoned the Chinese would win. By becoming the leader of the BNP she would increase her social standing and would use the more militant members to help drive the Pakistanis off the streets of Soho. But before removing the Pakis she would renegotiate the price per kilo with the Chinks.

Mikey was playing with fire and she knew she would have to tread carefully.

The Monro family founded the House of St. Barnabas-in-Soho as a charitable institution for homeless women in 1846.

It had been situated at number one Greek Street on the corner of Soho Square since 1863. At the present time Princess Alexandra was one of its patrons and she made an annual pilgrimage to encourage support. Several well-known members of Parliament had been associated with St. B's over the years. Michael Foot, a previous shadow Home Secretary and leader of the Labour party, had his 90th birthday party there before retiring for dinner to the Gay Hussar next door.

With its Establishment connections Mikey considered it to be the ideal conduit for her delusions of grandeur and decided to become one of St. Barnabas's patrons herself.

She rang the manager, who was also the fundraiser, explaining she had lived in Soho all her life and had always wanted to give something back to the area; she was a successful entrepreneur and wanted to donate £20,000 to the charity. An offer of that magnitude rarely came his way and not wanting to upset a potential benefactor, the manager did not ask the exact nature of her business. Mikey knew she would eventually be asked and decided that the description 'impresario' had a sufficiently vague yet glamorous interpretation.

Her new title was put to the test when she was introduced to Princess Alexandra and photographed for the Soho Gazette shaking hands with her as she handed over the cheque.

When the Princess asked her more specifically about her role as an impresario, she told of her luck as an angel for several successful West End productions. She guessed Princess Alexandra was unlikely to follow up on any conversation they had.

She felt she had arrived and as a Patron of St. Barnabas Michelle de Lavigne was welcomed into the arms of the Establishment.

In the middle of October Mikey received an invitation to the sale of the Monro family heirlooms to be held at St. Barnabas. To raise funds for the charity a Sotheby's auctioneer was going to be master of ceremonies and it was rumoured that the Prime Minister would also attend. With an election on the horizon he needed all the PR he could get.

This invite offered Mikey the golden opportunity she had been looking for. But before attending, she had to complete the trail of deceit that would lead to Group X's complicity in a significant assassination.

She did not have much time. And most importantly she had to make sure her involvement could never be discovered.

49. THE SOHO GAZETTE : (WEDNESDAY 11 NOVEMBER)

A couple of weeks after the invitation dropped through Mikey's letterbox, the editor of the Soho Gazette arrived at his office in Wardour Street to find an anonymous note pushed through his door.

The note said that the Prime Minister would be visiting St. Barnabas's at four o'clock on the afternoon of Saturday November 14th. He wondered who had left the note; if it was accurate he wanted an exclusive with this story. The national press would be told about it but he hoped they would not see the occasion as being of significant interest. With luck, there might be another event that day which would attract Fleet Street and distract them from following up on this one. He did not want any of the other newspapers treading all over his territory. He wanted only his photographer and his journalist to report the event, then he would have the sole rights on all coverage of the visit; or he might even write the whole thing up himself. Little did he know that the Soho Gazette's story and photographs would become international news and that he was about to make a fortune in syndication rights.

50. HARRY : (AFTERNOON, WEDNESDAY, 11 NOVEMBER)

After he had lost the man he was following, Harry bought fresh dressings for his burnt chest and returned to his flat.

He would need a clear mind for the job ahead but he had the evening in front of him, so he decided to have a couple of slugs of his vodka cocktail and a final toke of amylnitrate before cleaning up his act.

His heart was still pounding from the popper when the Brothers rang. "Whitey, we've got a punter wants to go to Croydon," said Saul.

Harry took a deep breath. "That's south of the river... that's the edge of the known world... what the fuck do I want to go there for?"

"Look Whitey, if you don't want the work then..."

"I'll tell you when I want the work," said Harry and hung up.

Then he remembered the poster he had seen at St. Barnabas's yesterday morning. He'd go for the free drinks and with luck he might come across one of those destitute and vulnerable women. He filled a small self-dispensing snuff bottle with speed and loaded a line into the neck.

It was eight o'clock when he headed towards Soho Square.

51. BRANEN : (EVENING, WEDNESDAY 11 NOVEMBER)

The Empire Room was a members only bar on the first floor above a French restaurant in Dean Street; it had always been there. It was where Branen had originally met the barrister who had helped him buy the podere.

The club's purpose was to enable its members to continue drinking legally through the day and after the pubs had closed. It fast became a venue for Soho's bon viveurs to meet and fall over in. The entrance was a single green door. A narrow wooden staircase led up to a door on the first floor landing that opened straight into the homely single-room bar. Like Costas, the owner Ayo Wood was in touch with Soho scandal, and like most small Soho club proprietors he also worked behind the bar.

Ayo was regaling an inebriated customer with one of his stories, while cleaning down the bar and getting ready for the evening's influx.

When he saw Branen he said, "How long is it since I last saw this man... don't you love me any more?"

Branen had his first whisky of the day and diluted it with as much water as he dared without upsetting Ayo. They talked of old times and Branen spun him a yarn about doing research for a book on Soho life; he had decided not to tell anyone other than Costas about Carrie.

Eventually he broached the subject of Snowman. Ayo told him he knew the man and had ejected him on a couple of occasions; most recently a couple of months ago when he had tried to deal drugs. Ayo made sure that the atmosphere in the bar was always convivial, and although not a big man, however drunk and obnoxious his members became they never disobeyed his order to leave.

As the evening progressed the members began to arrive and settle in for the duration. Ayo told him about a recent failed attempt by the Jamaican Yardies to infiltrate the Chinese monopoly of the drug scene and that the area was being taken over by Asian gangs. On the pretext of the book and in an effort to discover more about Carrie's contacts Branen asked him if he could introduce him to any of them. Ayo poured another whisky and explained that to keep his club open all the hours he wished and to renew his licence without police intervention meant he had to keep the dealers out; so he couldn't help him.

On his way out, filled with the courage gained from several whiskies, Branen decided to call Jane on her old number from the pay phone in the cloakroom. He prefaced the number with 141 to make the call untraceable. The woman who answered told him Jane no longer lived there. After reassuring her that he was an old friend, he managed to get the new number.

A man answered, "Who's calling?"

"A friend."

"Have you got a name?"

'Cocky fucker,' Branen thought to himself, but if he said 'no' he might put the phone down.

"I'm an old friend," he said, in an effort to put him in his place. The man chuckled to himself loud enough for Branen to hear.

"Hold on," he said.

Eventually Jane came on the line.

"Hello", she said in her cheerful manner.

All he could say was "Jane."

"Hello Benny." Her voice was gentle and he wanted to hug her. He hadn't realised the effect talking to her would have on him. He had dived headlong into the call without preparing himself. He'd forgotten she was the only person to call him Benny.

He managed not to let his voice falter. "Hello darling," he said, "I'm in London and I need to see you."

She understood him better than anyone ever had or ever would. He never had to explain his feelings to her, she already knew.

"I'll come to you... I'll bring my new baby to meet you."

He didn't know she'd had another child. It took him a moment to speak. "I'll be in Soho Square on Thursday morning at eleven o'clock. Is that okay?" he asked. She knew the significance of meeting there because it was where they had walked on their first night; where they had kissed for the first time.

He wanted to tell her he still loved her but it didn't fit; he shouldn't have had those whiskies.

"I'll be there... please be careful," she said.

He put down the receiver. The warning had surprised him. Her intuition had told her something was wrong.

He was on his way back to the hotel when he decided to drop in on Costas for a night-cap.

As he entered, Costas looked up from behind the bar and caught his eye; his expression was a warning.

Branen went over to him.

"Don't look round, he's here... Snowman's in the bar... at the table in the corner."

Branen pointed at a bottle of malt whisky and managed to see Snowman reflected in the mirrored wall behind the shelves. He was with a couple of men and a woman. His features were gaunt and the muscles in his face and neck were distinct. He reminded him of how they looked back in the Legion; starved, lean and fit.

"I'll have a shot of that, Costas."

He poured the drink and Branen reached for his money but Costas shook his head. Branen sat watching Snowman negotiate a deal. The chat, the exchange of tightly wrapped notes and the handshake that concealed the packet of drugs.

Then Snowman got up and went to the toilet. For the second time that night Branen acted on impulse. He emptied his glass, slid off the stool and the last thing he heard was Costas calling him back.

It was too late, his mind was made up. He pushed his way through the tables into the toilets.

From the sounds emanating from the cubicle he guessed Snowman was sampling his wares. He went over to the urinal and pretended to use it, hoping that no-one would come in. Snowman came out, glanced in his direction and went to the hand basin behind him. There was a mirror on the wall above the basin which meant that Branen had to move carefully. He turned slowly with head bowed and tried to relax his thumping heart.

Holding his breath, he stepped swiftly behind Snowman and passed his right forearm across the front of Snowman's throat. He tried to duck but it was too late. Using the same grip he had used on the transvestite in Paris, he pulled Snowman backwards. He tried to twist and jerk his elbow back into Branen's solar-plexus but he was expecting that. Branen let the elbow strike his ribs and pushed his knees into the back of Snowman's legs then took three steps back, jamming himself against the entry door. Now nobody could get in. He had him to himself.

Snowman's hat rolled off. He choked and made a futile effort to reach back for Branen's face before dropping onto his arse. Branen pushed his head into the nape of Snowman's neck as he flailed with both arms trying to grab and punch Branen. Branen dropped to his knees, and pulling Snowman down onto his back tilted his body-weight forwards forcing Snowman's head onto his chest with his forearm tight across his throat. Snowman gasped and choked and then went limp. Even under such duress he had the presence of mind to recognise his only chance was to play possum. Branen was impressed by his self-control but he knew the man wasn't finished yet.

He couldn't pretend for long and was soon gulping for breath. Branen loosened his grip just enough to avoid Snowman blacking out and to allow him to talk.

"If you try to struggle I'll throttle you," Branen said into Snowman's ear.

"What the fuck do you want?" he asked.

"Tell me about Carrie's murder?"

"What're you talking about… she's a friend." He was powerless to move with Branen's arm locked across his throat.

He tightened his grip again. "Tell me, you bastard."

Snowman was struggling for breath and going purple. He went limp and Branen eased off again.

He was choking as he said, "You're strangling me… I don't know nothing about her being murdered… I haven't seen her."

"What about the big man she met here last Saturday night?"

"I don't know what you're talking about."

There was knocking at the door.

"If you've got anything to do with her murder you're a dead man."

He tightened on Snowman's throat until he passed out. Then he let go and let Costas in. He went through Snowman's pockets, searching for anything that might connect him to Carrie's murder. He found half a dozen spliffs and a stash of wraps. He put them back. Snowman was coming round and gasping for breath. Branen grabbed him by the hair and banged his head hard on the tiled floor, stunning him. He had a roll of notes in an inside pocket and in his chest pocket he found his mobile phone. He took the money and the phone under Costas's angry stare.

"What have you done to him?" he asked.

"He'll be okay."

He picked up Snowman's hat and dropped it on to his writhing body. Then pushed past Costas and left the club.

52. MIKEY : (EVENING, WEDNESDAY 11 NOVEMBER)

Earlier in the year when she decided she wanted to stand for election Mikey had phoned Dean Beck, the chairman of the local BNP, and Lee the treasurer, who also happened to be his brother.

Dean told her that there were two other candidates and the rally and hustings were imminent. Mikey made a £10,000 donation, in the form of a membership fee to the association and a smaller donation to the National Party. It made Dean's eyes water; something which was to happen again when Mikey set about guaranteeing her nomination by organising a private party at Madame LuLu's, to which only Dean Beck was invited and which she secretly recorded in case she had to persuade him that she was his preferred candidate.

Now several months later with her nomination confirmed and without her having to resort to blackmail, Mikey persuaded Dean to hold the final BNP meeting before the general election, at the first floor reception rooms in the House of St. Barnabas.

"I know that the Prime Minister has planned a visit to St.Barnabas's in the lead-up to the general election and my speech will happen just three days before this," she said. "I think the timing is perfect and will enhance the party's credentials."

"Sounds good to me," Dean said.

She continued, "After my speech why don't you and Lee come back to mine for your own private party with all the trimmings."

After the rally Mikey planned that her limo would take Dean and Lee the five hundred metres from St. Barnabas back to Madame LuLu's and the action would be filmed as before to ensure their continued support.

53. SNOWMAN & COSTAS :
(NIGHT, WEDNESDAY 11 NOVEMBER)

Snowman came round with Costas crouched over him. His throat was raw and his head was throbbing and he was enraged at the indignity of lying on the lavatory floor.

His stash was safe but his cash had gone. Discovering that his mobile phone was missing, he kicked the door with frustration. He felt the small of his back to check if his revolver was still there. He had been unable to reach it when he was attacked. It was covered by his waistcoat and padded jacket; the bloke who had throttled him had missed it.

He grabbed Costas and banged him up against the wall. "Who was that fucker and where's my fucking cash?" Snowman rasped, and started to frisk Costas.

"Take your hands off me… I don't steal people's money," said Costas, pushing him away.

"Who the fuck was that cunt?" Snowman's throat was hoarse from Branen's throttling.

"I've never seen him before…" Costas fought back, "…and if you're going to get into fights, stay out of my bar."

"I want the bastard… and I want you to find him… I want to know if he comes in here again."

Costas shoved him away. "Fuck off."

54. SNOWMAN & SEAN :
(NIGHT, WEDNESDAY 11 NOVEMBER)

When Snowman bumped into Busby Bob that afternoon he heard that Sean wanted to see him. However bad he felt after the attack at Costas's, he still had to collect the rifle.

'He hasn't sobered up since last night,' Snowman thought, when he saw Sean standing behind the bar. He was feeling rough and Sean was looking rougher; he was obviously on one of his benders.

Slumping onto a bar stool, Snowman said, "Give me a drink, mate."

Sean had reached a state of inebriation where he had become detached from the real world. He obviously hadn't slept, he smelt of whisky and his eyes appeared to stare straight through Snowman. "Okay, mate." Then it dawned on him why Snowman was there. "I'll sort that thing out for you…" and, making a theatrical gesture, disappeared into his quarters behind the bar. He had already made enquiries amongst his old Irish acquaintances, now forcibly resident in London, and discovered there was a rifle available. It had been stolen a few weeks before for another job which had fallen through, and Sean's contact had been left holding the rifle.

Unsteadily, he reappeared with a long parcel wrapped in brown paper with an umbrella attached to it. Being an ex-provo volunteer he loved guns and in his drunken state he took great pleasure in leading Snowman by the arm to the side of the bar. Adopting a confidential tone he slurred, "It's a Tikka rifle... made in Finland... with a Carl Zeiss scope and silencer... it's ideal for big game and human beings... that's what you wanted, isn't it?"

Snowman didn't give a fuck as long as it did its job, but he listened patiently as Sean babbled on, anxious to show his knowledge. Snowman didn't want to upset the temperamental man because he was a sort of friend; about as close a friend as he could ever develop. Sean came out from behind the bar and put the parcel into the elephant's foot umbrella stand by the door.

When Sean returned, Snowman croaked, "Are you fucking joking... do you expect me to walk out of here carrying that?" His throat felt as if someone had pushed a cheese grater down it.

"Shh..." hissed Sean, holding his finger melodramatically to his mouth, and adding in a stage whisper, "Of course... and keep your voice down."

Snowman looked around. Apart from a couple in the far corner, the bar was empty.

"Don't think I'm keeping it here," said Sean.

55. MIKEY : (EVENING, WEDNESDAY 11 NOVEMBER)

While Mikey was rehearsing her speech for the BNP meeting her nerves started to get to her. She had a quaalude and smoked a joint to calm herself and slipped into a reverie, musing on her situation.

She was being lauded by the leaders of the BNP for standing up and representing the working classes in a minority party. If elected to Parliament, she would become an important figure in Soho society. She believed there were many voters out there who wanted the Pakistanis out of Soho. She was appearing regularly in the Soho Gazette and the attention gave her the respect she so desired.

Mikey whiled away an hour in the bath and then dressed in one of her more extravagant suits. Before leaving she made a call to Sabrina to check on the takings from the clubs and that the staff were performing well; she did not tolerate laziness. She asked Sabrina to check that the camera system in her private office was primed so that any movement in the room would trigger the recorder.

Then she made her way up Frith Street to St. Barnabas. She walked with short rapid strides, revealing her highly-strung and neurotic nature to anyone watching. Soho was her manor. She owned millions of pounds' worth of property and several successful clubs and bars, and she felt that she was in total control. She was Queen of Soho and nobody was going to relieve her of her throne, especially not those foreigners.

She decided to assume a deep authoritative voice and to speak with an Estuary accent to identify with her audience; she needed to sound convincing.

"Chairman, members of the executive and fellow activists.

For those of you who do not know me, my name is Michelle de Lavigne."

It had started well. Her reception from the shorn and tattooed, combat-clad members was warm by their standards; even if they didn't understand what was standing in front of them. Her bleached, cropped hair was a look their women had made familiar, but her deep, strange accent and androgenous suit left them confused but, fortunately for Mikey, not hostile.

"I would like to welcome you here tonight to the House of St. Barnabas, of which I am a patron. Last spring I rang Dean Beck, our chairman, and asked him to put my name forward as a candidate for the next election. I hope tonight you will realise that I am a worthy person to carry the local BNP banner for our great party. I am a proud, devoted and loyal member of this party. I want to bring the policies and beliefs of all of us here tonight to the attention of the people of our country."

Leaving a long pause she looked around at the crowd and was inwardly repelled by the moronic faces staring back at her. To her astonishment she saw a face she recognised; it was the fat man who Snowman had taken to the factory, the man she had plans for; there was no way he could have recognised her, was there?

Following his disappointment that none of the destitute women appeared to be at the party, Harry had sunk several glasses of the indifferent red wine and treated himself to a couple of lines of speed from his snorter. Even through his numbed nose, the surrounding mass of humanity smelt of stale sweat and cheap deodorant. Ignoring the frustration of his failed hopes he still felt euphoric and when this strange woman on the stage caught his eye he thought he'd show those around him that he was a thinking and intelligent man. He heard himself shout out, "Why should they vote for you?"

Mikey pretended not to know where the comment had come from. "Who said that?" she asked.

Harry froze. There was silence in the room and several of the thick necks turned to stare at him. The room remained silent.

Even though it was totally artificial Mikey assumed a smile and directed her attention towards Harry. "You should vote for me because we have put up too long with the downgrading of our society. The flood of immigration is oppressing the ordinary, hard working people of this country. The working men in our country are indeed the backbone of our society. They need our help to earn a decent living. They want to walk freely on our streets without being mugged... to survive without being tainted by other races... and not to have their jobs and housing taken from them."

Taking a slow deep breath, she looked around into people's eyes, trying to win their approval. She was impressed by her delivery and felt the audience was with her. She was settling into the role and felt the authority of a leader. It had come to her naturally and, although she would never admit it, she was surprised by it.

Harry tried again, "You're a fascist."

"That's because people like you are communists," Mikey responded.

Harry had found courage from the snorter and he decided to keep going. "I'm proud to be white."

For a moment Mikey did not have an answer.

Realising he had taken the initiative, Harry pressed on. "What are you going to do for this country? Why are you here?"

Mikey saw her chance. "I have to be here, sir, because I believe in this great country... but nobody is keeping you."

The crowd sniggered and a few applauded; hostile stares and chuntered comments were directed towards the heckler. The big men were getting pissed off.

Mikey continued, "I was born here in Soho and I love my country. My mother brought me up to work for a living. To have ambition and not to accept the threat to our livelihood from outsiders. I have worked hard all my life to get where I am. We don't want our businesses undermined by immigrants. Or by the perverts who infest the streets of Soho. We must decide our own future. Not have those foreigners come in and steal it from us. Not put up with the erosion of our basic values. All I have seen in my life here in Soho is the corruption of our principles, the contamination of our society and the dilution of our people. The politically correct do-gooders and the apathy of our politicians have made this possible. While we suffer unemployment, more and more businesses are being taken over and run by foreigners. It is time for all patriots to stand up and be counted."

"One, two, three, little pricks come to me." The amphetamine had kicked in. Harry had opened his mouth and it had just come out. The room fell silent and a few people turned to look at him.

Mikey only hesitated for a moment. "Okay, let's play the clown... in fact let's be the pantomime horse... I'll be the head and you just be yourself."

The assembled gang showed their appreciation.

Pleased by Harry's humiliation, Mikey continued, "I have spent my life working to achieve a pure Britain where we can all be successful... and where we are not compromised by people from other parts of the world."

She threw her arms wide, exalting in her self-importance.

"Like all of you here today, I have grown up in this beautiful country. I want to see it evolve into a place for our children to flourish in a pure and flawless society."

As the cheering died down, foolishly Harry tried again. "Even if you were God I still wouldn't vote for you."

"If I was God I would welcome you into my constituency right now," she said, pointing skywards.

Again the crowd roared its approval.

Harry was being out-manoeuvred and he could not compete. A space had cleared around him. It was a one-sided debate. He decided his best chance was to attack. "What's your game then?" he asked.

Mikey avoided the question with another question, "Why are you are here tonight?"

"Eating and drinking... you should try it," said Harry trying, too late, to get the crowd behind him.

Mikey responded, "And grow to look like you?"

The crowd enjoyed watching this weird woman destroy this subversive, and clapped her every answer.

Mikey did not want the effect of her carefully prepared speech to be diluted, but the idiot was feeding her the lines that allowed her to enhance her stature; while she was winning, she was prepared to encourage the dialogue.

Harry was blind to the danger. Had he not been a big, physical man he would have been buried by the crowd by now. The amphetamine convinced him he was equally witty and winning and could be master of the assembly. He was not prepared to give in and unwisely continued to heckle. "You're responsible for racism... why don't you stop it?"

"Why are you heckling me?" asked Mikey, smiling at the interruption. "If you want excitement go and show your ugly face down in Brixton... then see what kind of welcome you receive."

A body-builder covered in tattoos shouted something Mikey did not hear and the crowd cheered again. She turned her attention in his direction. "If you vote for me I will fight tirelessly to change the permissive... indulgent... politically correct... soft liberal corruption that infests this country and our community. Give me the power to change important issues, change our immigration laws and repatriate the strangers."

Turning to Dean Beck, she saw the look of approval on his face.

"I can and will influence our ruling class... I will address the issues that are crippling our country."

She paused, and Harry grabbed the moment. "Rubbish."

She turned to him and smiled, "I'll deal with your special interest in a moment."

She turned flamboyantly back to the audience. "With your help I will be your leader and your voice. Let the voice of the people be heard. This is our land... England for the English... long live Great Britain... I salute you all."

The cheering started and Mikey held up her fist in a fascist salute which increased the response.

Harry saw his last chance and shouted at the top of his voice, "Yes, you may leave the room."

The crowd went quiet again.

Mikey pointed at him. "If you don't like it in here why don't you get out?"

Harry shouted back, "In and out, it's coitus interruptus."

Mikey smiled, "Then you'd better quickly withdraw."

The crowd bayed in response and turned on Harry, they pointed to the door and started shouting, "Out, out, out…"

Harry had to walk through the howling mob and suffer his humiliation. "Go fuck yourself", he said under his breath.

'I hope I haven't over-egged it,' Mikey thought.

56. SNOWMAN, SEAN & HARRY : (NIGHT, WEDNESDAY 11 NOVEMBER)

Snowman rang him at eleven o'clock that night.

Harry had got back to his flat from the BNP party at about ten-thirty. He was angry and frustrated at the way things had turned out. It was five days since he had been tortured by Snowman and Mikey, and four days since he'd dealt with Carrie. He had tried but failed to stay clean for the last couple of days and the effects of the evening's consumption of cheap wine and speed were wearing off. He felt drained and exhausted.

Snowman reckoned that if Harry was in his flat, less than a hundred metres away, the safest thing he could do was to give him the gun as soon as possible. He pushed the rifle, still wrapped in brown paper, inside the umbrella gathering the armatures round the stock which was sticking out above the handle. He could carry it concealed under his arm the short distance to Harry's flat.

He was in the lavatory when he made the call from Sean's mobile. He didn't want to announce his name in case Harry recorded the message. "I'm coming round to see you in the next few minutes."

When the phone rang Harry jumped out of his skin. For a moment he did not recognise the hoarse voice. "What for?" he asked, then he realised who it was.

"I want to discuss something with you… are you alone?"

"Yes."

Snowman cut the call and returned to the bar.

Handing the mobile back to Sean, he said, "I need to borrow the five grand I gave you... I'll pay you back tomorrow."

Sean raised his eyebrows. "You've lost your money... your phone and your voice?" He started to laugh. "Have you been mugged?"

Snowman finished his drink and held out the glass.

Sean topped it up, "I wouldn't be doing this for anyone else, y'know." He disappeared into his office behind the bar and returned with the original envelope.

Snowman noted that it hadn't been opened. He smiled to himself; if he had tried to short change his friend he'd now be getting back exactly what he had given him in the first place.

Sean handed over the money. "Don't be forgetting now..... tomorrow."

Snowman tucked it into the rear pocket of his waistcoat. He flinched as he swallowed his drink; the brandy burned his throat. He went down to street level and stood in the doorway, looking up and down the street. It was dark and drizzling. He pulled his hood up and jogged down Dean Street with the rifle stock jammed in his armpit. As he crossed Bateman Street he glanced back at Carrie's door and felt a pang of remorse. It didn't last longer than the time it took him to cover the final twenty metres to Harry's doorway.

He rang the bell impatiently and was surprised when it buzzed open; he had expected Harry to come down. He looked up the dark staircase, switched the umbrella and rifle to his left-hand side and pulled the snub-nosed revolver from the small of his back. He released the safety catch and held it inside his jacket pocket.

Harry, with the bandages showing through the open front of his fleece, appeared on the top landing looking down on Snowman as he climbed the stairs.

Snowman didn't feel comfortable until he was at eye level with him. When he was sure that Harry wasn't tooled up, he pushed him into the flat. The smell of old cooking oil, sweat and burnt fabric greeted him. He scanned the room, checking that they were alone. All the blinds were drawn and the TV was whispering in the corner.

He let go of the revolver and produced the envelope full of money. "Here's the balance for the last job... five grand. We've got another bigger project for you... a lot more money."

Harry didn't react because he didn't understand what was on offer. But at least now he had the final five grand and he could think about getting out of Soho.

Snowman ripped the paper from the rifle. There was a cigar box taped to the forestock. He tore it off and laid the rifle on the coffee table. He stared at the sleek object. It lay there with its dark oiled gunmetal barrel and black polymer stock. He understood how some people could become fascinated by weapons. It was beautiful but deadly and reminded him of Myrtle.

Harry calmed himself as he opened the envelope and counted the money. Then he turned his concentration to the rifle. The smell of the oiled metal took him back to his sniper days and a feeling of confidence surged through him. He wondered what they wanted him to do with it? He picked up the cigar box and shook it. He prised it open to reveal half-a-dozen rounds in bubble wrap and a silencer.

Snowman went over to Harry's desk and dialled from the land line. "I've got the goods... and I'm with him now."

Replacing the receiver he turned to Harry. "Sit down and wait."

He turned up the TV and sat opposite Harry, keeping his hand on the butt of the pistol.

57. BRANEN :(LATE, WEDNESDAY 11 NOVEMBER)

After the phone call to Jane and the confrontation with Snowman, Branen returned to Hotel California.

Seeing Carrie's body and visiting her flat had left him feeling weak. On the way back he bought a half bottle of whisky from an all-night corner shop. He needed numbing. He lay on the bed and counted the neatly folded money he'd taken from Snowman; five hundred and fifty pounds. He scrolled through the numbers in the mobile. The names were all listed in initials. He put the money and mobile into his belt-bag.

He listened to the agitated street life outside the window as he hit the bottle. The cocktail of Soho sounds blended together to form an indigestible ratatouille of noise; the constant twenty-four hour to-ing and fro-ing of people who never seemed to work or sleep; the scream of abuse as a drugged-up prostitute argued the toss with a client who had deep pockets and short arms; the tuneless song of an out of town reveller who had imbibed enough alcohol to give him the courage to take on the wicked world of the Soho he had read about in his tabloid. All this and more echoed up between the buildings on each side of the passageway directly outside his hotel. The neon lights pulsed and bounced off the plastic net curtains; a stark contrast to the sunrises Branen had watched flickering through his bedroom window, back at the podere. For the first time in a long time he felt lonely; the same sensation he'd had before on assignments, but this time it had a particularly hollow ache.

Staring up at the peeling wallpaper, he tried to decide what his next move should be. The information from Costas, and the drugs found in her flat, led him to believe that Carrie had developed a relationship with Snowman. He had to assume that the Firm had instructed her to meet with him. He believed that they knew more about Snowman than they were prepared to let on.

Costas had told him about Snowman's strange reaction when he'd asked about Carrie; and that he'd seen her with 'some big bloke' in his bar just hours before she was murdered, but he said that Snowman claimed to know nothing about the man. If Snowman had been involved with Carrie he could have been the subject of the blackmail threats.

He opened Carrie's notebook. The note of the meeting in The Piano Bar with the weird officer made him wonder if he was the same bloke Costas saw her with. If he was, the Firm could be involved in her death. Who was that officer? Could he be the same person who had followed him? It seemed unlikely, given that he had been so incompetent.

The Controller had not mentioned Group X when he had first made contact on Tuesday night. But she had referred to the blackmail attempt. If it was genuine and not a set-up by the Firm, they must have got the information from Carrie's computer and left it there for him to find. He suspected that they had not found her notebook or mobile and that they didn't know about the existence of Group X or Snowman's meeting with 'a BNP politician' mentioned in the notebook. But the Controller could have been bluffing. If one of the people involved in Carrie's murder was in politics, he or she should not be too hard to find. Was it possible that Snowman had become suspicious of Carrie? Was that why she had been murdered rather than the implication from the Controller that she had been involved in a drug deal with the Chinese?

Because of the amount of money involved, and the bottle of Delamain he'd found at her flat, he decided to work on the premise that the blackmail demand was connected to her relationship with Snowman.

Then there was the beehive, with what looked like a camera in it. He was trying to sleep but it all kept nagging at him. He got out of bed and stood looking out of the window. There were lights on in the rooms across the narrow alley. A few feet from him life continued unabated, completely unaware of his grief. He realised that he had to go back to her flat. He might see signs of life in the flat below those beehives.

If the Controller changed her mind and pulled him in he didn't want them finding Carrie's notebook or mobile. He battled with the rusty, paint-filled screw-heads and managed to remove a window stay. Then he slid the plywood wardrobe out from the wall. The dust and cobwebs had not been disturbed for years. He rolled the parquet-printed linoleum back and searched for a short floorboard. He used the window stay to lever up the end of a board just high enough to enable him to slide the phone and notebook between the joists. He left it all as he'd found it. He was going back to Carrie's.

He replaced the battery and SIM card and turned on the Firm's mobile in case they had information for him. He was going through his kit-bag looking for the monocular when the mobile rang.

58. BRANEN & THE CONTROLLER : (MIDNIGHT, WED 11 NOVEMBER)

The Controller was frustrated that she hadn't been able to contact Branen, which had left her feeling impotent. He had disabled his phone and all she could do was set up a regular repeat dial in the hope that he would re-activate it.

She had instructed her researchers to find out anything they could about him but they had come back with nothing.

"There's no trace of the man... he's a bloody ghost," said the senior male researcher.

All she knew about Branen was based on a half-page summary given to the Chief by the Senior Civil Servant. The report stated that it had been seven years since he had last seen action and had been considered to be one of the most efficient solo operators in the service; he was not a team player.

The Controller wanted a psychological profile on him and had arranged a meeting with the Firm's human behavioural specialist. She didn't want someone as lethal as Branen running around out of control. She wanted to know what he was thinking and how best to get a handle on his mental state. She wanted to bring him under her control.

The psychologist had concluded that the summary was too vague, and since he had never known Branen he could only guess at how an ex-agent with his background might behave. But the Controller was sufficiently confident to believe that she could predict and stay ahead of Branen's strategies.

She had deliberately omitted to tell Branen about Michelle de Lavigne and the ongoing operation. If he managed to resolve the Snowman and terrorist problem she would hand him back to the SCS, who obviously had other plans for him. She had also omitted to give him any information about Whitey because she needed him to keep an eye on Branen. Even if Whitey was way below Branen's league, all he had to do was observe. They would not use him for any proactive action.

It was nearly midnight when Branen answered the call.

The Controller had been advised by the heads specialist that if she took the initiative she could establish a psychological advantage. "We have reason to believe that Snowman is connected to a terrorist group and that he was involved in your daughter's murder... it might be an idea if we met up for a briefing." She believed, even though the SCS had ruled it out, that with a face to face meeting she could establish her authority.

Branen wasn't sure. He was surprised by the 'might be an idea' suggestion because the Firm never dealt in maybe's, "Why can't you brief me over the phone..." he asked and before she could answer, "...what else have you got on Carrie and what exactly did she know before she was killed?"

"I've told you all we know."

It was still possible that the Firm was implicated in Carrie's murder and he wanted hard evidence before he removed Snowman or anyone else from the scene. "What more do you know about Snowman?" he asked.

"We didn't have much on him... that's what Carrie was put in place for. We think she was either killed by him because he had discovered she was working for us... or possibly she was killed by the Chinese because she got involved in a drug dispute they had with Snowman."

During Branen's first contact with the Controller she had mentioned a blackmail attempt and another agenda and a terrorist group. She wasn't giving him any background information, which made him wonder what they really wanted. Perhaps he was following a pre-planned path that would ultimately lead to his own death and provide the SCS with the security of his permanent silence. He was sure Carrie's notebook had given him a lead they didn't have. They knew there was a terrorist involvement but they didn't seem to know the name of the terrorist organisation.

The Controller read his mind. "What have you found out?"

"Nothing. What are you not telling me?" he asked.

There was silence. She ignored the question.

He persevered. "Has there been a post-mortem yet?"

"Yes."

"And?"

"We have no conclusive DNA details and no evidence that can help find out who did it. We brought you in because it was your daughter... we believed you'd hit this one hard. Find Snowman... find out what he knows. We want to know the extent of his involvement, if any, in the terrorist group. We want them all."

She obviously didn't know that he had already met Snowman, and realised that if he did not carry out their instructions he was useless to them. But he would also become useless once he had fulfilled their wishes. He wanted revenge and then to disappear off their radar.

They weren't going to give him any more information, so he decided not to wait for them to bait another hook and ended the call. He was sure they were digging a hole and waiting for him to fall in.

He removed the SIM card and battery from the mobile, put the kit-bag into the wardrobe, then set off for Carrie's flat.

59. MIKEY, SNOWMAN & HARRY :
(MIDNIGHT, WED 11 NOVEMBER)

Mikey arrived at Harry's flat about twenty minutes after Snowman's call.

On her way over from Madame LuLu's she heard chanting and police sirens. As she turned into Wardour Street she saw a fight between a gang of skinheads and the police at the bottom of Greek Street; the skinheads who had been at her meeting. She was still flushed with adrenalin from her speech and had left Dean and Lee indulging their fantasies with a couple of carefully chosen Eastern European girls, selected by Mikey for their willingness to fulfil any perversion that might be requested of them, and who probably earned more money for the night than their parents made in a month. But now she had more pressing matters on her mind.

Waiting for Mikey gave Snowman the opportunity to ask Harry what he had found out about what Carrie had been up to. "What did she tell you about me? I ain't heard or read anything about her since you got rid of her! Did you do her?"

In the sexual frenzy of the killing, Harry had not thought to question her. "I've done the job you wanted," said Harry, then stared at the floor, reluctant to say anything else.

Snowman grabbed him by the throat. "How'd you kill her?"

Harry gripped Snowman's wrist and forced his hand away, but remained silent and avoided eye contact.

Snowman was surprised by Harry's strength but before he could react, the doorbell rang and broke the impasse.

Snowman buzzed Mikey in. She entered with the balaclava over her face, dressed in a long dark Crombie coat.

Harry thought she looked like a large black vibrator.

When she saw Harry she smiled to herself, remembering how their paths had crossed earlier in the evening. She knew he had no idea who she was but she had to be careful that he did not recognise her voice.

Snowman ordered Harry to sit at the desk facing his computer and to put on the earphones. He doubted Harry's ability to complete the new assignment and he didn't trust him any more than he trusted Mikey. He had to watch his back; no one else was going to.

He gestured to Mikey to come to the far side of the room. "I don't trust him… he's a nutter."

She looked up at him. "Has he solved your problem?"

"He says so."

"Then we've got him where we want him. He's perfect for our job. We're not after brain of Britain, all we want is someone who has the nerve and can shoot straight… by chance we've found him. I don't give a fuck if he's got a screw loose… he'll do the job… he's done the first part which proves he's got the nerve. Anyway when he's done it we won't need him any more."

Snowman was agitated. "The creep makes my skin crawl… and I've had some cunt attack me in Costas's bar… asking about Carrie."

"Who was it?"

"I don't know."

"Well find out… you'd better straighten Costas out… tell him you don't want him giving sanctuary to an arsehole who is sticking his nose into other people's business… I don't want any hiccups with such a short time to go."

Snowman avoided telling Mikey that his mobile had been stolen; he didn't want her to think he was a weak link. She was powerful and vindictive and he didn't want to find himself on the wrong side of her.

Harry sat, ears muffled by the cans, wondering what they were going to do next. He felt safe that they would not make him suffer again because they obviously had plans for him. If they offered him enough money he would delay his escape.

Mikey glanced at the rifle lying on the table and went over to Harry. For the first time he noticed the cold clear stare of her grey eyes. He felt angry at the ignominy he had suffered at their hands.

"On Saturday afternoon, that's this Saturday, the Prime Minister is visiting St. Barnabas's hostel for an auction… he wants to show his support for the charity." She leaned towards him, trying to be as intimidating as possible. "He wants to demonstrate how caring his party is… and you are going to shoot him. Use all that military training, paid for by me and the British taxpayer, and make sure you don't fuck up… or we'll come after you instead. He's due at four o'clock. He'll have to use the entrance in Greek Street. That's your chance, unless you can shoot him through a window while he's being shown round. The election is next week and he will want to stop on the pavement for press pictures and to glad-hand people. He'll be welcomed by the local MP... so you'll have time to get your shot."

Harry hadn't expected his target to be so important. The idea of rediscovering the skills he had developed as a sniper and shooting the Prime Minister both excited and frightened him. His preparation and escape route would be crucial; that's what the army had trained him to do. He had thought about taking his revenge on Snowman; he knew where he lived and had picked him up with his black lover on a couple of occasions. He had toyed with the idea of going round there and sorting her out, but he would have to delay his revenge because they were now his meal ticket.

"Any questions?" asked Mikey.

He stared at the apparition with its high-pitched voice and mid-Atlantic accent.

"How much?" he asked.

"I'm going to give you enough to leave Soho and not come back... I've got access to property in the West Indies. I'll arranged a new ID and for you to take a very long holiday. We don't want you around after the job's done."

"How much will you pay me?"

"Fifty thousand pounds and a beach house... there's plenty of opportunities for a taxi driver there."

Harry had intended to bargain but because he was offered so much, he just nodded, thinking he would have done it for half that.

"If you accept the deal and succeed there could be more work in the future... do you need anything else?" asked Mikey.

"To be left alone... I'm used to working alone."

They watched silently as Harry put on a pair of latex gloves. He returned to the rifle. Snowman joined him and as a precaution removed the box of ammo. Harry operated the bolt action a couple of times to check it was in good condition and that there wasn't a round up the spout. Holding it up to his shoulder he lined up the Zeiss scope. "I'll need to sight it."

"Make sure you shoot straight," said Mikey, glancing over at Snowman, who had his hand on the revolver in his pocket.

Mikey stared straight into Harry's eyes. "Don't forget, this is very important... after you've done the job I want the rifle left in the boot of your car. Then take your car and park it outside Masonic Mansions... in Chinatown where he took you before... remember?"

She waited for any acknowledgement. Eventually he nodded.

Then pointing at Snowman, she said, "Ring the top bell and give the keys to him... he'll give you an air ticket and you'll leave the country at once... the money will be in an account at the Bank of Bermuda... he'll give you the details when you hand over the car keys. Leave any cartridge cases on the ground where you fire from... we want the rifle to be found even if you won't be." She handed a copy of the Qur'an to Harry. "I want you to leave this behind. Follow the instructions to the letter... they are crucial. Be ready to leave immediately after the shooting. Don't mess up or the whole deal is off... and if that happens, with what you've done already I'll make sure you're fucked by the law."

Mikey turned on her heel. As she got to the door she tripped on a worn patch of carpet. She cursed and pulled up her balaclava to see where she was going. It was just too soon and Harry got a fleeting but clear view of the back of her head. The short spikey hair with bleached tips, the expensive diamond ear-stud and the tanned complexion. It was enough for Harry to realise this was the second time he had seen her that night.

'It's going to work,' Mikey convinced herself as she went back down the grotty staircase.

60. BRANEN & HARRY : (EARLY HOURS, THURSDAY 12 NOVEMBER)

As Branen walked back to Carrie's flat, he felt that there was more there to be discovered; he had not checked the deleted messages on her computer.

The streets were quiet. It was a bitterly cold night and the inhospitable weather had kept people at home. Soho had temporarily lost its glamour, looking grey and unwelcoming; not just cold in temperature but cold in its heart. It reflected his mood perfectly.

Branen stood in the middle of the room; he could feel her haunting the silence. He made a promise to avenge her death; nothing would stop him.

Returning to the computer, he found a deleted message containing the word 'Office' in the address. It was dated Saturday November 7th and sent at 11.55am; the day she was murdered:

C.H.A.R.O.N. FATHER WANTS TO SEE YOU. MEET COSTAS LOUNGE – 16.00 HRS. TONIGHT – OFFICE.

The subject box said 'IMPORTANT'.

The message shook him. It had been sent from a different address to the blackmail messages, and he or she had used what he assumed to be Carrie's codename.

There were three possible sources of this message:

The first was the Firm. But why use him to trick her into a meeting?

The second was more likely. The message was from the fat man who she had met in Costas's. But if he had her codename he would have to be an officer from the Firm; and why would he want to lure her to Costas's by using him as bait? He could have just arranged to meet her there.

The third possibility was that The Associates was working with the Firm and had sent these emails to set him up.

He sat at Carrie's desk contemplating all the possibilities. The big man Costas had seen her with that night was now Branen's main suspect. If the man knew about him, he must be a rogue officer and all the messages could have come from that man.

As he was turning it all over in his mind he noticed a window in the building on the other side of the street, about fifteen metres to his left and at an acute angle. The light was on in the room but the blinds were down.

Branen decided to respond to the email; he had nothing to lose. He clicked onto the original address and typed:

WHAT HAPPENED TO YOU – I WAITED AND YOU DIDN'T SHOW UP. HOW ABOUT TONIGHT AT COSTAS AT SEVEN O'CLOCK?

Branen glanced up from the screen and noticed the light had been switched off in the flat opposite.

He clicked 'Send', hoping to stir things up. Then he made himself comfortable and waited for an answer. He would wait until the morning and then have breakfast at the Star and meet Jane at eleven o'clock.

It tore him apart that the bastard had set Carrie up knowing she needed to see him; if only he could have been there.

61. HARRY & BRANEN :
(EARLY HOURS, THURSDAY 12 NOVEMBER)

Harry spent a painful few hours trying to find sleep. His chest was throbbing and his mind would not settle. Each time he dropped off, any movement he made caused shooting pain from the wounds. It constantly reminded him of the humiliation inflicted on him; and now he knew who the person he now called the hermaphrodite was, revenge was at the front of his mind.

Harry was not instinctively a brave man but his sniper training had taught him how to overcome fear and deal with danger. He could not stop wondering who the man was he had videoed in Carrie's flat and what he was doing there. His demeanour and behaviour was not typical of a policeman. Harry put the recording back on and tried to examine his body language.

How had the man gained access to Carrie's flat? Could he be her father? He was tired of questions; it was all too much.

He climbed out of bed to play with his new toy, the Tikka rifle. He took a shower and put on a fresh checked shirt. He planned to make a ritual of the preparation of his weapon just like he used to do when he was about to be deployed on an army operation. These were exceptional circumstances and he allowed himself a cocktail to aid concentration.

He checked that all the blinds were securely in place and put on the rubber gloves. He sat on the sofa-bed and carefully presented the rifle on the coffee table in front of him. He checked for any identifying marks that might have been put there by the previous owner. If it was found by the police it could be traced by the manufacturer's number.

He opened the cigar box and took out the Reflex T8 sound moderator. He opened the bubble-wrap packet and emptied the rounds of .243 calibre ammunition into his hand. There were six rounds of soft-nosed copper-jacketed bullets. The lead tip was designed to disintegrate on impact with the target's body, causing massive internal hemorrhaging. Banned for warfare by the Geneva Convention they were used by the police, counter terrorist groups, and for game shooting.

He rolled the rounds over in his palm, feeling their weight. He was comfortable using this particular bullet as he was familiar with its flat trajectory. It would give him the accuracy he needed for a head shot. Even if he was an inch out in his aim, it would be lethal. At present he had not chosen his vantage point but he knew that the shot would not be much over a hundred metres at maximum because of the geography of the streets.

He flicked a round over. The headstamp NP was missing on the detonator cap but it was engraved on the base of the cartridge case. This told him that the rounds were precision hand-loads that the owner had assembled himself. It gave Harry a clue as to the origin of the rifle. He went over to his desk and tapped the computer into life. On the net he discovered that the rifle was a T3 Lite and was a recently introduced model. It was an accurate weapon. Returning to the rifle, he pulled back the bolt and made sure for a second time there wasn't a round up the spout.

He held the rifle up to his shoulder. The stock was short for a man of his size but it would do. He guessed it had been stolen from or supplied by a deer stalker. He knew that it was common for stalkers on Scottish estates to hand-load their own ammunition for greater accuracy.

He stripped down the action, removed the bolt and the magazine and held the barrel up to the light to examine the bore. It had hardly been used, there was no apparent wear in the throat where the rifling began; it was in perfect condition. He checked that the magazine was in good nick and reassembled the action, noting that the bolt operation was reassuringly quiet. He tested the trigger pressure and the safety catch with a few dry squeezes. He checked the muzzle and found a couple of dents on the end of the barrel, but he could hardly send it back to the manufacturer for repair.

Finally he loaded the magazine, and using the bolt to eject the rounds, caught each one with his right hand as it sprung from the breach. This took considerable speed and dexterity because he was left-handed and his fingers were thick. He had been forced by his instructors to shoot right-handedly during training. It had been twenty years and it pleased him to see that he hadn't lost his touch, even if he did get oil from the bolt on his shirt.

Harry was amused when he thought about the man who had assembled this ammunition; he would never know what these rounds were going to be used for. He was blessed with accurate ammunition and he was pleased with his new weapon; even if it didn't compare to his army-issue 7.62mm L42A1 sniper's rifle, with which he had learnt his craft, but beggars can't be choosers.

He was left with one major problem; how to set up the scope for an accurate shot. He remembered from the sniper course having to manually zero his scope in the field. He switched off all the lights and moved his computer to clear a space on the desk. Suddenly it chimed to tell him he had an email. He sat down clumsily in the dark room. Lit by the glow from the screen, he read the email out loud:

WHAT HAPPENED TO YOU – I WAITED AND YOU DIDN'T SHOW UP. HOW ABOUT TONIGHT AT COSTAS AT SEVEN O'CLOCK?

Who had sent the email? Was he fantasizing? Only Carrie had that address. His heart was thumping, he could hear it in his ears. His anxiety levels were soaring. Who the fuck had sent this? He stumbled over and switched on the beehive camera. The street lights reflecting on the window panes opposite prevented him seeing into Carrie's flat. For a moment he thought he could see the glow of her computer screen, but it could have been a reflection.

His nerves were shot and his heart palpitating. He sat for a while, breathing into his cupped hands. He had to ignore the email. There was nothing he could do about it. He grabbed a packet of diazepam from the drawer and dropped a couple of tabs to calm himself; he had to wait and see if anything developed.

It took at least ten minutes before he could settle his anxiety.

As the effects of the Valium kicked in he convinced himself that it was 'that fucking mutant fucking me around.'

He turned his attention back to his rifle. Using a block of wood and a roll of gaffer tape, he fixed the rifle firmly to the tabletop. He lifted the blind on the sash window overlooking Dean Street and, sitting well back, aimed the rifle up the road. It was four in the morning and most of Soho's lights had been turned off. He removed the bolt, and sighting down the inside of the barrel he aimed at a letter X on a hoarding a hundred metres away. Keeping the rifle dead still, he adjusted the turn-screws on the scope and focused it onto the same X. Before removing the rifle from its bondage he obsessively repeated the exercise three more times to make absolutely sure the sight was accurately zeroed.

Finally he went over the whole reassembled rifle and wiped it clean with an oily rag to ensure there were no prints or possible traces of DNA.

He was stretched out on the sofa trying to slow down the chaos in his head, but he couldn't forget that email. Even with the Valium his brain was buzzing with anxiety and making paranoid and chaotic connections. He got up and paced the room. He replayed the tape of the man who was in Carrie's flat yesterday. He was furious with himself for losing him in Soho Square. He sat and watched the recording over and over again, checking for any clue that might point to his identity.

The live feed from his hive camera was still running. He stared at the screen which showed the blank window opposite, remembering how he had sat for hours watching Carrie dressed only in her underwear. He missed her and wished he'd never succumbed to the threats of that mutant and the hermaphrodite.

He jolted up in his chair. "It's a fucking ghost," he exclaimed out loud. In the shadow of the window he saw the outline of a man holding a scope to his eye, staring straight into the camera. Without thinking Harry remotely operated the zoom.

62. BRANEN & HARRY :
(EARLY HOURS, THURSDAY 12 NOVEMBER)

Branen had hoped for a reply to the email, but by four o'clock in the morning he'd given up.

He couldn't bring himself to sleep in Carrie's bed, so he dragged the duvet from the bedroom and lay down on the floor. Then he remembered the beehive on the roof opposite. He tucked into the corner of the window by the desk and was focussing the monocular onto the camera lens when it moved. At first he wasn't sure if it was the reflection of the clouds moving over the moon. Then he saw the movement of the elements within the lens as they reflected in the moonlight. Now he was in no doubt that there was a camera hidden in the hive and that he was being watched. If he closed the curtains it would confirm to the watchers that he was in residence; that was if they didn't already know.

The figure was shadowy and Harry continued to stare intently at the screen trying to make out any movement. When the person disappeared below the window-ledge he watched for another half-hour, finally falling asleep where he sat.

Branen lay back on the cushions below the window so that the camera could not see him. He turned over on the makeshift bed and again became aware of Carrie's aura in the room. Perhaps it was her perfume on the duvet.

Harry woke at six-thirty, stiff from being slumped sideways in the chair. He had to find out who the man was. He decided to keep recording his surveillance.

It was 7am when Harry saw Branen in the flat again.

Branen washed, shaved and tried to smarten up ready for his meeting with Jane. Within clear view of the window he put on the belt-bag and his coat. He went down to the street, where he stopped outside the front door as if trying to decide which way to go. Walking at a slow even pace he turned out of Bateman Street and continued north up Dean Street.

He was sure he would pick up a tail and he needed to see if it was more professional than the last one. Without checking behind him, he cut through St.Anne's Court and walked to the Star café. On the way he dived into a newsagent. Once inside he pretended to look in the window and made a mental note of half a dozen people in the close vicinity. He bought a newspaper and back on the street opened the paper and dropped the inside pages. Cursing out loud, he crouched down to pick them up. Nobody hesitated. They all continued about their business. He walked back the way he had come and as he turned into Hollen Street he saw him. The fat bastard in the same ill-fitting overcoat who had followed him yesterday. He was doing up his shoe on the far side of the road. He had obviously panicked when Branen turned back towards him and copied his body language by crouching down. He was an amateur.

With his lack of tradecraft Branen decided that he could not be working for the Firm, but he needed to know who this fat fuck was. Could he have been Carrie's date on Saturday night? Was he behind the camera? Could he be working for Snowman and had he got Carrie's codename from him?

Branen was sure the man didn't know he'd spotted him, so he decided to let him follow and had his breakfast without worrying where the man would be when he'd finished. If he was following him he would always find the man again. It was still an hour and a half before he was due to meet Jane and he didn't want him observing them then.

It was ten o'clock when Branen finished breakfast and strolled back onto the street.

63. HARRY, BRANEN & THE CONTROLLER : (MORNING, THURSDAY 12 NOVEMBER)

When Harry saw the man in Carrie's flat getting ready to leave, he decided to follow him.

The man appeared to know Soho. Harry followed him to the café but got bored with waiting; he had other matters on his mind, he wanted to recce St. Barnabas's in preparation for his assignment.

When he arrived back at his flat the Firm's mobile rang. 'What the fuck do they want now?' he asked himself.

Carrie was dead and his role as her contact was obsolete. Hadn't he made himself redundant?

The Controller wasn't as blunt this time. "We have another job for you."

"I want more money," Harry said.

There was a hint of threat in the Controller's voice. "We'll talk about that when we debrief you concerning the Carrie affair."

This shook Harry. He didn't expect to have to be debriefed on her murder. "I don't have anything else to tell you about that."

She decided to push him. "Her father has become involved and he's dangerous... a risk to us."

The revelation that the man was Carrie's father confirmed his concern.

The Controller kept up the pressure. "We want you to keep an eye out for him... keep observing her flat. He has a key and we suspect he'll make a visit. We want you to report back if you see him there... have you seen anyone in the flat?"

The question caught Harry unawares. "No," he said, too quickly.

"So you can see into the flat from your apartment?" It was a rhetorical question calculated to keep him off balance and to confirm her concerns that Whitey knew more than he let on.

She had him cornered. He stuttered, "Not... not really."

"What's that mean?"

"Well I... if I look out at an angle from my window, I, er... can sort of see a bit... but not enough to see if anyone's in there."

"What about the front door?"

"Er, yes I can see down into Bateman Street... and the front door."

"Okay, keep your eyes open and we'll be in touch."

The line went dead.

Harry felt trapped. He had the mutant and the hermaphrodite on his back and now the Firm was harassing him as well. The last thing he needed was Carrie's father sniffing around. 'Fuck it, maybe I should get out now,' he thought.

He went over to the cupboard and poured a glass of neat vodka. Carrie had got him into this mess and now her father was looking for him; it was all her fault. And it must have been her father who had sent the email this morning. He felt exposed, even if the proxy email address was completely untraceable. The upside was that he had the ten grand from the odd couple. He would do the shooting and afterwards, on Saturday afternoon, he would be out of here. It was worth staying a bit longer for the extra 50K and the house in the West Indies.

Then the paranoia kicked in; after the last phone call the Firm might turn up to debrief him and search his flat. He couldn't keep the rifle and the money lying around. He stumbled over to the sofa.

Being careful not to let it rub against his chest, he strapped the rifle to his front with the sling over his back. He adjusted it so the tip of the barrel was level with the top of his shoulder and the stock didn't protrude below the bottom of his overcoat. He put the ammunition and the silencer into his pocket. He put the 5K cash into a heavy-duty dustbin bag and chucked dirty clothing on top. He checked in the mirror as he huddled up rehearsing his position for the walk up the road to his motor. As long as he kept slightly hunched against the cold wind the rifle was concealed well enough for him to get to his car without attracting attention.

64. BRANEN : (MORNING, THURSDAY 12 NOVEMBER)

When Branen left the café he walked through to Dean Street.

He couldn't spot the fat man and wondered where he'd gone.

He shivered; a cold November wind blew as he made his way towards Soho Square. He was fifteen minutes early for Jane so he bought a bunch of flowers and chose a bench on the east side of the square so he could observe all the approaches.

The square was fenced off with cast iron railings and divided into quarters by paths radiating out to each point of the compass from a central mock Tudor shed. The grass had lost its verdance. The rose bushes were looking ragged, the leaves brown and wilted, anticipating the fast approaching winter.

Branen shivered again; was it the cold or the anticipation of meeting her? Would she be pleased to see him? Would she kiss him or would she be distant, as she had been when they'd last met?

He was distracted by his thoughts and didn't see her arrive. There she was in the middle of the square, sitting on the bench outside the park-keeper's shed. She had her head down, tending to the child lying on her lap. As she lifted the baby across her body he remembered the first time he had seen her in the Marquee Club twenty years ago. He sat there for a moment watching her holding her child, conceived with another man. She was beautiful. He had fucked up and rejected her but he still loved her.

He hesitated for a moment then took a deep breath and walked over to her. She looked up and smiled. He put his arms round her and almost lifted them both off the ground. He went to kiss her mouth. At the last moment she turned her head. Having established where their relationship was now, he kissed her forehead and pressed his face into her hair and remembered her smell.

"Hello darling," he said.

She held his gaze. "Hello."

She stepped back and adjusted the baby, who was squeezed between them. She looked into his eyes for a moment and then without ceremony asked anxiously, "What do you want?"

He didn't know how to tell her. He gave her the flowers.

"I needed to see you," he said.

"Ben, I have another life... I came because I told you I would always be there for you and I knew when you rang that..."

"I have to tell you something."

She thought he was going to ask her to come back to him and held up her baby. "This is Georgie... it's her first birthday today."

He put his hand onto the baby's head but it didn't seem to notice.

"Carrie is dead."

The only thing that moved was Jane's jacket as the wind gusted under the eaves of the small shed. She didn't move her head. She was frozen in the moment. She stayed looking down at her baby and then she started to sink. Her body turned to jelly and she dropped the flowers. Branen grabbed the baby and at the same time tried to support her.

She turned her head up towards him, tears running down her face. "How?"

"She was caught up in a drug deal."

He was holding the baby and Jane was clinging to his arms with both hands. "How did she get involved with drugs... she had a job with the Civil Service... she was doing part-time modelling. How do you know about it... have you seen her?"

Jane sank back down on the bench. "Where is she?" Her voice was desperate and she was inconsolable. She knew he had something to do with Carrie's death.

"I wasn't in touch with her... the authorities contacted me."

"What was she mixed up in... what was your involvement?"

"After we split up I was recruited by the Government.... but I'd retired. I live abroad now." He had lived a clandestine life for so long that he couldn't bring himself to tell her exactly where.

He tried to explain. "She was approached by the Secret Service who hired her... I had nothing to do with it... unless they used me to persuade her to work for them..." He could hear his words; they sounded hollow and meaningless. "... I've done things in my life I regret but leaving you was the biggest mistake I ever made. My life changed then..."

Her eyes were asking him to stop. "You leave a trail of broken lives behind you."

"It's not what I intended."

She wasn't wearing a coat, just a jacket and skirt. She must have come by car. She sat weeping.

Minutes passed as he stood over her motionless. The smell of the damp earth wafted on the breeze, reminding him of standing at the graves of soldiers who had died in action in the Legion. In a vain gesture he offered her his handkerchief. "Let's go over to the café," he said.

Eventually she spoke. "I want to see her. What about her funeral?"

"Until I have sorted things, there is nothing we can do. Leave it to me... I'll contact you as soon as I know anything. Whatever has happened in the past you're part of me... I love you Jane... and I will always love you..."

She looked up at him. "I didn't sleep much last night... I've been worried about seeing you again. I didn't tell Paul... I agreed to come because I knew something was wrong..." She paused and looked up at him. "I had to let you go... and now I have to live without Carrie as well."

He pulled her up and put his arms round her. She was shivering. He took off his coat, wrapped it around her shoulders and put his beret on her head. She tried to put her arms into the sleeves and offered him Georgie. He took the baby and sat down; she stood over him.

"If only..." she stopped herself.

He looked into her eyes. "Most people go through their lives without experiencing what we had..."

65. HARRY & BRANEN :
(MORNING, THURSDAY 12 NOVEMBER)

The tranquil atmosphere within the square was in stark contrast to the bustle of Soho's streets. The parking spaces on Soho Square radiated out from the wrought iron fence and the cars were parked side by side, leaving just enough room between them for the drivers to leave their cages.

Harry made his way towards Soho Square. A casual observer would not have seen anything unusual about the figure huddled up against the cold wind, clutching a dustbin bag to his chest. They certainly would not have suspected he was carrying a rifle.

His car was parked facing the pavement on the east side of the square. He lifted the boot lid and pushed the bin bag right to the back. Anyone breaking into the car would only see filthy clothes spilling out of the bag and look no further. He was looking around to make sure he wasn't being observed when he saw the man.

Harry paused and watched him as he took a woman in his arms. He slammed the boot lid, opened the rear door and slid the rifle onto the floor behind the front seats. He adjusted his coat and squeezed into the driving seat. He sat for a moment, watching him, then started the engine and backed out of the parking bay.

It had all become clear. Fortune had smiled on him and the synchronicity of the moment did not elude him. In his tormented state, he saw it as a chance to simplify matters. He did a complete circuit of the square and parked across the front of two cars, blocking the still-empty parking space he had vacated a few minutes earlier. It offered him his best view. The pavement between the cars and the fence was less than a metre wide and hardly used by pedestrians. The boots and bonnets of the parked cars overlapped the narrow footpath and impeded the way.

Leaving his engine running, Harry wound down the driver's window and slid across into the passenger seat. Propping himself up against the passenger door he put his feet up against the open window on the driver's side.

Even after all these years his brain automatically switched into the conditioned response mode that had been drilled into him. He took the silencer and a bullet from the box in his pocket and reaching down behind the front seats screwed the sound moderator onto the rifle.

A taxi hooted and flashed his lights at Harry's double parked car. The driver pulled alongside and shouted abuse at Harry before driving off, but Harry's mind was elsewhere. He tucked the barrel of the rifle between his legs, loaded the round and leaned into the stock. He only needed a couple of minutes. The chances of a driver returning to one of the adjacent cars in that short time were remote. He estimated the shot to be fifty metres. He drew a bead on the back of his victim; the bottom half of his target was obscured by a park bench in the foreground. The song of the blackbird in the tree by the gate echoed in his ears as he took aim. Through the cross-hair sight he focused on the heart area on the back of the man's coat.

He fired and the blackbird soared into the air, squawking a warning call.

Branen was sitting on the bench in front of Jane as he passed the baby up to her.

She looked down at him. "You know whatever's happened, I will always love you…"

He looked into her eyes. "I know."

The bullet fragmented as it passed through her body, blasting her innards over him. The baby's body offered less resistance to the bullet which continued through the tiny child and thudded into the post above Branen's head. The baby had been wrenched from his extended arms. Jane's body was thrown over him, leaving him in her shadow. For a second he thought she had thrown herself at him but sticky warm blood was pumping from her chest onto his face and onto the flowers at their feet. Georgie lay beside him, lifeless.

For a moment he wasn't able to grasp what had happened.

He recognised the phut of the round as it left the silenced rifle but the location was wrong; this was the centre of London.

He pulled Jane down into his arms. He was shaking. He stared at her face. Her pallid complexion told him everything.

Involuntarily he let out a howl.

Harry slowly and deliberately slid the rifle back behind the seats and moved back into the driver's seat. He selected a gear and without indicating moved off smoothly behind a passing car. He took the first exit out of the square into Greek Street. There was one car in front of the car he had followed, and as they approached a junction another car pulled out in front of them. He realised he would be the fourth car in the queue when they stopped at the crossing with Old Compton Street.

There was nothing he could do about it.

Branen tried to makes sense of what had happened. He wanted to rewind time. He stared at their blood-soaked, distorted bodies. Valuable seconds passed before he could gather his thoughts and force his body to react.

Through the trees and bushes he saw a scruffy red car pulling away. Then it disappeared behind parked cars. The direction of the shot and the trajectory of the round was low because it had gone through Jane and Georgie's bodies and hit the shed above his head. There were no open windows in the office block opposite and no apparent low shooting position. The only possibility was the car.

He realised he had nothing to gain by staying where he was. He sprinted across the square to where the car had been and turned right out of the gates following the direction of the traffic. He was covered in blood and running like a madman down the middle of Greek Street.

The red car was caught in a queue of traffic and he was going to catch up with it. He couldn't see the number plate. There was a yellow Volkswagen directly behind it. He couldn't see enough of the red car to identify the make. Was it a Nissan, a Datsun or a Toyota? He couldn't tell. Vehicle identification hadn't been part of his job for a long time.

Through its rear window he could see a bulky man sitting in the driver's seat. Could this be the fat man who had followed him? Branen started to rehearse in his head what he was going to do when he caught up with the car. The driver was armed, certainly with a rifle which would be useless when he got close enough to open the door; he wouldn't be able to turn and aim it. If he had another weapon he would have to deal with the situation as it developed. He would use the back offside passenger door and would have the advantage of being directly behind the driver.

As Branen reached the corner with Bateman Street, at a full sprint, a pedestrian came out between two parked cars on his left. He tried to avoid him, slipped and slid under a car exiting the junction. The nearside front wheel trapped his lower left arm and the car stopped as the bumper banged against his head, leaving him concussed. But the adrenalin enabled him to free his arm and get to his feet.

Seeing Branen covered in blood the African mini-cab driver stepped back and leaned heavily on the bonnet of his car.

"You okay man?"

Branen observed through eyes and heard through ears that were deep inside his head, "Leave me alone." Turning to look down Greek Street, he saw that his quarry had disappeared. He staggered down Bateman Street trying to work out what he should do, where he should go. The excruciating pain in his arm stretched right up to the shoulder, but it did not feel broken.

The pedestrian he had avoided came after him.

"You need help."

"Leave me alone." But he was right, he needed help.

As Harry crawled in the queue to cross Old Compton Street he heard the squeal of tyres fifty or more metres behind him. In his mirror he saw a man getting out of a car.

As far as he was concerned it had been a good hit; her father was dead. He had no idea Branen had got so close to him.

Branen realised that he had to make cover without drawing attention to himself. He could not return to Jane. She was dead and there was nothing else he could do for her. They would find his coat and beret but fortunately he hadn't left anything identifiable in the pockets. They would establish the DNA from hair samples on the collar, but as far as he knew they did not have his DNA on record. His robbery conviction had been before they began taking swabs. Eye-witnesses and the angle of the bullet wound would provide evidence that he was not the shooter, even if he had run away. His shirt was covered with Jane's blood and his best bet was to behave like a vagrant who had fallen over drunk.

At the first street bin he stuck his head in and rummaged around. He found a beer bottle, and in the bottom someone had emptied a car ashtray. He found the biggest dog-end, a cigar butt, stuck it in his mouth and staggered across Frith Street, singing loudly, taking the occasional swig from the empty bottle and deliberately occupying the centre of the pavement. People stepped aside as he lurched towards them. Even covered with blood it was his best chance of blending in. As he approached Dean Street a police car, siren screeching, went past the junction. The trauma of the shooting had hit him hard and he started to go into shock. He sat down in a doorway trying to pull himself together.

A voice broke through his dizziness. "What d'you think you're doing? Get the fuck out of here."

He looked like a waiter. Branen pushed back against the wall and tried to lift himself up. As he got to his feet he realised he was in the entrance of a restaurant. His first reaction was anger, but not wanting to draw any more attention to himself mumbled, "I'm on my way, mate."

The waiter grabbed Branen by the shoulders and rushed him along the pavement. Branen stumbled but didn't fall. With his new-found power the waiter kept on pushing him. Branen could have knocked him over but instead he let him push him to the end of the street. He didn't know if the man was put off by the amount of blood on him, or if he sensed that Branen wasn't afraid, but he gave him one final shove, shouted, "Fuck off," puffed up his chest and strode back to his restaurant.

Branen made a mental note to go back and eat there one day.

66. HARRY : (MIDDAY, THURSDAY 12 NOVEMBER)

Harry drove over to Golden Square and found a residents' parking bay.

Golden Square was the smart face of Soho. The properties were well maintained with twenty-four hour security and occupied by established media and advertising businesses. His car would be safer there. All the same he removed the front of his radio and locked the steering wheel with a security clamp he kept in the boot. His car was scruffy and undesirable from a thief's point of view, particularly when surrounded by expensive limousines. He locked the rifle and the cash in the boot; safer than keeping them back at his flat. He was elated by his morning's work.

He stopped for a coffee in the Modern Café on Lexington Street. He sat in a corner, his back to the wall and with a clear view of the entrance. He needed to make a plan. He felt a weight had been lifted from his shoulders. All his attention had to be on recceing his shot, completing the assignment, getting his money and disappearing. He enjoyed observing the young fashionistas, dressed like tramps as far as he was concerned, as they drank their coffees and spouted their loudly proclaimed opinions on everything from film and politics to their careers.

He relaxed for a while, listening to them. He revelled in the satisfaction of his rediscovered power delivered from behind a .243 calibre rifle; he was strong and people would have to step aside for him.

After an hour of silently revelling in the success of the beautifully crafted termination of Carrie's father, Harry walked back to Soho Square. He tried to enter from Carlisle Street but found the police had closed all the roads into the square. He turned back, cut through to the top of Greek Street and stood at the entrance to St. Barnabas's behind the police barrier, amongst the small crowd that had gathered there watching.

The crowd were talking of a shooting and rumours of a witness; the gardener who hung out in the shed in the centre of the square. A woman on the steps of St. Barnabas's was holding forth and announced that a policeman had told her a woman and child had been shot and they were looking for a drug dealer who was seen running away. Harry was sure she had got her information wrong; he had killed the man. He noticed the woman was standing close to the position he anticipated the Prime Minister would be in on Saturday, the day after tomorrow.

He moved close to her. From that point of view he looked for a possible sniping position. Turning through a full three hundred and sixty degrees, he realised his best vantage point would be from a roof top. Directly above was too close and too acute. The view from the north across the square was obstructed by trees. Looking south down Greek Street there were well over a hundred windows overlooking the entrance to St. Barnabas's.

Trying to be inconspicuous he spent fifteen minutes slowly analysing each roof and window, rejecting one after the other. Either the angle was too acute or there was no background cover to stop him being silhouetted against the sky.

Finally he noticed three windows about a hundred metres down Greek Street, on the first, second and third floors above a record shop on the junction of Bateman Street. The corner where earlier, unknown to Harry, Branen had slipped and fallen under the mini-cab.

The building had a flat roof with a balustrade around it offering cover against the sky. The windows were on a forty-five degree angled brick face that cut off the corner of the block. All three windows were only just visible, being partially obscured by the building on his side, the north side of Bateman Street. The top window would give him the best angle of view and would avoid his having to shoot from the roof.

He stood for a while, facing south and away from the crowd, considering the angle of fire. He estimated that the shot was about a hundred metres and high enough to allow him to shoot over the heads of the Close Protection Officers and any surrounding civilians. He had to allow for the possibility that he might only get a head shot if the PM's body was obscured by the crowd. In the late afternoon at that time of year, if the sun was shining, from his shooting position facing north it would be setting to his left and would be to his advantage. At that distance with the scope he had been given, a head shot would not be difficult. He might use the sound moderator but even if he didn't, the echo within Greek Street enclosed by four-storey buildings would bounce around to such a degree that the source would be impossible to determine.

Harry walked back down Greek Street towards the junction, quietly counting his strides. He wanted to be seen by passers-by as an eccentric philosopher, head down meditating on the works of Sophocles, while in his deluded mind he was an undercover assassin employed to eliminate a rogue Prime Minister.

He established that it was almost exactly one hundred metres from the door of St. Barnabas to the window on the corner building. There were two red backlit 'MODEL' signs in the 1st and 2nd floor windows. But the top floor room, the one he wanted to use, appeared empty from the street. The front door was wide open, revealing a corridor leading to a flight of stairs. A hand scrawled cardboard sign read, 'Swedish Model – top bell / Italian Model – bottom bell'. At the junction with Old Compton Street there was a CCTV camera surveying Greek Street. The entrance to the tarts' flats was out of sight from St. Barnabas's and not watched by cameras; it was ideal for his retreat. He went into Bar Valentino opposite and sat in the window with a mug of tea staring up at his chosen building. The lack of recce time brought with it inherent risks and the danger of a cock-up. He had learnt that planning and preparation were crucial to success as a sniper.

From the safety of the café Harry looked up at the top window of the building. 'That...' he decided, '...is my firing position.'

67. BRANEN & COSTAS :
(MIDDAY, THURSDAY 12 NOVEMBER)

Branen needed cover and quickly.

His hotel was only a few hundred yards away but it meant going through the centre of Soho, which involved crossing a crowded Shaftesbury Avenue. He was covered in blood and couldn't risk the exposure. Then he remembered the alley running behind Costas's Lounge. Hoping he would not bump into the police, he crossed Dean Street and carried on with his drunken charade through Meard Street to Wardour Street. It was only a short walk but he didn't feel safe until he had entered the alleyway.

Costas's flat was above his bar, up a metal fire-escape on the first floor. It was midday when Branen banged on the security door. There was no answer. He guessed Costas was cussing in the kitchen, preparing brunch for his patients. He would open up the Lounge in the morning when his regulars arrived for their hangover breakfasts.

Branen was freezing and in shock. He slumped down in the corner of the metal landing. He couldn't be seen easily from the alley. He had been lucky to get here without being stopped, and dared not stay out in the open any longer than necessary. The lee of Costas's building offered little shelter from the icy wind and rain, and he slipped into a semi-comatose state.

68. SNOWMAN & COSTAS :
(AFTERNOON, THURSDAY 12 NOVEMBER)

Branen was still slumped on the fire escape when Snowman decided to visit Costas.

The club was quiet; it was the postprandial period between lunch and early evening drinks. The regular middle-aged couple was asleep on the same sofa to one side, the man now wearing a Panama hat and cuddling another champagne bottle. His head was resting on his small, carrot-haired partner, who was snoring with her mouth wide open. In the corner on one of the sofas sat three women whose conversation was becoming increasingly animated.

Melissa, Costas's buxom paramour, was slumped at the piano looking moody but not playing. Charlie, whose bar stool had become perfectly formed to his buttocks, sat in his usual place making indecent suggestions to Melissa and teasing Jack behind the bar.

Snowman hesitated inside the entrance. Looking through the glass door he saw Costas playing backgammon with Jack. Costas's Lounge was a valuable venue for Snowman because it was frequented by Soho's well-off showbiz crowd. He had already annoyed Costas and he did not want to permanently queer his pitch for future trading.

Costas's sixth sense made him look up from the board as Snowman sauntered in and leaned casually on the bar. The three women, who had drunk their lunch, turned to stare at the unusual-looking man.

Jack reluctantly went over to serve him. "What can I get you?"

After his conversation with Branen and the fracas in the cloakroom Costas was not pleased to see him.

"Just a beer," said Snowman, trying to look unconcerned.

Costas got up, lit a cheroot and moved behind the bar. "This is a private club... you're not a member."

"Since when has that mattered?"

"Since the Greeks pushed the Italians out of Soho."

Looking bewildered, Snowman said, "I'm not Italian."

"But I am Greek," said Costas.

Snowman was running out of patience. "Who's that fucking bloke who jumped me?"

"I've no fucking idea."

Jack stopped pouring the beer and put the glass on the bar.

Through a haze of alcohol Charlie, sensing the tension, peeled himself up off his stool. "I say old man…"

Snowman turned his stare on Charlie.

Charlie climbed back onto his seat.

Costas dropped a hand under the counter and reached for a sawn off pick-axe handle.

"What do you want him for?" asked Jack.

Snowman moved up the bar towards Costas, picked up a wine bottle and smashed it on the bar. He grabbed Costas by the throat and pressed the broken glass into his face.

"Don't fuck with me… lift your hands where I can see them."

Costas slowly lifted both hands.

"Where is he?" asked Snowman.

Jack smiled nervously at Snowman and pulled his mobile out.

"Don't even dream about it, arsehole," said Snowman and turned back to Costas. "Who was that bloke… where's he from?"

Snowman pushed the sharp glass between Costas's lips and slid it slowly to one side of his mouth. "If you don't tell me there'll be an accident… they'll burn you and your fucking club."

Blood began to trickle down Costas's chin.

Melissa left the piano and tried to push between Snowman and Costas. "What's the problem, big boy? You can see he doesn't know."

"Okay, do it the hard way… there's a lunatic out there who doesn't want you giving the bloke sanctuary. I'll be back and I want a name and an address." Snowman dropped the bottle and pushed past Melissa.

They stood in silence and watched him leave.

"Bloody freak," said Costas as he wiped the blood from his mouth.

Charlie turned to Jack. "Bravo… get him… and me a large brandy."

69. HARRY : (AFTERNOON, THURSDAY 12 NOVEMBER)

After the recce Harry returned to his flat.

The promise of fifty grand and the idea of living on a beach in the Caribbean suited him. If he ran short of cash he could always execute the occasional freelance mission for the hermaphrodite. He looked around; there wasn't much he really valued or wanted to keep. He put a few clothes into a hold-all and decided to go shopping.

As he passed the tarts' building he checked that they were still open for business, and after stopping for a coffee he made his way to Tin Pan Alley.

He browsed around for a while in Andy's Guitars. Having measured several guitars, he established that bass guitars were longer than normal, and about the same length as his rifle. Without the sound-moderator the Tikka rifle was one hundred and fifteen centimetres long.

He faffed around measuring cases, until the assistant asked, "What do you want it for... a machine gun?"

The question caught him unawares. "No, smart-arse, I've got a Fender Precision bass guitar."

"Wow," he said, looking like he didn't believe him.

Harry bought a case and strolled back to his car in Golden Square. Bent double inside the boot of his car, he fitted the rifle neatly into the case.

Then he walked back to his flat with it slung over his shoulder.

70. BRANEN & COSTAS :
(EVENING, THURSDAY 12 NOVEMBER)

Branen was soaking wet, and through the fog of his semi-conscious state he heard bolts being dropped and felt the metal security door being pushed open against him.

He didn't know how long he had been there but it was dark and the rain had turned to sleet.

The door was finally forced open and Costas, waste-bin in hand, came out onto the fire-escape. "Ben, my God... what's happened?"

From the expression on Costas's face Branen realised that he must look a mess. He tried to move his mouth to speak but nothing came out.

Costas lifted him up and pulled him inside. "You're freezing cold... shall I call an ambulance?"

The concussion had eased but Branen was hearing him as if through water; he shook his head. Costas dragged him onto the sofa where he sank into a disturbed sleep.

When he came to he was staring into the face of a blonde woman wearing a low cut top. Branen reckoned she had seen too many old Hollywood movies, because she was bathing his face with a flannel soaked in warm water.

"My name's Melissa, love. I'm a friend of Costas's..." She seemed to need to justify what she was doing. "I used to be a nurse."

'I bet you were,' he thought to himself.

Costas was standing behind her. "Can you sit up?"

He got up with Melissa's help. He was shivering like a drunk with a bad case of the DTs. They helped him to the bathroom, removed his bloody clothes and put him under a hot shower.

Costas gave him a tracksuit and back on the sofa they gave him a mug of tea. He refused the cigarette Melissa offered.

"I need to stay here tonight Costas... is that okay?"

Costas nodded, but looked troubled.

71. THE GARDENER : (THURSDAY, 12 NOVEMBER)

Eddie always wore his fake Barbour jacket, the waxed sheen worn down to the cotton base.

To enhance his image he had added an old leather belt round his middle and an army surplus scarf round his neck. His curly hair stuck out from the genuine Barbour hat he wore whatever the weather. The laces on his muddy boots were tied loosely so that he could slip them on and off with ease. He spent as much time as possible in The Basement Bar, just off Soho Square, where he would repeatedly tell anyone prepared to listen, "Sometimes I sit and think, and sometimes I just sit."

That was until the bullet thumped into his shed and gave him something new to discuss with his friends. He was the gardener and the first person on the scene of the shooting. In fact, he was at the scene before the shooting. Eddie was skiving, watching his tiny portable TV, locked inside the shed in the centre of the square. He had his boots off and his feet up when the bullet thumped into the shed's wooden frame and dumped a century of dust on top of him and his television set. His first concern was that the television had survived the assault. He thought someone had attacked the shed with a baseball bat. By the time he had pulled his boots on and peered out of the door, Branen was sprinting towards the garden gate.

The scene that confronted Eddie turned his stomach. The baby was at his feet. If it had not been for the blood running from its tiny body he would have mistaken it for a doll. His knees went weak and he regretted his fried breakfast. He saw Branen's profile as he swung through the wrought iron gate onto the street.

Eddie stood there staring at the carnage. The woman's body was kneeling face down on the bench, a bloody hole in her back and with an arm out-stretched towards the baby. He could not comprehend what he was looking at. He could not even reach for his mobile to call the emergency services; he just picked up the blood soaked bunch of flowers.

It was cold and there were hardly any people in the square. The only other potential witness was a homeless man who was sitting on one of the park benches that stood along the path Branen had run down. He was smiling and singing to himself when the police tried to interview him. Having consumed several Special Brews, he didn't even know the shooting had happened.

The police interviewed Eddie and took a detailed description of the back of Branen. Later on when Eddie had recovered his composure he remembered the three-quarter profile view of the fugitive he'd seen from fifty metres away. With help from the police and a degree of intuition and luck, he produced a reasonable e-fit representation of Branen's face.

The mini-cab driver who had run over Branen was eventually traced by the police and with his help a remarkably accurate e-fit was produced.

72. THE SOHO GAZETTE :
(AFTERNOON, THURSDAY 12 NOVEMBER)

The Soho Gazette was delivered to the newsagents at 5am on Friday mornings.

This Thursday, because of breaking news about the murder in Soho Square, the editor had been forced to delay the print-run until the last moment. It was a rare occurrence to be able to hold the presses. He loved the feeling. It made him a real newspaper man, an acknowledged editor, a man on whose decisions the printing presses waited.

He was having to choose between two leading stories. He finally decided the murders should take precedence over the rally, or riot as he preferred to call it. The riot had followed Michelle de Lavigne's speech to the BNP the previous evening. It was a good story and affected Soho's future. After the speech at St. Barnabas's a gang of skinheads had paraded down Greek Street shouting racist chants and making fascist salutes. They had broken the windows of an Indian restaurant in Old Compton Street before the police had split them up.

He managed to find space to keep both stories on the front page, which would guarantee increased circulation that week.

73. BRANEN & COSTAS :
(EARLY HOURS, FRIDAY 13 NOVEMBER)

In the warmth of Costas's flat Branen started to thaw out.

He was tortured by the image of Jane's contorted body being flung forward over him. He kept feeling the warm blood as it ran down his face and the taste as it crept into his mouth. He could not sleep, so got up from the sofa and sat at the kitchen table. He was there for an hour, struggling to control his grief, when Costas appeared from the bedroom.

"What's happening Ben... what have you got yourself into?"

Branen took a deep breath. "After Carrie was killed I arranged to meet her mother, to tell her... you remember Jane? Someone tried to shoot me... but they got Jane instead... if only I hadn't given her my coat..."

"Was that the shooting in the square? Everyone was talking about it in the bar."

Branen nodded, but didn't want to discuss it anymore.

Costas put his arm round him. "Who did it?"

"I'm not sure..."

"Is this a hangover from prison?"

"No."

Realising that Branen didn't want to say any more, Costas said, "We've got a problem... I had a visit at lunchtime from Snowman. He's looking for you... wants to know who you are. He was told to warn me off by some lunatic and not to give you any shelter... the word he used was 'sanctuary'... not really a gangster's word is it? I told him I didn't know you... but he didn't believe me. He said he was coming back."

"Costas, I want to keep you out of this... it's not your problem... you don't need to get involved."

"It's too late... they've threatened me and the club."

Branen said, "They tried to kill me yesterday... but if they thought they'd shot me then why did they come to you after that?"

"Perhaps they knew they'd missed," said Costas.

"Unless they had an observer... the shooter couldn't know he'd missed... unless he saw me running after the car." Branen continued, "I don't want you involved any more than you have been. I've put you in danger by coming here. I know you'd do anything for me but I can't take advantage of that... but you are the only person I can ask to help arrange Carrie's funeral... would you do that?"

"Yes."

Branen stood up and hugged him. "Thanks Costas. If I stay here we'll both be sitting targets... we won't stand a chance."

Costas held on to him. "I'm not like you Ben, I can't hide... I've got this place... but if there's any other way I can help."

Branen had a wash and shave and as he left he caught his reflection in the mirror. With the trilby and overcoat from Costas he looked like a well-dressed vagrant.

Costas watched Branen go. Friday the thirteenth had dawned and Costas felt uneasy.

PART THREE

74. BRANEN : (DAWN, FRIDAY 13 NOVEMBER)

Branen decided to go straight back to Hotel California.

As he walked through the early morning streets he was physically and emotionally drained. He was hungry but didn't want to eat. He thought about Jane's man and how he would feel when he heard he had lost her and Georgie. He wondered why the sniper had been waiting for him in Soho Square and how he knew he had arranged to meet Jane there? He had rung her from the Empire Room and was sure no-one could have overheard him. The sniper had mistaken Jane for him, which meant he couldn't have seen him give her his overcoat and beret. This was strange because a professional would have had the shot planned and prepared, possibly with a spotter, and they would have been in place well in advance. A spur-of-the-moment shot from a car left far too much to chance. This wasn't a professional hit. He could not imagine the Firm or The Associates being involved in such an incompetent attempt on his life. He reckoned it was a lone sniper shooting from a car. It had to be a chance encounter.

Who had sent the fat man to follow him and who had employed the shooter in the square? Was it the same man? Were they trying to stop him following up on Carrie's murder? The only way they could have known about his existence would have been by observing him through the beehive camera or if they had been tipped off by the Firm. But the Firm would never delegate such a sensitive wet-job to a bunch of amateurs. More questions and so far no more answers.

He stopped at a café on the corner of Wardour Street. There were a couple of tables on the pavement. He ordered two coffees and sat out in the weak sunshine. He had his back to the window so that he could observe the street. He pulled the brim of the hat down to hide his face.

The sun was low in the east and cut hard shadows down Peter Street, reflecting off a puddle of water left by the café owner when he sluiced down the pavement earlier.

As he sat there contemplating the two cups of coffee he dug up forgotten memories. He recalled the good times with Jane. Up all night at 100 Oxford Street and on to Ronnie's, only to turn out onto the street at dawn, to have breakfast and a cup of coffee, in this same café, at this table, waiting for Berwick Street market to come to life. They bought food from the stall-holders so that when they woke up later in the day they'd have something to eat. No responsibilities. Just them; the innocence and the simplicity of their life together; the lack of conniv-ance and duplicity that was to pervade his life later on.

A young woman sat down at the table next to him. She smiled. He was gazing at her when she was joined by a young man on a bicycle wearing sunglasses that had grown on him. They kissed and laughed together, leaving him to remember how it had once been.

There were two scenarios for Carrie's murder: either The Associates was responsible, in order to lure him back to London; unlikely because he was not a threat to them while Carrie was alive. Or more likely, Carrie had got mixed up with Group X through Snowman, who then found out that she was not kosher and killed her. This could explain the amateur attempt on his life which had killed Jane.

Now that Carrie was dead, as far as The Associates was concerned he was a loose cannon. They could not risk eliminating him in a friendly foreign country, so they had used the Firm to bring him over on the pretext of sorting out Carrie's murder and in doing so he might even resolve their problem with Group X. Whatever the outcome, The Associates would eventually have to get rid of him and the odds of survival were stacked heavily against him.

If he disposed of Snowman and the Associates hung him out to dry, the police would believe that his motive was revenge for his daugh-ter's murder; he would be the fall guy. He also reckoned that the Firm was controlling him without knowing about his previous involvement with The Associates or the Paris assignment. The Firm had its own disposals department and its operatives were very efficient; they had generations of experience. But the Controller never spoke to him as though she knew he was under a death sentence. He guessed that she saw him as an agent forced upon her to help solve the problem before he disappeared over the horizon.

He didn't know how much the Firm knew about his arrival or his escape routes, but he had to assume the worst and stay hidden to survive.

Although the streets were still quiet, he decided not to sit around for too long in case they had people out there looking for him. The couple got up to leave and pushed past his table as though he was not there.

He yearned to be back on his small-holding but he was driven to avenge the murders; he had to stay alive until then. He got up stiffly from the table and walked away. He was becoming too emotional and too sentimental to perform efficiently. He had to keep moving.

Soho still had and would always would have that unique village atmosphere. Throughout the dark hours its sleaziness soaked into the streets and buildings. In the early morning light it bled out of every orifice as if from a saturated sponge. That's why he loved it, and it was all the more apparent to him because he had been away for so long. He walked down Wardour Street to Tisbury Court. The contrast between the natural sounds and smells of his vineyards and the built-up refuse-strewn streets was particularly poignant. He had escaped the anxious existence of working for The Associates to the peaceful life of southern Europe, and now here he was back in this hostile urban world.

A bag lady stopped in front of him. She was wearing pink carpet slippers sticking out from below a full length, oversized raincoat. She was carrying enough luggage in plastic bags for a month on Capri. Staring deep into his eyes, she announced that he was her weight and speed.

He held out the change from his coffees. "How do I know you're not going to spend this on food?"

She put down the bags and took the coins. Looking him up and down, she handed back the money. "I think you need this more than I do, dear."

He approached Hotel California with a feeling of apprehension because he'd used the Firm's mobile from there. He didn't know if it was instinct or paranoia that fed his anxiety but he knew better than to ignore it.

75. THE CONTROLLER & THE SCS :
(EARLY MORNING, FRIDAY 13 NOVEMBER)

The Controller rarely lost her temper but she was under pressure from above and stressed out by the loss of one of her operatives.

She had lost contact with Branen and she hated not being in control of her agents, even if he did belong to someone else. Yesterday she had put a watcher on Hotel California but Branen had not returned or switched the mobile on again. She assumed he would want to stay in touch and had not expected him to keep the phone turned off. Now she had no idea where he was. To add to her frustration she had been contacted by the Chief, who told her to locate Branen urgently otherwise her desk was at stake. There was a new generation of graduates entering the service and the Controller's position was coveted by bright, ambitious new blood.

She called Antoinette, her researcher, into the room and slammed her fist down. "Get me all the CCTV footage of the Soho area... it's a village not a fucking metropolis. I want it reviewed now and I want him found."

Antoinette took a step backwards, "Have we got a photograph of him?"

"No. The Chief won't help us for some reason... he's too scared of the people upstairs and of losing his fucking pension..." said the Controller,"...now get me that footage."

"Ma'am, I think you ought to see this early edition of The Soho Gazette... it talks of a shooting in Soho Square yesterday... it wasn't mentioned on the news last night... but I wondered if it could be...."

The Controller grabbed the newspaper. It contained an e-fit picture of a man and reported that the police thought that the murders were related to a drug dispute. They were searching for the man to help them with their enquiries. The murdered woman's husband claimed he had no idea what his wife was doing in Soho Square that morning. He had left for work believing she was going shopping. He told the police about the phone call on Wednesday evening from his wife's previous partner. He only knew the man's first name, Benny, and so far the police had not been able to trace him.

At first the Controller was confused; could it be Branen? And why would he be involved in the murder of a woman and child in Soho Square?

She turned to Antoinette. "Well done... find out as much as you can about it... but whatever you do don't let the flat-foots suspect that we have any interest in it..." and holding up the Gazette she said, "...we've got this photofit in the paper and there a description of him here. Get on to the editor and find out if he's got any more details."

The recorded CCTV material from the previous week arrived within a couple of hours.

Antoinette briefed the other researchers. "Work backwards through the most recent footage... it will provide us with the most current information on Branen's whereabouts... we can look at the older stuff later. We haven't got much to work with."

Because there were only a few people around in the early morning's footage they found a possible suspect within an hour, recorded just after sunrise at a pavement café. They rushed the footage to the Controller and then carried on checking all the rest of the week's material.

Clearly visible on the camera was a man wearing a trilby hat, who could have been Branen, looking as if he was waiting for someone.

When the image was enlarged and enhanced the shadow cast by the brim of the hat made his identity uncertain. The description of the man seen running from the shooting could be the man in the blurred CCTV image and the Controller needed it to be Branen. Her career was at stake, so she took a gamble and showed her Chief the evidence. "At least I know where he was at sunrise this morning."

The Chief passed the information on to the Senior Civil Servant.

Pretending that it was not important the SCS said, "Just keep tabs on him."

Finding Branen was crucial to his plan because he was considering his options of where, when and how to delete him. He had three Operations Officers running companies and only one of them, the fruit and veg outfit, was suitably set up and based in London. This team was run by Dennis Leung.

The SCS knew that as soon as Branen had finished his work he would disappear. Leung would have to be ready to strike immediately.

There would be minimal pre-production time to identify the target, let alone plan the termination.

Completely unaware of the contract the SCS was preparing on Branen, the Controller briefed a team of watchers, including the one observing Hotel California. "I want an officer on every main street in Soho… saturate the area," she demanded.

"We don't have enough manpower, Ma'am… there must be a couple of thousand people in Soho. We only have six officers available at the moment."

"I want Branen to become dependent on us… we won't resupply him through the postbox at Giovanni's… when his money runs out he'll be in touch. Find him and follow him… I want constant updates on his location… and where he is sheltering at night."

The photograph, the e-fit picture and a description of Branen were issued to the watchers. All the Controller could do now was to wait.

76. DENNIS LEUNG :

Yee-Duk Leung wanted his son, Den-Fuk, to follow in his footsteps but at the same time wanted him to have a good education; something he never had.

When Den-Fuk was accepted at a public school in England, his father was sensitive enough to realise that his son would have to change his name to avoid ridicule from classmates.

With a little trepidation 'Dennis' Leung appeared in his smart new uniform on the first day at school. He excelled in many subjects and went on to university to read economics and become a rugby blue. After his graduation ceremony at Cambridge he was approached by a man who explained that because of his excellent qualifications and Chinese family connections he would like to offer him the opportunity to work for the Government. Dennis found the man a little too smooth but was intrigued by the offer and agreed to lunch with him the following day at the Garden House Hotel in Cambridge.

When Yee-Duk's son informed him that he had been offered a job in the Civil Service with the chance of promotion to a senior position, he was happy that his son would be joining the British Establishment because he considered a position in any Government to be very prestigious. Yee-Duk was a patient man and decided that there would be plenty of time in the future to initiate Dennis into the family business.

Dennis was a gregarious and sociable person and the idea of working for the British Government flattered his ego. After extensive psychological tests which revealed his aptitude for working under cover and his cool head under pressure, the SIS knew that they had a man who could offer them access to the secretive London Chinese community; this would prove to be invaluable over the next few years as China's worldwide industrial and financial influence increased.

After six months of intensive training, at SIS's instigation Dennis announced to his father that he wanted to leave the Civil Service and return to help run the family business. Yee-Duk was both disappointed that his son was leaving an esteemed job and at the same time pleased that his only child was joining him. He had no idea that Dennis was now an undercover officer for the Firm.

While he never really fitted into Chinese society Dennis was not completely comfortable with his English friends either. But he made sure he ingratiated himself with both communities by cultivating two contrasting personae. He threw extravagant parties and was careful not to mix the races. In each role he would have been unrecognisable to the other community. It enabled him to fulfil his Government brief without being suspected by the Triads. He saw his job with the Government as an opportunity to expand his father's business empire. If he made himself indispensable to the Secret Service he hoped they would overlook his involvement in crime, especially as his dealings only affected the Chinese community.

Over the next decade connections between the Chinese Embassy and the London 14K Triads developed into a significant problem for the British Government. Dennis had been working for the British Secret Service for fifteen years, successfully infiltrating and informing on his ethnic community, and was a crucial conduit into Chinese society.

When in the interest of British Government it became necessary to eliminate a particular Chinese official, Dennis came to the notice of the Senior Civil Servant. An insider with specialised skills was essential and Dennis was perfectly placed to become both an Operations Officer and an agent. It was decided by the SCS that he should be recruited to The Associates.

This action put MI5's nose out of joint. Relations between the Firm and the SCS became strained when they were forced to give up Leung without any explanation. They resented having him hijacked, and being kept in the dark about The Associates.

Telling his ageing father that he needed a sabbatical, Dennis disappeared for several months. He had excelled at sport at university and although this was fifteen years later, he had maintained his fitness and was able to complete the physical and weapons training demanded by The Associates.

At the age of thirty-six Dennis returned to his community a highly trained Government killer. Unlike other members of The Associates who were recruited and employed by specially formed commercial companies, Dennis already had his own company and therefore his cover story.

He developed his father's three storey row of warehouse buildings in Dansey Place into a super casino for the nouveau riche Chinese community. He introduced a harem of high-class prostitutes to his already lucrative mahjong school and lavish gambling den. And in the Triad tradition, he ran a side-line in protection rackets. It made the family business and him extremely rich. He was led to believe by the SCS that his present role within The Associates would allow him protection from the law. He gambled that his inside knowledge of the British Secret Forces would protect him from prosecution and enable him to strike a deal should the authorities ever decide to clamp down on his criminal activities.

His business and social activities meant that he led a twenty-four hour lifestyle, and to keep fighting fit he trained with a Wing Chun instructor every morning before work.

During the next eight years Dennis was to carry out several wet disposals within his community on behalf of the Government.

Without informing the Controller, it was Dennis to whom the Senior Civil Servant turned when he finally decided the time had come for Branen to be eliminated.

But before Dennis could be deployed they had to find Branen.

77. BRANEN & GIOVANNI :
(MORNING, FRIDAY 13 NOVEMBER)

Because he had used the Firm's mobile at the Hotel California Branen decided not to return there but to use his fall-back hotel in Chinatown.

The clothing he'd left at Hotel California wasn't essential and he needed to travel light. He had everything he would need in his belt-bag and he had to keep moving and use disguises whenever possible.

He had another old acquaintance who knew everything that went on in Soho, so he stopped off at Giovanni's deli.

Giovanni's father was from North Africa and his mother from Naples. When he was born they did not realise anything was wrong, but as other children grew, he didn't. He never cleared five feet. But what he lacked in height he made up for in other ways. He was not opposed to a little "back-handa" and ran one of Soho's most successful notice boards. "I sell the best tarts in the business," he would boast, holding up a bag of his mother's cakes. The girls liked Giovanni. At first he became their mentor, then their manager. At the beginning he dealt with general enquiries but as demand grew he saw the opportunity of becoming more involved and make more money. "Special tricks for special dicks" was his motto. He could procure any kind of sexual treats for select customers. He didn't make moral judgements and didn't ask questions, he just collected his percentage.

As trust in his discretion built, so did his customer base. Rumour had it that he had collected an infamous list of landed gentry and business-men, whose requests even he struggled to imagine. His girls would drop by for a chat and drink one of his coffees with added "Je ne sais quoi". Only Giovanni knew why he added French 'quoi' to Italian coffee. Transactions ranged from favours to financial and always ended up amicably resolved.

On the pavement outside the shop were his postboxes. There was a block of ten by seven lockable boxes at one end of the window. He rented out each box for £150 per year in cash, "No questions ask." Then he would forget who had paid for it: "After all, how can I remember seventy different faces?"

Should Branen need money or equipment, the Firm had given him the key to one of these postboxes. They could re-supply him without face to face contact. But he was sure it would be watched and that if he went to the box he would risk contact. He was taking a chance going to Giovanni's but dressed as he was, he considered it worth the risk. He needed information and what Giovanni didn't know about the comings and goings in Soho wasn't worth knowing.

Branen moved swiftly along the pavement and entered the shop keeping the hat pulled down. He wondered if Giovanni would remember his face. He shouldn't have doubted it.

Giovanni looked up from counting a pile of cash, "Hey, Benny boy...."

Branen remembered it wasn't only Jane who called him Benny; in fact, she had copied Giovanni.

"Hey, Benny boy, where you bin?" He stuffed the cash into his pocket and sprung down from an upturned crate.

He grabbed Branen's hand. "You looking pretty weary, Ben, what you bin up to?"

"Unfortunately not what you think," Branen said putting his arm round Giovanni's shoulder.

"Well fucka me man, good to see you... you just bin released?"

"Giovanni, that was nearly twenty years ago, and I got three years with good behaviour."

"Well, where the fuck you bin... you no come back to see me 'til now?"

"Well here I am."

"What you want... I can see sad in your eyes... what can Giovanni do for you?"

"A Gazette."

"You no want to talk?" asked Giovanni.

"Did you hear about the shooting in the square yesterday?" Branen asked.

"That paper you got is full of it," he said, holding up another copy, and there staring back at him was a photo-fit picture of himself. Someone must have got a good look at him.

"What's happening with the local elections?" Branen asked.

"Those National Front bastards... there's bin marches... my window broken. They call me a foreigner... a fuckin' foreigner, I live here all my life... or nearly."

"Who's their leader?"

"Michelle de Lavigne... good English name, eh...? Her friends call her Mikey... she bin in here, sometimes." He held up the newspaper showing a photograph of her, face distorted and arms aloft.

"Who is she?"

"Very rich... night clubs... property... they say she make her money from drugs. My girls they terrified of her. She has reputation... she hasn't stepped on my toes, but that's 'cos I'm not in her way."

"Where would I find her?"

"She got trendy flat in Soho Lofts... up Wardour Street."

Branen picked up a couple of sandwiches from the basket on the counter and handed him a five pound note.

"Thanks Giovanni," and he gave him a pat on the head, which Branen knew would annoy him. He couldn't trust Giovanni to keep his mouth shut.

Giovanni held up a copy of the Gazette and called after him, "You know Benny, he look like you."

Branen had just advertised the fact that he was in Soho. Soon the smoke signals would be going up and it would be on the village network. Was Michelle de Lavigne the lunatic Snowman had mentioned to Costas? Could she be the person connected with Group X that Carrie had written about in her notebook? And was she involved in the drug dealing and the other agenda the Controller had mentioned? If she was, she could be responsible for Carrie's murder. He was continually asking himself questions and had to find some answers.

Branen made his way back up Wardour Street to check out where Michelle de Lavigne lived.

He found the impressive building a hundred metres north of Old Compton Street. His best chance of spotting her was to keep watch on the entrance. He squatted down in Tyler's Court, a narrow passageway opposite the entrance to Soho Lofts. He settled in and ate his sandwiches, unfurled the newspaper and played the part of a vagrant; not too difficult at that moment.

On the front page 'Shooting in the Square' headlined above an article about 'The New Multi-millionaire BNP Candidate'. He read the report on Jane's shooting. The gardener claimed he had chased him out of the Square and he'd given a description of him which could have fitted a million other people, but the e-fit was pretty accurate. Apparently a mini-cab driver had also given a detailed description of him. He could barely bring himself to read the gory account of Jane and Georgie's murders. He had persuaded Jane to meet him when he could have told her about Carrie over the phone. He had drawn them in and was responsible for their deaths. He fought to control his despair.

Several passersby dropped coins into Costas's hat on the pavement in front of him. He was crouched down with his legs pulled up and his head resting on his knees. Even though he'd kept fit running over the hills near his vineyards, he ached all over. His arm and shoulder throbbed from the accident.

Eventually he slept: he was falling... below him stood Jane with Carrie... the tiny child he had left behind when he went to prison... they were staring up at him... he was flailing around and was falling very slowly... they were smiling at him... they kept going in and out of focus... his stomach was churning and he wanted to vomit. He descended, enveloping them into his darkness.

The next thing he knew there was a thump in his gut. He was lying on his side and there was someone standing over him pushing him with the sole of his boot.

"Do you want to discuss matters of importance?" The words were slurred and delivered in a broad northern accent.

All Branen could see was a brown leather boot standing close to his face; it had seen better days. His eyes tracked up a pair of dark trousers with frayed turn-ups to a dark overcoat. Sticking out of the top was an unshaven face with a fresh graze and a blue bruise in the middle of his forehead. His matted hair poked out from a skull cap.

"What?"

The figure, silhouetted against the sky, repeated himself. "Do you want to discuss matters of importance? If not fuck off!"

Bending down the figure held his face close to Branen's, his breath foul and thick with alcohol. "You're in my space and in my face, man... fuck off!"

Branen sat up. Even in his confused state he realised the threat the man presented was minimal. Branen continued his upward movement and thumped his elbow across the side of the tramp's head. He could have broken his nose but measured the blow just hard enough to knock him off his feet. The man rolled across the pavement in front of a couple of young women. They hesitated for a moment, staring at Branen.

"Charming," said one of them, as they stepped over the man and continued on their way.

The tramp was mumbling and pulling himself up onto all fours.

"Fuck off," Branen said between clenched teeth and just loud enough for him to hear.

The man looked carefully into his eyes and fucked off.

Branen needed to lift his spirits. A half bottle of whisky would be in character for his part as a vagrant and would fill the vacuum of waiting and hopefully deaden the physical pain; he was ever the optimist.

He already appeared drunk as he got to his feet. The couple of hours he'd spent crouched down on the cold pavement had left him partially immobilised.

He walked stiffly to Gerry's off-licence in Old Compton Street. The reception he got from the man behind the counter told him that he was not welcome. It was only the sight of the ten pound note that stopped him from throwing Branen out. He banged the half bottle of Scotch onto the counter and took the money.

Back at Tyler's Court his position was still vacant. The tramp had obviously thought better of it and conceded the space; at least temporarily. He sheltered from the cold wind and took a few long slugs of whisky. It began to work. He hoped desperately that Michelle de Lavigne had not left while he had been away.

Mikey spent the morning on the phone bullying and cajoling her way around her financial interests. She had left the apartment while Branen was away buying his whisky. She went over to Madame LuLu's to check the takings and go through the accounts before settling in at the bar for the rest of the afternoon and evening. She had an ulterior motive; she was feeling horny.

After a couple more hours of observation with no-one resembling Mikey leaving the building, Branen decided to cut his losses.

Apart from resting his body and getting drunk he had wasted five hours. He'd finished half the whisky and was hungry. He considered going back to Giovanni's to get something to eat but he knew he shouldn't have gone there in the first place; it was poor tradecraft and he'd been lucky to get away with it, but he had got Michelle de Lavigne's address.

The daylight was disappearing and it was getting colder. He decided to make his way over to Leicester Square. As he cut through Chinatown he saw a stall in Newport Place selling containers of chicken and rice. He sprinkled the chicken with sweet chilli sauce, and the hot food lifted his spirits.

After a wash and brush-up in the men's toilets in the square he looked and felt a whole lot better; he was ready to visit one of his old haunts that the Firm would not know about.

78. RONNIE SCOTT'S JAZZ CLUB :
(NIGHT, FRIDAY 13 NOVEMBER)

Branen had not been to Ronnie's for almost fifteen years.

If Errol had not been in reception he doubted that even in his cleaned up state he would have been allowed through the door.

Holding out a muscular arm Errol said, "Excuse me, sir," which did not mean excuse me at all. His eyes were friendly but there was a question mark behind them. Men like Errol who spent their lives dealing with the public understood body language better than any psychiatrist. He needed to understand why he was going to have to punch someone in the face.

Branen removed Costas's trilby and was engulfed in a bear hug. "Fuck me, man... Ben, where the fuck've you been, man?"

Branen flinched, his shoulder hurt. "Let go Errol..." He put him down. "I knew you always liked me, but take it easy."

Then the handshake made him wince; more by luck than judgement he had friends like Costas and Errol in his life; genuine, reliable and straight talking.

Errol stood back. "You're looking knackered, man."

"Just a bit, Errol... I've been busy."

"Come in, and have a drink," he said, as he pushed Branen through to the bar. The place hadn't changed; it was still painted matte black with circular wooden tables and rows of benches at the back. The walls were lined with black and white photographs of famous jazz musicians, some with an arm round Errol's shoulders. Small spotlights hung from the low ceiling, pointing at the stage. It brought back memories. It was bigger inside than it appeared from the outside and still had the same atmosphere.

It was early and the club was only about a quarter full. The usual mixture of people, the cool and the trying to be cool. Errol did not own the place but he was part of the fixtures and fittings. He loved a drop of liquor but that drop would lead to an ocean. Branen got a generous hand-poured whisky from a bottle that appeared then disappeared under the counter. They settled in at the corner of the bar and began to reminisce about the number of times they'd sat together in the same spot reminiscing.

An attractive, over-made-up woman, wearing a wrap-around top that did not leave much to the imagination and a wide belt instead of a skirt, pushed past Branen's shoulder and called to the bearded bartender.

The barman came over. "What can I get you?"

Errol always had an eye for a pretty girl. He undressed her in his mind and then looked around to check she was alone.

He leant over and hissed in Branen's ear, "She's with that dyke over there... maybe I can turn her."

Branen was stunned to see Michelle de Lavigne, smartly dressed in a man's suit and shirt, sitting at an adjacent table staring right at them. He turned away, hoping she hadn't noticed him.

Whisky and women were Errol's passions, and once he had the scent he would never let go of either. He leaned forward. "Let me buy you a drink.... what's your name?"

"Thank you..." She held out her hand. "I'm Sabrina, how do you do?"

"Well Sabrina, welcome to my club." Errol was straight into his stride.

Sabrina turned to the barman. "Can we have two daiquiris please?"

"Did you know the first daiquiri was made in the Floridita Bar in Havana for Ernest Hemingway?" asked Errol.

"What was the barman's name?" asked Sabrina.

"D'you know what's in a daiquiri, man?" The barman asked Sabrina.

"Rum, lemon juice and more rum... and I'm a woman," said Sabrina, rising to the occasion.

"You sound like my kind of woman," said Errol.

Sabrina was going to give as good as she got. "What's your kind of woman like?"

"To drink and fuck," said Errol smiling.

Sabrina picked up the daiquiris. "Well, you've bought the drink."

Errol just managed to say, "Would you like to join me for a drink later on?" before Sabrina gave him an 'I've heard it all before' look.

"Come on what have you got to lose?" Errol persisted.

"My virginity?" said Sabrina and started to walk away.

"If I walked like that I'd need talcum powder," said Errol, in an effort to have the last word.

Sabrina stopped and looked back over her shoulder, "If you walked like this you'd get fucked up the arse."

Shaking his head, Errol watched her sashay away.

Branen called to the barman. "We'd better have another couple of whiskies."

"Just like the old days," Errol said, still smarting.

Branen had sat for most of the day waiting for Mikey. And now after giving up, she had come to him. He decided he would wait until she left the club and follow her. He was not sure she would lead him to the truth, but the only other leads he had were Snowman and the beehive on the roof.

After the daiquiris Mikey and Sabrina started on champagne, and with Branen's help Errol finished the bottle of whisky. Branen had had enough alcohol to lessen the pain and loosen up his stiff joints. "Who's on tonight?" he asked Errol as the auditorium lights dimmed and four people came onto the stage. A young woman started singing.

"It's Kelly Angel... I persuaded senior management to give her a chance," he said, with feeling, "what a great voice... she's only been in London for a couple of weeks." He had obviously been counting the days.

Kelly was accompanied by a tenor sax, an acoustic guitar and a violin. She sang with a gravelly Janis Joplin voice. She was dressed in a blue, shiny dress. Errol was right about her.

At the end of the first set she got a standing ovation and disappeared through the door at the rear of the stage.

Errol sensed Branen's interest. "Would you like to meet her?"

"When she's finished the gig," he said, as casually as he could considering the amount of alcohol he'd consumed.

Errol nodded and winked at someone over Branen's shoulder and he turned to see Sabrina smile as Mikey led her out of the club.

Branen slid off the stool. "I'll be back in a moment."

He followed them out of the club. A cab was dropping off a couple directly outside and Mikey pushed Sabrina into the back of the taxi as the punters paid the driver through the window. The cab sped off up Frith Street leaving him standing there.

Back in Ronnie's he went down to the toilets. He ran a bowl of cold water and submerged his head. He stayed under until he was straining for air then he heard the door open.

Errol appeared, "Want a toot, mate?" he asked, holding out the wrap. Branen was not sure why he took it. He hadn't had coke in years, but anything that blunted the memory of the last few days was tempting. He needed a little oblivion even if it was only for a couple of hours.

Errol said he would see him in the bar and left him alone.

He looked in the mirror; he was knackered. He confirmed to his reflection, "You've ad libbed it... and fucked up." He was disappointed in himself. He was drunk and losing the plot. Confidence in his own ability had got him out of difficult circumstances in the past. If he was going to find those murdering bastards he had to concentrate.

Back in the bar Errol was distracted by Kelly Angel, who was sitting in Branen's seat.

"Kelly, I'd like you to meet an old friend of mine... Ben... but don't believe anything he tells you," said Errol, getting up and pulling up another stool.

Branen offered them both a drink.

"A glass of champagne, please," said Kelly, with a southern Irish lilt.

"These are on me," said Errol. "Anyone seen my barman?"

The barman popped up from behind the bar, wiping his nose.

Errol pointed at the white powder on his moustache. "Leave that shit alone and get me a glass of champagne."

"Please?" said the barman, wiping his mouth.

He spun a champagne flute into the air, caught it and pulled out a bottle of champagne.

"Don't bugger about, just pour it," said Errol.

"Any chance of my wages?" asked the barman.

"They're up your nose," said Errol, and handed the champagne to Kelly.

She turned and looked Branen straight in the eye. "Cheers."

He had not felt that frisson for a long time, not since Jane. It took him by surprise. She was about twenty and wearing a cocktail dress. She had long shiny black hair with dark almond shaped eyes and olive skin. She wore minimal make-up and had an aura of vitality. Whether it was aimed at him he wasn't sure, but it was there all the same.

"Do you live in Soho?" he asked her.

She turned the question round on him. "Why do you ask... do you?"

"Yes... kind of."

"Me too."

He had walked straight into that cul-de-sac and was none the wiser. He had nowhere to sleep that night and he did not want to end up on the streets. It was cold and wet and he needed to stay out of sight. The idea of her company seemed like a great way to spend the evening.

"Are you doing another set?" he asked.

"Yes."

"Then what?"

"Then I've got to wash my hair," she said.

"Perhaps I could hold the towel for you."

She was gracious enough to laugh. "Maybe... if I haven't got a headache." She finished her champagne and disappeared into the dressing room.

"Losing your touch?" Errol asked.

Branen shook his head. "I don't get out as much as I used to."

79. HARRY : (NIGHT, FRIDAY 13 NOVEMBER)

Harry's plan was simple enough. The tarts might not open up for business on Saturday, so he had to be in position before they closed for the night.

It had been drummed into him at sniper school. 'Don't over compli-cate, keep it simple, there's less to go wrong'.

It was fifteen years since he had been fully operational and, like Branen, he had lost the edge his training had given him. All missions had an element of chance and in an effort to increase the odds in his favour Harry spent the evening going over and over the scenario, trying to calculate where there could be problems or unpredictable moments that would need improvisation. Planning helped to stop him from thinking about the repercussions of what he was about to do, and from losing his nerve.

He had left his car in Golden Square and did not want to walk through Soho carrying the rifle in the guitar case straight after the shooting, so he collected the Datsun and drove back praying for a parking space in the residents' bay opposite his flat. He took it as a good omen when he found a gap by his front door.

Back in the flat he searched the chest of drawers and found a pair of stockings left behind after one of his sessions with a woman obtained for him by Giovanni. There was still a trace of her perfume on them; he shivered at the smell.

His training had taught him survival and evasion techniques. He'd learnt to live rough and wait for his target without leaving any trace of his presence. He packed the guitar case with all his equipment including cling film, an empty bottle to urinate in and a lead bag used for taking exposed film through customs X-ray machines. He also packed the Qur'an the hermaphrodite had given him and half a dozen Mars bars. He had to be able to eat, drink and defecate without leaving any evidence. He hid a kitchen knife down his sock and tucked the black-jack into his belt. He pocketed latex gloves, his vodka and mead mix and his drugs. He didn't plan to fall asleep.

At exactly midnight he set off along Bateman Street wearing his straw hat and with the guitar case over his shoulder; it was a misty November night.

He passed the tarts' doorway where he was going to return to in an hour. The door was open and there was a red light glowing in the corridor; the hand-scrawled message was still pinned to the door frame. He hesitated on the far side of Greek Street watching the entrance. He was wondering if he should go straight up. There might still be a punter with one of them or the girl on the top floor might not be working late that night. Normally her light was turned off by 1am, which was still half an hour away. Harry stood there trying to make up his mind when a young man in a dishevelled suit and tie came out of the entrance. He was greeted by another man who threw his arms round him then led him away giggling. Harry was about to cross over when another customer appeared and pressed the doorbell. He was taken aback; he had not realised someone else had been watching and waiting. He was irritated with himself, his lack of field practice was showing. He told himself, 'Stick to the plan.'

Bar Valentino was open late and from there he would have a view of the models' front door. He decamped there, waiting until he thought the girls might close for business. He'd brought a paperback about a sniper with him. With the dust-jacket from another book it appeared that he was reading Ulysses.

He had not been sitting in the café long when a stocky man in a raincoat walked in; he was the man Harry had just seen entering the girls' door. He looked official, which was out of character in the early hours on a Saturday morning in Soho.

When the man reached the counter a steaming mug of tea was already waiting for him.

"Evening Officer," said Valentino, who had met the policeman the previous day when he had been on the initial recce. "Here, have a winter warmer." He pulled a bottle of cheap brandy from below the counter and topped up the tea with a generous measure.

It was then that Harry realised his mistake. Of course they would check out the area in advance of the Prime Minister's visit. He wanted to kick himself, his heart went into overtime, the sweat instantly broke out on his face.

"How's it going?" Valentino asked the man.

"I had to tell the girls opposite that they couldn't trade tomorrow... I wasn't popular."

"You're lucky you got out alive, Guv... they sometimes come in here... they're tough girls."

"You bet." The officer picked up his tea and turned to survey the café.

The officer chose the table in the window where Harry was sitting.

"Evening," he said to Harry with a smile.

Harry mumbled back and stared into his book.

The copper cast an eye over his table companion, noticing the straw hat and the guitar case leaning against the wall beside him. The guitar case was nothing out of the ordinary. He was a local Special Branch policeman and was used to seeing musical instruments being ferried around the streets. Musicians were always hanging around Soho in the early hours, often left over from a late night gig.

The officer squinted slightly to read the cover of the book.

"I always thought that Leopold Bloom offered a view of the future... don't you?" asked the copper, uninvited.

Harry was forced to look up and acknowledge the comment even if he had no idea what the man was talking about.

"Yes," said Harry, guessing and hoping the copper was talking about his book.

"Is that an abridged version you're reading?"

Harry was completely out of his depth. He smiled weakly. His heart was going into overdrive and the palpitations were showing on his neck. He thought he'd planned for every eventuality, that he would be able to deal with the unpredictable, but this was totally unexpected and becoming extremely dangerous.

Dismissing the man's attitude as drug or alcohol induced, the officer asked himself, 'What is a drunk musician doing trying to read Ulysses at one o'clock in the morning?'

Harry had a tremendous urge to get up and run away. His face was flushed and the perspiration was dripping from his chin. He was afraid the buzzing was about to start and this added to his anxiety. He might lose control and ruin everything. His physical reaction had not gone unnoticed by the officer, who continued to dismiss it as alcohol induced.

Valentino broke into the officer's thoughts. "Would you like a top-up, Boss?"

The copper got up and went over to the counter.

With the pressure temporarily reduced, those few seconds gave Harry his chance to pick up his guitar case, reach the door, shout, "Thanks," to the owner and slip out before the policeman could take any further action.

But it had left a question in the officer's mind. He had noticed that the dust-jacket did not fit the book. It was, he thought, likely to be covering up pornographic material. Combined with the man's obvious anxiety, the questions were stacking up and fuelling his suspicions.

He went over to the door and watched Harry's retreating back as he headed up Greek Street towards Soho Square, slowly being enveloped by the mist. Should he stop the musician? He decided not to bother and let the door close. He went back to the counter. Then too late, changed his mind and set out after him.

In an effort to be less conspicuous Harry removed his hat then looped back down Frith Street from the square. He was unaware his change of direction had saved the mission. The policeman had entered Soho Square from Greek Street and carried on towards Oxford Street, assuming his prey had continued north.

Harry approached the tarts' entrance from the blind side of the café and tucked himself into the same doorway the copper had used. He noticed the smell of thrice-fried cooking oil that had permeated his clothes in the café. He carefully peered out from his refuge round the brick portico. The windows of the café were obscured by patches of condensation but he could see enough to be sure the copper had gone. He looked back in the direction he had come from. The Carlisle pub on the opposite pavement a couple of doors up from the tarts' front door was closed. Crowded into the doorway four youths were completing a deal. They all wore baggy jeans with hoodies. They were too busy to notice him.

He was keyed up, adrenalin coursing through his body. Now that he was in operational mode he saw everything around him as though for the first time. The decision to move was made for him. In the corner of his eye he saw the red back-lit 'Model' signs in the first and second floor windows being turned off. Then the red light in the entrance went out. He saw a movement in the darkened doorway. The tart was taking down the hand written sign and closing the street door.

Calling out, "Excuse me!" he dashed into the road. The prostitute pushed the door closed. In his rush Harry stepped off the kerb, straight in front of a taxi. The squeal of tyres caused the prostitute to open the door and peer round it. Harry froze in the headlights then leapt across the road with an athletic ability not normally associated with a big man.

The driver shouted, "Drunken fucker," and the tart closed the door.

Harry knocked gently on the door and in a reassuring tone said, "Excuse me," again.

"Fuck off, I'm knackered," said the tart through the door.

'Very nice,' Harry thought to himself, but he had to persevere.

"Last bit of business for the night darling?" begged Harry, "I'll pay anything you like for a bit of loving."

The tart slipped on the security chain and opened the door.

"It'll cost you top whack if you want me to open up for you," she said, missing the innuendo.

Harry reached into his coat pocket and pulled out a bunch of twenties and fifties. "Are you the Swedish Model?"

The tart's eyes lit up. "Yes love... pay me first, then I'll let you in."

"How about one hundred?" asked Harry meekly.

Realising she could make real money out of this last trick, she said optimistically, "Make it two hundred."

Harry did not want to spend any more time on the street in case he was noticed. He was prepared to give her anything he had, but he didn't want to raise her suspicions by agreeing too easily. "How about one hundred and fifty for half-an-hour?"

"Okay darling... you're my last one."

'You don't know how right you are,' Harry thought to himself, as he counted out the money and pushed it through the gap.

She slipped open the security chain and let him into the darkened hallway. "Nice coat," she said and started up the stairs.

Harry followed her, mesmerised by her muscular, swaying arse, encased in skin-tight red satin hot pants.

He reached down and pulled the knife from his sock and put it into his coat pocket.

80. KELLY ANGEL & BRANEN :
(EARLY HOURS, SATURDAY 14 NOVEMBER)

By the time they had finished the bottle of champagne it was time to go.

Branen told her he had nowhere to stay and explained how much she needed to be walked home and how much he needed a cup of coffee.

She had a first floor flat above a deli which looked out over Old Compton Street.

"What do you do for a living?" she asked.

"I've got a smallholding."

"What, in Soho?"

"Yeah sure, in the middle of the square."

Kelly went into her kitchen and opened the fridge. He followed her.

"Where do you live?" she asked.

"Abroad."

"Where?"

"Down south."

"South where?"

"Southern Europe."

"Why are you so secretive?"

"Am I?"

"What are you doing here?" she asked.

"You said I could walk you home."

"No, I meant in Soho."

"Looking for someone."

"Who?"

"You?"

"Tell me why you're in London."

"I had to come here... I have to sort out some personal stuff... where are you from?" asked Branen.

"I grew up in Ireland."

"That sounds like you don't originate from there."

"I don't think I do."

"What do you mean?"

She closed the fridge door and leant back on it. "It doesn't matter."

He pointed at the pendant round her neck. "Who's in that locket?"

"My mother."

"Where is she?"

Kelly didn't answer; she had made up her mind.

He felt their evening was coming to a premature end.

"Thanks for seeing me home."

"That's it… you want me to go now?"

"Yes."

"What about that cup of coffee?"

"I think we've had enough to drink."

"Couldn't I kip down on your sofa?"

"I'm sorry… this isn't my flat. One of the girls at Ronnie's is letting me crash here."

"Okay. It was good meeting you… maybe, I…?"

The look on Kelly's face answered his question and he couldn't explain why he had nowhere to go. At least she smiled as he let himself out.

He could not risk going back to either of the hotels at three o'clock in the morning and with CCTV cameras everywhere it was too dangerous to stay out in the open. The streets were beginning to empty as Soho shut down for the night; the only people left hanging out were late night clubbers.

81. HARRY & EUREKA :
(EARLY HOURS, SATURDAY 14 NOVEMBER)

When they reached the first-floor landing, the girl stopped and knocked on the door.

Harry thought, 'Fuck, I'm with the first-floor tart, not the top-floor one.'

She shouted through the door, "It's okay Dawn, I've got one more trick tonight."

He noticed her Slavic accent had become more pronounced. He was concerned now that his arrival had been announced, but there was nothing he could do about it.

There was a muffled reply from inside as though Dawn had her mouth full. Then the door opened and Dawn appeared in the gap. The only thing keeping her upright was the wall. "We're closed tomorrow... have you shut the street door?"

"Yes... do you want me to open it again?"

"Don't worry love... if I do the business for a bit longer I'll use the intercom," said Dawn, and slid behind the door.

Now that Harry had been seen, he'd have to deal with her later. He was relieved when they continued climbing.

Noticing that Harry's eyes were locked onto her arse the girl said, "My name's Eureka... it is easy for my men to remember that when they come."

Already Harry wanted his money back.

"This is my apartment..." she announced as they reached the second floor. She teased him. "Come on up to my boudoir."

"Ever thought of installing a lift?" asked Harry, panting heavily.

She turned and looked down at him, "If you think you're out of breath now darling, wait till I get you upstairs."

Her room smelt of marijuana and burnt candle wax. The bedside table lamps wore short skirts fringed with tassels. Eureka re-lit the candles while Harry got his breath back. He was careful not to leave any fingerprints. She opened a drawer in the dressing table and pulled out a packet of condoms.

"You've paid for full penetration... you must use these."

'It's like a consultation in a doctor's surgery,' Harry thought to himself taking the offered packet.

"Do I get anything out of the ordinary?" he asked optimistically. He wasn't ready for the girl but if she was prepared for the unusual he might be able to rouse himself sufficiently before he committed the final act.

"That'll cost you a whole lot more... and it depends what you want," she said pulling off her top and revealing a pair of medically enhanced breasts that stood apart and alone.

Harry changed his mind and stood up.

"Take the shorts off and get on the bed."

Eureka sensed a threat in his voice. She was glad she had not taken up the suggestion of unusual sex. She did as she was told and lay on the bed.

Harry reached over her. "I'd like to kiss you."

He had the knife behind his back. He bent over her and put his hand over her mouth; then pushed the knife up under her ribs and twisted.

As he withdrew the knife a hiss of escaping air came from her body and a gurgling noise from her throat. The knife had hit the aorta. He managed to pull away as blood pumped out and saturated the bed around her. Her face was contorted as though she was in orgasm.

Harry washed the blood off his hands and the knife in the en suite bathroom and sat down to wait.

82. BRANEN, DAWN & HARRY :
(EARLY HOURS, SATURDAY 14 NOVEMBER)

Branen was back on the streets feeling exposed.

He walked along Old Compton Street with his collar up and his hat pulled down. He didn't look up in case a camera got a full face view. He imagined a black and white photograph of him hanging on the pinboard in some nondescript office and it being emailed to a faceless killer assigned to knock him over.

He turned up Greek Street and was about to go into Bar Valentino to get a sandwich when the café lights went out. He went up to the door and waved through the condensation to Valentino, who was locking up. He flapped his hands and dismissed him with a supercilious grin.

He turned round, wondering where he could find cover for the night, and saw the red light in the first floor window across the street.

The knocking shop had been there when he was a teenager. He'd regularly have a bowl of minestrone in Bar Valentino, which used to serve the cheapest, most filling meal in Soho and he'd see the red lamp in the window turning on and off as customers arrived and left.

He crossed the road, pulled on Costas's gloves and rang the bottom bell. A spaced-out voice answered, "Yes."

"Want some business luv?"

"Come on up, darlin'."

The door buzzed open and when he arrived on the first floor the flat door was open. He saw the staircase continued on up, but the lights were off and he hoped they wouldn't be disturbed.

Harry sat at the end of the bed for almost an hour coldly contemplating the corpse in front of him. Her blood was coagulating and turning brown, it had soaked the bed and the room smelt of death. It was all-pervading and as difficult to remove from a room as the sulphurous smell of a skunk. The last time he'd experienced that stench was when he'd entered a bunker in Iraq, hours after a grenade had blown its inhabitants apart.

He was deep in fantasy when he heard the doorbell ring in the flat below. He crept to Eureka's door and checked that the hall lights were off. Then he heard a punter coming up the stairs. He waited with the knife ready. The punter stopped for a moment then he heard him close Dawn's door. He sat down and slowed his heart beat. Hopefully the bloke would leave within the hour.

She was so laid back and removed from reality she had to be on smack. Branen wasn't sure she really knew he was there. She was about fifty years old but looked a haggard seventy. She was exactly what he'd been looking for; no maid and hopefully no pimp. He watched her eyes, she might have been out of it but there were years of street experience looking back at him.

The room stank of cigarettes and an unusual perfume. The plastic laminate on the bedside table was peeling off, and on it stood an empty bottle of absinthe. Pavlovian conditioning guided her to switch off the red light and close the curtains.

She had not forgotten her price list. "All right darling, what do you want? A blow-job is a twenty, full sex with a johnny'll cost you a fifty note."

"I want you to sit down and let me stay 'til daylight."

"Fuck off, luv... I got business to do."

"I'll pay you enough to cover you for the rest of the night."

This old pro had seen it all before and however out of it she was, she could sense the desperation in him.

"That'll be a couple of hundred, luv," she said, appearing to sober up. She might have consumed the best part of a bottle of absinthe but the smack was helping her think her way through it.

"You won't make that much with what's left of tonight," he said.

She got to her feet. "Two hundred or fuck off."

He got up and reached into his pocket as though for his wallet. Stepping towards her he hit her on the side of the neck, hard enough to bring her to her knees. As she sank down he grabbed her and spun her onto the bed and gagged her with a pillowcase.

He turned her over and she was blue. 'Fuck...' he thought to himself, '...all I need is for her to die on me.' He pulled her up to a sitting position and vomit ran down both sides of the gag. He loosened it and she vomited again all over the bed and onto his sleeve. Her eyes were locked onto his. "Don't say a fucking word and you'll live... do you understand me?"

She nodded but he didn't believe her. He positioned himself so that if she screamed he would be able to hit her hard enough to knock her out.

He'd been there about half-an-hour when the doorbell rang. He put his finger to his mouth and sat on the bed next to her. The doorbell rang again. She looked at him with terror in her eyes. Her red light was off and the curtains were closed. The bell rang a third time and then a shout from the street, "Dawn... buzz the fucking door you drunken old slag."

Whoever he was, he wasn't afraid to interrupt.

"Is that your pimp?" Branen asked. She gave him a vacant stare.

A couple of very long minutes passed. He heard footsteps on the stairs. He pushed her down on the bed and pulled the grotty old bedcover over her. He took the SIG from his belt bag and screwed on the silencer. Keys rattled in the door. He managed to get behind it as it opened.

A hard looking skinhead walked in. He was dressed in a combat jacket and Doc Martens. He looked like he'd been born in the sixties and had never left the seventies.

Branen stepped out from behind the door. "Okay pal, let me see both hands, and slowly."

Harry had lost track of time when the intercom on the wall buzzed.

He jerked back to reality. 'Who the fuck is that?' He froze. It was so quiet that it seemed loud enough to wake the dead. He looked at Eureka but she was not going to be disturbed.

Then he heard the doorbell ring again in the flat below and a man shouting from the street.

Harry put on the latex gloves, unpacked the rifle and screwed on the silencer. He sat at the end of the bed waiting for the situation to develop. He heard the street door open and close again and another person going into Dawn's flat. The situation was getting over-complicated. As far as he could tell there were two men in Dawn's flat and he needed them to leave. But until then he would have to move around as little as possible.

When the pimp saw the silencer he knew Branen meant what he said.

Branen realised, 'I'm going to have to stay awake with these two until it's time to leave.' He indicated with the barrel to the bed. "Tear the sheet up into long strips and tie her hands and feet."

The pimp didn't like being told what to do.

"Now tie one end of a strip to your left wrist and lay face down on the floor." Branen tied the pimp's hands behind him and his feet together. "If you make any noise at all I'll shoot you." Branen meant it and the pimp believed him.

The three of them spent the rest of the night together, almost motionless. Time seemed to come to a standstill, tormenting Branen's hung-over brain. Apart from the occasional slamming car door and the odd abusive scream, Soho quietened down.

The seconds became minutes and the minutes became hours. Branen fought to stay awake. The smell of absinthe and cigarette smoke was slowly overtaken by the stale smell of sweat. Dawn's dimly-lit bedroom became an even more depressing hovel as it was slowly revealed by the early blue daylight. A picture of a Chinese girl with green skin hung on the wall at the end of the bed and Branen thought he saw a tear run down her cheek.

Dawn grunted and groaned for a while and then started snoring; loud enough that they could not have slept even if they'd wanted to.

The image of the skinhead, who must have weighed nearly twenty stone, lying face down in front of him, became engraved on his mind as he battled to stay awake; a halo of light seemed to surround him as he lay there.

Branen dropped off for a short while and woke with a jolt. The effects of exhaustion, alcohol and coke had left him strung out.

The pimp's voice had woken him. "I ain't got no feeling in me arms and legs… I'm in fucking agony."

"It's better than being fucking dead," Branen told him. He did not want to leave until the streets were busy again, but Soho did not come alive until after the rest of London had finished breakfast.

After another hour without hearing any movement downstairs, Harry retrieved his money from the corpse and began his preparations. He ran through every detail of his plan. Again he tried to predict the unpredictable. He did not want to be caught out again, as he had been by that copper in the café. He had plenty of time on his hands before he had to take the shot. To facilitate his departure with as little delay as possible, he practised removing the silencer and putting the rifle into the guitar case. He ran through the whole action at least half-a-dozen times, checking how long it took and making sure he did not snag it and that the case closed properly.

There were still the people downstairs to consider. It was 3am and he would be in residence for another thirteen hours, and could not risk anyone from downstairs coming up to visit Eureka. If they left before the Prime Minister's security was in place he would be okay. He didn't want to have to kill all of them; it could be noisy. But Dawn was a problem he was going to have to deal with; she had seen him. For now he would have to wait and see what developed. He ran through several potential scenarios planning his reactions. He visualised his escape route and ran through every movement several times. It was not ideal because there was only one safe way out; down the stairs and through the front door. The building would never pass fire regulations. Trying to escape over the rooftops would leave him exposed and isolated. It was important that he was out on the street mingling with the Saturday crowd as soon as possible after taking the shot. Most of the attention would be concentrated on the victim but the experienced Protection Officers would be trying to locate the shooter. There would be plenty of people in the area and by the time the CP mob were satisfied that the shooter was not in the immediate vicinity and had started to fan out, he hoped he would be long gone. To be seen leaving the tarts' front door, which was out of the eye-line of St. Barnabas's, a Close Protection Officer would need to have spotted his shooting position and have covered the hundred metres down Greek Street; but by then he would have walked away. All the odds were in his favour.

Predicting potential problems and calculating his responses kept his mind occupied and helped the time pass.

At about 4am he took a line of speed to get him through the early morning blues.

He had checked the weather forecast on the previous evening's news before leaving his flat and again at six in the morning on Eureka's bedside radio with the volume turned right down. He listened impatiently while the announcer read the shipping forecast; then she eventually let him know that after a clear start to the day, cloud and rain were due in the afternoon. It didn't really matter what the weather was going to do, he was still going to take the shot, but the attention to detail gave him confidence.

It started to get light at seven-fifteen. It was not real light, it was watery grey light that did little to lift his spirits. He was struggling to stay sober. His nerves were jangling and a drink would calm him down, but he needed to stay compos mentis for the job ahead. He could not stop playing with the idea that a drink would cheer him up and relax his mind. Finally he took a long slug from the vodka bottle.

He had decided to use the sound moderator after all. If he had to fire a second or third shot without it, the reverberation round the buildings would make the source more identifiable. There was also the chance of locating him by the muzzle flashes but that was a risk he had to take.

He had an eight hour wait ahead of him and he was getting more and more edgy.

It was 9am before Branen felt safe enough to move. He gagged the cursing man and tightened the bindings. Dawn never stopped snoring so he removed her bondage in case she vomited again; she could release her pimp when she felt like it.

He stood in the pavement doorway planning his day. A street-cleaning lorry trundled past, its heavy circular brushes sweeping up last night's detritus. He stepped out in its lee and followed it, hopefully hidden from any cameras. Back in Old Compton Street he made a mental note of the the mini-cab kiosk that had been there since the beginning of time. A bored looking guy was propped up inside the cubicle and by the expression on his face he had been there at least that long.

83. MIKEY : (MID-MORNING, SATURDAY 14 NOVEMBER)

As she often did, Mikey awoke nervous and shaky with mixed emotions and a rotten hangover.

Last night had presented its problems. She was still elated by the reception she had received after the speech on Wednesday, but not wanting to interrupt Sabrina's working week she had decided to wait until Friday night to celebrate.

After drinks with her at Ronnie's they continued with more champagne at Madame LuLu's. She'd got into an intimate conversation with Sabrina which stirred deep sexual fantasies, and they shared a gramme of Mikey's finest, shiny slate, uncut coke that she normally diluted by thirty per cent before selling on to Snowman. She sat staring at Sabrina as she excitedly chatted away to the others who had joined them at the table. Mikey's imagination went into overdrive. By now Sabrina had lost all her inhibitions. They went down to the toilets for another line and Mikey grabbed her and told her to collect her things. "We are going home."

"I don't want to go home... I'm having a fab time," said Sabrina.

"You're coming home with me... NOW."

"No I'm not."

Mikey slapped her hard, knocking her back against the wall.

"You bastard," said Sabrina.

Mikey screamed at her, "You're in big trouble, girl."

She kicked Sabrina's legs away so that she crashed down heavily onto the tiled floor.

"You'll learn to do what I tell you." She kicked her viciously and stormed out leaving her cowering in the corner, her face stained with running mascara.

Mikey went back upstairs to the table and pointed to one of the Serbian waitresses. "Come here."

Tilly obeyed.

"Go and get your coat, we're leaving."

Tilly was compliant; she had heard about Mikey's temper and without a work permit she couldn't disobey her employer. She only had a small command of English but that night back at Mikey's penthouse she learned a whole lot more and to do as she was told.

At 5am Mikey put half a dozen fifty pound notes into Tilly's hand and helped her to a waiting taxi.

She dropped a couple of quaaludes and prayed that she would sleep. Her heart was thumping and her eyes seemed to be glued open, she had to force herself to blink. Eventually with the light beginning to creep over the city landscape she fell asleep.

The paperboy had delivered half a dozen copies of the Soho Gazette to Soho Lofts the previous afternoon with the subscribers' names hand written on the top.

The African concierge delivered them to each apartment in his own good time. He had seen Mikey's photograph on the front page and read the article reporting her fascist views, and had not bothered to put the paper through her door until that morning.

It was just before midday when she heard him push the post through her letterbox. She stumbled out of bed and sank a glass of Fernet Branca. She had been taking the local newspaper since deciding to stand for the BNP. It kept her informed on Soho life and allowed her to show empathy with her electorate and their petty neighbourhood issues. She unfolded the paper and was startled to see a three column wide photograph of herself staring back. Leaving the blinds closed she sat down to read the article. In the exhilaration of the cheering following her speech, she had forgotten that she had spoken to a reporter.

Her speech was fully reported along with her 'clever put-down of a local heckler'. A reference was made to her patronage of St. Barnabas's and a quote from her saying that she would love to meet the Prime Minister when he visited the hostel tomorrow. The article was surprisingly unmalevolent, which made Mikey suspect that the reporter was sympathetic to her cause. She had made it public knowledge that the Prime Minister would be visiting St. Barnabas's. The information was now available to the 'terrorists' of Group X. In her still-befuddled mind she could not decide which way this information would be interpreted after the shooting. She sat for a moment trying to work out whether the quote would work for or against her once the Prime Minister was dead.

She looked up at the clock and threw the paper down in a panic. Due to the last twenty-four hours of over-indulgence she had forgotten that the visit was in approximately four hours' time and she had to be sure, doubly sure that everything would go to plan.

She got through to Snowman on his land line. He was still in bed with Myrtle, believing that after the events of the last week and his visit to Costas yesterday afternoon, his life was becoming a lot simpler; that was until the phone call from Mikey.

"I want to see you in an hour… at the factory… make sure the Illims are not there when we meet."

She slammed down the phone without waiting for a reply and dropped a couple of 'ludes.

84. BRANEN, MIKEY & SNOWMAN : (MORNING, SATURDAY 14 NOVEMBER)

After leaving Dawn and the pimp tied up, Branen wanted to get in position in case Michelle de Lavigne made an early morning move.

He avoided Giovanni's and bought a couple of rolls and a bottle of water and settled down just inside Tyler's Court, which offered him shelter from the wind and more importantly, meant that he was out of the eyeline of the cameras on Wardour Street.

The food settled his raw stomach and when he'd finished eating he fell into a troubled sleep: he was miles away pruning vines… the sun was setting… he was walking through the vineyard up to the stone house… then it was morning and the breeze was rustling through the eucalyptus tree outside his bedroom window.

A mid-Atlantic accent seeped into his reverie. "If you take, you have to give back." The quaaludes had caused a rare moment of generosity in Mikey.

He opened his eyes. It was spitting with rain and an hour must have passed. Michelle de Lavigne was bending over him. She threw a five pound note into his lap. Her voice echoed round his semi-conscious brain. In the past, lapses of concentration like that would have been fatal for him.

'Fucking hypocrite,' he thought; if it wasn't for her supply of drugs, a lot of her customers would not have ended up on the streets as addicts. He watched her strut away and started following her; the shiny suit she was wearing caught the light as she minced along. Branen could see her bleached hair as she turned into Brewer Street. He underestimated how fast she was moving and by the time he reached the corner there was no sign of her. He was frustrated by his incompetence; he had never lost a target before.

It had turned into a warm day when Snowman decided to walk to the factory for his meeting with Mikey.

He had meant to leave promptly after her phone call but he couldn't resist the temptations of Myrtle's body. He was in a post-coital flush as he cut through Chinatown. He crossed Gerrard Street and was bathed in orange shafts of winter sunshine. The warmth penetrated his clothes. His pork pie hat was perched on the back of his head as he smiled at any pretty young woman whose eye he was able to catch. He had slept in, made love and missed his breakfast; he was hungry surrounded by the smells of roast pork and stir-fry. He sped on, concerned that Mikey might turn up before him. She was crucial to his future and he did not want to upset her.

Branen scrolled through Snowman's mobile until he came across the initials MdL. He pressed the dial key, hoping that Snowman's name would appear on her mobile when it rang. He held a handkerchief over the mouthpiece, bent down close to a parked taxi with its diesel engine rattling away and stuttered the words, "Where are you?"

"Where am I, where the fuck are you? I'm at the factory… you idiot," she said, and rang off.

Branen flipped the phone shut and started to retrace his steps. He had no idea where the factory was. He was furious, he had no time to waste and he had managed to lose her. As he was wondering what to do next he had a second piece of luck. He saw Snowman heading down the other side of Wardour Street. Branen hesitated as Snowman crossed in front of him. Branen followed him onto the zebra crossing in Shaftesbury Avenue. Snowman moved athletically, avoiding people as he crossed over into Chinatown. Branen was caught off-guard as Snowman broke into a run. Had he seen Branen following him? He hadn't looked round or looked for reflections in windows; Branen was sure he didn't know he was there. He had to speed up because Snowman had turned the corner. In the hustle and bustle of Chinatown, he could easily lose him as well.

Snowman saw Mikey's bobbing bleached locks amongst the sea of Chinese heads about forty metres ahead of him and broke into a run. He caught up with her after she turned into Lisle Street.

Branen jogged on to the junction and stopped just twenty metres from them. Snowman was standing outside a doorway, talking to Mikey; he had to get out of their eyeline.

Acting drunk, he lurched into the George & Dragon pub on the corner and leant close to the window, watching them.

"Why meet here?" asked Snowman.

"I want to check that everything is in place... and that you're concentrating. Have you cleared the factory?" she asked.

"No... give me a few minutes and come back... I've left my phone at home. Can you lend me yours? I need to ring them before I go up."

"What are you talking about?" she asked, "You just phoned me."

Snowman went paler than normal. "Fuck, fuck, fuck."

"What's going on?" she demanded. The effect of the 'ludes was wearing off and last night's excesses were making her agitated again. She started to sweat. Because of the risks involved in the Group X project she had been forced to make him an offer that he couldn't refuse, but now she was beginning to regret it.

"I was mugged."

"You silly cunt, someone rang me a few minutes ago and asked me where I was," she screamed into his face. "Who was it.... the man who attacked you in Costas's?"

Snowman looked around to see if they were attracting attention. "I don't know", he said quietly, trying to calm her down.

She exploded with frustration. "Well find out and get rid of him...

225

have you straightened out Costas? I don't want any more fucking problems."

"Chill..." he said, trying to look unperturbed, "...if he asked you where you were then he don't know you're here, does he?"

She was losing it. "I told him I was at the factory."

"He wouldn't know where the fuck the factory is... would he?"

"Why the fuck did he ring me rather than anyone else in your phone?"

Snowman answered in a stage whisper, "Chill out man, maybe he rang other people as well... you're attracting attention right outside your factory."

Realising she was losing control she handed him her phone. "Make it quick and make sure, double sure, that the Illims are there tonight... no more fuck-ups."

Snowman rang the Illims and told them he was outside and to let him in. He pressed the bell push and pulled the hood up over his head.

Mikey grabbing her phone back, said, "I'll be ten minutes... exactly," and stormed off.

Still inside the pub, Branen was deciding on his next move when two Asian men dressed in white baggy clothes came out of the door that he'd seen Snowman enter. They hesitated for a while in the entrance, then went down the alley towards Leicester Square. Branen wondered if the men had any connection with the terrorist group. He waited and a few minutes later Mikey strode into view, pressed the bell and disappeared inside.

Branen left the pub and went to the entrance of Masonic Mansions where he saw a video entry camera pointing down directly at him. The middle bells were labelled in Chinese and the top and bottom ones were blank. He preferred the top bell for Mikey and Snowman, but not yet.

He was convinced that the two people who knew all about Carrie's murder were together in one place. He would never get conclusive evidence that they had done it, how could he? But he now knew enough to be as sure as he was ever going to be.

85. MIKEY & SNOWMAN : (PM, SATURDAY 14 NOVEMBER)

On the third floor of Masonic Mansions, in Group X's shabby office, Snowman was stretched out on the plastic sofa with his feet up and wearing latex gloves.

"Salaam Alekum," said Snowman as Mikey stepped over the threshold.

"Fuck off," said Mikey without a smile. "Who d'you think you are, a fucking Paki? Have you told them I want them to work overnight?"

"Yeah, no probs... they'll be back here in an hour," he said, handing her a pair of latex gloves.

On the coffee table in front of them was a hip-flask of brandy. Snowman reckoned Mikey needed the hair of the dog and now was a good time to humour her. The sunlight crept through the blinds; he thought it gave the room an air of optimism. But Mikey did not want any of it; she was annoyed by his lack of attention and was in no mood to humour him. She went through the plan again in detail and reminded him that the shooting would take place at four o'clock that afternoon. And afterwards, when Harry arrived at the factory with the car keys, Snowman was to check that the fat fuck had left the Qur'an and the cartridge cases at the scene of the shooting, and the rifle in the boot of his car. She explained that when Harry delivered the car keys she wanted Snowman to lure him up to the top floor and then stab, not shoot him, and showed him where to hide the body; it happened to be directly over the bomb at the back of the factory. The Illims were to collect the car and leave it in the Newport Place car park. She wanted the Illims to leave prints and DNA in the car, and with any luck Harry would have left prints on the Qur'an which would confirm his involvement with Group X.

"After you've dealt with him and organised the Illims you should go home and forget all about this." She looked into his eyes for any sign of doubt or fear, but saw none.

Snowman held her stare. "Don't worry about me... I've protected myself already."

She understood that he was protecting himself from her, and that if he died in suspicious circumstances he would probably have left a letter behind revealing her involvement with the group; she would've done the same in his position. Anyway she did not want to renege on her promise to him. 'I'm not a monster,' she told herself, '…he has been pivotal to my success.'

She told him she would meet him next week to arrange the laundering of his own money and that it would be deposited with an extra hundred thousand pounds in the Cayman Islands. With that and the beach house she was giving him, he would be set up for life.

Snowman assumed Mikey had made alternative arrangements for the distribution of her drugs and felt relieved at finally being able to get out of the business.

Without telling him about the explosive finale she had orchestrated for that night, Mikey made Snowman repeat the plan in detail before she got up and left.

As she strutted back across Soho she prayed that Whitey would not miss his shot.

86. HARRY : (DAWN, SATURDAY 14 NOVEMBER)

Harry was tense. He had experienced this anticipation before. Waiting for the moment to pull the trigger; his mouth dry, like an actor waiting to take the stage on a first night.

It was 9am when Harry heard the door to Dawn's flat close and footsteps on the stairs; he was sure it was only one man leaving. Then half-an-hour later he heard a man shouting and swearing before he too stomped down and slammed the front door.

Harry knew that he must act now. He crept down the stairs in stockinged feet carrying the rifle. He had realised much earlier whilst going through his plan that he could not continue without dealing with Dawn. He listened carefully at her door; he could hear what he thought was someone throwing up. He noticed the spy-hole in the door. He put the rifle out of sight by the door jamb and knocked. He had to keep knocking until Dawn responded, "What the fuck d'you want?"

She was just on the other side of the door and her closeness made Harry start. "Eureka's not well."

"Fuck off."

"Will you come and check…" Harry heard her shuffling around. "…

perhaps you can help her?"

"Fuck off… what the fuck are you still here for…? I'm gonna call the police."

She left him with no alternative. While still pleading for help he took a step back, slid the rifle across at waist height and fired a single shot through the door. There was a hollow grunt from inside the flat. He pressed his ear against the door. There was a sigh as the last traces of life escaped from her body. Then nothing at all, except for the sound of passing traffic. In the sullen silence, the raucous ring of the doorbell made his heart leap. He froze; had another punter turned up? He wondered if the suppressed shot had been heard outside. He didn't dare move. The doorbell rang again. He still didn't move. He heard the letter box lift up. A voice called, "Anyone at home?" It was relaxed and official-sounding.

There was silence and then the voice called out again, "Police here, just a routine check… nothing to worry about."

The letterbox stayed open for too long. Harry waited, his heart pounding in his chest, 'Are they going to force an entry?' he asked himself. The letterbox closed. Nothing happened.

After waiting for ten minutes he went back up to the top floor, one slow step at a time. He found a pad of decorated writing paper in Eureka's dressing table and with her lipstick scribbled 'Closed for business'. He went back down to the street door and pushed the page through the letterbox, trapping it in the flap, and put the security chain in place.

Harry sat in the tart's bedroom, nauseated by the smell. He turned on the transistor radio by the bed; it was tuned to a music station and The Bee Gees singing Staying Alive came on. He sat transfixed, staring at the floor. He was sweating and a feeling of paranoia swept over him. He punched the radio off button and went to the window with the view to St. Barnabas's. He slid the sash window down about twenty centimetres, leaving a small gap between the net curtains, and then drew the red velvet curtains behind the nets leaving a long strip of dull light. The window he had chosen was perfectly positioned for his purpose. If he kept it dark inside the room he would be invisible from outside.

He went to the roof-light outside Eureka's apartment. He put the kitchen table on the landing with a chair on top. He climbed onto the table and stepped up onto the chair, which creaked loudly under his weight; he was afraid the rig might give way and send him crashing down. Placing a pillow from the bed on his shoulder he was able to force the roof-light open. The table groaned beneath his bulk. A gust of cold air brought with it reality and broke the purgatory of the last few hours. He jammed a dildo from Eureka's bedside drawer into the gap, leaving the window ajar ready for his recce later. He climbed down and went back into the bedroom.

He'd only had three days to prepare the job. He'd decided on his shooting position on Thursday lunchtime and he'd had limited time to check out the prostitutes' habits and working hours. He'd walked past on Thursday night and three times yesterday. The policeman in the café said he'd told the girls to cease trading. Harry had to gamble that neither of the girls had a regular Saturday afternoon punter who might want to slip in. He'd noticed on the previous day that they had not put their sign up for business until five o'clock. If he was lucky no-one would interrupt him before he'd completed his mission. If the phone rang he'd ignore it. If anyone else had a key, he would have to ad lib it and deal with the situation as it developed.

He waited in Eureka's flat until three o'clock before climbing out onto the roof. A helicopter had flown over seven minutes earlier. He made every movement slow and methodical. He needed to check the location of any sharp-shooters or observers, and to make sure no-one had a direct line of sight into the bedroom below. He crawled to the back edge of the roof under the chimney stack and rolled the black stocking down over his face. He had been wearing it rolled up in the style of a black beanie for the last few hours. 'Like that hermaphrodite,' he thought.

Making sure he was not silhouetted against the skyline, he slid up until he could see over the edge of the brick parapet on the far side of the roof. He saw a police sharp-shooter on the roof of the building on the adjacent corner across the street. The policeman had his back to him and was looking in the same direction, towards St. Barnabas's. He was miked-up but was too far over to see into Eureka's bedrooom window. Harry carefully eased back down and edged slowly over to check the rooftops and windows in Greek Street. In a window opposite on the floor below, he saw another policeman who was positioned to observe the corner of the street by the tarts' front door.

He would have to remove this problem before he took the vital head shot. He had to expect sharp-shooters and observers but it worried him having them so close.

The observer in the window was about thirty metres away and as long as he hit the man's chest the soft-nosed ammo would do the rest. He estimated that it would take three seconds to pan the rifle thirty degrees, operate the bolt action and have the Prime Minister in his sights after his first shot. In the old days he could get off three accurate rounds at two hundred and fifty metres in six seconds. Allowing for the fifteen years without practice and his consumption of alcohol and drugs, he was confident he could still make the two shots within five seconds, and he would definitely have to use the silencer.

In an effort to avoid repetitive job fatigue the Prime Minister's Close Protection Officers were rotated. It ensured that they maintained concentration and kept a fresh approach to their assignments. Since 1984 and the attempt on Margaret Thatcher's life with the Brighton bomb, no-one had tried to assassinate a Prime Minister. All the training and role-play had been diligently rehearsed, but had never been tested in a real scenario. But after years of close protection without any attempts on the PM's life, human fallibility had inevitably allowed concentration to slacken. Complacency had entered the equation. Harry realised this and felt it gave him the advantage.

He belly-crawled back and lowered himself down onto the table. He moved the furniture into the bedroom and set it up against the far wall, opposite the window. He had seen this technique used by IRA snipers back in his Belfast days, giving him height for the correct trajectory down on to the street.

The smell coming up from the bed was even stronger. He stared down at the corpse and gagged. She lay in the middle of an island of blood. He wondered if she was up there with him looking down on herself. He nearly spoke out loud to her. He had to pull himself together; his future depended on the next few hours.

He focussed his attention on the cross-hairs in the telescopic sight. He pointed the rifle at the observer in the window below and panned across to establish a clear line of sight to the entrance of St. Barnabas's. His hands were steady. He had taken out targets that were far more inaccessible than this one.

By three thirty he was ready. He sat waiting on the chair on top of the table, resting the rifle on the back of a second chair in front of him. He watched as the Close Protection Officers at the entrance of the hostel fussed about making last minute checks, panning their binoculars up and down the buildings. With his dark mac and the stocking over his face he was invisible in the shadows. To ensure that there were no reflections bouncing off any of his equipment, he hung a piece of the stocking over the front of the scope. He wrapped the stock with cling film to avoid any DNA from his mouth getting onto the rifle. The guitar case was lying open on the floor ready to receive the rifle and the Qur'an lay on the floor in front of him.

The waiting was over. The fear and panic had left him and he found himself in a place of calm and clarity where he wished he could remain for the rest of his life.

87. BRANEN : (PM, SATURDAY 14 NOVEMBER)

Branen could not risk staying in Soho much longer and he was unlikely to have another opportunity to confront both Snowman and Mikey together.

How was he going to get through the front door of Masonic Mansions without being detected? Either he could wait for someone to come along and enter the building with them, or he could try to find another way in. There was no access round the back and he did not want to lose sight of the front door in case they came out again. A group of Chinese school children came towards him. He pulled out a handful of cash and stood in front of them, "If I give you ten pounds would you ring that top bell for me?" he asked, pointing at the doorway.

The kids were in their mid-teens, they giggled and looked at each other for moral support. Here he was scruffily dressed and standing in front of four teenagers with a ten pound note in his hand. A middle-aged woman stopped and watched him trying to complete the transaction. She commanded the children in loud Chinese to go on their way and led them off, giving Branen a look that made him feel like a child molester.

Pretending to read the menu, he checked his reflection in the window of the restaurant next door. He tried to smarten himself up but he didn't have much to work with. He took off his hat, smoothed down his hair and tried to look friendly. A young Chinese woman in jeans, carrying a briefcase, was walking towards him. He smiled and stepped in front of her. "Excuse me, I need your help."

She tried to push past but he kept smiling and held out the ten pound note. "Would you please ring the top doorbell and let me in when it opens? I'll give you ten pounds now and another ten if you succeed."

He was lucky; she liked the look of the money and hesitated. Still smiling and trying to reassure her he explained, "My brother won't let me in... we've had a row... I want to apologise to him but he's angry with me." Before she could respond he went on, "If you can persuade him you have a meeting with someone in the building he might let you in." He pushed the ten pounds into her hand. "Please..."

She took the money and tucked it into her pocket; he wasn't going to see that tenner again.

They were five metres from the street door when it opened and Mikey appeared. She hesitated, checked both ways, looked straight through Branen and the girl and scurried off in the opposite direction. Branen turned away to avoid catching her eye.

Even if Mikey had escaped, Snowman was still inside.

The girl looked at him suspiciously and asked, "Was that him?"

"No... she can't be my brother, can she?"

"Which bell?" "

"The top one... please."

88. SNOWMAN & BRANEN :
(PM, SATURDAY 14 NOVEMBER)

The ghetto blaster on the desk was playing a loud Arabic lament when the doorbell started ringing.

Snowman ignored it, he had a lot on his mind. He was concentrating on rolling a joint. "Fuck Michelle fucking de Lavigne, why shouldn't I have a blow? It's a lovely day... or it was before I came up here..." The entry phone kept up its insistent ringing. "Who the fuck is that?"

The small video screen came to life, showing a pretty Chinese girl. She pouted, giggled and played up to the camera.

Snowman said, "Yeah... what d'ya want?"

The woman's lips moved but he could not hear what she was saying. He let the receiver dangle on its coiled cable and switched the ghetto-blaster off.

He shouted into the mouth-piece. "What do you want?"

Her voice was muffled and there was interference.

"Hi, I've come for the audition," she giggled.

He stared at the screen, "What fucking audition?"

"You remember Mr Fung... I sent you my picture?"

Branen thought to himself, 'She's good.'

Snowman thought for a moment. He was not keen to let her in but she was drawing attention to the street door by shouting into the intercom. He convinced himself that, 'She must be for the geezer downstairs.' He pressed the entry key and took a deep toke on the spliff. 'I might pop down and interview her myself,' he mused.

The buzzer kept reverberating because the street door remained open, so he continued watching the screen until the girl disappeared inside. Then a figure pushed past the camera with his face obscured. Snowman did not recognise the man but it left him feeling uneasy. After a few moments the girl came out alone.

Snowman put down the receiver and drew the revolver from the back of his waistcoat. He opened the factory door and looked down the dark staircase. One flight down on the next landing was the toilet. He crept down and stood behind the door, leaving it ajar. He released the safety catch on the revolver and held it with both hands, exactly as he had seen on TV. In a moment of inspiration he flushed the toilet, making sure the door was open as far as possible without giving away his position.

Branen was fairly sure Snowman had answered the door. He gave the girl the rest of the money and ushered her back out. He didn't know whether his entry had been observed or not. He put on Costas's gloves and took the SIG from his belt-bag. He climbed the stairs slowly, alert to any sound or movement. He kept to the side of the steps where the wooden treads were less likely to creak. The building was quiet. All he could hear was the bustle of Chinatown outside. Then he heard a toilet flush a couple of flights above.

When he reached the last landing before the top floor he saw that the toilet door was wide open and the water-closet was filling up. He had not met anyone on the stairs so assumed that Snowman or another occupant of the top floor had been down to the lavatory.

He hesitated outside the toilet door and listened.

Inside, Snowman held his breath. The dope had slowed him down and he was relaxed enough to use the vibe to calm himself. He waited to see what the man would do.

Branen turned his attention to the door at the top of the short flight of stairs. He moved up the steps one by one and when he was three treads from the top he noticed, too late, that the door was not completely closed. Realising his mistake he started to turn when Snowman stepped out with a revolver pointing at him.

"Don't turn, I've got a gun... put both your hands slowly on your head," he said.

Snowman was seven steps and about four metres behind Branen; even an average shot would not miss from there.

Snowman saw the pistol as the man put his hands on his head. He didn't want to get too close. "Drop the fucking gun... drop it over your back."

Branen could not risk turning and shooting. He was penned in by the bannister and the wall. Snowman had the drop on him and he couldn't do anything about it. He let go of the pistol and it banged down the stairs. Snowman picked it up and put it into his pocket. Branen started to turn to face him.

Snowman recognised him. "I've been looking for you, you cunt... lie face down on the stairs... keep your hands above your head," he ordered. It was the first time he had done this and he was pleased with the control the gun gave him. He ordered Branen to crawl up the remaining steps on all fours. As long as he kept the man on his knees he would not be able to jump him.

235

He told Branen to push open the factory door and crawl in.

Branen noticed the smell of ammonia and the sweet aroma of marijuana. "You having a party?" he asked.

"Yeah, and you're the only fucking guest."

"I'll have a whisky sour."

He made Branen crawl into an office; he tried to look around, light filtering through damaged blinds at the one window in the room.

"Get up on your knees and take off your coat."

He was behind Branen and he was taking great care not to get too close. Branen was kneeling facing the back of an office chair with plastic arms. The seat had stained, torn fabric with the filling hanging out. On a cheap desk was a roll of duct tape and a gaudy radio murmuring Arabic musak. The patchy walls were stained with grey shadows where filing cabinets had once stood. On one side was a plastic sofa which had also seen better days. The windows had tattered metal venetian blinds hanging at different angles and under his knees the carpet was ripped and filthy.

"Take off your sweater," ordered Snowman, "...and get into the chair."

Branen pulled off the tracksuit top and sat in the office chair facing into the room. Snowman walked round behind the desk to face him. He had a .38 Smith & Wesson revolver, held in both hands. From where Branan sat the safety catch looked as though it was pushed forward. The gun was ready to fire.

Snowman picked up the duct tape and keeping the gun at arm's length, walked round behind him.

Branen heard the tape strip off the reel. Suddenly there was a heavy blow to the side of his neck. He felt his collar bone break but he managed to stay conscious. He had to make a move now, or this might be the end for him. Using the adrenalin from the blow to his neck he bent forwards and pushed up. He spun round to face Snowman but the impact had left him dizzy. Snowman hit him hard on the side of the head with the pistol. Branen went down and a kick from Snowman hit him in the solar plexus. He was on all fours again and fucked.

"Try that again and you're dead. Get back in the fucking chair," said Snowman, holding the revolver steady.

Snowman handed him the tape and told him to wrap his left arm onto the arm of the chair, then walked round him at a safe distance. "Put your other arm on the chair." Slowly and clumsily he bound Branen's right forearm.

Without being too obvious Branen flexed his muscles, trying to produce as much slack as he could. Snowman put the revolver on the table and stuck a piece of tape across Branen's mouth. Blood oozed from the cut on the side of his head and dripped onto his chest.

Snowman left the room and came back carrying the blow-torch. He turned up the radio and took a penknife from his pocket. "Who the fuck are you and what d'you want...?" He leant down and screamed into Branen's face, "You fucking bastard."

Holding Branen's left hand and keeping to one side, he pushed the blade up Branen's middle finger nail and levered it off. Branen reared up in the chair. Then Snowman pushed the blade up Branen's index finger nail and levered that one off too. The pain was excruciating.

Snowman had lost all control. This bastard had mugged and robbed him and as far as he was concerned he wanted to hurt him as much as possible.

Branen tried to play possum.

Snowman lent forward and screamed into his ear, "Fuck-head... who are you and what d'you want?"

He lit the blow-torch and started to run the blue flame across Branen's injured hand. The pain was so severe it felt unreal. His brain was tripping as though he was on LSD. Nothing appeared real any longer. In an effort to control the pain he tried to detach his mind from reality. The room was spinning and a wave of nausea made him wretch behind the tape. Snowman's prime motivation was to inflict maximum pain; he wasn't bothered about an answer. He was so angry that he had lost all reason.

Then the doorbell rang.

Snowman swore and went over to the entry-phone. He saw the Illims staring vacantly up at the camera. He told them to fuck off and come back in an hour.

Branen realised the inevitability of the situation; it was unlikely that

Snowman was going to allow him to live. If he was to survive he had to gamble and the doorbell had offered him a chance. He knew that most opportunities for escape came immediately after capture and he had left it late. He threw his legs up over his head and flung himself backwards off the chair. The backward somersault took him over and onto his feet. The right arm of the chair broke free, leaving it hanging from his forearm; his broken collar bone shot almost unbearable pain through his body but the adrenalin was just winning. The momentum had broken the stem on the back support and the remainder of the chair was dangling behind him, still attached to his left arm. As Snowman ran towards the table Branen stepped forward, measured the distance and stamped onto Snowman's knee. The knee twisted sideways and he lost his balance. Branen changed legs and caught him in the groin with a whipping front kick. He went down and his hat slid over his face. Branen turned, stumbled over the chair and launched himself towards the desk. He fell short but managed to tip the flimsy desk towards him. The revolver dropped to the floor. He picked it up with his right hand and checked the safety with his thumb. He fired in Snowman's direction. The bullet went through Snowman's stomach as he made a desperate lunge towards him. The round stopped him in mid-flight, twisting him back at an angle. It hadn't hit a bone but it had torn his guts. He crumpled in agony. He lay curled in the foetal position on the floor, clutching his stomach. His eyes were still open searching Branen's face. Branen wanted him to suffer. He tore the tape from his mouth and put his face close to Snowman's. "Who was the fat man with Carrie in Costas's?"

Snowman's voice was strained and weak, "Fuck you...."

Branen shouted at him, "You killed my daughter." Snowman stared blankly back at him. There was complete silence as Branen watched him die.

Branen slid down and sat absolutely still. The acrid smell of cordite reminded him of a scenario from the past that he didn't want to remember. He didn't feel any satisfaction from killing Snowman even if he was sure that he was involved in Carrie's murder. In his anger he had sought revenge, but killing one of the people responsible for her death did nothing to relieve his grief. Seeing his body lying there didn't resolve anything. Minutes ago he'd been full of life. Killing people can be surprisingly easy and pointless.

As Branen got to his feet a police car with its siren screaming drove past. For a moment he thought someone had heard the shot, but the police car kept going. He put the gun down and pulled the tape away from his left arm, releasing the chair. His hand was swollen and his shoulder was throbbing.

He reached into Snowman's jacket to retrieve his pistol and noticed a wad of notes in his inside chest pocket. He pulled out a dozen fifty pound notes. Snowman wouldn't be needing those any longer. Branen put his coat back on and went out into the main factory area. He noticed several copies of the Qur'an lying around. He went to the sink and washed his wounds. He taped up the two injured fingers leaving the blistering uncovered, hoping the burns would repair sooner in the open air. He'd left traces of DNA and finger prints in the office but as far as he knew all that information was confidential to The Associates and not available to any of the other services. He searched around and found a couple of paint cans and a plastic container of white spirit which he poured around the office and over Snowman. He put the Smith & Wesson revolver into Snowman's hand. He took one last look around then tossed a lit match into the office and shut the door. Putting the SIG back in the belt-bag, he picked up a mobile lying on the table and went down the stairs and out onto the street. He walked a hundred metres up Lisle street and dialled 999. The local fire station was two hundred metres from Masonic Mansions in Shaftesbury Avenue. They would have plenty of time to prevent the fire spreading beyond the top floor.

Branen waited. He was anxious to reassure himself that the Fire Brigade would arrive before anyone else in the building was hurt.

The Fire Brigade received the emergency call and were outside within ten minutes. Smoke was curling up into the darkening sky. The Chief Fire Officer sent one of his men into the pub to clear it of Saturday afternoon drinkers and another fireman was sent to ring Masonic Mansions' doorbells. When he did not receive any response he broke down the door.

Fifteen minutes after Branen had set the fire the remainder of the white spirit in the container burst into flames. The flaming liquid seeped through the floorboards and ran between the joists. The fire brigade were on the first floor when the flames finally reached the pressure cooker at the factory's front door. The heat generated caused it to explode which in turn triggered the other pressure cooker and the can of diesel under the window. Within moments the factory was blown apart.

The TV in the pub was turned up loud, the last race at Cheltenham was underway and the punters were refusing to obey the frustrated firemen urging them to vacate the premises; they had more important matters to consider: whether to order another drink and to decide which horse would win. When the bombs went off, the whole building shook and their minds were made up for them.

Branen turned and saw yellow flames curling up into the sky with debris raining down onto the road. There were people shouting and running. He was shaken by the size of the explosion and puzzled by the faint but familiar smell of M118 explosive. At the end of Gerrard Street he wiped the Illims' phone clean of finger-prints, turned it off and threw it into a skip and continued up Wardour Street. The air was alive with emergency sirens as he crossed over Shaftesbury Avenue from Chinatown back into the heart of Soho.

89. HARRY & MIKEY & THE PRIME MINISTER : (4.08PM, SATURDAY 14 NOVEMBER)

In the bedroom of the prostitute's flat, one second after the top floor of Masonic Mansions had blown up, Harry tightened the rifle stock into his shoulder, squeezed the trigger and shot dead the police observer in the window opposite.

The explosion on the corner of Lisle Street was two hundred and fifty metres south as the crow flies and it was loud enough for Harry to hear. He wondered briefly what it was, but being focussed on his next shot didn't give it a second thought.

The noise of the blast caused Mikey and the Prime Minister to turn and look in Harry's direction.

Mikey had planned to activate the bombs when she returned later that night after the Prime Minister was dead, but her plan had been brought forward by Branen. The explosion took her by surprise as she stared in the direction of Chinatown, wondering what had happened.

In the couple of seconds that followed, Harry panned the rifle across towards the Prime Minister as the Close Protection Officers surrounding him started to react to the explosion. Filling the frame of Harry's scope was the person shaking hands with the Prime Minister. Harry saw the bleached hair, the expensive diamond earrings, the tanned complexion and recognised the cunt. He could not believe his eyes. He only hesitated for an instant. There in front of him was that BNP arsehole who had humiliated him in front of the crowd, who had demeaned him, made him beg for mercy, who had told him to shoot the Prime Minister and who was now shaking hands with him. Harry realised that he'd been set up. He would never be allowed to escape. Michelle de Lavigne was never going to send him to the West Indies with fifty thousand pounds in cash.

The Prime Minister's office had been told that Michelle de Lavigne was a major financial donor to St. Barnabas's charity, which was why they had approved her introduction to the PM. The PM did not want to upset or alienate anyone, because the results of recent polls showed his lead was as thin as a cigarette paper. Mikey had been granted all the necessary security clearances, even though it was on record that she was standing for the British National Party. And the security team's attention had been distracted from the activities of Michelle de Lavigne by the recent shooting in Soho Square. With this shooting in mind, the bodyguards had intended to whisk the Prime Minister straight inside the building. However the PM had other ideas; it was one of his last public appearances before the General Election. He wanted the press to photograph him glad-handing the local dignitaries and to be seen publicly helping a local women's charity. It had been planned that he was to shake the local vicar's hand, but Mikey had grabbed the initiative and the PM hadn't realised who Mikey was. To the chagrin of the security men she stepped in front of the vicar. She believed the most advantageous place for her to be that afternoon was here shaking hands with the Prime Minister; even though Harry White was going to shoot him while she stood next to him. She would be seen smiling and being welcomed by the Establishment. There was no conceivable way she would be linked to the assassination.

It took milliseconds for Harry to react. 'To think I believed her... that weirdo must think I'm a fucking idiot to put this rifle in my car then give her the keys.' With that thought, he pulled the trigger and the rifle kicked against his shoulder for a second time in just a few seconds. "Die you bitch."

The bullet entered Mikey's brow between her eyes and removed the whole of the back of her head. The shot pulverised her skull. Brain tissue and bone blasted over the bodyguards and the dignitaries standing behind her. They stood motionless, covered in her blood.

Harry realised he had a hard-on.

He left the two ejected cartridge cases and the Qur'an on the floor and wrapped the barrel of the rifle with the lead bag he'd brought with him, then packed it into the guitar case.

Now the hermaphrodite was dead the only reason for leaving the spent cases and the Qur'an was to cover his own trail.

When he reached street level on this memorable winter's afternoon, dusk was beginning to fall. By the time the Close Protection Officers had rushed the PM back to the armoured Range Rover, and the Chief Operations Officer had realised he was not getting any response from one of his observers it was too late.

Harry walked briskly away and blended into the afternoon crowd, who were completely unaware of the chaos going on round the corner a hundred and fifty metres away. He crossed over Dean Street to his car, which was parked in the bay opposite his flat.

The helicopter, with its blades thrashing the air just a hundred feet above Harry, was dashing backwards and forwards like a demented dragonfly. He knew its thermal-imaging camera would not be able to penetrate the lead bag and would not identify the heat residue from the rifle barrel.

A police car skidded to a halt across the end of Dean Street, closing it off to all traffic and pedestrians. As its siren faded away Harry dumped the guitar case back in the boot. He congratulated himself as he watched the police setting up crime tape. 'They'll never know how close they were to catching me...' He slammed the boot lid.

He hoped Snowman would not know about Mikey's death yet. He would move the Datsun over to Masonic Mansions as soon as possible and then he could collect the money. He had rid himself of one torturing cunt but the other bastard was still around, and he was determined to kill him too. He wondered what the mutant would do about it if he found out that he had shot the hermaphrodite instead of the Prime Minister. He locked the car and crossed back to his front door. He briefly checked the end of the street where the police stood in bullet-proof waistcoats, clutching Heckler & Koch submachine guns to their chests. He smiled to himself as he watched them pace self-importantly backwards and forwards across the junction.

Harry waited to see how the rest of the day panned out, unaware that Snowman was already dead.

90. BRANEN – (4.15PM, SATURDAY 14 NOVEMBER)

Branen walked unsteadily from Masonic Mansions towards Dean Street.

His wounds were throbbing and the pain made it hard to think about anything else.

He made his way along Old Compton Street. Soho was crawling with police cars; why were they in central Soho and not down in Chinatown checking out the factory fire? He saw the police car slewed across the end of Dean Street and wondered if someone had seen him leave Masonic Mansions and if there was an APB out on him. He stepped into a shop doorway and watched for a while. Further up Old Compton Street a Range Rover, followed by a Jaguar, hung a left out of Greek Street and with squealing tyres accelerated away. He couldn't understand why they were closing down central Soho; maybe there had been another incident. The place was crawling with armed police. Soho was getting too hot for him.

He still had to settle the score with Michelle de Lavigne and check out the beehive camera, but he was going to have to lay low for a few hours and wait until things quietened down. It was too risky to continue through Soho so he decided to return to his fallback position until things cooled down. He stopped off at a chemist where he bought the strongest painkillers available, sterile dressings and a bottle of blonde hair dye.

He crossed back over Shaftesbury Avenue and headed to the China Hotel; he was confident the Firm did not know about this place. He had not used their mobile from there and had not been followed. It was the safest place for him to hole up for the next few hours. He had no idea what was ahead of him but he knew that the next few days would determine his future.

The street door was locked and there wasn't a bell. He knocked and waited. Eventually the Chinese woman opened the door just wide enough with the security chain attached. He thought, 'This is meant to be a fucking hotel.'

She stared at him, looking as if she wasn't going to let him in. He tried to keep the SIG out of sight as he searched through the belt-bag to show her the room key. He smiled, hoping she remembered he had paid in advance, then without a word she opened the door and disappeared into her cupboard under the stairs.

He needed to sleep but first he had to sort himself out. The collar bone seemed to be a clean break. It ached like hell but it was not too debilitating. His left hand was another problem. The fingers were swollen and throbbing and he did his best to burst the raw blisters and bandage the wounds. Then he took a double dose of painkillers.

After a complete overhaul and a cold shower he lay down on the bed to make a plan for a sequence of events that he had no real control over. He'd been in situations before where missions had got out of hand and had learned to cope with the unpredictable and ad lib the moment. He had always come out alive, but now he was too close to the people who wanted to get rid of him and who knew too much about him.

He tried to put himself in their shoes. If he could get out of Soho alive he knew they didn't have the infrastructure to follow him; they would have to use the Firm and probably the police who possessed the manpower. But as the Firm did not know him as well as The Associates did, this would be to his advantage. He could run but he was not prepared to let Carrie, Jane and her baby die unavenged. Their deaths had been a meaningless waste. The bastards had destroyed the most important people in his life and he needed to find the fat man.

He turned this over in his mind as he lay there listening to the sounds of Chinatown echoing down the empty mews. Occasionally a car headlight would cut a sharp swathe through the room and after it had passed across the ceiling, the corners would dissolve back into darkness. He got up and opened the window. A breeze carried the smell of rain and the sound of traffic into the room; it was preferable to the stale odour of the room.

91. BRANEN & THE CONTROLLER :
(2AM, SUNDAY 15 NOVEMBER)

A few hours later Branen was awoken by the pain in his shoulder.

There was a strong, familiar smell in the room which confused him; then he remembered the truffles. He opened the wardrobe; the fumes would have worked instead of smelling salts. Three thousand pounds and hours of searching wasted.

After another cold shower he re-taped the damaged fingers and bound the hand to keep the swelling down. He snipped away at his hair with nail scissors until it was as short and neat as he could make it, then bleached what was left. It didn't quite turn out as planned; instead of blonde it turned an orangey red and the chemicals made his head itch; it wasn't Vidal Sassoon but it was good enough. The nagging pain in his shoulder slowed him down and the whole exercise took over an hour. He put his arm into a sling and tucked the remains of the medical kit into the belt bag. It was the early hours when he crept out of the hotel.

He was hungry and after a plate of stir-fry, a couple of beers and another double dose of painkillers his spirits lifted as much as could be expected considering his predicament. He wanted to get back and suss out whether Mikey was at home and then decide what to do about the camera in the beehive, so made his way back into central Soho. Even though it was the early hours the streets were still fairly busy, mostly with young clubbers and drunks looking for action. He tucked back into Tyler's Court opposite Mikey's apartment and decided to sit it out for a few hours, hoping she had been out for the night and would return home while he was there.

No such luck. By about four-thirty in the morning the streets were a lot quieter and he was freezing, mainly because he had cut off all his hair. While he was turning things over and considering his options, he remembered that he still had Snowman's mobile. Wondering if Mikey knew about Snowman's death he dialled her number.

The Controller's watchers had scoured Soho for the last two days without finding Branen and now she was forced to withdraw the night surveillance team to save on overtime payments.

The Controller's office was the operation's nerve centre; it was a sectioned off glass box with venetian blinds, offering privacy when she needed it. Directly outside the office were her four researchers, sitting at computer consoles surrounded by telephones.

After the police had removed Mikey's possessions from her corpse and logged them, the Firm requisitioned them. On the table in the centre of the meeting room Mikey's phone and other personal effects had been neatly lined up.

James, the senior researcher had taken a break and was fast asleep when Mikey's phone rang. He took it straight into the Controller's office without knocking.

She ordered a trace on the call and then answered, "Yes."

Branen didn't think it sounded like Mikey's voice. "Can I speak to Mikey?" he asked, imitating Snowman's hoarse voice.

"Who's calling?"

The voice sounded familiar. "Tell her it's Snowman," he said.

"Where are you?" she asked.

Branen recognised the Controller's voice; he rang off and removed the battery.

It had been a brief exchange but the Controller had also recognised his voice. It took another ten minutes to confirm that the call had been from the Soho area, but it was too short to locate accurately.

92. BRANEN : (5.30AM, SUNDAY 15 NOVEMBER)

If the Firm had Mikey's phone they were bound to have her as well.

Why had they picked her up? What had happened to make them

change their strategy? Branen was wasting time continuing to watch her front door so he decided to concentrate on the beehive.

Soho had gone quiet and the last stragglers were heading home. The streets were intimidatingly dark and empty. He thought back to his teenage years and wondered if time had glamourised those early adventures.

He had another three hours of darkness but if the watchers were out looking for him, their job would be much easier because there weren't many people left on the streets. His only advantage was that the cameras didn't have enough resolution to identify him at night.

He was running out of time and had to keep moving but his problems were escalating. He swallowed more painkillers and walked over to Carrie's flat, trying to avoid pedestrians and cameras. He scanned the roof on the opposite corner. He couldn't see the beehives from the pavement so he looked round the building. Forty metres up Bateman Street was the restaurant doorway he had been ejected from, next door to a recording studio. Between them a fairly solid drainpipe went straight up to the roof. A forty foot climb would get him onto the flat roof and to the beehives. Normally he'd manage it but his injuries were severe enough to compromise the plan. But he had to do it for Carrie, and the more he thought about it the more problems would enter his head and the more likely that he would not attempt it.

He looked both ways down the street; there was no-one around. He took off the overcoat, tied the arms round his waist and climbed up onto the railings. A spear of pain shot through his shoulder as he tried to lift his body weight. After a couple of attempts to grip the pipe he started up. Hoping that the cast iron joints were properly attached to the wall he climbed, resting at each intersection, with his feet jammed behind the pipe. The wind was gusting and the higher he got the more vulnerable he felt. But the adrenalin dulled the fear. Taking the initiative with positive action gave him a psychological boost. He climbed as silently as possible in case anyone was sleeping in any of the rooms he passed.

Close to the top he started to shake uncontrollably. He was on the final stage and if he managed to climb the last few metres nothing would stop him after that.

At last his hands gripped the coping stones surrounding the roof.

He was almost there but the pain had made him light-headed. His muscles were turning to jelly but all he could do was terrify himself by looking down at the railings thirty feet below. He could not rest for too long in case he was spotted. With one last thrust he managed to get his right arm over the edge and pull up and over the balustrade. He lay pressed against the sloping tiled roof, looking up at the dawn sky that was beginning to show between the scudding dark clouds. The relief of conquering the climb left him feeling euphoric.

He allowed himself a few minutes to get his breath back and to stop shaking. Everything ached but he had made it.

93. HARRY : (SATURDAY NIGHT AND SUNDAY MORNING, 15 NOVEMBER)

Harry settled back into the sofa and sat revelling in the success of his mission.

It had been a busy week and the satisfaction of seeing the hermaphrodite's head disintegrate had left him feeling good.

'Fuck it, why not?' he asked himself as he went round to the dinette and opened the chipboard cupboard. He pulled out a bottle of mead and the one bottle of vodka he had left.

"Fuck it, why not?" He enjoyed the sound of his own voice; he didn't manage much conversation. He chopped out a line and poured himself a generous cocktail. He took a long slug, slumped back into the sofa and stared at the ceiling.

The idea of living in the West Indies for the rest of his life was a fantasy that had seemed attractive at the time, but he was happy and except for the money his life had not changed dramatically. He was a man of the city; he was street-wise and he enjoyed the big smoke, the dingy dives, the tarts and the hustle of his city existence. In fact he would have been lost without it. He didn't regret a thing. He had shot that measly queer and watched through the scope as the life was blasted from her body. He had enjoyed that moment. If only he could have slowed it down, making her suffer gradually. He'd wanted her to realise it was him who had pulled the trigger. She would never know, but fuck her, she was dead now just like that prying bastard he had shot in the square. He was, unusually, smiling to himself; he felt invincible. He had the final solution for any problem he might come across in his life. Maybe he would keep the rifle although he knew this would be foolish because it could be traced back to the killings, but he didn't need to decide right now.

The hours slid away. They disappeared like minutes, as they always did when Harry snorted speed and drank his cocktail watching more porn on the internet. He had decided not to take his car over to Snowman at Masonic Mansions until the next morning when he could recce the route before driving it. Not knowing that Snowman was already dead, he was gambling that he could do it before Snowman found out about Mikey's death.

It must have been about six in the morning when he heard a noise on the roof above his head. By now he was in an acute state of mental and emotional turmoil. He tore his obsessed mind from the computer screen and stared up at the ceiling.

94. BRANEN & HARRY : (6.15AM, SUNDAY 15 NOVEMBER)

Branen recovered his breath and edged his way along the roof and onto Harry's flat roof and the beehives.

As he lifted the cover off the middle hive, a lump of the edging-strip fell away. It seemed to fall in slow motion and as he tried to catch it, it clattered onto the roof. He froze, hoping that anyone in the flat below would be asleep. He listened for a couple of minutes then removed the top box. On the next level he discovered the video camera. There were cables running through the hive and across the asphalt to a roof-light where they disappeared.

Harry dragged himself to his feet. The wind must have blown something off one of the hives. Then he panicked, imagining that someone was up there. He stumbled to the television and turned on the hive camera. It was still pointing towards Carrie's empty window. He had a moment of regret as he remembered the hours he had spent watching her; that would never happen again. His heart began pumping violently from fear and amphetamines and there was the buzzing in his head. And then his nose started to bleed. In Harry's confused mind he translated it as the bees calling to him.

As Branen stared at the camera the red power light came on. He realised it was being operated from the floor below. He moved silently behind the roof-light. Within minutes it creaked open on its rusty hinges.

Breathing heavily, a hulking man wearing a sweat-stained shirt appeared through the opening. As he climbed from his burrow onto the roof he was lit by the glow from inside the flat. He was fat but looked strong; the effect was eerie and menacing. His hair was dishevelled and his feet were bare. His movements were laboured and convulsive as though he might at any moment have an epileptic fit. Then Branen recognised him. He was the man who had followed him four days ago and now he knew why; he had seen him in Carrie's flat through the hive camera. He must be the bloke Carrie had met in Costas's. He still had his back to Branen.

"Who are you?" Branen demanded.

Harry's whole frame convulsed with the shock of Branen's voice. He swung round from the waist and the rest of his body followed. Even with his injuries Branen knew he could take him. Harry stood transfixed, staring at Branen, his nose bleeding. For a moment Branen felt sorry for the pathetic figure, but the image of Carrie's body in the morgue filled his mind.

"Why did you kill her?" he asked.

Harry stared at Branen. He was confused. He recognised the face but the hair was different. He was sure this was the man he had shot dead in Soho Square but here he was re-incarnated on his roof. He was here for retribution. This was his nemesis.

In November the bees were dormant but the buzzing was getting louder and fiercer.

"You killed Carrie, you bastard..." Branen heard himself shouting, "DIDN'T YOU?"

Harry dropped to his knees, "She needed me." He had tears in his eyes as he stared at him.

"Then why kill her?"

"I was told to."

"Who by?"

"The hermaphrodite."

Branen hesitated. "Who…?"

"That fucking queer… that fucking fascist… but now it's all over… I've settled the score, she's gone… I blew her away."

"You've shot Michelle de Lavigne… why?"

Harry didn't answer; he just stared at Branen.

"You killed my daughter… and you shot Jane too?" He wanted confirmation that this was the man who had murdered his family.

Harry crawled forward on all fours. "I shot you," he mumbled. Buzz… buzz… BUZZ… they were swarming again… they were swarming in his skull… FUCKING BUZZ BUZZ BUZZ. Their black furry bodies were exploding in front of his eyes. He clambered back to his feet and staggered over to the hive that he'd stolen the Queen bee from. He picked it up and held it above his head. With a howl from deep inside his stomach he hurled it down into the street. He leant back into the prevailing wind and watched. The hive seemed to float down before smashing into the road. He stared at the wreckage. The angry bees began to swarm. They surged back up between the buildings, spiralling up like a massive shoal of krill moving in perfect unison. They passed Harry as he held his arms out to them. They formed themselves into a serpent-like configuration above him. Then the demonic mass swooped down and swamped his upper body, turning him into a ferocious black cloud of insects. He became a buzzing, brown mass, infested with stinging bees.

Harry let out a howl of pain and stumbled over the balustrade. He reached out as though clutching for his departing soul. He held out his wings and attempted to fly. As he fell the four storeys, he imagined he was being carried far away by the sheer energy of fifteen thousand bees.

Before he hit the road, they left his doomed body to its fate and swarmed away into the distance.

Branen heard the heavy, sickening thump as the man's body hit the road.

He didn't go over to the edge; instead he turned and went down into the flat. There was a collection of Polaroid photographs laid out in front of the man's computer. They were all pictures of Carrie, naked except for a pair of briefs. The shock of seeing his own daughter posing for these pictures caught him like a punch in the solar plexus. Tucked under the end photograph he found one of her lying naked on the floor of her flat. The bastard had photographed her mutilated body. His head was spinning. He grabbed the back of a chair and took several deep breaths. Then he gathered up the pictures. He had to get out of there as soon as possible. He grabbed a set of car keys he found by the door and ran down the stairs. By the glow of the street lamps shining through the fanlight he could just about read the numbers on the key-fob.

Luckily six-thirty on a wintery Sunday morning was about as quiet as Soho could be. The fat man's body was spread-eagled in the middle of Dean Street with his arms out above his head like a hollow fallen oak tree. He lay amongst the debris of the crushed beehive. There was blood oozing from his ears and nose. Branen checked the car number plates in front of the building before starting to search the street.

A drunk couple on the opposite pavement fumbled with their mobile phone.

Branen found the car parked right in front of the couple, who were calling the police.

He realised it was the same car he had chased down Greek Street. If he'd had any doubts about the fat man shooting Jane and her baby, he didn't now. He tried to keep his face turned away from the couple as he unlocked the driver's door. The man on the mobile pointed to the body. Slurring his words he called out to Branen, "Hey, man, see if he's okay."

"He'll be fine," Branen said in an Irish accent and got into the car. He had to back up to pull out of the parking space and avoid the broken body beside the car.

Hoping the couple were sufficiently drunk not to note the number plate, he drove off.

He parked in Soho Square and waited for daylight. It had only been a week since the satellite phone had rung informing him that Carrie had been murdered. Within seven days he had lost Carrie and Jane and the people responsible were dead as well.

Now he had to get out. He represented a critical and unpredictable risk to The Associates and they knew he suspected that Carrie's murder was due to their negligence. Since they no longer had an emotional hold or any other leverage over him, he was too dangerous to be left alive. Because of his history they would use their best operatives to execute the job while he was on home territory.

He had no reason to stay in the UK any longer; he would return to his small-holding, but even there he would have no future. Even if he could get back safely he would have to disappear again.

The UK government would think twice before compromising the sovereignty of an ally by murdering one of its own citizens on foreign soil. Years before, the CIA station chief in Milan and twenty-six agents were prosecuted for kidnapping an al Qaeda suspect in Italy. The deliberate use of lethal force in an allied country was considered to be an act of terrorism. Without careful planning to ensure that it would be a deniable operation the UK Government would not risk it. If they tried at all it would have to look like an accident.

The Firm was efficient and thorough. As soon as they were briefed by The Associates to find him, they would check out the passengers on all incoming flights from Europe arriving around the time that he collected the cardboard box. When they discovered his name was not on any of the flight lists they would know he had not flown into Stansted. Then they would check other means of transport and ports of entry, and all the registration numbers in the Stansted airport car parks, looking for his method of entry. This would be a long process. He had to keep delaying them to give himself as much time as possible below their radar. He couldn't risk leaving the country by any of the conventional routes so he decided to try to convince them this was exactly what he would do; travel to France via Dover.

He sat in the car until just after eight o'clock when the sun rose. Then he left the Datsun parked in Soho Square and walked to Brewer Street where he'd seen a twenty-four hour internet café.

There was one other customer; he looked up guiltily from his screen as Branen entered and waved to the assistant behind the counter who beckoned him over. "How long?" he asked.

"A few minutes will do," Branen said, noticing the assistant was pierced like a dart-board and had 'Fuck You' tattooed in the middle of his shaved head. He had enough jewellery dangling from every orifice to own a share in a gold mine.

"That'll be a pound for 'alf an hour."

Branen gave him a coin.

"You pervs are all the fuckin' same… something for nuffing."

Branen was tempted to knock his 'Fuck You' head off but he didn't need the attention at that moment.

It took a few minutes to log on to a ferry service and book a one-way ticket on the 12.15 ferry from Dover to Calais using the Branen credit card. He gave the Range Rover registration number with the booking, knowing this would give the Firm another lead. He wanted to delay them by having to search for the car. At last he had the initiative and as long as he kept it he was in control. He had to keep selling them dummies which would allow him to keep moving on undiscovered.

He returned to Soho Square and replaced the battery and SIM card in the mobile, allowing the Firm to locate him. He keyed in number 7.

When the voice answered he spelt out, "V.I.N.T.A.G.E."

"Yes," the Controller spoke quietly. She asked herself, 'Why has he left it until now to call, what's he up to?'

Branen said, "I don't know whether you have heard but events have progressed."

"The call is secure, you can speak freely," said the Controller.

Her calm tone belied the fact that she was about to implode but he decided to let her have what he knew.

"Michelle de Lavigne's fake terrorist cell was in Masonic Mansions where they were producing crack… I think that the building was rigged with explosives and that Snowman was her main man. Snowman was responsible for the plan to kill Carrie. He's dead and so is the sniper who murdered Carrie and shot her mother and the baby in Soho Square…" He paused to let it sink in. "…The same man who shot Michelle de Lavigne… was he working for you?"

The Controller was confused, "Who is this sniper?" she asked, thinking that it might be him. "…The police think that the PM was the target. Are you telling me de Lavigne was the mark?"

Branen did not want to get that deeply involved, so he didn't answer.

The Controller decided that if she let him know how much intel they had, he might let something slip. "They've found the shooter's position… a police observer and two prostitutes dead… and a copy of the Qur'an with two cartridge cases left at the location. If you know who shot de Lavigne, you must know more."

"That shooting had nothing to do with me... my job is over. I want you to call the dogs off," he demanded.

The Controller just managed to suppress her anger. "There are no dogs... I need you to come in for a full de-briefing and then you can go on your way," she lied, aware that the SCS had other plans.

Branen thought she sounded genuine. She probably didn't know that he could not be allowed to live now Carrie was dead.

"I need to have some sleep."

"We can arrange that for you."

"What do you suggest?" he asked.

"I will send a car for you in half an hour... at the junction of Dean and Old Compton... same as before. Can you be there?"

He was tempted to tell her she already knew where he was but resisted. He needed that half hour and didn't want her putting out an emergency pick-up on him.

"I'll be there," he said, sounding resigned.

She rang off. "Fuck," she screamed.

Within five minutes of calling the Controller, Branen was standing at the mini-cab kiosk in Old Compton Street. It was early but a couple of cabs stood outside on double yellow lines with the engines running. Beside the kiosk was a newspaper poster with the headline, 'Attempted assassination of Prime Minister'.

"How much to do a collect and return from Folkstone ferry port?" Branen asked. "I want the cabbie to pick-up an envelope from a white Volvo in the arrivals area. He can't miss it, it's got foreign plates... I'll collect it from you later this afternoon."

While Saul worked out a price Branen picked up a newspaper and read the front page which described the shooting of Michelle de Lavigne; according to the journalist, the shooter was attempting to assassinate the Prime Minister.

"It'll be a hundred and fifty quid including an hour's waiting... and that's cash, mate," said Saul.

He took the money and led Branen over to speak with the driver.

Branen had already switched off the ring tone on the Firm's mobile and while he explained it all again, he got into the back of the cab and slipped the mobile down between the rear seat cushions. "See you later," he said, then got out of the car and watched the blue Toyota with music blaring drive to the end of Old Compton Street and pull out into the traffic on Charing Cross Road.

Now every minute counted.

95. THE CONTROLLER & THE SCS : (9AM, SUNDAY 15 NOVEMBER)

After she'd received Branen's call the Controller phoned the SCS.

He had dined with one of his 'chargé d'affaires' until the early hours of Sunday morning. They had started with an excellent Mersault followed by an '83 Chateau Pichon-Lalande, a new wine to the SCS that was too good to leave alone. The last thing the SCS wanted, as he sat in bed sucking indigestion tablets, was to hear from his office, but the call of duty had demanded that he leave the mobile on.

"Branen's been in touch... and I've arranged to have a car pick him up," said the Controller, anxious to be seen to be on top of this case.

"Good," said the SCS. "What makes you think he'll be at the RV?"

"He sounded exhausted and I got the feeling he wants out," said the Controller, trying to sound optimistic. Her lack of knowledge and control of the situation left her feeling frustrated and angry.

Her senior female researcher, Antoinette, barged into the room. The Controller saw the expression on her face and put her hand over the receiver.

"Branen's call was made from Soho Square... but he's still got the mobile turned on and he's on the move, Ma'am."

The Controller put her finger to her lips and spoke to the SCS. "I've got breaking news... I'll get back to you." She ended the call.

"I told you I wanted someone to collect him straight away..." she shouted at Antoinette, "...where's he heading?"

"Through east London... he's travelling fast... he's done six miles in the last ten minutes... I think he's heading for the M20 and Folkstone or Dover... shall I cancel the car that's meant to collect him, Ma'am?"

"Keep me informed on his location... get on with it." She waved Antoinette away.

She had missed breakfast. Her blood sugar was low. She slumped back and closed her eyes. 'Why...' she wondered, '...has he left the phone turned on?' The question virtually answered itself.

She rang the SCS back. "Branen's leaving London and heading east."

"Has he got his phone turned on?" asked the SCS.

"Yes, sir."

Knowing Branen was too smart to leave a trail unless he wanted to the SCS asked, "Are you sure he has got the phone with him?"

"No, sir," admitted the Controller, beginning to feel her job disappearing in her ear, "...but I'm about to check the ferry companies for any advance bookings."

"Before you do that ring his fucking phone and find out if he's on the other end of it, and bring him in immediately... if you can find him," said the SCS and rang off.

The Controller wanted to scream, but she rang Branen's phone anyway, knowing that she would not get an answer. They would still have to catch up with the phone, whether or not Branen was accompanying it. Meanwhile he could still be in Soho and she would have to continue searching for him there.

Realising that she was going to need more resources, she put a call through to her Chief. She made it clear that to find Branen it was essential she be given the freedom to use any facility she required; she would need the helicopter as soon as possible to catch the vehicle carrying the mobile.

The Chief needed to know who was going to pay for all these extra overheads and told the Controller he would get back to her after he had spoken to the SCS.

He was back on the phone minutes later. "You have special authorisation... you are in charge of this case and you can use any resource you need, as long as you don't let anyone else know what it's about. That's a lot of power... don't fuck up... you know your job depends on it," he said, relieved to pass on the responsibility. He was glad he only had a short time to serve before his carefully planned retirement. In fact with the current pressure on him, given half a chance he would retire today.

The Controller knew that if she succeeded in capturing Branen it would put her at the top of the list to inherit the Chief's post; and then she would be beyond the reach of the hungry young Turks snapping at her heels. In fact it would put her in total control of them; a role she longed for. The feeling that she was partly responsible for Carrie's death concentrated her mind and made her more determined; it was a matter of personal and professional pride that she catch the bastard, whatever he had or hadn't done.

96. THE SENIOR CIVIL SERVANT & DENNIS : (9AM, SUNDAY 15 NOVEMBER)

Branen had disappeared off the radar and the SCS was beginning to regret ever getting involved with the Firm.

He blamed their bureaucracy for the Branen fuck-up; he preferred his own system of autocracy. He was reminded of the example made of Group 13, even though its actions were secretly condoned by the Government.

This was the first time one of the SCS's agents had gone native, and now the existence of The Associates was in peril. He went to the wall safe and removed the satellite phone and the code book he used to contact his Operations Officers. He dialled Dennis Leung but the phone went straight to voicemail so he left a coded message.

When Dennis's mobile rang in his briefcase, he was leaving his Dansey Street Club having spent the night with his favourite concubine. He returned to his wife and daughter in the penthouse apartment in Gerrard Street and using the secure mobile called the SCS.

"We've got a rogue agent who has to be dealt with..." snapped the SCS. "...He's on the run and presents a major threat... we must eliminate the problem once and for all. Put your ear to the ground and check if anybody has seen him in Chinatown. I hardly need tell you the matter is top secret... wait there and I will fax through his description." The SCS preferred unidentifiable faxes to emails or texts.

Dennis Leung asked, "What's the priority rating?"

"It's a top priority wet-job... immediate," the SCS confirmed.

The SCS ended the call with a sense of relief. He had finally authorised the removal of the politically damaging problem that Branen represented. His worry was that Branen had already flown the nest and that Leung would have to wait until that inefficient female Controller had found him.

97. BRANEN : (9AM, SUNDAY 15 NOVEMBER)

Branen returned to the Datsun in Soho Square and headed west out of London avoiding the major routes, which would be covered by CCTV.

The Firm would eventually discover he was not heading east towards the ferry ports but in the Datsun going in the opposite direction. He had gained valuable time because by not flying into Stansted his passport had not been recorded on arrival. They would have to find his entry point and then trace the Range Rover. And he had added to their problems by dumping the mobile in the minicab so that they would have to follow the phone to rule it out. But he was dealing with professionals and they would be calculating what his fall-back plans might be.

Getting out of London without being picked up on traffic cameras was going to be impossible. He headed north towards Barnet and on to the A41. He paid cash and filled the car with petrol before reaching Hemel Hempstead. He was looking for a minor road off to the west, out of range of any cameras. After about ten miles, near Berkhamsted, he found a turning and wound his way south-west, sticking to minor roads and lanes. The low sun was an ideal compass point to keep to his left. It was a cold, bright winter's day and the trees had little foliage left on them. He was surrounded by the soft browns and verdant greens of late autumn. The natural beauty of the English countryside was in stark contrast to the monochrome of Soho.

Keeping the sun in his face, he meandered on, not knowing exactly where he was. Every time he came to a main road, if he could not cross straight over he turned back and found an alternative route south. Having allowed them to see him heading north he was determined to avoid the cameras from now on.

He passed under the M4 west of Reading between the villages of

Tidmarsh and Bradfield. A direct route to Reading from London was about sixty miles and took just over an hour. He checked the tripometer and saw he had done over two hundred miles since leaving Soho and it had taken him more than six hours.

It was now two-thirty in the afternoon and it felt as if he was running waist-deep in water. By attempting to hide he was using up valuable time.

98. THE CONTROLLER : (9.30AM, SUNDAY 15 NOVEMBER)

The Controller was furious with herself.

She had not given Carrie's case her full attention from the beginning and now she had to deal with the repercussions as well as with Branen's unpredictable behaviour.

It was nine-thirty in the morning when the information about Branen's booking on the 12.15 Dover ferry reached her. The reservation for a Range Rover begged the question: had Branen arrived in the UK in this vehicle? The Controller beckoned to one of her researchers through the glass screen. "Trace the Range Rover... and send UK Customs the e-fit and passport details. Tell them we do not have a photograph so they must double-check all single males between thirty and fifty years old who try to leave the country today. Tell them to keep it up until further notice. If they detain any suspects they must contact us straight away with photographs. And they must only notify us... not the police. This is a matter of national security and must not become general knowledge. Make them feel important, that they've been entrusted with classified information... they must not release anybody until we give permission... I don't want any mistakes. I've had the helicopter assigned and I want it airborne right now. Locate the vehicle with the mobile in it... find out if it's the Range Rover... he might be conning us." She waved him away and then asked herself out loud, "The trail is all a bit too easy and obvious... why doesn't he just buy a ticket when he gets there?"

Wondering if his boss needed an answer, the researcher hesitated in the doorway. She waved him away and looked up at the ceiling. "Where the fuck are you, Branen?"

The report on the two murdered prostitutes and the police spotter only compounded her problems. During door to door enquiries the police had failed to get a reply from the prostitutes. When they broke down the door they discovered the carnage. The police suspected that the Qur'an found on the second floor, the shooter's location, could be connected to the explosion at Masonic Mansions where more copies of the Qur'an had been found. The building had blown up at about the same time as the shootings; something the police had initially put down to coincidence. The fact that Michelle de Lavigne had her head shot off was thought to be inaccuracy by the sniper; they still considered the Prime Minister to have been the target.

As far as the Controller was concerned the accuracy of the bullet in Michelle de Lavigne's forehead was not a mistake or a detail to be ignored; Branen was capable of the task and had the motivation; and there was still Harry White to consider.

"Where's the helicopter?" she demanded.

The researcher looked at her warily. "We're having problems getting through to the pilot, Ma'am. He was initially out of reach... it'll be in the air anytime soon."

"It'll soon be too late. I need to know his movements after he arrived in the UK... on Monday or Tuesday the ninth and tenth of November... and I need it now." She was shouting again and she didn't want to.

Then the Chief rang. "The Police Commissioner has told me about an accident in Soho involving a Tommy Farr. The man's blood tests showed high alcohol and narcotic content... and he was covered in bee stings. They're saying he was drunk and started messing around with his bees and fell off the roof... they also found a camera hidden in one of the hives and they're trying to find out what he was up to. I want your assurance that the police know nothing of Carrie's murder. The police must not know that Tommy Farr was one of our officers. I want you to investigate any possible connection between Branen and Tommy Farr's death."

The Controller asked, "Can you arrange for Tommy Farr's blood and saliva samples to be sent to MI5's forensic laboratory?"

"Why?" asked the Chief.

"We need all the clarification we can get," she said.

"I'll see what I can do."

The Controller put the phone down without telling the Chief that she wanted to compare the DNA with the semen found in Carrie's flat; even if Tommy Farr was dead the results could finally clarify his involvement in Carrie's murder. She also kept quiet about the call she had received from Branen; she needed ammunition in case the Chief tried to feed her to the wolves. And she reckoned that Branen was involved in Farr's death.

Now another individual involved in Carrie's case had died. The pressure on her was mounting and her chances of failure were increasing. She remembered from Tommy Farr's records that he had been in the army. She asked herself, 'Was he filming Carrie... and did Branen get to him?'

She decided to dismiss the ridiculous information given to her by the SCS suggesting Branen had entered the country to kill his own daughter. There was no reason why he should have done this.

She turned to her team and said, "We've got to catch Branen before he disappears. Use SIS's records to get a full picture of Tommy Farr AKA Whitey and find out from the police if there were any witnesses to his death. Remember everything is at stake here... including our future."

99. DENNIS LEUNG :
(LUNCHTIME, SUNDAY 15 NOVEMBER)

Because Branen knew that the Chinese community was reknowned for its secrecy, he had deliberately rented the room in Chinatown.

He believed it would provide him with good cover from the Firm, but as far as the Chinese were concerned he stood out like a steak and kidney pie on a dim sum trolley.

Dennis discovered the whereabouts of the gwilo during lunch with his hung kwan, lieutenants; the owner of the China Hotel, Ng Kwok was one of Dennis's hung kwan. When he asked him if any white ghosts had come to his notice he reported that a gwilo had rented a room five days ago and had reappeared in his hotel last night. Dennis showed him the e-fit and Ng Kwok nodded vigorously. "Yes, that's the lei lo mo... but his hair is different."

Dennis finished his lunch before leaving to search the hotel room himself.

He noticed the smell as soon as he entered the room and when he opened the wardrobe he had to take a step back. He was not used to truffles and having eaten more than was comfortable and drunk a considerable amount of Elixir de Chine, the musky smell turned his stomach. A thorough search of the room produced the A4 envelope Branen had hidden in the mattress.

Dennis sat contemplating the photograph of a girl crossing Dean Street and read the report of her murder. He decided to keep the information to himself. However important this operation was to that stuck-up Civil Servant he had other pressing matters on his mind, so he returned to his club.

100. THE CONTROLLER : (4PM, SUNDAY 15 NOVEMBER)

The helicopter finally caught up with the blue Toyota as it approached junction 12 on the M20 on the outskirts of Folkstone.

The pilot managed to drop down low enough over the mini-cab to get the registration number, photograph the driver and establish that there was no passenger.

Within minutes of the Controller getting the message she telephoned her Chief to organise a stop and search of the mini-cab without giving the police the reason.

It took until 4pm before all the information on Branen and Tommy Farr had been assembled. She took her time digesting it then stood for a while at her window watching the winter sun disappear. "You're out there somewhere… and I'm going to find you."

She had originally notified Branen of his daughter's murder on the morning of Monday 9th November. She estimated that the earliest he could have arrived in the UK would have been that same afternoon, fourteen hours after Carrie's body had been discovered. She knew that he was in Soho at 1am on Wednesday because that was when he had first contacted her using the mobile from Left Luggage. She calculated that Branen's online booking for the midday Easyjet flight to Stansted on the Monday meant he should have arrived at Stansted at around 3pm.

Allowing for delays, the parcel of equipment at Left Luggage should have been collected by 5pm. But he did not collect it until 9.30am on Tuesday 10th. And if he had entered the country through the airport there would have been a Customs record of his passport being scanned.

She ordered her exhausted researchers to contact the French and UK Customs again. "I need to know when Branen arrived in the UK. I want a manifest of all the Channel port traffic between 2pm Monday the ninth and 9.30am the following day. Start at Dover, followed by Folkestone and Portsmouth... if you find nothing there then check Newhaven, Poole and Weymouth. Also contact Eurostar for the train records... and get French Customs to check all solo male drivers who paid cash on every train and ferry."

The problem the Controller had with ferry crossings was anyone could purchase a ticket with cash and after a cursory check of their documents the French authorities would let them through. French bureaucracy compounded her problems; however urgent the enquiry, French Customs' officials would have to interrupt their family's Sunday déjeuner for their rosbif colleagues. Cars disembarking from the ferries in the UK were recorded on CCTV but unless they were stopped by British Customs they could drive straight into the country. If Branen had arrived by ferry, which was what she believed, he had made himself difficult to trace.

When she discovered the ferry companies had no-one available on a Sunday night to search the records she was forced to wait.

101. BRANEN : (SUNSET, SUNDAY 15 NOVEMBER)

Branen crossed under the M4 and headed into the setting sun, keeping to country lanes.

He could not risk using the fat man's car for much longer. If they discovered it was gone they would suspect he had stolen it. Then they would go public with a top priority 'Wanted Missing Report' through the Police National Computer and it would be broadcast to police forces throughout the country. He had seen it done before when he was involved in a UK operation towards the end of his career. The police would not be given the full story or told why he was wanted, but a priority rating would be given to the case and they would have to react accordingly. The police would definitely be told that he was armed and he could not expect to be treated gently if they caught up with him.

By five o'clock dusk was closing in. He planned to spend the night in the car, parked up somewhere out of sight. He needed to find some woodland off the beaten track but within striking distance of a small town.

He drove on heading west on minor roads and followed the River Kennet for a while and passed a couple of pubs. He reckoned he could stop for a pint and a pie without raising any suspicion and without being located as long as he didn't use either of his credit cards. But for the moment he needed to keep going.

North of Marlborough he turned north-west towards Lyneham, where he had flown out of the country to a military airfield in France for the first recce of the mission that had got him into this mess. It was dark now and he risked a short stretch of the A3102 before turning right and skirting north of Chippenham. After a twenty minute drive along country lanes he found himself at a T-junction with the A4 towards Bath. He could not remember having passed a lane off to the west for several miles.

The tiredness was kicking in and against his better judgement he decided to turn onto the A4 and hope that he did not hit any villages with cameras. He passed through the sleepy villages of Corsham and Box and arrived at a roundabout on the edge of Batheaston village. Ahead of him the A4 turned into a dual-carriageway bypass. He decided he had pushed his luck far enough and turned off on to the old A4.

Batheaston village had two pubs, a village shop and not much else. He parked the car and got out to take a breather. His whole body was telling him to stop; his shoulder ached and his hand was throbbing.

The pub was lit up and the warm smell of food and beer wafted out on the cold night air. Unlike in France and some other European countries, hotel records were not registered with the authorities and he could have booked a room for the night. But he had taken a risk by using the A4 and it was in these moments of imagined safety that missions were wrecked.

He allowed himself twenty minutes in the pub. The locals didn't take much notice of him as he finished a sandwich and a pint. He had to force himself to move on. The time had come to change vehicles but he couldn't risk stealing one.

He noticed a small sign to The Fosse Way, the old Roman road leading north from Bath.

He climbed back into the car and started up the hill.

102. THE CONTROLLER : (7PM, SUNDAY 15 NOVEMBER)

It was 7pm when French Customs finally got back to the Firm.

Over a thousand private cars and five hundred vans had entered the UK via the six ferry ports in the south of England on the Monday afternoon and the following morning.

The Controller had just put down the telephone after her evening's de-brief with the SCS when her junior researcher stood up waving the computer print-out in his hand. He announced in a falsetto voice, "We've traced a grey Range Rover entering the UK on the 6am ferry into Dover on Tuesday the tenth… he didn't use a credit card… it's the same car that was booked on the 12.15 ferry leaving today… but this time paid for using his Branen credit card."

"Trace all transactions on that card at once… and I want all CCTV records on the roads leaving Dover on the tenth of November pulled… search for any sign of the Range Rover. And I want all the Stansted long term car parks to check their records… now get on with it."

She closed the door, got out the gin bottle and asked herself, 'Branen gave away the details of the Range Rover when he bought the ticket to Calais today, but if he had no intention of using that route why didn't he just invent a car registration number? Either he was going to use the ferry, or it was a bluff and he was trying to make me spend time looking for the car while he uses another escape route. It's all taking too fucking long.' Then she poured herself a large gin with a small tonic.

It took an hour for the Range Rover to be found. With this vehicle eliminated from her search she had to go back to square one, but she didn't know where to start looking.

The report on Tommy Farr had shown what she already knew. He was a low-grade operative recruited by the Firm for one mission and provided only with need-to-know information.

The final paragraph of the report caught her attention. It described his history including the fact that he was a trained sniper and it gave details of the car he owned. She was still waiting for the DNA report but she was coming to the conclusion that Whitey was directly involved in Carrie's murder. She assumed that because his body had been found in Dean Street in the early hours, his car must still be parked in the area. She ordered her officers to conduct a search of all the parking bays, car parks and garages in and around Soho and to check with the police for any stolen vehicles.

It only took an hour to establish that none of the local hire companies had rented to anyone resembling Branen or anyone who had paid with cash. No new transactions on either of his credit cards had shown up. When all these leads drew a blank and Tommy Farr's Datsun could not be found, the Controller concluded that there could only be one reason for its disappearance.

Then she heard that the police had traced two witnesses to Whitey's death and that they'd seen a man drive off in a red car shortly after the incident. They could not give a description of the man, except that he spoke with an Irish accent; and unfortunately they did not know the car's registration number or make.

The Controller's neck was on the block so she decided to back her hunch and launch a country-wide search for the Datsun. But with limited resources she needed the help of the police. Issuing a D Notice to silence the press would only arouse their interest. The Controller had no option so she rang the Commissioner.

"We need a top priority wanted missing person and vehicle search for a man we're after... he's armed and dangerous and under no circumstances is he to be approached. When you find him let me know and my people will pick him up. I want him taken alive."

"What's this man's name?"

"I can't tell you that... just find him for me... I'll do the rest." She rang off.

"And fuck you too," said the Commissioner to the dial tone.

Then she rang the SCS back with the new information.

With this news, the SCS rang Dennis Leung leaving the usual urgent call back signal.

At that moment Dennis was finishing a second bottle of Elixir de Chine with another of his favourite whores in the apartment above his gambling den.

The SCS's second call was to the Police Commissioner. "I want to make sure you know all about the 'Wanted Missing' request we asked you to expedite... would you deal with it personally, old boy...? And contact only me immediately the suspect is found. One of our own has gone bad... we want to take care of it in-house... I'm sure you understand that I can't tell you any more... but he must be found."

The Commissioner was amused to hear that the SCS and the Firm were both wanting to deal with this man. There was obviously conflict between the two and he enjoyed watching their petty disputes. But he didn't need this powerful civil servant on his back.

The SCS went on, "One of my agents will be dispatched by helicopter as soon as your officers locate the vehicle. I will personally supervise the capture of the deserter. It's connected to the affair with the Prime Minister in Soho yesterday... I know this is a matter for the police and assure you I will assist you in every way I can... and I do want to include you in but please, for the sake of the Nation keep it to yourself for now. Let's have a quick drink at my club... what do you say, old boy... in about half-an-hour...? as soon the man has been caught I'll fill you in."

He put down the receiver and smiled to himself as he imagined the cock and bull story he would invent.

103. THE SCS & DENNIS LEUNG :
(9PM, SUNDAY 15 NOVEMBER)

The SCS was back at his apartment and still drinking port having had, '...a splendid hour,' at his club with the Commissioner.

The conversation had been about, "Some fucking little dyke, mixed up in God knows what, got it in the head instead of the PM... and we've got a bastard who's left our employ and gone rogue." Wondering if the Commissioner's acceptance of the situation, the evening drink and his somewhat gentle manner suggested he was AC/DC he continued, "... anyway I promise you I'll watch your back if you keep this hush hush."

When Dennis eventually got back to his penthouse in Gerrard Street he returned the SCS's call. "A man resembling the e-fits spent last night at the China Hotel in Horse and Dolphin Yard. Apparently he was scruffy and appeared injured, but we don't know where he is now."

"A bit fucking late..." was the SCS's response, "...now that the monkey's flown the nest."

Dennis put the phone down and swore; he did not like to be spoken to in such a supercilious manner by a gwilo. He was one amongst many Chinese who had not forgotten about the arrogance of the British bureaucrats during the Boxer Rebellion, even though it was over a hundred years ago.

104. BRANEN : (8PM, SUNDAY 15 NOVEMBER)

Branen wanted to head west into Wales, but if he tried to use the Severn Bridge he would be caught by the unavoidable cameras.

He was forced to head north towards the A40 and to cross into Wales beyond the Severn Estuary. By now the Firm could have discovered that the Datsun was missing and conclude that he had stolen it. If he was going to evade them he had to get rid of the car.

The old Datsun was pulling hard in second gear as it climbed up out of Batheaston. Branen pressed on, over several cross-roads, sticking to the Fosse Way that had now become a single track lane. After ten miles he passed under the M4 again, heading north. He went through Hullavington village, keeping to the 30mph speed limit so as not to attract unwanted attention.

Eventually he came to a junction and saw a sign to the 'Historic Town of Malmesbury', hopefully a place where he could rent a car and buy a mobile phone in the morning. A couple of miles short of Malmesbury he began looking for somewhere to hide the car and spend the night. He slowed down to walking pace searching for a hiding place. After about a mile he caught a 'Byway' sign in the headlights pointing into what appeared to be solid bushes. He stopped and walked back to explore. He had not seen another car for the last five miles. The byway was overgrown and looked ideal. He turned the car off the road and drove into the undergrowth. He kept in first gear and managed to push on up the track. The deep wheel ruts caused the sump to sink into the mud and grate against the rocks and branches strewn across the path. After fifty yards, the rear wheels spun and the car became bogged down and was forced to a stand-still in a swamp; he wasn't going any further. He turned the engine off and the silence was deafening, particularly after the commotion of the charge through the undergrowth. He put a foot out and sank into the quagmire up to the top of his boot.

He wanted to recce Malmesbury and needed a plan for the morning. He slid around in the mud as he removed the number plates and buried them further up the track. He returned to the road and cleaned his boots before setting out to walk the mile into the centre of town.

It took nearly an hour to check out Malmesbury's pubs. He decided that The Guildhall Bar, which lay behind the town car park, might provide the local knowledge he needed. It was frequented by locals, not tourists like the other smarter pubs.

A man stood leaning on the bar with one leg behind the other. Dressed like a farmer, he looked like a local and would probably know local stuff.

Branen moved in beside him and ordered a drink.

The man turned to him. "You a stranger?" he asked.

"Not to my friends, mate."

"What're you doing here?"

"Looking for a drink."

"Seems like you come to the right place then…" The man turned to the woman behind the bar. "…stop polishing those glasses Gwen, we've got someone here who wants a drink… mine's a pint of the usual."

"Are you keeping the bar up or is it holding you up?" asked Branen.

"Do you know who I am?" the man asked.

Holding out his hand Branen said, "No, can anybody help…? My name's Ben."

The man spent some time deciding then said, "Tom," and shook hands.

"Silly question but can I get that drink for you?" asked Branen.

Tom condescended, "Not so silly… it's a question of need."

After half an hour, another pint had disappeared before Branen could finish his and Tom was just lucid enough, if Branen could be patient enough, to get the information he needed. He told Branen about his genealogy and the state society was in and eventually Branen managed to tease out of him the fact that there were no car hire places in Malmesbury. However he did suggest that in the morning he should try Williams Autos across the car park. When Branen asked him about a mobile phone shop, he had no idea if there was one in town.

Branen hoped that in the morning Tom would not remember ever having ever met him.

Three hours hunched up on the back seat of the car allowed Branen to take an objective view of his situation. Even if he made it abroad, it would not be long before they worked out a way of getting to him without upsetting an allied Government. Wherever he hid he would always be in danger and always looking over his shoulder. As far as they were concerned, he had committed the act that threatened their existence and that meant he could never remove their insecurity and paranoia. His only escape would be to match their threat with an equal counter-threat which could not be neutralised. For the next couple of hours he lay there planning and calculating the risks. He was convinced that he had been set up by The Associates, and that Carrie's murder was just a device to bring him back into the country.

He would be pursued for the rest of his life. And to negate the threat he knew he would have to return to London.

105. BRANEN : (5.30AM, MONDAY 16 NOVEMBER)

He managed a couple of hours' sleep before cramp finally woke him up.

Costas's overcoat had kept the cold out and another couple of pain-killers had helped him to sleep. It was 5.30am and still dark as he lay in the fat man's car re-living the events of the past week.

He decided to search the car. In the boot he found the guitar case with the rifle inside and the bin bag jammed right at the back with filthy clothing spilling out. Branen assumed it was the gun the fat man had used to kill Jane and her baby. He also found a sound moderator and the paraphernalia of a trained sniper, including a bottle of urine.

He dumped the gear into the boot and waited for a couple of hours before walking back into Malmesbury with the rifle in the guitar case slung over his shoulder. The air was bracing and as he walked he was treated to a sunrise that would have cheered him up under different circumstances.

It was about 8.30am when Branen arrived at Williams Autos but they were still closed. The sign in the window said the opening hours were 9am till 6pm. He wandered through a walkway to a café on the High Street and ordered sandwiches and a take-away tea. Then he walked to the town square and sat watching the locals going about their lives.

However successful he was at blending in to an environment, he always felt an outsider. His training had given him the ability to deal with the danger that was a constant on any mission; but sometimes he wished that he could change places with the man whose sole ambition was to make enough money to support his family and enjoy himself.

Branen ate the sandwiches, drank the tea and meditated on his plan. He had to find out who ran The Associates. But if he succeeded there would be no point in killing this person because even if he managed to cut off one head, a more determined one would appear in its place and pursue him with increased vigour. But could he intimidate him or her sufficiently to make them remove the threat that hung over him? It was a gamble with long odds but it was a gamble that he had to take if he was going to survive.

The time had come to change his appearance; by the end of the day he had to change clothes and assume another character.

The clock in the square struck nine and interrupted his reverie. He picked up the guitar case and strolled back to Williams.

The woman on reception said they didn't hire cars. She had a kind face so Branen pressed her, explaining how tough a musician's life was and told her about a gig he had in Manchester that night; it was a job he needed to take. He saw by her expression that she was trying to believe him but she was looking at his bandaged hand and wondering how he could play the guitar. Branen took out one hundred pounds and explained that it was all the cash he had but he could earn four hundred pounds if he could get to the venue by this afternoon. The money took precedence over reason and she disappeared into the workshop. She spoke to the mechanics with the authority of someone who was not just a receptionist. Then Branen heard one of the mechanics address her as Mrs Williams.

She returned saying they had a second-hand pick-up being prepared for the forecourt. If he had a driving licence or passport and a credit card to prove who he was, she would hire it to him. She meticulously recorded the details from his driving licence and queried the London address. He explained that he had come down by train to spend the weekend with friends and then this gig had turned up. She decided not to pursue it any further. But she wanted a guarantee that he would not run off with her car and so using Branen's credit card, she asked him to sign an imprinted slip which she promised not to cash unless he didn't return with her car.

Within fifteen minutes Branen was driving out of Malmesbury on the bypass heading south in an old Toyota pick-up that was hardly worth the one hundred pounds he had paid to hire it.

When he reached the M4 he turned east back to London, not at all sure what he was going to do when he got there.

When Branen worked as a freelance photographer he would visit his Operations Officer who also acted as his photographic agent. The agent was based in a top floor apartment, in a block of flats in the Viale Corsica near the centre of Milan.

After an assignment in the Commores, Branen was editing transparencies in the agent's office when a call came in from London. The agent initially took it on the speaker-phone but when he realised who the caller was he picked up the remote handset; but not before Branen had time to recognise the voice. He had never met this anonymous person, but it was the same voice that had given him all the catch-words and the classified information needed to authorise a mission.

The agent left Branen on the light-box and as he went into his office, closing the door behind him, Branen heard him say, "Yes, Herbert."

All Branen had was a Christian name; was it going to be enough?

The hire car would protect him from the motorway cameras as he stuck religiously to the 70mph speed limit. The weather was a compete contrast to the previous day. In the rear-view mirror the dark clouds blended with the tarmac as the motorway dissolved into the mist behind him, hiding what had previously been the direction of his escape. The thinning trees and leafless woodland on each side had submitted to the seasons and were beginning to shut down for winter. The year was dying and he was heading back into the smoke not knowing whether or not he would survive.

And he didn't know how far behind him they were or whether they had discovered the Datsun.

106. THE FARMER, THE POLICEMAN & THE CONTROLLER : (MONDAY 16 NOVEMBER)

At about 8.30am, an hour after Branen had left the Datsun, a farmer walked up the byway.

He carried a shotgun in case a rabbit showed its head. His wife made a very good rabbit version of jugged hare and the mere thought of it made his mouth water. Like all impecunious men hoping to find their fortunes, he had spent the weekend fantasizing on how best to capitalise on his acreage. Arable and cattle farming were so unprofitable that farmers all over the south-west were searching for new ways of making a living. He believed he had discovered a demand for plants such as marigold and lavender for the newly burgeoning homeopathic market. As he pushed his way through the bushes, he noticed the tyre tracks and broken branches. He imagined that a courting couple had driven up there last night seeking a quiet spot.

Clearing the byway would have made it easier to access his already fallow fields where he planned to plant the flowers and herbs, but it all took time.

Up went his dog's hackles and it froze like a python ready to strike. The dog had detected a fresh scent and the farmer urged it on, releasing the safety catch on the gun. Fifty metres further up the track he found the red car buried in the bushes.

He didn't get back home for his coffee until 11am; and only then remembered to phone the police. He told Sergeant Brian 'Nosey' Parker that the car had no number plates. Brian had read the Wanted Missing Report and realised that at last an important case had landed on his patch and he might finally see some action. He got on to his HQ and reported the find.

It was after midday when Brian arrived at the car. Wearing latex gloves, he discovered the ten thousand pounds buried in the bottom of the dustbin bag.

The Controller finally heard about it at 1pm via the Commissioner. In the ops room she had a large-scale map of England pinned up. She stood for a while, trying to put herself into Branen's shoes. 'Why dump the car there rather than anywhere else... where's he heading?'

107. BRANEN : (MONDAY 16 NOVEMBER)

It was lunchtime as Branen ploughed his way through the London traffic.

It started to rain and the grey clouds created a premature dusk. He had made an incomplete plan and needed to get started before the pitfalls became too daunting.

The multi-storey car park behind the Ship in Wardour Street was mainly contract parking, but there were always a few spaces that could be bought from the attendant with a bribe. He dropped off the car, picked up the guitar case and headed for the toilets.

Fifteen minutes later he had cleaned the wounds and re-bandaged his hand. He polished his boots and reappeared on Wardour Street returning to his favourite internet café.

He re-introduced himself to his 'Fuck You' friend who seemed almost pleased to see him. Branen fired up a computer and typed Home Office into Google, searching for the senior management. He found that the Director General of Crime, Policing and Counter Terrorism was a woman. From the website he got a complete list of names of who was in charge of all her departments. The name Herbert did not appear anywhere; but one name was missing and that was the head of Counter Terrorism and Intelligence.

He went to 'Advanced Search', typed in Herbert and got a dozen results, mostly for a politician who was very unlikely to be the person he wanted. After an hour of searching the net he had drawn a blank;

he or she was too well hidden. He made a note of the names of all the relevant junior civil servants and signed off. He needed to eat.

Everything you wanted in life was within easy reach in Soho. The Pasta Place was a few doors down and Branen needed carbohydrates. His next stop was a barber's shop at the bottom of Frith Street.

"Give me a number one and a shave", said Branen.

The old Italian barber stood back and asked with a shake of his head, "Did Hannibal have a go at your hair or did you do it all on your own?"

In a menswear shop opposite, Branen bought some clothes which included a white shirt and T-shirt, a tweed off-the-peg suit that almost went with his boots, a raincoat, a trilby and a pair of extra large leather gloves to cover the dressing on his left hand. The whole lot cost nearly four hundred pounds, but thanks to Snowman's cash he looked the business. Branen was left with about five hundred pounds. In the tailor's changing room he wrapped the rifle in his old clothes and folded them inside Costas's overcoat, then packed it all back into the guitar case. He dropped into the chemist and for ten pounds bought a pair of reading glasses with heavy frames.

He was a new man. The major obstacle he faced was time; he didn't know how long it would take to execute his plan and to find the head of Counter Terrorism and Intelligence; and he had no idea how soon the Firm or The Associates would catch up with him.

But for now he believed he still had the advantage.

108. THE CONTROLLER : (2PM, MONDAY 16 NOVEMBER)

The Controller briefed James. "Branen will know that the car will be found so we must react quickly. He'll also want to change appearance and transport. Find me four agents and chopper them down to Malmesbury immediately."

"Yes, Ma'am... what do I say we're doing there?"

"Get the Wiltshire Police to supply details of all vehicles stolen in the previous twenty four hours within ten miles of Malmesbury... and that our officers will be requisitioning the local nick... tell them it's connected to the attempted murder of the PM and it must be kept quiet."

Malmesbury was a small market town and it would not be difficult to find Branen if he was still there. But the Controller did not have enough manpower, and she was frustrated by the SCS insisting that the search was too sensitive to be made public. If she could have informed the press that there was a suspect at large, they could have published the photofit countrywide.

Sergeant Brian Parker was in charge of the small police station and was the man with the local knowledge. His nose was put out of joint when, an hour later, a helicopter landed in the fields behind his station and the team of three men and a woman took charge.

"James, get them to check out all guest houses, hotels, pubs, restaurants and cafés, also car hire and bus companies," said the Controller.
"Okay, Ma'am."
"Show them the images of Branen but make sure they don't leave any behind... I can't have the press anywhere near this."

A young man in a council house on the edge of Malmesbury was dragged naked from his bed by the Controller's armed officers. He had been drunk the night before and had stolen a car from the town square and left it outside his own house.

The woman in the café who had sold Branen his sandwiches earlier that morning only worked until midday, so when an officer visited the premises the owner did not recognise the CCTV image.

When an officer interviewed Gwen, the barmaid in The Guildhall pub, she mentioned a stranger resembling the e-fit engaging old Tom in conversation the previous evening. The officer asked Sergeant Parker to follow up on the lead.

As dusk was descending, no definite trace of Branen had been found.

At 5.30pm Tom arrived for his tea-time pint and was greeted by Sergeant Parker, who had decided to wear plain clothes so as to not appear too intimidating.

"Hi Tom, how are you doing?"

"What's it look like to you, Nosey?" said Tom, looking intimidated.

"Would you like a pint?"

"Do I look like I wouldn't?"

"Gwen… give Tom here a pint of his favourite and a Coke for me, please…" Turning back to Tom, "…Gwen tells me that you had a drink with a stranger in here last night."

"Why, is that a crime?" asked Tom.

"No of course not but…"

"I'm not saying anything without my lawyer."

"Come on Tom…"

"I might incriminate myself."

Gwen put the pint in front of Tom.

"Drink up Tom, and tell me about him."

Tom took a long drink. "I don't remember much… I was tired…"

After another pint Tom became more affable. "He was looking for a car to hire…."

"Yes…." said Nosey, trying to encourage him.

"I recommended Gladys…"

"At Williams Autos?"

Nosey went round to see Gladys Williams just as she was closing up for the night.

"What do you remember about this man… was there…?"

"Would you like a cup of tea?" she interrupted.

"It's important that you tell me what you know otherwise you might be seen as aiding and abetting a criminal."

"I don't want to get into trouble but… you see my situation, don't you?"

"Look, Gladys, you know me well enough…"

"All right Brian, it was like this… I took a one hundred pound deposit from a nice-looking man and allowed him to rent a pick-up. Apparently he was a musician who had fallen on hard times and needed help to get to Manchester… I had to help him… you understand, don't you?"

"What else?"

"Well I got him to sign a credit card slip…"

The Controller received the information about the truck and the credit card at 6.30pm and the search now became a countrywide alert.

When the information had been disseminated on the PNC there was little she could do but wait for the pick-up to be found; hopefully with Branen still in it. She was left trying to read his mind and predict his next move.

The last place she would have considered looking was Soho.

109. THE SOHO GAZETTE : (4PM, MONDAY 16 NOVEMBER)

The windows of the local newspaper office overlooked Wardour Street.

A gold leaf transfer, 'THE SOHO GAZETTE est.1832', was attached at eye-level to the inside of the window. For a moment the sun found a gap in the leaden sky, and as he entered Branen noticed the transfer cast a legible shadow on the wooden boarded floor. A long mahogany counter stretched the width of the room with a bar-room style flap in it to allow the staff access. The newspaper had been passed down through three generations of the editor's family, and he placed great significance on the traditional appearance of his office. He had reluctantly moved into the computer age twenty years ago but still had an old aluminium Grant projector to enlarge illustrations, and a microfilm scanner with a full library of microfiches for reviewing back-copies. Because of the 'Attempted Assassination of the Prime Minister' scoop, the potential earnings from the syndication rights would be enough to update the computer system. And for the first time under his ownership, The Soho Gazette would be financially liquid.

His first reaction to Branen, dressed in the tweed suit and library framed spectacles was, 'Who is this smart alec?'

Branen told him the story of a novel he was writing about the Home Office, the SIS and the involvement of the head of Counter Terrorism and Intelligence. The editor's attitude to him changed when he dropped the name Herbert into the conversation.

"I think you mean Herbert Redcliffe..." said the editor, "...not many people know much about him... a very secretive fellow, and full of himself."

"That's right…" Branen said, "…and I hear he runs some pretty clandestine groups."

"So they say," said the editor, tapping the side of his nose and trying to give the impression he knew more than he did.

To distract the man from the real purpose of his visit Branen moved the conversation on and talked for another five minutes, before thanking him for his valuable time and going on his way.

Back at the internet café, 'Fuck You' did a double take when Branen entered, dressed to kill.

"I think I preferred you before," he said. They were now firm friends.

Branen typed Herbert Redcliffe into Google. Five hundred and thirty-four matches came up but only five related to the man he was interested in. There were references regarding meetings at the House of Commons concerning European legislation on terrorism going back ten years, but no reports of him doing anything since then. He appeared to have disappeared, which supported Branen's theory that he was now involved in top secret work.

He returned to the Home Office website and did an 'Advanced Search', without any luck. There was no home address, but on a link to the BBC website he found that in the New Year's Honours List five years ago Redcliffe had received a CBE. His address was given as London W1. Branen followed the link and found an article about him on the Telegraph newspaper website, again five years old, mentioning that he was a high-flying member of the Civil Service considered to be capable of reaching the top and a member of The Athenaeum Club. That was all.

Branen Googled The Athenaeum Club and found it was frequented by politicians and lawyers, but there was no published list of members – just the address.

110. BRANEN & THE SCS : (6PM, MONDAY 16 NOVEMBER)

Branen collected the pick-up from the car park and it was six o'clock when he arrived at the Athenaeum. It occupied a grand detached Georgian building on the corner of Waterloo Place and Pall Mall.

He strolled down the central reservation, noting the times left on the meters nearest the club. The bays radiated out from the central island in a similar layout to Soho Square. He decided on a particular bay, with a clear view of the entrance but without leaving him in clear view of anyone exiting the club.

There was a dark green Lexus saloon parked in the space he wanted, with ten minutes left on the meter. He waited with the engine running. The chauffeur was sitting with the interior light on reading a paperback and then Branen saw him answer his mobile. He pulled out and Branen reversed in, thirty metres away from the entrance to the club.

Earlier he had bought a fountain pen, paper and an envelope; the type with string and a button on the back to seal it. It looked official and that was what he wanted.

In his best calligraphy he wrote: 'To – Herbert Redcliffe Esq. c/o The Athenaeum Club, Waterloo Place, SW1.' And at the bottom of the envelope wrote 'By Hand' and underlined it.

It was dark and raining as he ran up the wide stone steps, trying to look as though World War Three might be about to break out. He approached the commissionaire, who was behind a window within the classical portico, beside the tall mahogany and glass entrance doors.

"I have urgent papers for Mister Herbert Redcliffe." Branen spoke in his most cultured English but with his tongue stuck in the roof of his mouth. It sounded as if he had a cleft palate and was hopefully enough to disguise his voice.

"Mister Redcliffe is not here at the moment, sir."

"The office told me he had left to come here," Branen said, looking disappointed.

"Well sir, can I pass them on to him when he arrives?"

"Unfortunately I have to deliver them personally," he said holding the envelope so he could see the 'By Hand' note.

"Well sir, unless you are a member I cannot allow you in."

"Couldn't I wait in the reception area?"

"Come round to the inside," he said.

He was wearing a uniform with gold binding, greased hair and with half-frame glasses; he'd spent a lot of time looking in the mirror.

"You could of course sit over there," he said, pointing to a dark polished wooden armchair.

"Thank you, would you be kind enough to point me out to Mister Redcliffe when he arrives... in case I miss him?"

"Of course... I'm sorry we can't offer you a drink while you're waiting... I'm sure you understand, sir."

Waiting had always been part of Branen's job and he did not know whether Redcliffe was going to visit the club this evening or not. He had no definite evidence that he was the civil servant responsible for The Associates or whether he had ever seen a photograph of him but Branen had changed his appearance, with the hat and spectacles, and hoped to remain anonymous. He settled down with a copy of the club's Telegraph.

An hour of slow reading passed, made difficult by the magnified spectacles. He kept practising his speech impediment by reading the articles quietly to himself.

The commissionaire came over. "Are you okay, sir?"

"Yes, thank you... we did try to phone Mister Redcliffe from the office but his mobile was turned off... I'll have to wait," said Branen.

Branen took a handful of notes from his inside pocket. "I would love a vodka and tonic if that is at all possible?"

"I'll see what I can do for you, sir," he said, taking a ten pound note.

Another hour and another expensive drink passed while he was trying to work out a plan B.

A handsome man with swept-back silver hair came up to reception and handed over his umbrella and trench coat. He was dressed in a subtle pin-striped suit and a tie from a regiment Branen did not recognise; he was accompanied by a doppelganger.

The commissionaire leant over the desk and pointed in Branen's direction.

Herbert Redcliffe strode over, "What can I do for you?" he asked.

He was younger than Branen expected. He stood up with the raincoat over his left arm covering the gloved hand. He touched the brim of his trilby and said, "I'm very sorry to trouble you, sir, especially this late, but the office asked me to deliver this to you personally... by hand." Branen was impressed with his speech impediment. He had put two sheets of blank A4 paper inside and sealed the envelope making it awkward to open.

"They said it was important, sir..." he wanted to keep the initiative,

"… but that I shouldn't wait for a reply… goodnight, sir." Without giving him the chance to ask who he was, he touched the brim of his hat again and started to walk away.

"Just a moment… which department are you?" he asked.

Branen turned to see Redcliffe looking at him suspiciously. He had to gamble; he stepped back towards him speaking in a stage whisper. "The Controller, sir."

The man Redcliffe had come in with stepped up behind him and put his hand on his shoulder. "What can I get you, Herbert? The usual?"

Redcliffe's suspicion had turned to confusion. Branen took the moment's hesitation to head for the door before Redcliffe could ask any more questions.

Now Branen knew what Redcliffe looked like.

Back in the pick-up Branen decided to look more casual; he took off the jacket, hat and tie, retrieved the belt-bag and re-bandaged his hand with a new dressing. Then he settled down to wait for Redcliffe.

The SCS took the envelope to the lavatories. When he found two blank sheets of paper he rang the Controller.

"No envelope has been sent over from this office… perhaps it's from another of your projects," she assured him.

He thought, 'Somewhere, something has gone wrong. Who was that man who delivered the envelope?' He couldn't picture his face, just the hat and spectacles and the awkward diction. He had wondered at the time who could be uncouth enough not to remove his hat in the club. It was not the first time papers had been dropped off to him at his club, and only his office would have known where he was going that night. The blank papers must be a mistake by some idiot junior. He dialled his personal assistant but got no reply. He was furious; the man was meant to keep within reach at all times. He would have to deal with the matter in the morning and he made a mental note to have a word with security. But that was tomorrow; now he had more visceral pleasures on his mind.

He pulled himself together; it was important that his guest did not see him flustered. He was doing his duty by having dinner with the Home Secretary, who dictated the annual budget for his department. After this he planned a night of indulgence and in the morning, a lie-in. He had warned his secretary to postpone his diary until midday because he had, "Personal affairs to sort out."

It was 12.30am when a maroon Jaguar pulled up outside the Athenaeum. It parked with its indicator lights flashing until Herbert Redcliffe finally appeared on the steps with his dinner guest. A close protection officer appeared and waited by the back door of the car.

Redcliffe went through the motions of a jovial parting; they shook hands and the Home Secretary stumbled into the limo. Then, without a moment's delay, Redcliffe crossed Pall Mall and was off up Regent Street on foot.

Branen set out after him. Redcliffe moved swiftly, as though anticipating a tryst. Across Piccadilly Circus he turned into Shaftesbury Avenue then left up Great Windmill Street. The street was busy and Branen followed about fifty metres behind. He turned first right into Archer Street and Branen crossed to the other side. Then Redcliffe stopped at an entrance with enough stainless steel on its facade to keep a Sheffield factory in business for a year. It was the Red Label club; a typical Soho joint that could go bankrupt at any moment, change its directors and open up again the next day. It might have another name by the time Herbert Redcliffe left.

Branen watched him have a brief conversation with the doormen and slip them some money; he was obviously welcome there.

Branen waited for a couple of minutes across the street. Both the doormen had earrings in their right ears and their manner and body language was friendly.

The noise was deafening; the room lacked any soft furnishings. It was lit by dozens of small spotlights and the interior was hi-tech industrial. There was a long bar surrounded by men, posing with bottles of beer. There was standing room only; mostly because there weren't many seats and Branen noticed there were hardly any women.

There were pretty men dressed in tight trousers and T-shirts designed to show off their pecs; shy men hiding in the shadows, trying to catch any passing eye. The camp extrovert men shouted louder and more provocatively. They were not remotely interested in anyone else but themselves; they were the most vulnerable.

At the bar Branen ordered an organic, healthy, bottled beer. It cost about the same as a small brewery in Romania and was delivered without a glass. He removed his raincoat, tied the arms round his waist and undid several buttons on his shirt, then perched on a bar-stool with one of the retiring types right behind him. He attempted to drink from the bottle, the gas went up his nose and the beer ejaculated from the neck. A giggle went up behind him and he turned to meet his newest friend.

"I bet you can't do that twice in an evening," he said.

"That depends on the company," Branen said. The man hesitated and Branen used the pause to slide off the stool and cruise the room.

The bar was full and he stuck to the outside edges. Redcliffe was nowhere to be seen. Was there another floor? Branen doubted he had come in and gone straight out again, so he went to the lavatories at the end of the corridor. As he reached them he saw a metal staircase going down to a basement room.

He went into a cubicle and took off the raincoat and shirt and hung them on the back of the door hoping they would still be there when he returned; they were hardly fashion's latest creations. Branen wet what was left of his hair and checked the look in the mirror on the way out. He looked hot and sweaty, as though he had been in the bar for some time. The bandage on his hand was clean and his shoulder ached but he was going to have to suffer that.

He went downstairs and found himself on a dance floor. He pushed through the gyrating bodies to a garishly lit bar. Redcliffe stood out in his smart suit surrounded by young men, and he was buying the drinks. If his crew were not dressed in white T-shirts they were in black; Branen felt like a clone. He eased as close to Redcliffe as he could and ordered another beer, this time with a glass. Redcliffe was drinking whisky by the tumbler-full and was the centre of attention as he held court over his subjects. Even a couple of metres from him the music was too loud for Branen to hear what was being said.

He leant on the bar and turned towards Redcliffe, trying to give an impression of relaxed confidence and hoping Redcliffe would notice him. Fortunately for Branen age did not seem to be a problem here; he was in the mature range. He wanted to catch Redcliffe's eye before he chose his beau for the night. Branen emptied the rest of the beer into the glass and sprang off his stool, deliberately knocking into the back of one of the groupies.

The little fellow turned on him. Hidden behind tinted shades was a made-up face. "Careful," he said loudly.

Redcliffe stopped talking and looked round. Branen wondered if he would be recognised. He hoped that the combination of the whisky and his change of clothes would work. He smiled at the young man and caught Redcliffe's eye.

Redcliffe didn't hesitate. "I haven't seen you here before."

"That's because I haven't been here before." This time Branen's accent was London.

Redcliffe levered himself from the bar and pushed through his entourage towards him. "A virgin… eh, what."

Branen smiled, "In your dreams," he said with as much provocation as he could summon.

"Let me buy you a drink, my boy… and perhaps I could introduce myself."

Being addressed as 'my boy' at forty years old amused him. "You can introduce me to whatever you like."

He noticed that his apparent humility appeared to excite Redcliffe.

He came close to whisper. "There's an awful lot I'd like to introduce you to," he slurred.

They spent another thirty minutes at the bar, with him waving away several younger men; finally he suggested they went on somewhere else.

When Branen went to get his coat Redcliffe asked if he should come with him.

Branen told him, "All good things are worth waiting for…" and promised to return soon.

His clothes were still hanging on the back of the cubicle door. He put the raincoat on, stuffed the shirt into the pocket and left the belt-bag slung round his waist. As he headed back to meet his date he glanced at his watch; it was two-thirty.

Redcliffe put his arm through Branen's and they strolled back across Soho. "Tell me all about yourself, dear boy…"

Without mentioning his female friends Branen was able to stick pretty much to the truth about his early life in Soho.

"What about money… how'd you get by?"

Branen was warming to the yarn. "I work as an estate manager in

Scotland… for an Arab from Dubai. A lot of foreign entrepreneurs are buying up Scottish estates, you know… they see it as an investment."

"So what are you doing in Soho… isn't it rather louche for you country types?"

"I holiday in London every year… I like to meet new friends… they might even come and visit me in Scotland… that would relieve the boredom."

Redcliffe either wanted to believe him because he wanted to keep him happy or his story was sufficiently plausible. They were getting along fine and stopped at Balans bar in Old Compton Street.

During the drink he asked Branen, "How did you damage the hand, old chap?"

The question caught him off guard. "Caught it in a bear trap… they rampage the highlands, you know."

Redcliffe smiled and asked, "Would you like a Mitsubishi?"

At first he thought Redcliffe meant a cocktail and held up his drink, "I'm fine at the moment."

Redcliffe shook his head and repeated the question. Branen asked him what he meant. He was glad he had spun Redcliffe the story about working on the Scottish estate because his naivety became excusable.

Redcliffe reached into his pocket and pulled out a silver box. He flipped the lid open and produced a couple of pills.

"Have you ever taken ecstasy?" he asked.

"Yeah… I've had a Dove."

"You are a sweet thing…" he said, "…you're so old fashioned."

He waited while Branen pretended to swallow it.

"Aren't you having yours?" he asked.

Redcliffe smiled and took his tablet. If there had been any doubt, it was now taken for granted that Branen would be going home with him. He got rid of the ecstasy tab before it dissolved and had one more tequila before they left.

From Dean Street they turned into Bouchier Street; a narrow, typical Soho cul-de-sac with a paved walkway through to Wardour Street. They came to a smart, three storey block of flats with a penthouse on top. It was very white for Soho and very secure. It was the kind of building smart people live in when they want to say at dinner parties they live in Soho, but they don't have the balls to really live in Soho.

The building was a modern version of Corbusier architecture, with simple curved bay windows and balconies to each apartment. Herbert Redcliffe obviously had money, possibly inherited money, or maybe he was just overpaid.

Branen tried to note the code Redcliffe typed into the security lock on the metal gates but his view was blocked; he thought it was 4,6,5,4. The gate closed behind them with a reassuring clunk. In the front courtyard the entrance had a modern glass canopy over it and inside, the wide central staircase curved up to the penthouse. A bunch of keys appeared from Redcliffe's coat pocket and he opened three deadlocks. Branen looked up expecting to see a sign saying Fort Knox above the door.

He had heard of, even seen minimalism in magazines but this was minimalistic minimalism. It looked as though no-one had ever set foot in here before. He took his shoes off without being asked. Whoever was employed to clean the place must have done it with a toothbrush.

"Let's have a drink," suggested Redcliffe.

Branen slipped his raincoat off and hung it over the back of one of the Eames chairs.

Redcliffe went behind a long white counter and from a frosted glass cabinet took out a bottle of tequila and two frozen glasses.

111. THE POLICE, THE COMMISSIONER & THE SCS : (3AM, TUESDAY 17 NOVEMBER)

Branen's pick-up truck was discovered in Waterloo Place at 3am that morning.

As part of central London's security checks, all night-shift officers had to note down any distinctive, suspicious, or out of town number plates. The copper had wandered up and down the rows of parked cars in Waterloo Place and then returned to his patrol car to run the numbers through the DVLA. The plate on the pick-up came back to him with a red alert attached. When he checked his pocket-book for the night's briefing notes he found the number and a memo for 'immediate action'. He radioed in.

"Stay within view of the vehicle but out of sight. If the driver returns and help has not arrived, back-off… under no circumstances attempt an arrest," said the Incident Officer.

As soon as the Incident Officer had briefed the constable, he informed the Police Commissioner. The Commissioner then contacted the SCS to tell him what his officers had found.

112. BRANEN & THE SCS :
(3.30AM, TUESDAY 17 NOVEMBER)

When Redcliffe turned round, Branen had already got the SIG out and was pointing it at him.

His face showed no fear. "Do you know who I am?" he asked.

"More to the point," Branen said, "Do you know who I am?"

The bottle of tequila, wet with condensation, slid from his hand and smashed on the floor. If you had to spill anything in this flat it had to be a clear liquid in a plain glass bottle; it went with the decor.

It dawned on him all at once. "It was you at my club… fuck you, Branen."

A mobile phone started to ring.

"If I don't answer they'll trace its location and be round here straight away," he said.

Branen had to let him answer it. "One wrong word or phrase and you're dead," he said.

Redcliffe flicked the phone open. "Ah! Commissioner…" He raised his eyebrows at Branen. "Okay…okay. Look, I'm tied up…" He listened for a moment, "I'll get back to you as soon as I can." He flipped the phone shut.

"What was that all about?" Branen asked.

"The Commissioner of Police… they've established you were in Malmesbury yesterday… were you?"

"What else? He didn't phone you to tell you that at three-thirty in the morning."

"They think you're in Manchester…"

"They've found my vehicle," Branen said, testing to see if Redcliffe was lying; he was dealing with a professional bluffer.

Redcliffe smiled at him. "I don't think so but they're searching

289

Manchester for it... I didn't want to get into a long conversation in case you misinterpreted it... I don't want you to shoot me. The Commissioner's under strict instructions to keep me updated... even in the early hours... that's how important you are."

Branen didn't know whether to believe him about Manchester or not, but there was nothing he could do about it; he had to keep moving.

"Let's not fuck about, Herbert... have you got a camera?"

Redcliffe opened a cupboard. "Take your choice." He was suffering from bravado.

"I'll have the Polaroid... bring it here and take your clothes off."

Branen took two photographs of each pose, one for Redcliffe to keep as a memento and one which he put into his back pocket for his own use. He photographed him attempting to jerk off and made him smile at the camera.

He put the camera on the kitchen counter, set the time delay, and photographed Redcliffe kneeling in front of him with Branen's naked back to the camera and his trousers and pants round his knees. He had the SIG out of shot in his left hand. Again he insisted that he smiled.

"I don't suppose you'd like to do this for real...?" Redcliffe asked, "... it's quite a turn-on."

Branen took a couple more shots of Redcliffe lying back on the sofa fondling his cock and one kneeling, his naked arse in the air, turning towards the lens and still smiling.

Branen had finished with him.

"Let me explain the way it is, Herbert... if I removed you now, another head would take your place... it's in my interest that you have a long and successful career. I'm keeping these photographs as insurance. If you send anyone after me you'd better order yourself a coffin, 'cause if they don't get me I'm coming after you, and as you know from my file, I've never failed. My own life won't mean fuck-all to me... all that will matter to me will be watching you die slowly and painfully. Do we have a deal?"

Redcliffe didn't insult him by trying to deny he had the power to authorise what he demanded; and by not denying it, it was understood that he could do it. He nodded. Branen looked into his eyes and he nodded again. Redcliffe's arrogance covered a vulnerable and susceptible human being.

As a last insurance policy, Branen took out the copies of the two 6" by 4" photographs he had taken in Paris in 1997 and handed them to Redcliffe. He had the negatives locked up in his safe, hidden in the podere.

"I know the Security Services raided many of the paparazzi's studios after the event... but no-one knows about these... they prove I was there. A lawyer has a sealed copy of my testimony which tells the whole story and I've hidden the negs in a safe place... to be published if I have an accidental or violent death. They are my guarantee that the Government won't come after me."

Redcliffe studied them. "If you can get out of the country without the Firm catching up with you, I'll obstruct any further Associates or MI6 investigations... I'll make sure they don't pursue you after that. Until then, I cannot stop the nationwide search... there is nothing I can do about that now. You'll have to make your own luck... and may God go with you."

"Get it right, Herbert, or you're fucking dead with your arse splashed all over the tabloids," Branen said, hoping he was not being naive in believing what he wanted to believe; that his acknowledgement meant an implicit agreement between them. He was trusting the understanding he saw reflected in Redcliffe's face and hoped it was not the effects of the ecstasy tab he had taken earlier.

If he was lying about the call from the police, or changed his mind, Branen needed to get away before Redcliffe could release his blood hounds. Branen asked him for a roll of adhesive tape and pushed him into the bedroom; made him lie on the bed and bound his wrists to the bed-head. It would take him at least an hour to free himself and by then he would have got back to his vehicle and cleared London.

As he left the apartment, he wondered if Redcliffe would keep to his word or pursue him for the rest of his life. But letting him live was Branen's only option.

113. THE SCS, THE COMMISSIONER, DENNIS & THE CONTROLLER (4AM, TUESDAY 17 NOV)

As soon as Branen left the room, Redcliffe began to wrestle with the tape binding him to the bed-frame. The filigree metalwork was sharp enough to cut into the tape, but it still took him fifteen minutes to free himself; it was a lot sooner than Branen had anticipated.

The Commissioner had just managed to get back to sleep when his mobile rang again.

"I couldn't speak when you rang... what did you want?" demanded the SCS.

"Sorry to have troubled you at this early hour, Herbert, but we've found the fugitive's pick-up truck in Waterloo Place... in the West End."

Realising the urgency Redcliffe said, "This operation is now outside your remit... it falls under my command... I will take charge of it. I want all police personnel withdrawn... my agent is on the way."

"We only have one officer at the scene," said the Commissioner.

"Get rid of him... but if there is any contact with my agent, the password for the operation is 'Fugitive'."

The Commissioner was relieved to be able to withdraw his officer and to avoid having to make the arrest. He did not want the responsibilty for this breach in national security to fall on his or his officers' shoulders. If the security services fucked up, he wanted to make sure they carried the can.

Then Redcliffe rang Dennis, who was in the middle of a game of mahjong. He briefed him and described the pick-up truck, the location and comfirmed the password for the operation.

"The target could already be back at the truck. The police have been withdrawn... bring the body back and we will arrange disposal... make sure you get there, fast!" ordered Redcliffe.

As usual Dennis's limousine was outside his club in Dansey Place. The bodyguard got into the front passenger seat cradling the Diemaco M4 rifle.

Dennis's staff knew nothing about his involvement with the British; sometimes they wondered what he was up to, but they never asked.

The moment Redcliffe slammed the mobile shut it rang again; it was the Controller.

She had been sitting on her hands waiting for somebody, somewhere to turn up with information she could work with. She had not heard anything since early evening and there was little else she could do but pore over the intelligence, trying to predict Branen's movements. She was pissed off. She couldn't go home to bed because intel could arrive at any moment; she had resigned herself to another night at the office. At midnight she finally decided to get some sleep, instructing her team to wake her up if there were any developments.

News of the discovery of the pick-up finally reached the Controller's office at 4am after a call from the Firm's overnight Duty Officer. He had got the information from the Incident Officer at Scotland Yard who he knew. There was a priority incident in Waterloo Place and the police officer at the scene had been withdrawn at the orders of the Commissioner; and then everything had gone quiet. On a hunch, the Duty Officer called the Controller's investigation room to let her know about it.

She rang the Incident Officer. "I've heard there's a priority incident in the West End... what can you tell me?"

"I'll need the catch-word before I can tell you anything..."

"You told my duty officer about it, why can't you tell me?"

"It's more than my job's worth to give you the details... I just thought your department should know..."

"Well, thank you anyway... I'll contact the Commissioner... don't worry, I won't mention your contribution."

She rang the Commissioner. "I need to know if you've found the pick-up..."

The Commissioner had given up all hope of sleep. He smiled to himself when he realised the Secret Services were, as usual, not talking to each other. And just to irritate the SCS, he decided to give the Controller the intel she needed. "We located Branen's pick-up two hours ago, in Waterloo Place."

She was furious. "Why the hell didn't you notify me?"

"Redcliffe wanted it kept to himself," the Commissioner said, enjoying the moment.

Leaving the Chief out of the loop, she decided to call the SCS directly.

The SCS had instructed her to telephone him only when she needed immediate action or for the 7pm daily report. She risked disturbing him in the middle of the night, using the excuse that he might not know the latest developments.

When she spoke to the SCS she got short shrift. "The case is out of your hands… go and make yourself useful somewhere else," Redcliffe told her and put the phone down.

The Controller was stymied; there was nothing she could do but wait.

114. BRANEN : (4.15AM, TUESDAY 17 NOVEMBER)

Branen decided to return to the pick-up.

If he was to believe what Redcliffe had told him, they were still looking for it in Manchester. Redcliffe had said he would not pursue him beyond the borders of the UK and he accepted that Redcliffe couldn't stop the search already in progress. It was ingrained in him to keep changing his transport and appearance, and he was breaking a cardinal rule by returning to the vehicle, but it would be just as risky to travel by public transport.

It was cold and he'd only had three or four fitful hours' sleep in the back of the fat man's car nearly twenty-four hours ago. He put the shirt back on and buttoned up the raincoat. He was anxious to get out of London and the fastest way was to use the pick-up.

He stopped in a doorway at the bottom of Regent Street and looked across Pall Mall. In the middle of the square was a stone plinth with a bronze statue of Edward VII on horseback. On the east side of the plinth there were random pock marks in the stone that looked like bullet holes.

At this time in the morning there was hardly any traffic and apart from his pick-up there were only six cars parked around the central reservation. There were no signs of life but he kept watch for nearly ten minutes before walking down the pavement opposite The Athenaeum. He stopped behind a tree and examined the parked cars. They all appeared to be empty.

As he kept watch, a black Mercedes limo swung into Waterloo Place and cruised up to the far end, then turned round the central pavement and headed back towards Pall Mall. It was not out of place in its surroundings, but from habit Branen made a mental note of the number plate. It slowed down on the far side of the parked cars and for a few seconds was out of sight. Then it reappeared and turned left into the one-way system. He had not seen anyone leave the vehicle and was curious as to why it had driven round the square.

He crossed Pall Mall and waited fifty metres from the pick-up until he was sure the coast was clear.

115. DENNIS LEUNG & BRANEN :
(4.45AM, TUESDAY 17 NOVEMBER)

The drive to Waterloo Place had only taken the Mercedes four minutes, and as soon as he arrived Dennis saw Branen's pick-up truck.

There didn't appear to be anyone else around and he assumed that the police had already been withdrawn. He checked for a vantage point with cover and saw that the evergreen cotoneaster bushes beside the Athenaeum had a direct line of sight to the pick-up.

"Drive round the central pavement and drop me on the far corner... drive off as soon as I'm out of the car... then park out of sight on the far side of Pall Mall and wait for my call," said Dennis.

"I come with you Boss?" asked the bodyguard.

Dennis gave him a look that told him to keep quiet and with exceptional agility he slid out of the car and rolled over the wrought iron fence. He hardly had enough time to get into position when he saw the man walking up the central pavement. Lying on his back, he extended the butt-stock on the rifle. It snapped into place. He gently rolled onto his stomach and lifted the telescopic sight to his eye. The man looked straight at him and Dennis hesitated; he resembled the e-fit and fitted the description despite the short hair. He would have to wait for the man to approach the target vehicle before he could be sure.

As Branen approached the rear off-side corner of the pick-up, he saw a glint of reflected light and a movement under the bushes in the gardens beside the Athenaeum. It could be a tramp, but this was not trampland and anyone bedding down there for the night would soon have been discovered. Pulling the SIG from his belt-bag Branen ducked, sprinted ten metres and hid behind King Edward's plinth. The glint of light was too sharp to have been reflected off a leaf, and he was sure he had heard a metallic clunk.

Dennis instinctively reached for the single shot catch on the rifle as Branen dashed for cover. Caught off balance, Dennis hadn't had time to settle on his target and he didn't want to take a pot-shot even though he was only 25 metres away. In the moment it took for him to steady himself, Branen had gone. He had seen the pistol in Branen's hand and was relieved that the man had not run straight at him, because at close range the rifle was not as manoeuvrable or as effective as a handgun. The stone plinth was at least three metres wide and Branen could run directly away from him without showing himself again.

He had to gamble. Using the plinth as cover Branen sprinted across the road and sprung up and over another statue into the gardens opposite. Not a shot had been fired and he was in cover. He lay flat on the ground under the edge of a bush trying to suppress his breathing. When Redcliffe told him they were looking for the pick-up in Manchester, he had lied, and by returning to the vehicle Branen had taken an amateurish risk. It must be The Associates and not the police who were after him, because if the Secret Service had organised this they would have used CO19 to arrest him, and by now he would have been lit up and surrounded. Redcliffe had double-crossed him, called off the police and sent in one of his assassins. The shooter might be good but he had also just fucked up; we all make mistakes.

All Branen could hear was the occasional taxi as it rattled down Pall Mall. He cursed because the noise offered cover for his assailant's movements. He could not stay still as he did not know if he or she had moved or if there was more than one person out there. He ran through the gardens towards Pall Mall until he reached the side fence. As he climbed over the top, a surge of pain in his shoulder caused him to fall and he landed badly on wire grids securing access to the basement of a building. He ran fast, keeping down behind the stone balustrade that separated him from the pavement, hoping that the security grid would not give way under his weight.

Dennis was fucked and he knew it. Branen had gone and there was no point in trying to pursue him. Then he saw him doubled up and running behind the balustrade opposite. He panned the rifle and fired a single shot. The round hit the balustrading beside Branen and with a high whine ricocheted up into the air.

Branen had to keep running and hope that if his attacker fired again he would miss. He ran the last thirty metres still using the balustrade for cover, anticipating another round in his direction. He finally reached Pall Mall, vaulted over the stone coping and sprinted across the road. Everything was unnervingly quiet and in the silence of the early hours in the city he felt foolish, but self-preservation ruled and he had to find cover. The Associates had access to all MI5's resources and if he was picked up on CCTV the information would be passed on to them within minutes.

Dennis was deep in thought on the way back to Chinatown. He did not tolerate failure in other people and was disappointed with his own lack of success. He wasn't going to phone the SCS and tell him he had missed the target. It occurred to him that Branen may not know that his room in China Hotel had been discovered and might head back there.

When they pulled up in Dansey Place he told his bodyguard to hide in Horse and Dolphin Yard and call if a gwilo turned up.

Then he went back upstairs to finish his game of mahjong.

116. BRANEN : (5AM, TUESDAY, 17 NOVEMBER)

Branen had to find refuge for the rest of the night and plan his next move.

They had the truck, the rest of his clothing, the guitar case and the fat man's rifle. With his DNA from the truck and forensic and ballistic tests they could ignore any other evidence and accuse him of the attempted

297

assassination of the Prime Minister, and frame him for the murders of Jane and her child.

The attempt to kill him meant that Redcliffe must have escaped the bonds and reneged on their agreement. There was no reason for Branen to leave him alive and in charge of The Associates, but it would be too dangerous to return now; he would settle with him sometime in the future.

It was 5am and he was in a shop doorway in an empty city. It would not be long before they found him again. His chances of survival were minimal. He heard the rumble of a bus and a number 94 turned up Regent Street from Pall Mall. He ran up the pavement and the driver must have seen him because he pulled up at a bus stop not more than fifty metres from where he had been hiding. The doors hissed open.

Branen was planning how to get out of the country when he remembered his old lawyer friend Anthony, who held his sealed testimony to be opened in the event of his violent death. Branen had promised him a share of his produce for helping him buy the podere. A couple of years earlier their share-dealing relationship had slowly declined and they'd lost touch. Branen remembered that Anthony had talked about his yacht on the Solent and he was always inviting him down for a weekend trip across the Channel. He used to describe standing on the teak deck, with the sun rising over the sea to the east, eating bacon sandwiches and coffee laced with whisky as he sailed into one of the small French harbours; he was a lawyer with a romantic streak. If he still had the boat this could be the moment for Branen to take advantage of his offer.

He could not remember Anthony's phone number and the only way he could think of finding him was through Ayo at the Empire Room. He would have to wait until lunchtime when the bar opened. If he returned to China Hotel he could hole up there for a few hours.

He went forward to the bus driver. "I've just realised I've left my briefcase at home... could you drop me off as soon as possible?"

Branen cut off Regent Street to avoid the main thoroughfares; there were hardly any people around. The unrelenting sound of the city had temporarily abated, the smell of refuse replacing the traffic fumes.

As he turned down Rupert Street four smartly dressed men left The

Rupert Street Bar. They were loud and animated; they'd obviously been up all night. He joined the back of the group as they walked south. He would try to hide amongst these boys to avoid any cameras. They looked at him, wondering what he was doing. Branen wished them a good morning and when they turned left at Shaftesbury Avenue Branen broke away and ran across the road and down into Chinatown.

There were a couple of twenty-four hour cafés in Chinatown. Instead of returning to the one he'd been in forty-eight hours earlier he decided to go to the other restaurant. As soon as he got there he went to the toilets to check that the kitchen had an exit into the alley at the back. He ordered steamed dumplings and green tea and sat with his back to the wall facing the entrance. After the food he had a battle to stay awake; the lack of sleep and the stress of being hunted was taking its toll.

He must have dozed off because it was half an hour later when he paid the bill, giving the waiter twenty pounds and telling him that he wanted to leave through the back of the restaurant. The chef and a bottle washer barely glanced up as he left through the kitchen and out into the narrow cobbled mews.

A narrow archway led into Macclesfield Street from Dansey Place and a single street lamp created an eerie and ominous feeling between the high buildings. The air smelt of Chinese food and the only sound was the hum of extractor fans.

Branen hesitated in the fire-escape doorway and poked his head out, checking up and down the cobbled mews; there was the black Mercedes he'd seen in Waterloo Place; what was it doing here?

He put the SIG into his coat pocket, turned up the collar and deliberately walked unsteadily towards the car. The exhaust pipe was silently pumping out fumes into the cold air. He saw the chauffeur watching him in the wing mirror as he walked up behind the car. As he passed his partially open window Branen felt the warm air-conditioning and could smell marijuana. He wondered if this car had dropped off the shooter who had fired at him earlier?

He walked through the archway out of sight of the Mercedes and ducked into Horse and Dolphin Yard heading for the China Hotel. He felt uneasy and wondered how it could be just a coincidence that the Mercedes was parked there.

Realising he was in a cul-de-sac he changed his mind and turned round; had they found his room and were they waiting for him? He gripped the gun and slipped the safety catch off; he wanted to take the initiative. He decided to go back and hijack the car and get the chauffeur to drive him out of London.

As he neared the entrance to the mews he heard the echo of footsteps, then a screech of tyres as the Mercedes braked violently, blocking his exit. There was a shout and he turned to see a Chinese man, five metres away, pointing a sawn-off shotgun. The chauffeur sprung from the car also holding a sawn-off 12 bore. Branen had nowhere to go. Having a gun gives you confidence, but surrounded by men with shotguns this confidence can be delusional.

A tall, well dressed man squeezed down the side of the limousine. As he approached the chauffeur followed, keeping a clear firing position. The man stopped three metres away, his face in shadow. He pulled a Walther pistol from his right-hand pocket. "Let me see your hands."

Branen didn't stand a chance of getting off three accurate rounds without being blown away by a load of buckshot. He slowly lifted his hands clear of his body.

"Are you Branen?" the tall Chinese man asked.

When he heard his name he knew he was in trouble.

The Chinese man spoke with an educated English accent. "Lie face down with your hands together... above your head."

From his prone position Branen saw the chauffeur take a thick cable-tie from his pocket and had a temporary feeling of relief; at least they were not going to finish him off here and now.

The boss slipped the cable-tie over his wrists and pulled it tight. His two accomplices picked Branen up and searched his pockets, then took his belt-bag and the SIG.

They led him back into Dansey Place and the boss followed.

117. DENNIS LEUNG & BRANEN :
(6AM, TUESDAY 17 NOVEMBER)

Back in Dansey Place Branen was led under a small awning and through an unprepossessing entrance. He looked up at the breaking sky and had the feeling that he was drawing his last breath of fresh air.

Behind the shabby maroon door was a modern steel staircase with wire rails. The walls were painted white and decorated with red and black Chinese motifs. It was not what he'd expected to see inside the rundown exterior.

As they climbed the stairs Branen's senses became heightened. Every smell and sound was magnified as though for the last time. They passed the first floor and he saw a collection of one-armed bandits calling gamblers to worship. Occasionally their prayers would be answered with a repetitive, metallic rattle as the meagre winnings were spewed out. Branen breathed in the sweet smell of marijuana again. Three men sitting at a bar with deadpan expressions watched his progress up the stairs. There must have been nearly a dozen Chinese men losing their hard-earned wages. Wages toiled for in hot, sweaty kitchens, wages that took them weeks to earn and minutes to fritter away.

The boss was behind him and the two heavies were each side. He was being led like a lamb to slaughter and there was no way he could escape. He decided to save his energy rather than try making a pathetic break for freedom.

On the second floor landing he was presented with another tableau. A completely red room full of gambling tables and another bar. Three shiny – very shiny – gold Chinese women turned away as they passed. They were drenched in dangling jewellery, with glistening eyelids and fingernails, and they were available for business. Punters sat at tables with spinning roulette wheels, playing poker and mahjong. This world went on night after night into the dawn, hidden behind sooty city walls, making a fortune for some people and slaves out of others.

As they went on up, the noise began to diminish. They stopped at a solid metal door. The chauffeur pushed past and unlocked it. Instead of entering a hallway they were in a square room, with cream sofas on the right and left. A polished rosewood Wing Chun dummy lit from above stood ominously in the corner like a silent guard. In the opposite corner was a grey Chubb safe the size of an en suite bathroom, but probably still not large enough to hold all the cash this building must generate for its owner.

The boss went behind a glass desk and for the first time Branen saw his face; he seemed familiar. He searched his memory but couldn't remember where he'd seen him before and wondered what he had in mind for him.

The two heavies pushed him into a chair and stood behind him on each side. He had three armed men surrounding him and nowhere to go. Escape was impossible.

The boss reached into a drawer slung below the table and took out some papers and a photograph; he let Branen get a glimpse of Carrie crossing Dean Street. It was from the envelope he'd hidden in the mattress at China Hotel. He wondered how long they had known that he was staying there, but it didn't matter any more.

The boss took his time looking at the photograph and reading the report. There was a dull silence; the room must have been soundproofed.

The boss leant forward. "We're in the same business, Branen."

Branen realised that the man must work for The Associates.

He sat staring at Branen, then appearing to make up his mind held up the photograph. "Who's this?"

"Nothing to do with you."

The boss gestured to one of the heavies who proceeded to empty the belt-bag onto the desk. He removed the ammo and handed the Polaroids of Carrie to him. The boss slowly examined each one.

Branen came out of the chair, "Those pictures are none of your fucking business."

The bodyguards grabbed him and threw him back into the chair. One of them picked up a can of lighter fuel from the desk and squirted it over his head, then flicked open a cigarette lighter holding the flame where Branen could see it. He wondered if his hair was too short to catch fire.

The boss held up a Polaroid of Carrie in her underwear. "Who's this girl?" he asked again.

Seeing the photograph made Branen react to the question with emotion that he didn't want to show. "Some fucking maniac... a pervert raped and stabbed her." He felt tears prick his eyes and blamed it on the lighter fuel running down his forehead. He was facing the end of his life in a fucking Soho brothel.

"I heard she was killed," said the boss.

"Who told you, Redcliffe?"

"Who's Redcliffe?"

Branen thought, 'If he doesn't know who Herbert Redcliffe is, Redcliffe must have used a codename.' So Branen told him, "The man who gives you your orders."

"You mean the man responsible for your daughter's death."

"How the fuck do you know that?"

"He told me."

Now Branen was never going to have the chance to avenge Carrie's death.

"That's why I've got to get rid of you," he said.

Branen didn't react, it wouldn't make any difference. They hadn't found the Polaroids of Redcliffe in his back pocket but they wouldn't help now.

The boss looked at him without blinking, his expression completely cold. Then he threw the photographs down on the desk. "You don't seem to care."

"I've got nothing left to lose."

"What about your life?" he asked.

"I'm already dead." Branen stared into the jet black eyes. He'd chosen the job a long time ago and it was too late to regret it now. Redcliffe had lied and he had only minutes to live.

After a few moments, and with the first sign of any emotion, the boss said, "I have a daughter, too."

"I HAD a daughter", Branen said, bitterly.

The boss hesitated, then said, "I'm going to give you a break."

His words hung there in the silent room.

"My arm or my leg?" Branen said, trying to force him to elaborate.

Ignoring his defensive glibness the boss leaned back in the chair, "I have to report back to that Civil Servant... the same arrogant gwilo that you work for."

A couple of hours seemed to pass while he made up his mind. "I'm going to sleep... then I'm going to tell him I lost you."

Branen took a deep breath trying to believe what he had just said.

Apart from using the word 'arrogant' when he spoke about Redcliffe he didn't understand why he was letting him go, and he wasn't about to ask.

"Do I go now... or can I shelter here?" he asked.

"You can't stay here."

"Can I have the pistol back?"

Dennis shook his head.

"How about the photographs?"

The boss pushed them across the desk.

Then Branen remembered where he'd seen him before. The man didn't realise that their paths had crossed eighteen years ago. But there was nothing Branen could do now about their past history. It could turn out to be the boss's biggest mistake, only time would tell.

Branen stood up slowly, anticipating a blow from behind. No one stopped him. His wrists were still tied together and he had to reach for the photographs with both hands. He folded them clumsily and put them back into his belt-bag. He turned towards the door and held out his arms. One of the heavies took a flick-knife from his pocket and cut the cable-tie, then escorted him down to the street door.

It closed behind him, and he walked away.

PART FOUR

118. BRANEN : (7AM, TUESDAY 17 NOVEMBER)

Branen had unfinished business with the Chinese man, but for now he needed to hide up until lunchtime when he could blend amongst the crowds and prepare to make his move.

Earlier he had noticed a skip full of junk and food waste, at the other end of the alley. He left the club and headed towards it. It was still dark when he collected a couple of cardboard boxes and a handful of Chinese newspapers from the skip. He laid them down in the narrow space between the skip and the wall, then found two dustbins to block each end of the gap. He had just enough room to crawl in under the overhang. He was well concealed and if the rubbish was not collected he could hide there for as long as he was able to put up with the smell of rotting food.

He needed to sleep but the cold and damp seeped up through the cardboard. Any part of his body in contact with the ground went numb. He finally gave up and lay there waiting for daylight.

An hour passed before a ray of sunlight appeared down the alley, bouncing off the wet cobble stones. He felt that he deserved some compensation after such a bleak night. Without the hill running and weight training back at the podere he would have been wiped out by now.

The low sun slid away behind the buildings and the cold wind made his teeth chatter loudly enough to generate morse code. More rancid food was dumped into the skip but fortunately no-one saw him and no dogs came sniffing round.

While Branen lay there he reflected on what Herbert Redcliffe had told the Chinese agent about Carrie and his broken promise to him. He'd been in control of all the operations Branen had been involved in and had been instrumental in Carrie's recruitment and death; he might as well have killed her himself. Branen decided to keep his half of the bargain.

He left his burrow, carrying the cardboard bed and headed back to the rear of the restaurant he'd eaten in earlier that morning.

The fire exit to the kitchen was ajar so Branen stuck his head in and looked around. If anyone asked, he was begging for food, but all he could hear was muffled snoring. He edged in and behind the steel racks he saw the same old chef stretched out in a plastic chair, fast asleep. There was no sign of the bottle washer. A thin filleting knife lay on a chopping board on the stainless steel unit that separated them. He crept over, slipped the knife into his pocket and walked out into Dansey Place.

Branen collected his bedding and, hoping he didn't smell too bad, headed back up into Soho.

119. THE CONTROLLER : (7AM, TUESDAY 17 NOVEMBER)

The Controller slammed her hand onto the desk. "He's back in London and there's no way I'm going to stop searching for him."

Over the last three or four hours she had become totally frustrated; her attempts to sleep had been unsuccessful and that final order from the SCS had infuriated her. She'd be damned if she would give in that easily. She was determined to find Branen.

She didn't have enough authority to demand information on his whereabouts from the Commissioner but she could use her influence with her Chief. She planned her approach while she waited for him to arrive at his desk. He was always in his office by 7.30am.

She hoped that she hadn't alienated him by going over his head to the SCS, but he might not have heard yet.

She dialled his extention, "Morning sir," she said brightly.

"What do you want?" he said.

He rarely showed his feelings so she pressed on. "I didn't want to trouble you during the night, sir, but apparently Branen's car was found in Waterloo Place at two o'clock this morning. The SCS has taken over the case personally and has told me to make myself useful somewhere else… I wondered if you could find out if they've caught him and if so where he is now?"

"If you've been instructed to stand down, I suggest for your own good you do so."

"Look sir, if we let Mr Redcliffe get away with this we will always be at his beck and call... let me see what I can do discreetly... I'll keep you posted at all times."

She knew the Chief would be irritated by Redcliffe's behaviour because it was general knowledge that he had been overruled by the SCS and the Home Secretary on previous occasions. She gambled that he might still be carrying a grudge and as long as he wasn't risking his pension he would want to get one over on Redcliffe.

"Don't do anything yet... leave it with me," said the Chief and rang off.

'He's taken the bait,' she thought as she replaced the receiver.

She checked herself in the mirror and decided her tracksuit looked fine for now. She opened the blinds to her office and was pleased to see all four researchers working away, surrounded by sandwiches. She told them to be prepared for an 8.30am meeting and went back to her desk.

When the Chief finally got hold of the Police Commissioner, he was informed that the fugitive had got away and confirmed that the SCS was taking charge of the operation. The SCS was cutting the Firm out of the loop and now the Chief was sure that there was another agenda for Branen. He decided to let the Controller know that Branen was still on the streets and let her pursue what had become her obsession. It would give her the chance to put one over the SCS.

All the time she had been tracking Branen, he had been in Soho. She decided that it was the only place he had friends who would give him shelter. Again she decided to go over her Chief's head. If she showed initiative and came out smelling of roses she would be guaranteed his job when he retired. "Nothing ventured nothing gained," she said to herself and dialled the SCS's number.

120. HERBERT REDCLIFFE, DENNIS LEUNG & THE CONTROLLER : (EARLY MORNING, TUESDAY 17 NOVEMBER)

After the SCS had spoken to the Police Commissioner and activated Dennis, there was nothing more he could do. He lay back on his bed in a state of anxiety, waiting and hoping to hear from Dennis that Branen was dead.

A couple of hours later he woke from a disturbed sleep wondering why he hadn't heard anything. He rang Dennis and getting no reply, attached a priority ring-back flag.

After releasing Branen, Dennis had returned to his penthouse in Gerrard Street. He was asleep when the phone in the suitcase rang, and his hung kwan decided not to wake him.

Eventually Dennis rang back at 7am and reported that he'd lost Branen. Redcliffe was incandescent with rage. He knew that Branen would realise The Associates, not the police, had authorised the attempt on his life and he was now in extreme danger. He needed Branen caught as soon as possible but he was not in a position to supervise his capture. That was, until the Controller rang him.

She launched straight in. "I understand Branen has gone AWOL again, sir."

The SCS did not respond.

"Why don't you let me find him for you, sir… you know you haven't got the resources I've got."

Herbert Redcliffe realised the Police Commissioner must have been shooting his mouth off, but he also knew the Controller was right.

"What do you suggest?" he asked.

"Give me the authority to find him and I won't let you down. If he did kill his daughter I want him as badly as you do," she said. It was less than twenty-four hours since she had requested the DNA comparison on Whitey's semen and blood, so her suspicions about his involvement were as yet unconfirmed.

"Are you recording this call?"

"No sir, it wouldn't do me any good if my Chief knew I was dealing directly with you… this is strictly off the record."

"Firstly I want you to organise a close-protection team to meet me at my apartment at 11am... and unofficially get on with the search, but keep your officers to a minimum. When you find him you must let me know and I'll tie up all the loose ends."

"Okay... I'll do that," said the Controller, crossing her fingers.

She showered, dressed and went into the meeting with her team. She asked them to dig deeper to find Branen's true identity and unearth his history. Then she sent Janet, a junior, to the Westminster CCTV control room to monitor the live feed from the whole Soho area including Regent Street and Waterloo Place. She briefed Antoinette to arrange for the close protection team to collect Redcliffe at 11am, and then to visit as many bars and clubs in Soho as she could with the e-fit and CCTV image.

She told them, "This is an off the record project so we can only use three watchers to cover Soho, and they have to keep their mouths shut. I want three armed officers on standby in the unmarked van. The minute we have a reasonable ID I'm sending them in to arrest him."

She was not going to let the SCS mess it up again. It was her prize to be won and flaunted.

121. BRANEN & THE TRAMP : (9AM, TUESDAY 17 NOVEMBER)

Branen made his way up Wardour Street looking for the tramp who had accused him of stealing his accommodation.

There he was, bundled up in a filthy blanket in Tyler's Court where they'd had their fracas last Friday.

Branen crouched down and shook his shoulder.

"Fucking hell," he said, even though he was still asleep. His eyes opened and an expression of horror spread over his bruised face. "Fuck, not you again... it's my fucking space."

Branen tried to appear friendly. "I don't want your space... what's your name?"

He was struggling to his feet. "What's that got to do with you, pal...? I don't have a fucking name for people like you."

Branen reached into his belt-bag. "I'd like to buy your hat and coat."

The tramp moved his hands up his body and over his head; Branen guessed he was checking that he was all still there. "That'll be five hundred pounds," he said.

Branen counted out five ten pound notes and held them in front of his face. The man propped himself up against the wall, took off his skull-cap and a mop of greasy curls flopped down. Then he pulled off the coat and held it out with his left hand as he grabbed the money with his right. "You won't regret it..." he said, "...they're from Savile Row."

Branen dragged the coat over the top of his raincoat and pulled the cap down over his forehead. "Don't worry, you won't see me again." The smell of alcohol and urine turned his stomach.

The tramp looked up from counting the money. "It's you who'll have to worry if I see you again, pal."

He watched Branen walk away and when Branen looked back the tramp was counting the money again, just to make sure he wasn't dreaming.

Wearing the new hat and coat and with his bed under his arm Branen assumed a shuffling walk and turned into Bouchier Street. It was gone 9am and he hoped he wasn't too late. There was no-one around when he tried the entry code on Redcliffe's gate. He tapped in 4,6,5,4, the numbers he thought Redcliffe had used, but the gate didn't open; he would have to revert to plan B.

Seven metres from the gate there was a recess in the wall where he could lay out his bed. He arranged the cardboard so that he could roll out of it fast when needed to. He had the filleting knife in his hand. Would Redcliffe go into the office this morning? Or had he already left? Branen decided that if he wasn't disturbed he would stay in his foxhole until midday.

Branen had to strike now or he would have to wait for months until Redcliffe had forgotten about him. He hoped that Redcliffe would think it too risky for him to come after him straight away.

122. BRANEN, REDCLIFFE & THE TERRIBLE TWINS : (11AM, TUES 17 NOV)

At 11am a BMW limousine reversed into Bouchier Street.

The passenger checked the man lying in the shelter of the building adjacent to Redcliffe's gate. The tramp was wrapped up in cardboard and newspaper and looked innocuous enough; he dismissed any potential threat.

The registration plate told Branen it was the same car that had collected him to view Carrie's body with the same terrible twins inside.

Less than a minute later he heard the clunk of the metal gate closing. Redcliffe appeared on the pavement. The driver stayed at the wheel and his doppelganger slid from the passenger seat and opened the back door to let Redcliffe in. As the close protection officer turned to get into the front, Branen rolled out of his bed and leapt forward. The officer was just slamming his door when he reached the car and pulled open the rear door. He dived in and grabbed Redcliffe by the throat.

"I thought we had an agreement," Branen said in his ear as he pulled him across his body. "...you're responsible for my daughter's death and now you've broken your word you're useless to me."

The passenger was already out of the car and had drawn a Browning pistol from his shoulder holster.

Branen had the filleting knife in clear view at Redcliffe's throat.

"Get back in the car or he's dead... I've got nothing to lose."

The officer knew that before he could raise his weapon and shoot, he would have killed Redcliffe.

He got back into the car and Branen closed the rear door. The driver must have flicked a switch because he heard an electrical click as the door locks engaged. There was a solid glass partition separating the front and rear compartments.

"Is the intercom on?" Branen asked.

"Yes."

"Drive up onto the pavement... close to the wall on your side."

The driver had no choice.

"Unlock the doors."

The same electrical click as the locks disengaged. The driver couldn't open his door far enough to get out but the passenger door opened onto the street.

"If you get out of the car I'll slit his throat."

He dragged Redcliffe out of the car backwards towards the alley to Wardour Street. They were forty metres from the car and into the alleyway when he said, "I made you a promise, Herbert."

311

"Please, Branen, don't…" he was begging.

The bodyguard in the passenger seat would be assessing when it would be safe to exit the car. It would be very soon. Branen slid the slim blade into the back of Redcliffe's neck between the vertebrae. Death would not come instantaneously. He would see and hear for a couple of minutes but he would not be able to react physically because Branen had cut his spinal column.

He kept dragging Redcliffe along the alley until he was ten metres from Wardour Street. As Redcliffe's slumped body dropped to the ground his head twisted, and with vacant eyes he stared at Branen unable to speak or breathe. A minute later he would be dead.

Branen sprinted left then right into Brewer Street. He had a fifty metre start on the bodyguard and he knew Soho. After turning into Percy Street he hid in a doorway, took off the tramp's hat and coat and crossed over to Berwick Street market. He looked totally different in his raincoat and it was easy to blend in with the throng in the market. He took his time examining the fruit and veg as he meandered through the stalls. He bought an apple and nobody seemed to take any notice of him. Halfway up Berwick Street in a second-hand clothes shop he bought a bright red hoody with Los Angeles emblazoned on the back, a blue cap with NY embroidered over the peak and a shoulder bag. He changed into the new kit and put the mackintosh into the bag. He threw the Polaroids of Redcliffe into a waste bin; they were no further use.

123. THE CONTROLLER : (AM, TUESDAY 17 NOVEMBER)

The Controller's researcher did not find any record of Branen's existence. His identity had been so well hidden that even the most sophisticated searches had revealed nothing.

Antoinette was an hour into visiting Soho clubs and bars with Branen's image when she arrived at Costas's Lounge.

As she entered she saw Jack with his back to the door, pretending to clean the optics but helping himself to a large measure of vodka.

Just as he was knocking it back, she said, "Hello…"

Jack jumped out of his skin. "What do you want?"

"Aren't you open yet?" said Antoinette, looking around the empty room.

Jack did a double take, the woman was attractive. He came out from behind the bar and started slowly wiping a table. "It's early..." then wiping his mouth and pointing to the row of spirit bottles, "...I was just levelling out, man."

Antoinette got closer and held out Branen's e-fit and CCTV images. "I wondered if you've ever seen this man before?"

"You a policeman?"

"Have you seen this man before?"

Jack had been out the previous night on a bender and was taking his time.

He held out his hand. "My name's Jack..."

Antoinette ignored him.

Jack looked at the pictures. "...err, yes that's Ben, he's Costas's mate... he had a bit of trouble in here last week."

Then it dawned on him that he might be speaking out of turn. "Hang on a minute... I'm an innocent bystander... do you want a drink?"

Antoinette gave up on him. "Is the owner here?"

Jack rang upstairs. "Costas, we've got a visitor I'm sure you'd like to meet."

Antoinette showed the images to Costas and noticed the look of apprehension on his face. "Jack tells me he was in here last week..."

"Don't believe anything he tells you... and who are you anyway?" asked Costas.

He tried to convince her that Ben was just another customer, but with Jack's verbal and Costas's reluctance to talk she decided to have him taken in for questioning. She also ordered one of the watchers to keep an eye on the entrance to Costas's Lounge in case Branen showed up.

When the Controller heard from Antoinette she went to West End Central police station so that she could question Costas personally.

In the interview room she explained that if he did not co-operate she had the means to make his life a misery. "Think of the excuses we could dream up to close you down... drugs, under-age drinking and that's just for starters."

"I've no idea who the man is… but he might be the bloke who came into the bar last week… he was drunk and made a nuisance of himself… but he left peacefully enough and I haven't seen him since."

Despite Jack's statement to Antoinette, the CCTV photograph and the Controller's threats, Costas was not as compliant as the Controller had hoped. After an hour of intensive questioning he was still adamant in his denial. Her final frustration was that she could not detain him without having him charged by the police and decided that he was a lost cause and had to release him.

As she was leaving, her phone rang. Her researcher informed her that Herbert Redcliffe had been stabbed in Soho. She turned back to the station sergeant. "Has there been an incident in Soho?"

"Yes Ma'am, we've been called out to a stabbing in Bouchier Street."

She ran to her car and instructed the driver to get her back to the office.

124. BRANEN & THE BARRISTER :
(MIDDAY, TUESDAY 17 NOVEMBER)

Dressed in the jacket and cap Branen looked like any other tourist on Dean Street.

He kept his head down and went up the stairs to the Empire Room and straight across to the cloakroom before Ayo could see him. He needed to change back into the mac and have a wash and brush-up. He put the jacket and cap into the bag and hung it on a coat hook. He checked his money; he had under two hundred pounds left. He could not risk using the Firm's key to the postbox at Giovanni's, or the credit card for the account at Barclays. He was going to have to make do with what he had left.

The usual hard drinkers were propping up the bar and breaking in the new day. A few people were grouped round the chairs in the window overlooking Dean Street. Several had seen better days and better times. They talked too loudly and only listened to themselves. They were pouring increasing amounts of alcohol down their throats until it was lapping just behind their dentures. In such a small room you had to speak up to make yourself heard.

Ayo was behind the bar. "Ben… twice in a month… to what do we owe this pleasure?"

As he came closer his expression changed. "You look fucked! What have you been up to? You told me you were photographing Soho life…" he turned away and poured a large whisky. "You look as though you've been to war since I last saw you." He pushed the glass across the bar and waited for an answer.

"Things got a bit rough… I'll tell you some other time," Branen said, as casually as he could.

Ayo reached over and put his hand on Branen's bandaged hand. "You haven't got yourself into trouble again, have you?" He sniffed. "There's a smell of petrol in the air."

Branen had put his head under the tap but he still smelt of lighter fuel.

He asked Ayo for Anthony's phone number and called him from the pay phone in the cloakroom but it went straight to his message service. Anthony was his best chance of escape so he decided to keep calling every fifteen minutes.

After an hour there was still no answer. Branen knew all the ports, train stations and airports would have his description and he was becoming increasingly desperate; it would be only a matter of time before they caught up with him. He returned to the bar and Ayo pointed to a man who was sitting with his back to the window staring morosely into a tumbler of whisky. Branen hadn't noticed him at first because he was against the light.

"There's your man, Ben…" said Ayo, "…he arrived while you were making the call."

"Would you like a drink, Anthony?" asked Branen.

He looked up and a wry smile crept across his face. "What are you doing here?"

"It's good to see you, Anthony."

"What do you want?"

"A lift…"

"If you think I'm driving after a skinful…" he said, raising his glass, "…I'd never practise law again if…"

"I meant across the Channel… in that fucking swanky yacht you're always bragging about."

"When?"

315

"It has to be tonight... have you still got it?"

He nodded. "It must be important."

"I wouldn't ask if it wasn't."

He looked into his drink. "I suppose I shouldn't ask why."

Like Costas and Errol, Anthony knew Branen had dodgy connections, but without asking any questions he was prepared to take a risk for an old friend.

Branen reckoned that Anthony had seen Humphrey Bogart in Key Largo once too often and fancied himself as a bit of a buccaneer.

"How are we going to get down to Buckler's Hard?" he asked.

Branen held out two fifty pound notes. "Here's a hundred pounds for the train and taxi... see you there?"

"Why don't we go down there together?"

Branen looked him in the eye. "It wouldn't suit you... when can we sail?"

"Sorry I asked," he said and finished his drink.

"Do you want another?"

"Not if I drive to the yacht. We have to sail before ten tonight... be with me a least a couple of hours before that."

He appeared to have changed his mind about driving and about the drink. While he savoured it he used the time to tell Branen where Buckler's Hard was, how to find his yacht and about the difficulties of catching the tides to sail out into the Solent. Branen was sure it would have been fascinating if he had been interested in sailing.

Draining the glass Anthony pushed the cash back. "This one's on me... see you later."

With a wave to Ayo he left the bar.

Branen needed a road map of southern England to plot the route to Lymington. When he explained to Ayo that he did not want to leave just yet he sent the barman, Michael, to buy the map for him.

Ayo wanted to know what he had been up to; he loved intrigue and gossip. Branen told him he had been entangled in an illicit love triangle and the boyfriend had caught them out, and hence his injuries. The more he pursued the story and the more he drank, the more convoluted the story became until he ended up believing it himself.

Branen was getting anxious to leave and if he was going to avoid the motorways he had a journey of at least a hundred miles in front of him. Michael finally returned with the map. Branen checked the route out of London; the A3 to Guildford, then the A31 junction from there across the north of Southampton towards the New Forest.

Ayo insisted he had one for the road and Branen flinched as Ayo grabbed his shoulder and shook his hand.

He collected his bag from the cloakroom and left to sort out a mode of transport. He had to move fast and he had to avoid the cameras.

It was 3.15pm when he walked back to Soho Square wearing the hoody and cap. The sky was leaden and the streets were getting busier; early Christmas shoppers offered him some cover. He was looking for a motor-scooter with a crash-helmet attached and no security chain through the wheel. The seat and steering locks on older scooters were cheap and vulnerable, which was why so many of them were stolen by joy-riders.

He walked around the square past the scooter bays checking for an unsecured bike. Out of twenty or more scooters, only three had helmets attached and they all had thick security cables locked through the wheels. Motorbike owners in London had learnt the hard way.

125. JANET, PHIL & BRANEN :
(3.30PM, TUESDAY 17 NOVEMBER)

The mundane job of watching the screens at Westminster's CCTV Monitoring Centre had fallen to the most junior of the Controller's four researchers.

Janet had arrived at the secret location at 9am.

"Let me explain how all these cameras work round Soho," said Phil, the jovial man who spent his working life sitting in front of the screens.

After six and a half hours of scanning the monitors Janet was getting hungry and her eyes were sore. Nothing had been seen of Branen and she was convinced that her boss believed he had got away. She went over to the kitchen and made herself her fifth instant coffee of the day. Her stomach was raw and she needed food. She returned to the desk, put her coffee down and turned to Phil. "Be a darling and keep an eye on the screens for me... I'm going to pop over to the bagel shop."

But as she swept up her jacket, she knocked the coffee over. Cursing her luck, she grabbed a handful of tissues and managed to stem the flow before it poured into Phil's lap. As she was mopping up the coffee Branen was walking round Soho Square. Phil glanced up at the monitors and a figure wearing a hoody and a cap caught his attention. He could not see the face but the man appeared to be hiding his identity.

He called Janet back. "Jan, hang on a moment... have a gander at this fella..." He pointed at the screen.

Janet looked at the man and reckoned he was worth checking out. As she dialled her mobile she said, "Thank God I spilt the coffee."

James had stayed with the Controller. He sensed she was climbing up the slippery pole and he wanted to stop her sliding down. He took the call and switched it to speaker-phone.

"There's someone in Soho Square..." said Janet.

"That's unusual," said James.

"No, seriously... he's a definite maybe... it's got to be worth checking out."

The Controller pushed in. "Whereabouts in the square?"

Janet had to check with Phil. "He's on the south-west corner near Frith Street."

The Controller patched through to the watchers. "Check out a man wearing a hoody, a cap and carrying a duffle bag, in the south-west corner of Soho Square."

One watcher, disguised as a bag-lady, who had been watching Costas's Lounge, was at the junction of Old Compton Street accosting pedestrians and asking for her fare home.

A second watcher in Greek Street, dressed as a new age punk, was forty metres from Soho Square leaning on the wall outside the Pillars of Hercules pub with a pint of shandy in his hand. He put the glass on the window sill and strode up to the square. As he made his way along the south side, Branen turned down Frith Street.

The bag-lady was heading up Frith Street towards him, holding a can of pepper spray in her pocket. The third watcher in Chinatown was too far away.

Like Branen, they carried bags containing hats and alternative clothing in case they needed a change of disguise. It was all turning into one big fancy dress party.

The Controller shouted to her watchers, "Do you have eyes on him?"

"No Ma'am." The answer was in duplicate.

The Controller switched back to Janet. "Where is he?"

"He turned into Frith Street... and we've lost him for the moment."

"Find him... NOW."

Branen had disappeared into the newsagent's. He was flicking through magazines and checking the street through the window when he noticed the punk on the opposite pavement who was moving quickly and scanning up and down the street. Branen had to assume the worst and take evasive action. Hiding behind the central magazine rack, he slipped off the hoody and put the mac back on. Leaving the bag and clothes on the floor he headed back to the square. A taxi was crawling towards him. He hailed it and jumped in. Handing the driver a twenty pound note he told him to go round the block and back up Dean Street.

He stopped the cab at St Anne's Court, jumped out and walked past the window of The Piano Bar where Carrie had first met Whitey. As the crow flies he was fifty metres from where he had hailed the taxi, but for the moment he had evaded the watchers and the cameras. He was looking for another motorcycle bay and didn't see the camera situated high up on the north corner of Berwick Street Market.

Meanwhile Janet's ears were beginning to bleed as the Controller harangued her with instructions. Phil was scanning all the monitors when he saw a man with a crew-cut resembling Branen. "Who's that, Jan... walking towards the market?"

Janet took one look at the man and decided that even with shorn hair he resembled the suspect sufficiently to risk her career.

She shouted into her mobile, "I think we've found him... he's got short hair and wearing a mid-tone raincoat. He's in Broadwick Street." Her heart was trying to climb out of her body.

The Controller was stressed out. Were they now chasing another suspect or had Branen changed his clothes?

She decided to go with Janet's hunch and radioed through to the Renault Espace alerting the three armed officers. "I want him alive."

126. BRANEN : (3.45PM, TUESDAY 17 NOVEMBER)

Branen had struck lucky on the corner of Berwick Street. There was an old Honda scooter with L-plates and without a security chain.

He stood on the opposite corner watching the stall-holders selling all kinds of exotic vegetables. Dusk was closing in. It wasn't going to be easy to break open the seat and force the steering lock without drawing attention to himself from the endless procession of traffic and pedestrians.

This time he didn't have the benefit of The Associates' R&D department to make him an ignition key. He had learnt how to short the ignition on various vehicles, and hopefully the technology had not changed too much since then.

He pushed between the parked bikes and bent over the scooter, using his body as cover. He could not risk riding the bike without a helmet and hoped he'd find one locked in the storage compartment below the seat. He wrenched the back of the seat and nearly shouted out as a bolt of pain shot down his arm from the collar bone. Fortunately the lock failed first time and the seat sprang up revealing a crash-helmet, which he put on and snapped down the visor. He managed to rotate the handle bars in both directions forcing the steering lock to shear; again his collar bone reminded him that it was broken.

Now he had a problem. He had to break into the front fairing and short out the ignition socket. He saw some lads walking down Berwick Street towards him. On the corner behind him was a chemist so he retired into the shop doorway.

The men passed by without giving him a second look.

127. THE RENAULT ESPACE, THE CONTROLLER & JANET : (3.45PM, TUES 17 NOVEMBER)

The Renault Espace was parked in Kingly Street and two of the officers were in the 24-hour café buying sandwiches when the call came through.

It took two minutes to get them back on board and with siren screaming they made the five hundred yard dash through the afternoon traffic.

Janet kept an open line to the Controller and was patched through to the Espace driver. "Branen has gone into the chemist's shop on the corner of Broadwick and Berwick Street," she said.

The Espace was thirty metres down Berwick Street when they came across a white van stationary in the middle of the road with its flashers on; the driver was delivering a carcass of meat to Myrtle's restaurant.

The officer in the passenger seat jumped out shouting, "Police, move your van NOW..."

"Yeah, and I'm the Pope... fuck off," the driver replied.

The officer set off at a sprint down Berwick Street towards the chemist.

The Controller was listening to the conversations between Janet and the Espace's driver.

Branen reappeared on the screen.

"Hurry up, he's come out the shop..." said Janet, "...and he's trying to steal a scooter."

"I'm stuck behind a fucking van..." said the driver, "...and my officer has legged it down Berwick Street to head him off."

She saw Branen hesitate, look around and stare up at the camera. He seemed to make eye contact with her and she found herself shrinking away from the screen.

"It's okay, he can't see you," Phil said, laughing.

The relentless wailing of the Espace's siren and the hooting taxis had finally persuaded the delivery driver to dump the carcass in Myrtle's entrance. He was crawling down crowded Berwick Street trying to get out of the way of the Espace, but there were cars parked down both sides all the way to Broadwick Street and there was no room to pull over and let the aggressive driver past.

It was getting darker and it had begun to rain; Branen didn't know when the scooter owner might return. He heard the siren and saw the inverted smokey glass dome of the CCTV camera up on the wall. They were on to him. He had to move. He unzipped the belt-bag and took out Carrie's key and pushed it under the front fairing and twisted. He got his fingers under the plastic panel and snapped it back, revealing the wiring loom and the ignition plug. He kept his face down as the noise of the breaking plastic echoed round his head.

The officer ran past Branen to the junction outside the chemist. He dived into the doorway that Branen had been sheltering in and reappeared within moments. Branen had his back to him, bent over the scooter with his body blocking the view. He wrenched the two wires from the top of the plug and twisted them together. Moving as swiftly as he could he straddled the scooter and jumped on the kick-start. He turned on the lights and pushed the scooter out in front of a white van which, in his haste, he hadn't seen coming. They both managed to brake. The driver swore at him and tried to force past. As Branen pushed out in front of him he noticed the doors of a Renault Espace following the van fly open and two men jump out. He knew who they were.

They shouted to their companion as they ran towards Branen, "That's him... stop him."

He had a ten metre start on them and accelerated away. He headed south down Berwick Street knowing the van would not be able to negotiate the market stalls, which took up the whole road, but three men were chasing on foot.

Branen wound up the throttle and with his thumb on the hooter drove like a maniac down the centre of the market between the stalls. The crowds began to part like the proverbial Red Sea. He saw two of his pursuers in his mirror about twenty metres away sprinting after him shouting, "Police, stop."

Branen doubted they really were policemen. There were several abusive shouts from people who had to jump for their lives but everyone was getting out of his way. That was until just before the bottom of the market when the punk stepped out in front of him. He was wearing a skin-coloured ear-phone; it might have been a hearing-aid but Branen had to gamble. Instead of trying to drive round him he opened the throttle and went straight at the punk. If he managed to stop Branen, he was finished. At the last moment Branen avoided the swinging truncheon that had appeared in the punk's right hand and crashed into him; the punk left the ground and flew over him. Branen nearly lost his grip on the handle bars and skidded sideways for several yards, but just managed to stay on the scooter.

He turned left and, as he accelerated away, looked back and saw that one of the officers chasing him was only a few metres behind. The street was clear as he sped down to the junction with Wardour Street. As he turned right he noticed the police tape on the far side across the entrance to the pedestrian section of Bouchier Street where he had left Redcliffe's body, five hours ago.

He had a thirty metre start on the chasing officers. He drove along the kerb against the one-way traffic down to Shaftesbury Avenue and turned south, leaving Soho behind.

One of the officers chasing Branen had got the last three letters on the scooter's number plate and this information was instantly circulated on the PNC.

As soon as he was clear of Soho, Branen stopped the scooter and checked the rear number plate. It was covered in city grime and was fairly illegible but he couldn't risk keeping it for long. If they had got the registration number the technology built into the traffic cameras could locate him.

He had to steal another vehicle. He needed to find a parking bay of motorbikes not covered by cameras. He headed west through the tunnel under Hyde Park corner. He could never enter an underpass without being reminded of the events in Paris that had changed so many lives. He emerged from the tunnel into Knightsbridge and turned left down the side of Harrods into Hans Crescent. He drove beyond the store where the road narrowed and there on the right was a motorcycle bay. The scooters were much more expensive models than the ones in Soho which would make them harder to steal. In the middle of this array of bikes was a polished bright red scooter with a wire basket on the back. 'One careful lady owner,' he thought as he tested the steering lock. It didn't have a chain through the wheel and the steering wasn't locked. The tall hedges bordering the pavement gave him cover from the houses and again he levered off the front panel and shorted out the ignition. He swapped the scooters over, rode back up to Knightsbridge, turned left and headed south-west.

There was nothing the Controller could do but wait. It was gone midnight when she went into her office and poured a couple of fingers of gin.

128. BRANEN : (EVENING, TUESDAY 17 NOVEMBER)

The ride down from London was tough and debilitating.

Branen was buffeted around by passing lorries and the side winds sucked and pushed him across the road in front of oncoming traffic. The small wheels on the scooter meant that the handling was unpredictable and he struggled to concentrate through the pain of his injuries. The constant battering from the cold wind and driving rain cut straight through his thin mackintosh and shirt, but as the effects of the alcohol wore off adrenalin took over.

The route was straightforward as far as Winchester. Before he reached the M3 he stopped at a garage and filled up with petrol. He paid cash and checked the map for the final part of the journey. He was running very late and it had taken him over three hours; he was drained mentally and physically. He was close to escape but one mistake or lapse in concentration and he could be caught. If he didn't get to Anthony before 10pm they would miss the high tide and they'd be stuck in the harbour. Using the motorway was a chance he had to take. He was on a different scooter and far enough away from London to risk the twenty miles of motorway that would take him to the edge of the New Forest. Motor-scooters rarely use motorways but to make up time he had to gamble that the police would not stop him.

With a sense of euphoria he left the motorway and entered the New Forest. One moment the clouds separated, leaving luminous gaps lit by a bright moon, and then the rain would start. The New Forest felt surprisingly remote as he followed the winding road through the moorland and pine forest. Even with the rain driving into his face he was overcome by a feeling of exhilaration.

It was nearly 9pm when he turned left off the main road into Lyndhurst towards Buckler's Hard. He followed the signs to the yacht harbour and emerged from a tree-lined avenue into the marina. He pulled up short of the car park in case it was covered by cameras. There were three vehicles parked there. He guessed at that time of year and time of night only a couple of boat-owners would be on their yachts. But the harbour master would probably be in residence. He looked around and saw a wide footpath leading into woodland with a signpost pointing to Beaulieu House. He checked all round and could not see anyone, so drove the scooter along the footpath and turned into the wood. He rode another hundred metres through the trees and found a ditch full of autumn leaves, where he buried the bike.

He had to meet Anthony on Jetty 'E' at the end of the marina; he had told him that he would be moored on the outside of the quay in a Tradewind 33 yacht, which meant nothing to Branen.

129. ANTHONY & BRANEN :
(9PM, TUESDAY 17 NOVEMBER)

When Branen arrived on the jetty alongside the yacht, Anthony was standing on deck, a dark figure against the moonlight.

Anthony was pacing impatiently and unlike his yacht he looked the worse for wear.

"I was about to abandon ship and sink a drink..." he said, "...there's a force eight gale blowing out there in the Channel... it could reach storm force. You're an hour late and we've got to get out of the harbour before the tide prevents us crossing the sand bar... with just me, and you a novice crewing we might not make it in such a blow."

Reeking of whisky, he stepped unsteadily into the cockpit and started the engine. "Cast off... to stand any chance of getting across the channel just do everything I tell you."

Branen realised that there might be a gale out there but Anthony had hit his own personal doldrums.

Anthony called the coast guard to complete the radio check.

"Are you sure you know what you're doing in these poor conditions, Anthony?" asked the coast guard.

Anthony reassured him that he had sailed the Channel in all kinds of weather before; but he didn't sound convincing to Branen.

Branen said, "I wanted us to slip away without anyone noticing..."

Anthony explained, "If we didn't make contact, it would arouse suspicion."

They slowly pulled away from the quay while Anthony pointed to various ropes and pulleys, explaining which bit did what. They motored out into the middle of the Beaulieu river.

Anthony offered Branen the tiller. "Maintain the course ahead...
I'm going below."

He disappeared into the cabin and reappeared holding a tumbler
and a pewter flask. "We could do with a top up," he said, refilling the
flask from a bottle he held tightly under his arm. He poured a generous
measure into the tumbler, handed it to Branen, then drank from the
bottle. He described the water in the estuary as sloppy but it seemed
rough to Branen and he was going to have a debate with his stomach.

They motored out of the river and into the Solent without bottoming
on the sandbank. It got seriously sloppy. The driving rain started as
they left the comparative shelter of the marina. The strong winds were
pushing the dark clouds across the sky with unnatural speed. The
moon would burst through, then with a squall of heavy rain the clouds
would hide it from view again. The waves were breaking over the bow
and causing the boat to see-saw. Branen had no idea what they were
facing out in the Channel.

"I've decided to motor out of the Solent... past the pinch point
between the Isle of Wight and Hurst Point... and into the Channel...
then we'll raise the sail..." muttered Anthony. "...we're heading west,
bypassing those bloody Needles."

"Hoist the mainsail and keep a couple of reefs rolled round the
boom," said Anthony.

There was a sudden vicious squall causing him to stumble. "I've
changed my mind... just unfurl the jib while I keep the engine running."

Branen was agile enough to move about the deck but Anthony said,
"Make sure you stay clipped on otherwise we'll lose you overboard."

Anthony had sailed across the Channel with friends several times
before, but never on his own or in the dark. The wind was bitterly
cold as he took another long tug of whisky and tried to rationalise his
reasons for agreeing to this trip. The man he was helping to escape from
the UK had always fascinated him. He had an affection for the street-
wise loner, who represented a totally different way of life. Branen had a
freedom of spirit that he and his other friends at the Bar had given up
when they took on families and mortgages. There was something going
on in that man which intrigued him. He had never asked the question
and so far it had never been revealed but he suspected that Branen was
running from the law. When Branen had asked him to take him across

the Channel he'd detected a note of desperation in his voice and against his better judgement he had been drawn into his friend's predicament. With these heavy seas and with no-one else to help him, he was out of his depth. He was torn between the excitement of the moment and his responsibility to his ex-wife and daughter; he was taking a gamble which would put his life and their fortunes at stake.

Another squall brought him back to reality. Just one more shot and he felt he could beat the elements.

They were both wearing life jackets and harnesses and Anthony told Branen again to clip on; which meant clipping the carabiner attached to his harness to a wire running round the edge of the deck. Even that was difficult. The boat was rolling around and Branen was still a long way from gaining his sea legs.

With the tide now turned and the wind coming from the west into their faces, the sea conditions worsened. Branen began to worry that he had pushed his friend into a situation that was getting out of control.

Anthony called out, "Breaking seas." It wasn't directed at Branen, more of a shout to the elements telling them he knew what they were up to.

"It's too dangerous to put up too much sail in this weather... we'll roll out the foresail... we'll keep the engine running otherwise we'll make no headway in this wind." He wasn't looking at Branen and he wasn't shouting at him. Branen felt that Anthony was trying to convince himself that being here was okay and what he was doing was correct. It didn't convince Branen and he was becoming more anxious that Anthony didn't believe it either.

"Clip on over there Ben... over there!" he yelled, pointing forwards. There was a note of suppressed fear in his voice. Earlier he had shown Branen which ropes to use to release the sails but his instructions had been vague.

Branen climbed out of the cockpit onto the deck and was aware of a feeling of insignificance and vulnerability in the face of the force of nature.

"Look..." shouted Anthony above the noise of the crashing waves on the hull, "...there's St. Catherine's lighthouse."

He was pointing to the port side and Branen could see a flashing light that at one moment appeared to be dipping beneath his feet and seconds later rising way above his head; then it would completely disappear behind a wave. Branen crept forward and the yacht yawed viciously. He grabbed the handrail and nearly did a forward roll over the side. He braced himself as the boat rose and fell on tumultuous waves. He moved away from the edge of the deck to clip his carabiner on to the bars at the base of the mast. Anthony shouted something he could not hear. He was waving his arms and shouting. Eventually he understood that he wanted Branen to release the roller mechanism to raise the foresail.

When Branen had managed it Anthony wound up the throttle and they picked up speed; they left the Solent and entered the Channel. Then the sea became even rougher, the wind was relentless; they were soaked and getting very cold.

Anthony took another long drink from the flask and switched to the chart-plotter screen on the GPS navigation instrument in front of him. He set the cursor to the port of Cherbourg and pressed the button. "It will be far safer to sail into a major harbour like Cherbourg... where we'll be anonymous, than to dock in a small harbour where they'll be much more curious."

The Raymarine bleeped back at him, setting the course; they would follow the map straight to Cherbourg.

"Whatever happens with currents the instruments will automatically correct the course... it's simple enough, even for a novice like you to follow. Providing nothing goes wrong and we average five knots, we should make landfall by tomorrow morning."

A couple of hours had passed and they were about five miles out into the Channel when Anthony drained the flask. They were passing through sea mist and low cloud which would disperse and then close in again to envelop them. Visibility was varying from between three hundred metres down to twenty or thirty metres. Anthony was annoyed by Branen's incompetent seamanship so when he decided to raise the mainsail he climbed unsteadily out of the cockpit and headed forward along the lurching deck to show how it was done.

There was a deep and thunderous sound. A sound resembling the roar of a crowd in a stadium, but the noise included the deafening hiss of a huge snake.

Suddenly out of the mist came the massive bow of an oil tanker.

It was the most frightening sight of Branen's life, totally overwhelming. The ship thundering towards them was no more than fifty metres away. It looked like a huge mountain approaching at an impossible speed; an enormous steel hull towering above them, bearing down on their boat; the outcome seemed inevitable. They were going to be driven down by this vast black metal mass and swallowed up by the sea. It was unreal. It was like being in a 3D horror film in the middle of a malevolent maelstrom of noise and water.

Anthony had not clipped on. He turned to face Branen with his back to the ship. He must have seen it, he certainly could hear it because it drowned out the noise of the sea. He had a look of disbelief and resignation on his face as though he had already accepted his fate. Branen had to take a chance. He swung the tiller arm towards him, hoping to steer down the side of the ship. The wrench of the tiller caused a searing pain down his arm but he held on as the bow wave from the ship hit them; they rose up and took off. They hung in space before belly-flopping back down onto the next wave with a bone-crunching crash. Anthony was up in the air at an angle, a couple of metres above the deck. The yacht sailed away from beneath him and he descended out of sight, below the boat and into the chasm between the yacht and the tanker.

Branen leapt to the edge of the cockpit expecting to see Anthony, but he was gone. Another giant wave and Branen nearly followed him over the side. It was his white-knuckled grip on the tiller handle that kept him in the boat. His friend had disappeared and he could not help him. He was dwarfed by the giant hull speeding past and deafened by the thump of the engines; he was shooting down a dark tunnel towards death. Using all his strength, he pulled the tiller again to the left and waited. If he'd reached out he would have been able to touch this beast as it rushed past. It was a kind of hell he would never have dreamt could happen. He doubted if he was going to survive the final propeller thrust, even if he got that far without being consumed by this gargantuan monster.

It must have taken no more than thirty seconds to pass but time had stood still; there seemed to be no end to the ordeal. Eventually the boat was flung out in the wake of the ship. Then the gigantic thrusting propellers sucked and spat the yacht out over the wash from the stern wave.

Like waking from a nightmare Branen saw the titanic hull receding, and then it was gone. The noise diminished until he was left alone on the boat with the eerie whistling of the wind through the rigging and the stench of diesel fumes. He scanned the rolling mass of water but Anthony wasn't there. He shouted his name but his voice disappeared into the wind and spray. He gripped the tiller and forced the boat to circle.

Precious time passed as he searched for his friend. His voice became cracked and hoarse; he refused to accept that Anthony had been consumed by that black ocean.

Branen fought to overcome his emotions. The boat was being thrown around like a cork and he had lost any sense of direction. White-capped waves slammed relentlessly into the hull; he didn't believe that it could withstand such an onslaught. He was at the mercy of an overwhelming force and defenceless in the face of the storm. He kept searching the waves, hoping to see Anthony, but in these seas he knew that there was no chance of finding him.

With a helpless sense of sadness and after an hour, he finally gave up. He reckoned that he had little chance of survival, but if he could point the boat into the oncoming waves he might get through; but the waves were not approaching from any one direction and he had to rely on the buoyancy of the boat. Landfall seemed a long way off.

He ripped off the life-jacket and belt-bag and put them to one side. He tore off his coat, shirt, trousers and boots and threw them down into the cabin. If the boat capsized he didn't want to drown because of the weight of his wet clothes.

He hung on to the tiller with his inflamed hand and pulled the life-jacket and belt-bag back on over his T-shirt.

In the cockpit the illuminated screen showed the yacht pointing west, sideways across the plotted course. Could navigation be this simple? Ignoring the pain, he pushed the tiller arm away from him and turned due south into the wind. The image on the screen turned with him. Anthony had set the route and he was going to follow it. There might be more tankers in front or behind but if he tried to turn back there could be ships anywhere. He decided to leave the foresail how Anthony had set it. The engine was working and as long as it didn't run out of fuel he stood a chance.

He sailed on for more than seven hours.

At first he was hunched up in the cockpit, checking the route every few minutes. After an hour had passed he was losing too much body heat and beginning to drift off, so he tied the tiller with a rope and went below. He was being thrown from one side of the boat to the other, feeling horribly seasick as he pulled on his clothes. He threw up the water he'd been trying to drink.

Eventually streaks of light appeared between the clouds turning the sea from black to grey. And at last the storm abated. He checked the screen and tightened the tiller ropes again. The adrenalin was wearing off and exhaustion was setting in.

Time passed as he drifted in and out of sleep.

It was 7am and on the horizon he could see a narrow black strip dividing the silver water from the sky. There was no colour; it was a black and white image. It reflected his feelings as another of his friend-ships had ended in disaster. He would never forget that because of him, Carrie and Georgie were dead. And through their generosity Jane and Anthony had both lost their lives. He had destroyed them when all they had done was to try to save him from himself. He was responsible for the death of three of the most important people in his life and an innocent baby.

He realised he did not have the skills to sail into a harbour and moor up unnoticed. If he fucked up the mooring or said the wrong thing to the harbour master over the radio, assuming he could work out how to use it, he would attract attention. And if he was interrogated he would not be able to bluff his way through awkward questions.

He adjusted the tiller and took the boat to the right of the designated path on the navigation screen. He was aiming a few miles further west up the coast, hoping to find an uninhabited landing point.

It was another couple of hours before he turned directly west a few hundred metres from the jagged French coastline. Fortunately so far he had not hit any underwater obstructions. He noticed that he was heading into the wind. He moved forward and clung to the mast as he furled the foresail. He was faced with miles of dark cliff face and occasionally the sky cut jagged spaces into the daunting black rock. To make land without being seen, he would have to abandon ship and swim to one of the inlets. The yacht would motor on for miles before it ran out of fuel and then be discovered unmanned. If Anthony's body were to be found it might be concluded that he had been washed overboard on a solo crossing of the Channel. Branen was fairly sure he had not been noticed boarding the yacht back at Buckler's Hard; the memory of it seemed like a dream from the past.

He tied the tiller to ensure that the boat would travel in a straight line. When the yacht was found he wanted them to assume Anthony had done this to allow him to go forwards to adjust a sail. He went below and found a roll of heavy duty dustbin bags; packed his damp belongings into one bag and knotted it tightly. He put that bag with air trapped inside into another bin liner, knotting it again. He repeated it a third time, again trying to make sure it was water-tight and usable as a float. The water was going to be freezing and he would have to swim strongly. A few years ago on an assignment he had to swim for his life in an Irish loch in the middle of winter, and he was familiar with the sleepy feeling of not caring as hypothermia sets in.

He watched the coast for a while until he saw a small inlet that appeared to go deep into the cliff face.

Dressed in the life jacket, T-shirt and pants he took a deep breath and dived into the sea with the polythene bag.

Fuck it was cold. The shock took his breath away. For a moment he could not take in any air at all. He swam frog fashion as hard as he could, trying to generate as much energy as possible. The water was cold enough to numb the broken collar-bone and he was losing feeling in his whole body. He managed to move his arms sufficiently to hang on to the floating bag which was acting as a sail. He kicked out but the wind and current pushed him off course, back in an easterly direction. He pumped away, counting each stroke out loud to encourage himself forwards. He had to generate enough energy to stop himself succumbing to the cold. It was about two hundred metres to shore and every kick of his legs seemed to be harder than the last. His energy was disappearing faster than he could have anticipated. He wasn't even halfway and he was exhausted. It was his will to survive that enabled him to swim the last hundred metres. He could easily have let the sea carry him away. He was in a trance and was sorely tempted to let go and give in to the elements.

He was semi-conscious when he was picked up by the breaking surf and washed towards the beach and into shallow water. He no longer felt cold and had an irresistible urge to float away in a dream. He tried to stand up but he had no strength left. He had turned to jelly and he just wanted to sleep. Part of his brain was still aware of what was really happening. He crawled from the freezing water shivering uncontrollably, but strangely still not feeling cold. The sun had risen and was squeezing its early rays over the cliff-face and on to the beach where he had landed. This wasn't warm sunshine, but it felt like it.

He removed the soaking underwear, which was sucking out what little remained of his body heat. At the base of the cliffs he dug with numb hands at the sand and buried his underwear. Naked, he forced himself to run along the beach. Gradually he managed to get his body moving and after ten minutes he returned to the bags to retrieve his clothes. He started to do a set of feeble star-jumps; slowly the blood returned and he regained some strength.

130. BRANEN : (SUNRISE, WEDNESDAY 18 NOVEMBER)

The bay was less than a hundred metres long and cut off from the rest of the coast by cliffs stretching out into the sea.

It was cold in the shade of the rock face but he was relieved to be back on land and alive, which conflicted with the guilt for the lives that had been lost. He was entering another world that they would never be able to see.

The sheer rock face in front of him swept up to a blue sky, presenting a horizon over which lay freedom. The sun appeared from behind a cloud casting elongated shadows across the beach, instantly warming his body and lifting his spirits.

He followed the inlet, fearing that he would have to climb those intimidating crags. A narrow strip of sand wound inland between the steep cliffs for seventy or eighty metres.

He was beginning to believe that, however weak he felt, he was going to have to climb out of there, when in the far corner he saw a steep track winding its way up through the rock face. The climb was not for the faint-hearted and he wondered who or what creature had formed the path. But it led to freedom and with every step his optimism increased.

At the top he emerged into the sunshine and found himself on an empty coastal footpath. Ahead was rough heathland and beyond that, hedgerows and fields with a strip of woodland running inland. He cut across the scrub skirting a bog and entered the wood. Keeping out of sight he followed an animal track for four or five hundred metres until he came out into a field. While he was walking, he worked on his story should he bump into a local. He had entered the country illegally and this would be sufficient to return him to the UK authorities. He didn't know if the British had contacted the French to be on the lookout, so he could not risk using any form of public transport. This was a rural and unpopulated area and he decided he would tell anyone he met, in his passable French, that he had arrived in Cherbourg and was looking for a friend who lived in the area. Plenty of English people owned property in Normandy and his story was totally credible. He would explain why he was on foot by telling them that his hire car had broken down and he wanted to rent another.

But now he was exposed in open country, and to avoid arousing suspicion he needed to find a road. He followed a hedgerow for another few hundred metres and came to a track which led to a collection of farm buildings and which he was sure would lead to a road. He was skirting the edge of the farm when an old dog woke up and started barking. Fortunately no one bothered to investigate.

The farm was on a narrow lane which led to the tiny rural village of Eculleville, with a sign which someone had peppered with shotgun pellets. He found a small local shop which had a petrol pump outside and a tiny bar beside it.

He was hungry so went into the bar and introduced himself.

His accent made it obvious he was English, so before offering his euros he tried Madame out with a ten pound note. She held it up to the light and without any debate gave him a fresh, warm baguette with charcuterie and a café au lait in a cup large enough to swim in. He had a cognac to complete the experience and began to feel a whole lot better.

He made small talk to an old man in a cap beside him on the principle that if he explained his predicament before he was asked, it would allay any suspicions before they grew heads.

"Can I get you a drink?..." Branen asked in French. "...I need to hire a car... is there anyone local who can help?"

"I'll have a cognac... why don't you go back to Cherbourg and get them to sort out your hire car?" the man asked.

"I don't have time... I've arranged to meet my friends tonight and I can't contact them."

Branen was worried that the man would start cross-questioning him about his friends so he distracted him by buying him another cognac. "Do you know anyone who might have an old second-hand car for sale?"

Branen's new friend accepted another coffee and another cognac, "I might be able to help you there..." he said and swallowed the cognac.

Branen paid the bill and they walked arm in arm back down the road to the farm he had circumvented earlier. The weather-beaten farmer looked like Branen's new friend's brother. They sat in his kitchen for half an hour drinking Pernod before he led them out into the yard. Tucked away in one of the barns was an old rusty Renault 4 van. If Branen wanted to remain inconspicuous he could not have chosen a better car. After much bargaining, drinking and waving currency around, with his friend holding it up to the light as the patron had done, they reached an arrangement.

With the deal finally done Branen was one hundred pounds lighter, which left him with seventy pounds and a handful of euros for petrol. He planned to use the route le chemin de l'école to avoid major roads. The journey was going to be at least a thousand kilometres without being able to afford anything more to eat, but that was a small price to pay for freedom. If he took it easy he reckoned he could average about ten kilometres per litre of petrol. A hundred litres would get him close to the Italian border; and after the last fill-up he might have enough money left for a sandwich. He could not risk crossing into Italy in this old van; he did not have any insurance and if customs or the police stopped him it could lead to embarrassing questions. But for now it would do.

At about midday, he watched in the rear-view mirror as the two old boys, with satisfied smiles on their faces, waved goodbye.

Branen headed south with too many Pernods in him.

131. THE CONTROLLER : (WEDNESDAY 18 NOVEMBER)

The Controller had been in the office all night and the gin hadn't helped.

Herbert Redcliffe was dead and the watcher, who'd tried to stop Branen on the scooter had ended up on life-support. The only redeeming feature in this case, as far as she was concerned, was the report on Whitey's DNA which confirmed that it matched the semen found in Carrie's flat; her suspicions had been correct. But she kept this information to herself in case her rivals used it against her.

"The trail's gone dead..." she told the researchers, "... get back on to Customs and re-check all the ports, airports and Eurostar trains."

While waiting for news of the watcher and hoping Branen or the motor scooter would be traced, she finally fell asleep, fully clothed on the futon in her office.

Herbert Redcliffe's death had been the lead on last night's TV news channels and in the evening papers. It was front page news in the early editions of the national newspapers. The Firm had spread rumours that it was a homosexual jealousy killing, but the press suspected there was more to the story.

The motor scooter Branen had dumped near Harrods wasn't found until 11am on Wednesday morning.

Eventually the Controller had to accept that Branen had irretrievably escaped her clutches. With the lack of further intel she did not have the authorisation to spend any more money on the case. The watchers and the armed officers were stood down and her researchers moved on to other business.

She was forced to surrender the case which was left open, marked 'No Further Action' and handed over to MI6.

She would never forget Branen and longed that one day their paths would cross again.

132. BRANEN : (WEDNESDAY 18 NOVEMBER)

On a previous journey down through Europe, Branen had come across a motorway service station, a hundred kilometres west of Lyon near

Chambéry. That aire du service was his destination. It was an overnight hang-out for long-haul lorry drivers before they followed the A43 across the Italian border to Turin and Milan.

As long as he did not get too held up in the many towns he had to pass through, he could make Chambéry in fifteen hours, which would get him there in the early hours. Now that he was on the road, the first priority was to change his sterling into euros. He spent the first part of the journey getting used to the agricultural smell permeating the van and to the gear-lever which was located on the dashboard.

Saint Lo was a hundred kilometres south of Eculleville. In the centre he found a Bureau de Change. He bought petrol, water, a map and the cheapest rucksack he could find, and was soon back on the road again.

Using the less congested straight routes de liaison interrégionales allowed him to contemplate the overwhelming events of the last two weeks. He would never recover from the trauma of Jane's and Carrie's murders. And the tragedy of losing Anthony overboard meant that gone from his reach was the testimony; because of its highly inflammatory content, Anthony had hidden it where only he could access it. Now Branen would have to risk returning to the podere to retrieve the negatives of the massacre in Paris in 1997. Without the negatives, he no longer had the protection of that evidence which left him vulnerable should The Associates want to eliminate him.

When he was approached by The Associates he knew he was being employed to kill. At first he justified it in the belief that he was protecting his country's security. But he had to ask himself, why should his life be more valuable than the one he'd been ordered to take? With this question came the knowledge that his own life was equally disposable. Eventually he had numbed himself to the reality of what he was doing and he lost the fear of death; the ideal state of mind for a successful killer. But after each kill, he realised murdering someone reduced the humanity within himself; from which he could never relinquish the responsibility. The problem came when he decided to stop. The full consequences of his actions were burnt into him despite the fact that he'd aborted the Paris mission; something the authorities would never know.

The only major city he passed through on his way to Lyon was Orléans, one hundred kilometres south of Paris. From there he felt safe enough to use the trunk roads, but he still avoided the autoroutes.

He motored on for mile after mile through avenues of poplars and rolling French countryside, never exceeding eighty kilometres per hour. As he left each village behind Soho became more remote, a recollection defiled by the suffering of Carrie, Jane and her baby. He had loved the place and had grown into adulthood in those streets. He loved it and hated it at the same time, but knew he would not be able to leave it for ever.

He was treated to a cold, sunny day. The light was low and the scenery was beautiful. A family in a classic old Citroen DS convertible overtook him heading south with the roof down. The mother was trying to control the children as they climbed over the seats. It reminded him of the times he'd spent with Carrie and Jane.

He knew that while he remained alive he was a threat to The Associates. He represented an open wound that could be healed only if he was disposed of. He would have to change identity and attempt to disappear again. No rest for the incriminated.

The afternoon crept by as he drove relentlessly on. He watched where he was heading and forgot where he'd been. The sun dropped down through the right hand passenger window and the night closed in. He had to keep splashing his face with water to stay awake and his eyes began to feel as though they had grains of sand scratching around under the lids, but the exhilaration of escape kept him going through the hunger and exhaustion.

He finally arrived at the autoroute service station west of Chambéry at 3am. He parked in the furthest corner of the car park and turned off the engine. He let his head drop and fell into a deep sleep.

When he woke up, he had no idea where he was or how long he had been there. It was still dark and he had to find a lift over the border. His watch said 3.45am but France was an hour ahead and he wanted to catch the early lorries. He found an old piece of cloth and an ancient toolkit in the back of the van and folded them into the rucksack to make it look convincingly full. He put the bottle of water into a side pocket and slung the bag over his good shoulder; he looked like a hitch-hiker on his way south.

The drawl of Charles Trenet singing La Mer coming from the

jukebox and the smell of good coffee gave him a feeling of optimism. There were three men at the bar; two in traditional blue overalls sitting together at one end. The other man was perched on a high stool at the far end. Branen moved between them and ordered half a baguette and a coffee. The barman wiped the counter in front of him and slid a tall glass of coffee across, tucking the bill under it. A minute or two later he returned with the sandwich.

The food and warmth restored his energy. He had finished with the Renault and would leave it there. Eventually it would be traced back to the farmer, who'd say it had been stolen and he hadn't bothered to report it. Somehow today he was going to cross into Italy, even if he had to hitch-hike out on the road. After crossing the border he would call Salvatore and ask him to drive up and collect him.

"Where are you heading, monsieur?" he asked the man at the end of the bar.

"Turin…" he replied. "… I'm delivering a generator… I can take you there if you like."

Within half an hour, after buying the man another coffee with the last of his euros, Branen was high up in the air-conditioned cab winding along the A43 into the Alps.

It was not long before the regular rhythm of the engine and the hot air from the air-con seduced him into a deep sleep and he started to dream about the night, five days ago, when he had tried to stay with Kelly. She knew her mind and wasn't afraid to say what she wanted, or in his case what she didn't want. There was something about her he couldn't forget.

He must have slept for more than an hour before the hissing air brakes jolted him back to reality. They were entering the tunnel at Fréjus and the border crossing into Italy. The driver appeared to know the border guards and they hardly gave Branen's French passport a second glance. The warmth of the cab had increased the agricultural smell of the cloth in the rucksack but fortunately the driver seemed too polite to mention it. Branen wanted a meeting point with Salvatore but he didn't know Turin and he didn't know whether Salvatore did either.

The driver had a St. Christopher medallion hanging from his mirror which prompted Branen to ask, "Do you know where the Turin shroud is kept?"

"Mais oui," said the driver, crossing himself.

133. BRANEN & SALVATORE :
(LUNCHTIME, THURSDAY 19 NOVEMBER)

At midday, eight hours after they had set out the driver dropped Branen off on the edge of an industrial estate in the suburbs of Turin.

By then the porcine stench from the rucksack had permeated the fabric of the cab; Branen was sure the driver couldn't wait to see the back of him. The fact that he'd pulled into a lorry park with a restaurant but did not mention eating together confirmed Branen's suspicions. He only had a couple of euros left and was going to need them to telephone Salvatore. Branen's podere was more than five hundred kilometres south and it would take Salvatore an eight or nine hour drive in his old pick-up, so he set out to walk to the Cattedrale di San Giovanni Battista in the centre of the city.

At the first phonebox he called Salvatore. "Salvatore, can you meet me…?"

Salvatore interrupted. "My friend, where are you…?"

"In Turin, can you meet me at the Cattedrale where the shroud is kept…? And please bring enough cash for a hotel… I know this sounds crazy but I'll explain later."

He left the rucksack inside the phone kiosk and continued towards the town centre. He found a small hotel near the Cathedral in Via San Domenico and reserved two single rooms; he did not expect to see Salvatore before 10pm.

Branen spent the rest of the day wandering aimlessly around the centre of Turin, trying to ignore his hunger and avoiding the smell of food and coffee that radiated from the ristorantes.

Around 11pm as he was pacing up and down the Cathedral steps trying to keep warm, wondering where Salvatore had got to, he heard the familiar sound of his van. Salvatore ran up the steps, put his arms round Branen and then stood back staring at his bleached hair. "You look like shit my friend… are you in trouble?"

"No problems Salvo… everything's okay now… I'll explain one day."

After they had checked into the hotel they walked to a trattoria that Branen had lined up several hours before.

They shared a bottle of wine and had the best spaghetti vongole since

Salvatore's wife, Francesca, had last cooked it for them. The meal and Salvatore's company temporarily revived Branen's faith in humanity. They had a couple of amaros and were back in the hotel by one in the morning.

The food, the drink and the stress of the last three weeks meant that Branen slept like the dead.

134. BRANEN & SALVATORE :
(9AM, FRIDAY 20 NOVEMBER)

The next morning he woke at about nine o'clock and Salvatore was nowhere to be found.

Salvatore was used to getting up with the sunrise so Branen wasn't too worried. He had breakfast and checked out of the hotel, using what was left of the two hundred euros Salvatore had lent him. He wandered round the corner to the Cathedral and there was Salvatore kneeling in front of the altar, probably praying for the Inglese's soul.

With his faith sufficiently restored, they set out on the journey home. It was a relief for Branen to be able to travel on the autostrada without worrying about CCTV cameras.

Seven kilometres south of Castiglione del Lago, on the banks of Lago Trasimeno, the broken road wound up through the hills. They turned onto a deep rutted dust track and climbed for five kilometers through woodland before pulling into the driveway of Salvatore's farmyard; it was late afternoon.

The door opened and Eduardo ran out to meet them. He jumped up and Branen lifted him into his arms, trying not to show the pain in his shoulder.

"Hello Ben, hello Ben, I learn Inglese now…" Eduardo paused, staring at Branen, much as his father had done. "…what funny hair you got." He was seven years old and used to get frustrated with Branen trying to speak Italian. They were pleased to see each other.

Standing in the door behind him was Francesca in a soft cotton floral dress and white apron. She came forward and cuddled Branen. "Ciao, mio amore."

He felt her warmth. She was beautiful. He remembered when

he'd first met her, she had taken his breath away. She was classically Mediterranean; dark, voluptuous and sexy. Reeking of sins that could only be dreamt of, because she was Salvatore's wife.

"I need to get back to the house, Francesca..." He wanted to be on his own to deal with the last three weeks.

"No, Ben," insisted Francesca, "...I have made your favourite pasta with funghi, which Eduardo picked for you... you're staying to eat with us."

135. BRANEN : (EARLY HOURS – SATURDAY 21 NOV)

When the time came to leave, Salvatore suggested, "You take my pick-up now and I get it back if I need it..."

Branen wanted to return to his house unobserved in case he had unwanted visitors. "It's only a couple of kilometres across the valley and I'll enjoy the walk."

Branen set out along the woodland track round the hill. The air was cold and he was accompanied by the calls of a pair of owls and the barking of foxes in the distance. In the moonlight he surprised a boar foraging on the side of the track. They both started, and when it recovered it looked at Branen with disdain and strolled reluctantly back into the wood. Seeing it took him back to Soho and the legend of the hunting call when Henry VIII chased wild boar.

The path dipped down to a ford across the stream. By taking the lower track instead of walking up to the road which connected the farms, he could get back to the podere through the woods.

The Security Forces couldn't be sure where he was, but by returning to this place he was gambling again and he had to have those negatives from Paris; they could save his life. He had to assume that during the six years the satellite phone was switched on at the podere, they had traced the location. Although he'd destroyed the phone before he left for London, whoever took over control of The Associates would still have that information. The compromising Polaroids of Redcliffe were now useless. Since The Associates had failed to kill him in the UK, he was hoping that they would hesitate before trying to kill him abroad. The little he owned and valued was in the farmhouse but by returning to it, was he letting his emotions overrule common sense?

He slowed for a moment, trying to be logical. Redcliffe's replacement would take time and he reckoned that The Associates thought he was still in the UK. He decided to go to the podere briefly, but he could not risk staying for long.

Keeping off the track so as not to leave footprints, he made the final climb up to the edge of his land. He undid the rope and lifted the thin tree trunk that was his back gate then crouched down and examined the ground. There were no signs of tyre tracks and the only prints in the dust were clove-shaped deer tracks and a large paw-print, which looked like a dog fox. The main entrance to the farmhouse ran down a track from the road on the other side of his land.

He approached the house silently through the woods, looking for any signs of life. He belly-crawled through the vineyard and came within three metres of a badger before it panicked and scurried off into the long grass; it could have compromised his approach. He lay under an oleander bush fifty metres from the house, watching and listening. Other than wildlife nothing stirred inside or out.

After an hour of observation he crawled over the rutted track that wound up to the house and spent another half hour in the shelter of a wall beside the barn.

Having reassured himself that no-one was around, he took the door key from a beam on the outside of the barn and crept over to the house. The hinges squealed like a pig as he let himself in. It smelt like it hadn't been opened for a while. Nothing appeared to be disturbed or out of place.

Hidden upstairs in the bedroom he kept a belt full of cartridges and a shotgun with the stock sawn off and the barrels cut at three-quarters; still long enough to bag a rabbit or a pheasant at thirty metres. He'd never imagined he would ever have to assault his own house but he had to take the chance. He moved silently across the kitchen and picked up the poker from the fireplace then sprinted up the creaking staircase and stormed the three rooms. The house was empty.

Back downstairs with the shotgun tucked into the cartridge belt around his waist, he retrieved the negatives from the safe under the bottom tread of the staircase.

At last he was home, even if it was only temporarily. He climbed the creaking stairs again and from the bedside cabinet took the letter Carrie had given him when he had last seen her alive, when she was fourteen. He also took out a photograph taken eighteen years ago, before he went to prison. In the picture he was twenty-two years old, holding Carrie's hand; she was just three. Jane was holding her other hand and it reminded him of what he had missed out on. Then he remembered Carrie's mobile and notebook he had hidden under the floorboards in Hotel California and wondered if they would ever be found. He put everything except Snowman's phone back into the belt-bag with the negatives and strapped it round his waist.

He couldn't risk falling asleep in the house so he pulled a blanket from the bed and put on a thick fleece jacket. As he left he hung a thread between the front door and the frame and smoothed out a patch of sandy soil by the door.

Back in the woods he removed the SIM card and battery from Snowman's mobile and buried the phone. He returned to the oleander bush where he had a view of the house and scraped a shallow dip in the rich soil. He lay down, pulled the lower branches down round him for camouflage and made himself as comfortable as he could. It was a couple of hours until dawn and he needed to see Salvatore before he left. He would give him the tractor and the podere and he could pay for it in instalments, which he would collect when Salvatore could afford to pay it. Branen would persuade him that he could take care of his money instead of the bank. It would allow Branen a source of funds without him being traceable. He would return briefly in a few months to sign all the paperwork, which would show that he had sold the farm to his neighbour and moved on without leaving a forwarding address.

He listened to the wind rustling through the leaves of the eucalyptus tree that stood sentry over the house. It was strangely reassuring.

136. BRANEN : (SUNRISE, SATURDAY 21 NOVEMBER)

It was still dark when Branen awoke. The cold and damp had penetrated the blanket and he ached all over.

He rolled over to face the house and flinched as the sawn-off shotgun dug into his crotch. He had to repeat the whole routine of checking out the house to make sure no-one had visited during the couple of hours he'd been asleep.

By the time he got back to the cover of the barn the sun was rising behind the mountains. He crept up to the front door, checked the patch of soil for footprints and saw that the thread had not been disturbed. Confident that he'd had no visitors, he went inside and brewed a mug of tea.

Then he picked up the key to the barn from the hook in the kitchen and went out onto the stone terrace overlooking the vineyard. He realised he would have to leave this sanctuary for ever. He could hear the brook tumbling down through the hollow on the far side of the olive grove. He looked out at the view between the hills, down to the lake below. The breeze on his face was raw and had the rusty smell of autumn, reviving memories of that fateful night when he had ridden the motorbike away from the Pont d'Alma. He had been the oily rag used by the secret forces behind the Establishment to wipe away any possible connection to the tragedy. He was the last remaining threat. But even if he had not committed the final act, he had accepted the job and dear friends had died because of it. He had exploited the two most important people in his life and now they were lost to him for ever. And he had deprived himself of seeing them laid to rest. Their presence in his life had revealed so many conflicting emotions, and they would always return to him when he least expected. This was both the hope and the sadness he would have to live with.

He sat on the old wooden lounger dazzled by the flickering sunlight, his vision blurred with tears. The vines and olive trees stretched away down to the row of cypress trees. The landscape had been laid out by man but was not man-made; its history stretched back in time long before men arrived to plunder it.

He walked through the vines, checking how much damage the boar had done while he'd been away. The dew was fresh on his skin and the birds' autumnal attempt at a dawn chorus provided the sound-track. He came upon a deer grazing on the last of the summmer's foliage and it scrambled back into the bush when it saw him.

He was going to have to leave all this behind him today; it was too dangerous to hang on. He was left with a feeling of despair; he was free but was lost in his life. While he was still alive he would be a hunted man, always looking over his shoulder; they would never let him survive.

As he walked back up the hill the sunlight bounced off the tips of the vines; the day was beginning to warm up. The thrush's song was telling the other birds that winter was coming. It was time to pack their bags and move south, and he had to join them. He was going to drive the old Ferguson tractor round to Salvatore and tell him what he had decided.

The tractor was locked in the barn. The old rusty padlock opened easily. Perhaps Salvatore had popped in while he'd had been away. He climbed up and wiped the dew from the cold metal seat with the cuff of his jacket. He stretched down and pulled on the starter knob, more with hope than expectation that the battery would have any life left in it. Not even the slightest murmur from the starter-motor. He would have to give the battery a booster charge, which would take half an hour.

A robin flew down, landed on top of the bonnet and cocked its head to look at him. His red breast matched the painted tractor and for a moment he wondered whether he'd migrated from the UK and like him had flown a long way south. He opened his beak and Branen thought he was going to throw up but instead he chirped at him. He didn't know if the robin was trying to say something but it was good to see him and for a moment he took Branen's mind off the reality of his life.

The pain in his shoulder was easing and his hand was on the mend, but he was still weary from the emotional onslaught of the previous three weeks. He cursed those bastards and could not get them out of his mind. He didn't want to be important enough for them to waste time and resources on, but he knew he would never achieve that insignificance. As much as he regretted it, if he wanted to survive he had to move on.

He wondered if the tractor was out of petrol and as he climbed down he noticed a sprig of oleander trapped in the zip of his jacket. He tried to pull it away but it was firmly entwined. The petrol filler-cap was under the bonnet and as he went to lift it he heard a noise outside. He turned to see little Eduardo drop his bike in the doorway and run towards him.

Branen picked him up and Eduardo hugged him. "Hello Ben, what you doing...? I glad you back!"

346

Branen treated him as though he were his own son. He would follow Branen round, giving opinions which echoed his father's. They had seen him through all the problems of insect infestations and mildew infections, and had helped save the vines. Last night Eduardo had wanted to stay up with them and talk but at eight o'clock Francesca insisted he went to bed.

Branen turned back to the tractor and lifted the bonnet open with his spare hand. The robin darted up on to one of the beams.

Eduardo pointed. "Look."

Branen saw the red, ten centimetre long, corrugated cylinder strapped below the petrol tank. He thought for a moment how close the colour was to the red painted engine. He saw a black cap dangling from a piece of string inside the bonnet.

Someone had been here.

They had used a modified Breda Second World War hand grenade, known as the 'Red Devil', to make it look like a local dispute. When Branen opened the bonnet the safety lever had been released by the string.

Desperate to protect Eduardo, he tried to turn. He pulled him close to his chest. They must have reduced the time delay fuse; within a second he was overwhelmed by a feeling of unlimited hopelessness. He thought his head was exploding as everything seemed to be moving outwards. He could see himself being blown towards the light that shone through the barn doors.

In the following milliseconds he wondered if anyone in the world was better off because he'd been there. He doubted it.

Then blackness.

* * *

CPSIA information can be obtained at www.ICGtesting.com
Printed in the USA
BVOW08s1952270416

445873BV00004B/39/P

9 781911 110248